A Fictional Natural History of Cryptids

Drums and Dragons

A Field Guide to *Mokele-mbembe* and Other Living Dinosaurs in Africa

A NOVEL BY RYAN J. LYONS

Book cover design by ebooklaunch.com.

ISBN: 0-578-51596-2
ISBN-13: 978-0-578-51596-0

CONTENTS

AUTHOR'S NOTES

This book is a work of fiction, but the dragons depicted here are inspired by reports of unknown animals in Africa. The exception is *sasabonsam*, which is an evil, winged spirit of West African folklore. To my knowledge, it has never been identified as a flesh and blood cryptid, but I have taken some artistic license and depicted it as a *kongamato* type.

This book also takes place before *Sojourn with the Sasquatch* even though *Sojourn* was published first. The details of why I have chosen to publish out of order are probably only interesting to me, so suffice it to say that I wanted to polish this book more before putting it into print. Hopefully the extra time has allowed me to do *mokele-mbembe* and its fellow African dragons some justice.

Finally, as in *Sojourn*, I have followed the style advocated by the late J. Richard Greenwell of the International Society of Cryptozoology when referring to unknown animals. The native name of an animal, such as *mokele-mbembe*, is italicized; and, although most unknown animals in this book are referred to by their native names, Western names would be capitalized but in normal typeface. Although Westerners also use names such as *mokele-mbembe* and *emela-ntouka* when referring to these creatures, we do not seem to have anglicized those terms (as opposed to Sasquatch, which is not, strictly speaking, an unaltered native name), so I have chosen to retain the italicization.

RYAN J. LYONS

ACKNOWLEDGEMENTS

Once again, I have to thank my husband, Joe, and our two neurotic dogs, Nemo and Logan, for giving me time (and, in the dogs' case, the occasional, grudging few minutes of quiet) to write this book. This time around, I would also like to acknowledge some marvelous mentors I have had over the years: Mrs. Besch, my art teacher from some years ago at Minetto Elementary School; Valerie Hutchinson, my former tutor; and Kimberly A. Steele, Esq., my current supervising attorney. Aside from inspiring me with their intelligence, kindness, and assertiveness, they also encouraged me at various points in my life. Without them, I don't know if I would have had the self-confidence to take on a project like this, the gumption to follow it through, or the bravery to put it out there not knowing how it will be received.

I would also like to acknowledge real-life cryptozoologists like Dr. Roy P. Mackal, who took the risks of actually going out into the Congo to look for these animals and bring the rest of us news of their possible existence. Walter Spink's eccentricities should by no means be taken as representative of these unsung heroes who not only ask the question—what if—but also look for its answer. I don't profess to know whether *mokele-mbembe* and its fellow dragons are real, but because of Dr. Mackal and his colleagues in the cryptozoological community, we know they might be, and there is a little more magic in this world because of it.

FOREWORD

The idea of dinosaurs existing in modern Africa has generally been dismissed as a fantasy along the lines of Sir Arthur Conan Doyle's *The Lost World*, but in fact, tales of living dinosaurs predate and undoubtedly inspired Doyle's novel. In any event, accounts of prehistoric survivors meet great skepticism, which explains why Walter Spink's success finding living dinosaurs—or dragons, as he called them—was neither widely believed nor widely publicized in any reputable source when he originally reported it.

For this reason, the reader will doubtless be surprised to learn that Walter Spink located and studied several species of living dinosaur in West Africa over the course of approximately one year during 1983 to 1984. Although he has since passed on, Walter made copious notes documenting his experiences, and these have come to me as the executor of his estate. What is more, I can vouch from my own personal knowledge that Walter observed and interacted with these creatures more closely than any Westerner before or since, for I was with him and witnessed the wonders that I am about to describe in this memoir.

For many years, I kept my knowledge a secret for fear of ridicule and damage to my career, but I break my silence now for several reasons. For one thing, I'm getting old enough now that I just don't give a damn whether anyone believes me. At the same time, I also find that Walter's work with unknown animals in general has gained credibility in light of his accepted findings regarding the North American Sasquatch, about which I hope to write in the future. Thus, I am cautiously optimistic that this memoir will be received better now than it would have been in the 1980s.

More importantly, I feel that it is safe for the dragons themselves if I reveal their existence now. During our study of these animals, it became painfully and tragically clear that some Westerners would destroy the dragons if they knew about them, so my silence was meant to ensure the dragons' own well-being in addition to securing my own reputation. More recently, however, the Republic of the Congo has established the Lac Télé Community Reserve, which protects a 1,695-square-mile area that includes the habitat of the Congolese dragons. Thus, I am confident that my revelation of the dragons cannot invite catastrophe into their lives as Walter and I inadvertently did during our time with them.

With this newfound sense of freedom and security, I finally present my own detailed account of studying the African dragons in the wild with Walter Spink. Within you will find our observations regarding the behavior of *mokele-mbembe* and other living dinosaurs, as well as the questions that we were forced to bequeath to those who will follow us. My intention is that this work will both guide future dracontologists when studying these animals and inspire the general public with the awe and wonderment that Walter and I felt at witnessing these miraculous survivors of a lost world.

Matthew Preston
Northern California
September 30, 2014

CHAPTER I
EX AFRICA SEMPER ALIQUID NOVI

The story of my experiences pursuing the African dragons begins when I met Walter Spink. Before I knew him, I certainly never dreamed of being a monster hunter (or, more properly, an assistant monster hunter), and I had no reason to suspect that it would ultimately be my fate to do so. Indeed, for the first 20-some-odd years of my life, it did not occur to me that anyone outside the pages of a Victorian novel might actually pursue such a pastime, but then I was hired, just out of graduate school, as assistant curator of the F. Donald Hagstrom Museum of Natural History in Fairview, where Walter found me.

Although he has since become somewhat infamous for his discoveries (and his unorthodox methods), Walter was by no means as well-known in those days. I first heard of him from the museum's austere curator, Dr. James Stoutenger, and I might have thought it was a joke but for the fact that Stoutenger did not, according to popular belief among his colleagues and employees, have a sense of humor.

"Have you ever heard of someone called Walter Spink?" he asked me shortly after I had joined his staff.

"No," I said. "Is he someone important?"

"That's very funny." (Dr. Stoutenger's face, as always, remained solemn despite his words.) "No, he's not important. He's something of an eccentric. You see, he fancies himself a—*hmmph*—monster hunter."

"You mean vampires and werewolves?"

"Nothing so gothic, no. Sea monsters, abominable snowmen, that sort of thing. I suppose it's all the same, though; all make-believe, I mean."

"Of course."

(It may surprise some readers, given the reputation I have since earned, to know that I was originally quite skeptical of legendary animals.)

"I'm telling you all this because you'll probably hear from him at some point," Dr. Stoutenger said. "Every once in a while, he brings in some hair or bone for identification, hoping we'll tell him he's discovered a new species. We look at his specimens—just to humor him, mind you—and politely explain what they really are."

I confess that I scoffed along with Dr. Stoutenger at the time, not suspecting that I would not only meet this Walter Spink character but join him. For some time, he put in no appearance and remained as legendary to me as the monsters he pursued, but finally I met Walter when he called upon the museum's expertise, just as Dr. Stoutenger had predicted.

When lay people find animals, plants, fossils, or rocks that they cannot identify, the local natural history museum is often their first resort. An unusual bone, turned up by a farmer plowing a field or a homeowner breaking ground for a swimming pool, might be presented to determine whether it once belonged to some long-extinct creature. More to the point, museums are frequently consulted regarding purported evidence of unknown animals; Sasquatch enthusiasts, for example, have availed themselves of the expertise of museums and their staffs in identifying hair samples found in their pursuit of the apemen (but have generally succeeded only in proving the prevalence of bears in the American wilderness).

It was in such a capacity that Walter Spink contacted me one day in late 1982.

"Hello? Hello?" a squawking voice greeted me when I answered my telephone. "Is this the curator?"

"Actually, I'm the assistant curator," I said, "Matt Preston."

"Just the assistant curator, you say?"

"The curator is a busy man, but I'd be happy to help you if I can. May I ask who I'm speaking to?"

"To whom."

"Come again?"

"You should have asked 'to whom am I speaking.' You mustn't end a sentence with a preposition. And you should know who I am. I would be greatly surprised if somebody hadn't warned you that some crazy old fellow would be calling eventually, although I won't ask you to admit it."

"Is this Walter Spink?"

"I am he, for whatever that is worth."

"What can I do for you, Mr. Spink?"

"It's nothing, really; just a small favor. I was hoping you could take a look at a specimen I picked up in Gabon."

"What is it?"

"It's a country in West Africa."

"No, I meant to ask what you found."

"Oh, of course. How silly of me! It's the remains of a dragon."

"A dragon?"

"Well, I call them dragons, but the natives call this one *mokele-mbembe*. Anyway, I have been led to believe that it's the remains of a *mokele-mbembe*, but I need your help to verify that. Can you look at it for me?"

"Of course. Bring it by any time."

"Actually, I was hoping you'd come to me. I don't drive, and this particular specimen is difficult to move."

Thinking little enough of the exercise, I took down Walter's address and arranged a time to call upon him and his purported *mokele-mbembe* specimen. At the time, it seemed like an intellectual placebo to satisfy Walter's desire that his specimen be investigated, even if his suspicion of its nature would undoubtedly be proven unfounded. I certainly did not sense any foreboding, nor could I suspect what turn my life would take in the wake of my introduction to the pursuit of legendary animals.

Mokele-mbembe, a Lingala phrase meaning "one who stops the flow of rivers," is one of many names for a creature that is known throughout West Africa from Cameroon to the Democratic Republic of the Congo.[1] Unusual tracks discovered by 18th century missionaries in the Congo, evidently belonging to a large but unfamiliar animal, first hinted its existence to Europeans, and colonial explorers relayed native descriptions of an animal the size of an elephant, with a quadrupedal body, a small head perched atop a serpentine neck, and a long, powerful tail.

Perhaps the best early description of *mokele-mbembe* and its habits comes from a German, Captain Ludwig Freiherr von Stein zu Lausnitz, who wrote as follows:

> The animal is said to be of a brownish-gray in color with a smooth skin, its size is approximately that of an elephant; at least that of a hippopotamus. It is said to have a long and very flexible neck and only one tooth but a very long one; some say it is a horn. A few spoke about a long, muscular tail like that of an alligator. Canoes coming near it are said to be doomed; the animal is said to attack the vessels at once and to kill the crews but without eating the

[1]Other names include *nsanga, jago-nini,* and *n'yamala* (also transcribed as *amali*), all of which seem to describe a similar creature. *Mokele-mbembe,* however, is the one that is best-known to Westerners.

> bodies. The creature is said to live in the caves that have been washed out by the river in the clay of its shores at sharp bends. It is said to climb the shores even at daytime in search of food; its diet is said to be entirely vegetable. The preferred plant was shown to me, it is a kind of liana with large white blossoms, with a milky sap and applelike fruits.[2]

To many, the creature's reputed appearance and habits called to mind a sauropod dinosaur, and undoubtedly the romanticism Westerners feel at the thought of prehistoric reptiles surviving into modern times has sustained their interest in the legend ever since.

In light of the foregoing, it was perhaps foolish of me to have initially expected Walter to bring the purported remains to me at the museum and blasé of me not to have had a more emphatic reaction, either of skepticism or interest, to Walter's claim. In my defense, I knew nothing of alleged living dinosaurs before my acquaintance with Walter, so I was completely ignorant of the appropriate reaction to someone purporting to have found the remains of one.

Upon keeping my meeting with Walter Spink, I found myself reflecting that even the man's house was eccentric. The majority of the houses on George Street boasted proud Victorian façades with sharp gables like upturned noses, and Walter's residence, with its dilapidated appearance, might well have been the source of their offense. Beyond a conspicuously overgrown lawn, a building the color of bread mold with sloughing paint and sagging roof snubbed the convention of its neighbors just as Walter snubbed the convention of the scientific community.

At the front door, I let myself in under the direction of a handwritten sign that read *Bell broken—please come in* and began calling into a seemingly empty suite of rooms.

"Who's there?" a voice demanded.

"It's me, Mr. Spink," I said. "Matt Preston."

---

[2]Ley, Willy. *Exotic Zoology.* New York: Capricorn Books, 1966, 70. Print.

"Who?"

"From the museum."

"Oh, *that* Matthew Preston."

A disused door groaned open, and after adjusting the level of my eyes to account for his height, I beheld a diminutive gnome of a man with tousled white hair and beard framing a face with a beakish nose, beady eyes, and a tracery of wrinkles as intricate as the tattoos of some South Seas potentate. This was my first sight of Walter Spink, and I confess that on sight alone he was the last person from whom I would have believed a story involving living dinosaurs.

Hobbling toward me and brandishing a gnarled hand to shake, Walter welcomed me and then led me into the room from which he had just emerged, which proved to be a study walled with bookshelves.

"I apologize for the frosty reception," Walter said. "While I was in Africa, my beastly niece got it into her head somehow that I was dead and told the whole family. Now every time I turn around, some relative is poking around hoping to pilfer my estate. Imagine!"

Once our introduction was out of the way, Walter wasted no further time before getting down to business. Initially, this consisted of probing my familiarity with *mokele-mbembe*, becoming scandalized to learn that my educators and colleagues had neglected to apprise me of the legend, and relating substantially the description I provided above (albeit with more emphatic insistence that it must be a living dinosaur).

"You said you came into possession of the remains of one?" I asked dubiously. (Now that I had been briefed on *mokele-mbembe*, I was suitably incredulous at the magnitude of Walter's claim.)

"I can tell that you're skeptical," Walter said, "and I suppose I only have myself to blame. I may have been somewhat facetious when I told you I had the remains of a *mokele-mbembe.* To be more accurate, I have the partial remains of a *mokele-mbembe*. Its heart, to be exact."

"How did you come by that?"

"I didn't slay a dragon and cut the heart from its chest, if that's what you're thinking. In parts of Africa, the remains of certain animals are believed to possess magical powers, and they are consequently kept or ground up for traditional medicine. A horse's leg is supposed to kick away evil spirits, for example, and ground pigeon heart goes into a love potion. I have yet to learn the purpose of dragon parts in West African fetish magic, but with some asking around, I located a feticheur who possessed the heart of a *mokele-mbembe*."

As he explained, Walter beckoned me to follow him to the far side of a desk, where I was able to view a large specimen jar that had previously been obscured by precarious skyscrapers of books. Did I say jar? Actually, it was the size of a propane cylinder, but it was made of glass, and a shape the size of a watermelon—but textured more like a huge lump of liver or some other organ meat—lurked in a draught of preservative fluid. It might have been the heart of a large animal, although that by no means settled my mind regarding its origin.

"Have you weighed it?" I asked.

"It's 57 pounds," Walter said. "The size of an elephant's heart, I might add."

"Have you considered that it might really be an elephant's heart?"

"I have indeed, and that is precisely why I need your assistance. I imagine it is possible to determine by microscopic analysis from what type of animal this organ came?"

"Yes."

"There you go, then. If the tissue is from a mammal, then this may just be the remains of an elephant, and I am the fool that you have undoubtedly been led to expect. If the tissue is reptilian, on the other hand, it would be a reptile the size of an elephant. Though I am not a zoologist by profession, I have studied animals and seen them in the field, and I know of no reptile of that size—certainly not the crocodiles and monitor lizards that are endemic to Africa—so at the very least we would find ourselves with a new species. I believe that would indicate that there is truth to the stories of African dragons such as *mokele-mbembe.*"

I was forced to acknowledge the soundness of Walter's reasoning even if I lacked his faith in the result of testing. In any event, I agreed to investigate Walter's specimen and took custody of the heart with strict admonitions from Walter to guard it with my life.

"Remember, you mustn't let anything happen to it. Why, I suspect it's the most valuable specimen in the history of zoology!"

Getting away from an elderly person can sometimes be an awkward affair, but Walter Spink was eager to see me off so that I could more quickly make my inquiry. As I got into my car, I reflected that he really was an amiable enough old coot, although this did not impart any faith in his hypothesis regarding the supposed dragon remains. My life would certainly have been easier if my impression of a kindly but mistaken old man had been correct, but my dismissive attitude regarding Walter's discovery was destined to change.

Lest I give the reader an inaccurately favorable view of myself, I freely admit that I considered doing nothing with Walter Spink's specimen and simply telling him that it had turned out to be an elephant's heart. I suspect that many of my colleagues, possessing limited free time and certain that testing was a mere exercise, might have done so. Ultimately, however, I am too timid to break a speed limit, to say nothing of telling an out-and-out lie, so the temptation was only fleeting. I made a good faith effort to test whether Walter's specimen came from a reptile, in which case his hypothesis might be borne out.

There are several features that distinguish the heart of a reptile from the heart of a mammal. The reptile's heart generally contains only three chambers, consisting of two atria and one ventricle, as opposed to the four-chambered mammalian heart; this feature is, of course, impossible to observe from visual inspection alone.[3] At the microscopic level, on the other hand, reptilian cardiac tissue lacks the transverse tubules that are present in its mammalian counterpart, and reptilian red blood cells possess nuclei that are not found in those of mammals. Thus, tissue analysis at the microscopic level is the most certain method of distinguishing the tissue of one from the other.

At the risk of disillusioning the reader, I do not possess the expertise to perform microscopic examination of animal tissue. Thus, I probed the museum's network of contacts until Linda T—, a herpetologist affiliated with a university out west, agreed to look at a slide taken from the purported dragon heart.[4] I did not, however, brief her as to Walter's hypothesis regarding its origin, seeing no need to embarrass myself or to taint the results by suggesting an answer.

While museums and academic institutions frequently consult with lay people to identify biological specimens, practical concerns dictate that their paying work comes first. Consequently, side projects such as the examination of bric-a-brac specimens from lay people tend to be placed on the proverbial back burner. For this reason, I did not expect an immediate response to my inquiry, but Walter Spink lacked my perspective. He called me daily, and our conversations ran essentially as follows.

"Did you get my results yet?" Walter would ask.

"Not yet, Mr. Spink," I would say.

"All right, then. I shall call you tomorrow."

After several weeks of this, which I confess caused me some irritation, I received a call from Linda with the results of her examination, and suddenly I found that Walter's impatience was the least of my concerns. You see, in spite of all my expectation to the contrary, the heart turned out to be the remains of a reptile, although Linda had no idea of the shock she was delivering and was quite

---

[3]Moreover, the crocodile heart has four chambers, so the structure of the heart alone is insufficient to rule out the class entirely.

[4]I omit her full name and affiliation for fear of the consequences to her career if she should be openly affiliated with monster hunting, consequences with which I am all too familiar.

routine when she made her report.

"It's definitely from a reptile," she said.

I was so prepared to hear otherwise that I did not immediately register her words.

"Thank you so much for clearing that—huh?"

"I said that the tissue you sent me is from a reptile."

"Are you sure?"

"Absolutely sure."

"Is it cardiac tissue?"

"Yes, and I'm absolutely sure about that, too. Now I've got a question for you: why are you so surprised?"

"Because I was absolutely sure that it was from an elephant."

Perhaps the prospect of discovering a new species of reptile should have thrilled me, but for some reason I felt a disquiet that I could not explain. At the time, I ascribed it to cognitive dissonance because the test results challenged my expectation. In any event, it was with such heavy footsteps and such a somber countenance that I visited Walter, bearing both his specimen and my unexpected news, that at first Walter misapprehended the outcome of his inquiry.

"It's about the test results, isn't it?" he said. "Good heavens. It was just a mammal after all, wasn't it? The more fool me for getting my hopes up."

"No, Mr. Spink," I said. "It's not that."

"Then what the devil is it?"

"You were right. It is a reptile's heart."

"But that's wonderful! Why the devil do you look like you're suffering from a sour stomach?"

I was not called upon to explain my mood because Walter's attention quickly reverted to the significance of his discovery.

"This proves beyond a doubt," he said, "that there is a massive, unknown reptile in West Africa. Now, you'll say that this still doesn't prove that it's a living dinosaur, and you're right, but it's certainly encouraging, and who knows? I may just wind up being right about that, too. Now, the first order of business is to alert the scientific community to what I've found. I think a letter to the *Proceedings of the Northeastern Zoological Society* should do. And of course I'll have to describe the creature. At the risk of coming off egotistical, I think I shall call it *Mokelembembe spinki.*"

After sharing a celebratory glass of champagne, I left Walter building these and other, similar castles in the air in anticipation of how his discovery would be fêted. For a few moments at least, I was actually able to feel that I had been involved in something positive, and I reflected, perhaps prematurely, that Walter's quest was not as quixotic as people claimed.

It goes without saying that Walter's hopes were dashed, and *Mokelembembe spinki* was not acknowledged as a species; certainly the discovery of a giant, possibly prehistoric reptile in Africa would otherwise have become widely known long before the publication of this memoir. If, in my naïveté, I believed that the scientific establishment would accept such a claim from the likes of Walter Spink based merely on the evidence in hand, I underestimated the bias against creatures such as the African dragons. Skeptics, like believers, tend to view evidence in the light of their own preconceived notions, so I should have known that Walter's specimen would not be so easily acknowledged. I am also ashamed to report that I played a part in sabotaging his success.

My role in the denouement of Walter's discovery was unintentional and can be ascribed to an excess of enthusiasm. When Dr. Stoutenger made one of his usual comments at Walter's expense, I cited Walter's recent success in his defense. In doing so, however, I unwittingly delivered intelligence into the hands of an enemy, though he gave me no reason to suspect at the time.

"In that case, I'm very happy for him," Dr. Stoutenger said (though, as always, his face did not express such feeling). "It's been a long time coming. Tell me more."

And I told him. Fool that I am, I told him everything.

The result of my indiscretion was to afford a decided skeptic the means to take preemptive action against Walter's discovery. I do not know whether Dr. Stoutenger was concerned about the museum being connected with what he deemed to be pseudoscience, or if instead he bore some personal grudge, but whatever his motivation, he developed an alternative theory regarding Walter's specimen. More importantly—and more unfortunately, at least for Walter—he published his hypothesis first. I quote the below from Dr. Stoutenger's article.

> While the specimen has been demonstrated by microscopic examination to be the heart of a reptile, there are several possible explanations for its size. Poste (1968) has described the occurrence of gigantism in certain species of agamid lizards, and Bryant et al. (1977) observed the incidence of myocarditis in the frilled lizard (*Chlamydosaurus kingii*) and American alligator (*Alligator mississippiensis*). In all of these cases, known species of reptile presented with substantially enlarged hearts.
>
> In the absence of additional remains, or preferably a complete cadaver, it is impossible to determine whether the size of the anomalous specimen indicates a reptile of unusual size or a reptile with a pathological condition. While this does not disprove the legends of an unknown West African reptile, it does preclude identification of the present specimen with an unknown species. For the time being, the most likely identity of the specimen appears to be a Nile crocodile (*Crocodylus niloticus*), the occurrence of which in Gabon has been described by Kingsley (1897) among others, with one of the

medical conditions described above.[5]

By the time I finished reading this, I suddenly understood the foreboding I had initially felt when I had been confronted with the unexpected results of Walter's inquiry.

The next act in the saga of Walter's dragon can be guessed by anyone familiar with the literature concerning unknown animals. The principle of Occam's razor states that the simplest explanation is the most likely to be true, but all too often the explanation that does not involve the existence of a new species—regardless of whether it is actually any more likely—will be accepted as true. Thus, Dr. Stoutenger's hypothesis satisfied many authorities, who saw no need to inquire further if even a remote possibility avoided the existence of the dragons. Moreover, because Stoutenger's opinion appeared first, the scientific community viewed the matter as being resolved and saw no reason to entertain Walter's hypothesis. Consequently, Walter's write-up concerning *mokele-mbembe* was rejected by the *Proceedings of the Northeastern Zoological Society* and every other scientific journal that considered itself reputable.

I learned this when I visited Walter, whom I found railing against the entire scientific establishment.

"If I'd known that nobody was going to listen to me anyway," he said, "I would have just stayed dead when I had the chance and saved myself all of this grief."

When I confessed to my part in Walter's disappointment, he took it surprisingly well.

"I appreciate your honesty, Matthew," he said, "but I think I have only myself to blame. Knowing the scientific community, I was a fool to ever get my hopes up. If that beastly Stoutenger fellow hadn't discredited *Mokelembembe spinki*, someone else certainly would have done it."

---

[5]Stoutenger, J. "Review of Anomalous Partial Remains Attributed to Unknown African Reptile." *Proceedings of the Northeastern Zoological Society*, vol. 67, no. 9, 1982, pp. 127-31. Print.

As my comments on this matter have already suggested, I disagreed with Dr. Stoutenger and the skeptics. A typical Nile crocodile heart weighs approximately three pounds, so Walter's specimen was 19 times what would be expected. Needless to say, I am not aware of an instance in which gigantism or myocarditis enlarged an animal's heart to such an extent.[6] Dr. Stoutenger's explanation seemed as strained as the idea of a living dinosaur, if not more so, and I told Walter as much.

"Wait a minute," Walter said, brightening. "You're not taking that beastly Stoutenger fellow's side?"

"Not at all."

"I knew from the moment I met you that you were an intelligent young man. If I've made a new friend who hasn't yet written me off as a complete lunatic, then I suppose some good has come of this whole affair, after all."

In this manner I became acquainted with Walter Spink, then acknowledged as his friend. This incident was undoubtedly the genesis of my schism from the scientific community, but I was not immediately enlisted into the ranks of the monster hunters, either. I may have had a more open mind than some members of the zoological community, but it was only when monster hunting seemed my only option that I made my first foray into what Walter and I would come to refer to as dracontology.

---

[6]Nile crocodiles are known to exceed 16 feet, so a crocodile with this degree of gigantism could theoretically make for an improbable 304-foot long monster. Ironically, a behemoth crocodilian called *mahamba* is actually rumored to exist in the Congo, but even the wildest fish stories do not put its length at more than 50 feet.

CHAPTER II
THE FORTUNES AND MISFORTUNES OF A MONSTER HUNTER

Monster hunters tend to experience more setbacks than successes, although to my knowledge Walter Spink is the only one who ever blamed them on black magic. To their credit, monster hunters also tend to be persistent; thus, whatever agency Walter ultimately credited with the nonstarter that came of his discovery of the *mokele-mbembe* heart, he was by no means dissuaded from continuing to seek African dragons. Moreover, as a result of a misfortune that I suffered (whether magical or material in origin), I would be joining him in his pursuit.

I learned of Walter's unique explanation for his woes when he telephoned me shortly after the debacle I described in the previous chapter.

"Hello?" he squawked. "Matthew? I'm embarrassed to ask, but I honestly don't know anyone else to call. Can you help me? I'm bleeding."

I might have envisioned Walter Spink, the victim of some robber's bludgeon, flailing uselessly in a spreading pool of his own blood, but in fact he was simply plagued with varicose veins, one of which had burst. When I drove him to the hospital, however, I observed that he also sported a constellation of blisters on his left forearm and could not help expressing some concern.

"That's nothing," he said. "You have no idea of the terrible time I'm having. First, no one believes me about *Mokelembembe spinki*, and since then I've been burned, bruised, and attacked by a crow, and all my chest hair has fallen out. It's my own fault, I suppose."

"How do you figure that?" I asked.

"There's something I didn't tell you about the *mokele-mbembe* fetish, Matthew, because I thought the museum might take issue with its questionable procurement. Now that it's been discredited anyway, I suppose it doesn't make any difference if you know. I didn't buy or barter for it. I took it."

"You stole it?"

"You don't have to use that word! And what was I supposed to do? That beastly sorcerer wouldn't part with it no matter how much I offered him, and I needed it more than he did, anyway. If it makes you feel any better, I'm paying for it now. I'm obviously cursed."

"Cursed?"

"Well, how else do you explain it? The run of terrible luck I've been having can't just be the result of coincidence. Obviously this witchdoctor put some sort of spell on the fetish to pay back the damned fool who stole it from him."

Even in modern times, to say nothing of ancient mythology, one hears of stolen objects bringing misfortune down upon whoever possesses them against their true owners' rights. The spirits of Pompeii have a legendary reputation for inflicting personal suffering on tourists who pilfer pieces of mosaic or pottery from the ruins. Similarly, stomach problems and hauntings, attributed to the curses of angry shopkeepers, befell looters in the wake of Mwai Kibaki's election in Kenya. Skeptics would say that these are psychosomatic symptoms arising from guilt coupled with an atmosphere of superstition, and the thought certainly occurred to me in Walter's case, though I was too tactful to advance such a hypothesis.

If I was initially skeptical at the idea of a cursed African fetish, I was tempted to consider the possibility of cursing when I was notified, around this same time, that my services were no longer needed at the museum. My involvement with Walter Spink was not expressly cited as the reason for my dismissal, but considering my disagreement with Dr. Stoutenger on that subject and the timing of the decision, I could not help suspecting a connection. Then, just when I had resolved myself to the life of an unemployed person (to wit, viewing substantial amounts of daytime television and neglecting to shave for days at a time), I received the job offer that would change the course of my life.

"Hello, Matthew?" Walter squawked. "This is Walter Spink. I tried you at the Hagstrom Museum, and some unpleasant man told me that they let you go. Well, I certainly gave them a piece of my mind about that! Are you working yet?"

"No," I said.

"Excellent! Well, not excellent that you're out of work, of course, but excellent for me that you're available. I have some work, you see."

"What type of work?" (As if I didn't already know.)

"Why, assisting me on my next expedition, of course! I have no intention of giving up just because of a few skeptical scientists. I'm going back to Africa, and I'm going to take you along, if you'll go. I'll cover all the expenses, and give you something for your time, to boot."

Although it may disappoint the reader, this was the genesis of my participation in the study of unknown animals. Even if I did not believe it was possible to find a living dinosaur in Africa, I had no other employment option at the time. I agreed to accompany Walter to Africa, little suspecting what my new employment would actually entail. If I had, I imagine I would have turned him down flat, even if I would unwittingly have deprived myself of many wonders (while quite consciously saving myself from many dangers).

"Splendid!" Walter said. "There's only one matter I have to address before we can make our plans. As much as it pains me to give up any piece of a *mokele-mbembe*, even if it's no use to me as proof, I shall have to consider getting rid of that cursed fetish. We'll certainly never succeed in finding any more dragons—to say nothing of risking our very hides—if that thing is still around when we go out into the field."

"What if your trouble doesn't stop once you give it away?"

"Don't be absurd, Matthew. The curse will just pass on to whoever has the fetish."

For some time, divesting himself of the fetish occupied Walter and presented no small amount of consternation. He initially tried advertising it for sale in the hope of recouping the sum he had invested in traveling to Africa for its procurement, but the only response was an inquiry seeking to know what a *mokele-mbembe* was. Ultimately, Walter grumblingly resolved himself to take a loss, and he sold it cut-rate to an acquaintance who dealt in would-be relics of unknown animals, where it would be offered alongside casts from purported Sasquatch footprints and the remains of a supposed sea monster that was actually a decomposed raccoon.

It may perhaps strike the reader as strange that Walter Spink would part with the only known remains of an African dragon for what, in Western culture, would be considered a dubious reason. I myself privately condescended toward his faith in fetish at the time, but I have since seen too many things I cannot explain to chock Walter's abundance of caution on this subject up to silly superstition. In any event, once Walter had rid himself of the fetish, his mind was eased on this particular subject enough that he could focus on continuing his pursuit of the dragons.

Deciding to hunt dragons is easy enough, but the venture is constrained by several practical concerns, not the least of which is financing. The costs of travel, lodging, meals, and visas—to say nothing of the wages of guides and translators that the dracontologist needs in the African bush—mount quickly, and precedent in the field of cryptozoology suggests that it is unlikely for a *mokele-mbembe* (or any other legendary animal) to obligingly present itself for examination so as to lessen a dracontologist's expenses.

Given the state of Walter's home, it should be no revelation that he was not independently wealthy. Thus, once he had divested himself of the troublesome fetish, he set himself to the task of financing his next expedition. The easiest way to do this would be to find an individual of like interest with the means to pursue it through our efforts, and in fact there is an entire group of such individuals, though I was not aware of this fact until Walter announced the discovery of a prospective patron.

"Good news, Matthew," he said. "I've located a fellow who's interested in African dragons, and more importantly he has the money to support our work. Thank heavens I got rid of that cursed fetish. Our luck already seems to be changing!"

To say that I was curious about (and somewhat suspicious of) the type of person who would fund work such as Walter's would be an understatement, but Walter was tight-lipped if I asked for more information.

"He's quite conservative," was all that he would say.

After a relatively brief correspondence, Walter arranged a meeting with our mysterious prospective benefactor, whom I shall simply identify as Mr. F. I suspect that Walter only included me in this assignation because I was his sole means of transportation, and despite the invitation, he remained cagey about our would-be patron. Even with all this secrecy, though, I began to guess that something was unusual when Walter met me at his door clutching a Bible in one hand and wearing a crucifix around his neck that would have shamed the most flamboyant vampire hunter.

"What the devil are you staring at?" he asked.

"I didn't realize you were so religious," I said.

"I'm not, but I need to make, er, a good impression."

Nor was this the full extent of Walter's preparations to win over

Mr. F. Before I could interrogate him further about his religious regalia, he also presented a rather attractive young woman who would be accompanying us. How he recruited her for his scheme was a mystery at the time, but more to the point, his reasons for including her deepened the foreboding surrounding our new acquaintance.

"This lovely young woman is Vanessa," Walter said, "and if anybody asks, she's your significant other."

"What?!"

"I'm sorry, but I couldn't have you show up, an attractive young man without a young woman, and risk Mr. F. taking you for a homosexual. He's very conservative."

(Suspicious as it was that Walter felt the need to go to such lengths to convince Mr. F. of my heterosexuality, I was not about to object to being associated with an attractive young woman. Truth be told, I could hardly help falling in love with Vanessa once the idea had been put in my head by Walter's scenario, and I nursed a yearning infatuation with her for some time afterward.)

If Walter's uncharacteristic dress and his paranoia lest I be taken for an itinerant homosexual did not clue me in to the nature of our would-be benefactor, Walter's final warning immediately before our meeting should have.

"One last thing," he said. "Whatever you do, don't mention evolution, or carbon dating, or the big bang theory, or role-playing games. In fact, if you have to say anything, it might be safest if you just talk about the weather and your health."

With this admonition, I accompanied Walter to a dinner meeting with Mr. F., where everything appeared normal for approximately two minutes before Mr. F. said something that explained both his interest in African dragons and Walter's desperation to appear conservative.

"If you don't mind my asking, Mr. Spink," Mr. F. said, "when did you first accept the Divine Story of the Creation as taught in the Bible and reject the Devil's Counterfeits?" (Mr. F. spoke seemingly random words as if they were capitalized, and he occasionally added syllables that are not traditionally enunciated.)

"You know, it feels like only yesterday," Walter said, quickly adding, "but I'm sure that's just because I feel such passion for the divine word."

As the reader has undoubtedly guessed by now, Mr. F. was an evangelical Christian and a Young Earth Creationist. As best I can tell, this belief system rests upon the unerring, literal truth of the Bible and places the age of the Earth at somewhere between 6,000 and 10,000 years. Consequently, it rejects any scientific doctrine or theory that runs contrary to that literal truth (in other words, essentially all of them); paleontology, for example, is disregarded as being at odds with scripture, and fossils are ascribed to animals killed in the Noachian flood or hoaxes perpetrated on gullible secularists by Satan himself.

In the absence of any particular religious sentiment, Walter's sudden conversion can be explained easily enough: Young Earth Creationists accept accounts of living dinosaurs in Africa. If paleontology errs in representing that prehistoric reptiles are extinct (or so the Creationists reason), then it follows that science is wrong in general and the Bible the more credible natural history account. In addition to a desire to prove the continued existence of dinosaurs, Young Earth Creationists also frequently enjoy tax exempt status and surplus monies to fund the search for creatures such as *mokele-mbembe*, and Walter could overlook a theoretical disagreement if it meant advancing his research.

I will spare the reader a word for word transcript of the dinner meeting with Mr. F. Suffice it to say that Walter and Mr. F. took turns expressing their devotion to the Bible's unerring transmission of God's word, and it was fortunate that I was largely ignored, because I would undoubtedly have been exposed as a secularist heretic if I had been called upon to speak. Rather than questioning our study methods or experience, Mr. F. inquired no further than Walter's acceptance of the biblical account of creation, and Walter must have been convincing, because the Creationist seemed satisfied.

"I will Pray for your success in finding Behemoth in the Jungle," Mr. F. said finally.

"Behemoth?" Walter squawked. "What the devil are you talking about?"

"The animal that the Heathen calls *mokele-mbembe*."

"Oh, of course. How silly of me. Your prayers are appreciated, of course, but will you also be contributing any money?"

"As the Lord is my Witness, I will."

"Praise be! I can pray to that!"

As a result of Walter's pandering, we left our meeting with Mr. F. assured of his financial backing for the foreseeable future. This feat being accomplished, Walter waited just long enough to be out of sight and earshot before brushing himself off as if he had been sullied by his hypocrisy.

"Between you and me, Matthew," he said, "I haven't the faintest interest in all that religious fiddle-faddle, but I would have said anything to get some money out of that fellow."

Even if Walter's religious affectation was not strictly sincere, Mr. F.'s funds were genuine, and he promptly remitted an amount that was substantial enough to finance many months' field work in Africa. I suppose some people might question the morality of Walter accepting monies under such a pretense, but his charade was certainly less outrageous than that of the average televangelist who purports to be godly but lives tax-free in a mansion while allowing his fellow human beings to starve. Indeed, unlike the televangelist, Walter made productive use of Mr. F.'s contribution, and he ultimately delivered so much information regarding the African dragons that I think he can be forgiven a bit of sham Christianity.

*

The trouble with pretending to be good Christians in order to earn our benefactor's goodwill was the continuing threat of being caught and called out for the apostates we actually were. I was frankly surprised that Walter had successfully masqueraded as a believer during our first meeting with Mr. F., and their follow-up telephone conversations in the following days seemed rife with opportunity for him to slip up. The better the Creationist got to know Walter, the more certain I felt that he would sniff out Walter's insincerity and demand his money back, and the snippets of conversation I overheard on Walter's end did nothing to alter that feeling.

"Oh, of course," I heard him say frequently during these calls. "How silly of me."

Somehow, Walter's ruse was not discovered regardless of how inauthentic his portrayal of Christian zeal seemed to me, but that did not stop me from worrying while we underwent a battery of examinations and vaccinations, secured our visas, and made sundry other preparations for our forthcoming expedition. After waiting for the other shoe to drop in this manner for several weeks, I felt certain that my grim prediction had been realized when Walter called me late at night in a panic.

"Matthew," he said, "thank heavens you're awake. How soon can you be ready to leave?"

"I guess I could be packed in a few hours. What's wrong?"

"It's about that Creationist fellow, but there's no time to explain. Just get packed as quickly as you can and come over as soon as you're ready."

By the time I had packed and made my way to the ramshackle house on George Street, I had convinced myself that Walter meant to effect a midnight flit so as to dodge an unpleasant confrontation with our patron, but Walter disabused me of this belief when I confronted him with it.

"Found out?" he asked. "Don't be ridiculous, Matthew. I still have him eating out of the palm of my hand."

"Then why the sudden hurry?" I asked.

"It's that damned fetish. You know, the cursed one. Would you believe that Mr. F. bought it?"

As it turns out, the fetish that had been so eagerly disposed by

Walter had been found and purchased by Mr. F. with equal enthusiasm. This the Creationist reported triumphantly to his fellow believer in African dragons, little suspecting that Walter knew the provenance of the remains all too well.

"This is a catastrophe," Walter said. "Who knows what dreadful things will start happening to him with that thing around?"

"Did you, er, warn him?"

"I tried, but he said I was just being superstitious. Imagine!"

"I'm still not sure how this affects us."

"Don't you see? That fetish is going to jinx Mr. F. and everyone around him—including us, if we don't get the hell out of here. Personally, I have no intention of resting until I've put at least a thousand miles between me and the damned thing."

Whether the disposition of the fetish actually made any difference in Walter's fortunes is, of course, a matter of debate. Regardless of the possible influence of magic, Walter and I made our way to Africa like a modern St. George and his squire sallying forth in search of dragons. With enough money, all things are possible—even an elderly monster hunter with no scientific background and his reluctant assistant putting together an expedition to find living dinosaurs—and before we knew it, we arrived in Africa, there to discover whatever fortunes and misfortunes awaited us in our quest for dragons.

CHAPTER III
DISCOVERING *DRACOPTERYX*

As I indicated in the foreword of this memoir, there are several distinct types of large, unknown reptiles in Africa, and the sauropod-like *mokele-mbembe* is just one of them. Their behavior, habitats, and appearances differ widely from type to type, but all resemble prehistoric reptiles. Being just as happy to study one living dinosaur as another, Walter Spink and I followed up on leads to any variety of dragon whenever we found them, and our first observation of a live dragon was actually a winged reptile rather than *mokele-mbembe* itself.

We came upon the winged dragons while searching for *mokele-mbembe* in Cameroon in West Africa, but until our arrival in the capital city of Yaoundé, I could not guess what form our investigation would take. It was not until I asked Walter if he meant to look for another *mokele-mbembe* fetish that he shared his plan (while vehemently resisting the possibility of becoming entangled with African magic again).

"I've learned my lesson when it comes to tangling with witchdoctors," he said, "and I won't do it again anytime soon. No, I mean to ask around for people who have seen dragons. Hopefully, we'll find someone to show us where they live so that we can see them alive in the wild."

Having decided upon our methodology, we abandoned the steel skyscrapers and asphalt boulevards of Yaoundé, where *mokele-mbembe* and other dragons are understandably absent, and headed north through Bakweri villages comprised of tidy *ndaw'a ngonja* mat houses and past the 13,200-foot green ziggurat of Mount Cameroon. Accompanied by the *boom-boom-boom* of village signal drums trading gossip over our heads in their inscrutable code, we crossed plains of undulating hills like seas of waving grass alternating with lush tropical forests, led by Walter, clad in full formal attire right down to a tweed blazer, at the head of a half-dozen bearers and guides. Initially, Walter thought to visit Mamfe, where biologist and animal collector Ivan T. Sanderson had an encounter with a monstrous animal resembling *mokele-mbembe* on the Manyu River in 1932, but we only found that *mokele-mbembe*-type animals, by whatever name, were unknown in the area as of the time of our visit.

I will not linger over the fruitless weeks that Walter and I spent seeking long-necked dragons across northern Cameroon, but suffice it to say that our failure to discover them was not for lack of inquiry. Aside from asking after the dragon by its local name, *m'koo mbemboo*, Walter had also brought along a book of now-dated illustrations of dinosaurs, which he offered to everyone he met like a Jehovah's Witness peddling *The Watchtower*, hoping that one of the beasts in the pictures might be familiar to someone from live observation.

"Pardon me," he would say, "but have you seen any of these animals?"

Regardless of Walter's diligent querying, the sauropods were not recognized as he had hoped they would be, and for some time there was little he could do but sulk at his lack of results.

"That last fellow barely even looked," he said after one particularly cursory dismissal.

Even if long-necked dragons were not known from the Mamfe area, we began to hear of a carnivorous winged reptile called *sasabonsam*. Several residents claimed to recognize one of the pictures in Walter's book, but their knowledge of the creature was of dubious value because it came from second-hand reports. Eventually, though, we obtained a more promising identification from a young man named Kosi Menya who had not only seen a *sasabonsam* but been attacked by one.

As a consequence of the dragon in question having attacked the witness, our inquiry felt like a police investigation, with the young man scrutinizing the pictures in Walter's book just as seriously as if he were choosing from among the potential suspects in a police lineup. Early in his perusal, he raised a finger and slowly planted it on the page in front of him, and Walter, ever eager, pounced on the possibility of a positive identification.

"Is that what you saw?" he asked.

"No," Kosi shook his head. "That's not the one."

Again the young man skimmed the pages of Walter's book, and again his seemingly accusing finger came to rest on one of them.

"Is that it?" Walter asked.

"No," Kosi shook his head again. "Not that one, either."

After this exercise had been repeated a half dozen times, and with excruciating deliberation, the witness finally pointed out a picture of the animal that had attacked him.

"Are you sure this time?" Walter asked.

"That's the one," Kosi said. "I would know that cruel mouth and those merciless eyes anywhere."

"Wonderful! Now let me see."

Walter squinted over the watercolor facial (and wing) composite of the young man's assailant and nodding knowingly.

"Just as I expected," he said. "It's the pterosaur again, Matthew, and this young man actually saw it! Just imagine what people back home will think when we tell them we found pterosaurs!"

After an interrogation that would have earned high praise from MI6, Walter was satisfied that our witness had seen a living pterosaur, but I was privately skeptical. Presenting someone with a book of dinosaurs and asking him if he's seen any of them was a leading form of questioning, to say the least. I confess that I was also somewhat biased against the idea of a second species of dragon: it would have been miraculous enough for one prehistoric creature to have survived into modern times, so the idea of an assortment of African dragons seemed too good to be true. This was how I felt at the time, but it was of course fortunate that Walter pursued the investigation of the putative pterosaur, for we would have been deprived of some fascinating discoveries if we had been guided by my more conservative thinking.

⁕

Though references are fairly obscure, dragons resembling pterosaurs have been reported from several parts of Africa. To the south, winged reptiles called *kongamato* are said to swoop down upon unwary intruders in the Jiundu and Bangweulu Swamps in Angola and Zambia. In East Africa, the Kitui Watamba tell of similar dragons that soar about Mount Kenya and the surrounding savanna. In West Africa, where Walter and I focused our field work, these creatures are referred to as *olitiau* by some ethnic groups and *sasabonsam* by others. At present, it is not possible to say whether these are different species, for our knowledge is limited to *sasabonsam.*

Before we could know anything about *sasabonsam*, we first had to find them, and in this we relied upon information from the people of Mamfe and the surrounding villages. The consensus among residents was that *sasabonsam* lived in the forests to the north and east, some distance from any human habitations. Being so advised, we took up temporary residence in a small village called Foulagou and spent our days hiking the equatorial forest looking for signs of the winged dragons.

Mamfe and Northwest Cameroon are part of the Cross-Sanaga-Bioko Coastal Forest, which so far inland consists primarily of mixed moist semi-evergreen rainforest. In addition to winged dragons, this forest's animal population includes western lowland gorilla (*Gorilla*

gorilla diehli), drill (*Mandrillus leucophaeus*) and leopard (*Panthera pardus*), and its numerous tree species including bokanga, mahogany, ebony, and kapok form a canopy some 160 feet high. It was the latter tree, *Ceiba pentandra*, that chiefly interested Walter and me, for that is the species in which *sasabonsam* reportedly roost.[7]

In light of the almost universal agreement among our native informants that *sasabonsam* live in kapok trees, Walter and I began our search for *sasabonsam* by looking for specimens of kapok. These were easy enough to find, for kapok are some of the largest trees in the forest with their 30 foot thick trunks and winding buttress roots like petrified snakes at their feet, and we quickly located several of them. Assuming that a winged reptile would be fairly visible, and further operating under the assumption that a flying animal would most likely be spotted in the canopy, we scanned the branches almost 200 feet over our heads hoping to make out the gargoyle forms of lurking dragons in the treetops.

"Are they up there?" Walter asked, squinting fruitlessly into the canopy before adding, "It's no use, Matthew. I can't see anything. What about you?"

"Nothing," I said.

"Bother. Wherever could they be?"

For our first days in the forest, we catalogued numerous winged creatures, but none that could possibly be *sasabonsam*. There were raptors such as the majestic crowned eagle (*Stephanoaetus coronatus*) and chestnut-flanked sparrowhawk (*Accipiter castanilius*), but neither was as large as the dragons that had been described to us. There were also several species of parrot-like turacos in vibrant blue or green plumage, including the great blue (*Corythaeola cristata*), Guinea (*Tauraco*

[7]Specifically, kapok trees with red earth at their feet are said to be the homes of *sasabonsam*, which supposedly sit in the branches and dangle their feet to ensnare unwary passersby so that the creatures can eat or at least exsanguinate them. This appears to represent the mythification of *sasabonsam* by some ethnic groups, for Walter and I did not find unusually red earth at the site of any actual *sasabonsam* roost trees, nor did we observe them to hunt in the manner attributed to their legendary counterparts.

persa), and yellow-billed (*Tauraco macrorhynchus*) varieties, as well as African dwarf kingfishers (*Ispidina lecontei lecontei*), orange like tiny licks of flame, and black bee-eaters (*Merops gularis*) with red cheeks and blue breasts. There was accordingly enough flapping and cawing to make the forest feel primeval enough to harbor all manner of prehistoric creatures while simultaneously giving Walter no end of false alarms for the appearance of the dragons that he had been promised.

"Gracious, what was that?" he would ask, obviously hoping he had perceived the rumor of a winging dragon, when the flap of great wings carried one of the eagles in pursuit of a crowned guenon or other small primate.

"It was an eagle," I would say.

"Bother. Normally, I'm all for a little birding, but I was really hoping to finally see dragons."

Or, after hearing some primordial shriek:

"What was that? Is it one of them?"

"It's a hornbill."

As diligent as we were about watching over our heads for *sasabonsam*, our first evidence of their presence was found, ironically enough, under our feet. We were so preoccupied with what was over our heads that we might almost have missed it, but my innate talent for making a mess of myself ensured that we found this particular dragon spoor. Over the years, I have found no small number of awkward and clumsy ways to stumble upon evidence of unknown animals, and our search for the winged dragons inaugurated this tradition: while traipsing about the rainforest paying too little heed to where I was going, I stepped in it. Literally; not figuratively.

I planted my right foot in a pile of *sasabonsam* feces at the foot of one of the kapok trees.

Because they share a common ancestor, reptiles such as *sasabonsam* leave similar droppings to those of birds. Both consist of darker lobes of solid matter and a splatter of white liquid urates. On the other hand, the size of the droppings is proportionate to that of the creature that leaves them. *Sasabonsam* are several times larger than the largest raptor in the rainforest, so their feces can be distinguished by sheer size. The pile into which I stepped, for example, was longer than my foot (which, as you may imagine, made the circumstances of our finding evidence of *sasabonsam* bittersweet, at least for me).

"You really should be more careful, Matthew," Walter said once I had brought my find to his attention and we had agreed on its likely provenance. "That could be an important scientific discovery that you smashed into the bottom of your shoe."

Fortunately for science, there were plenty of other piles of dragon droppings, in fact so many that it was surprising none of us had stepped in them sooner. Although the incident did nothing for my personal dignity, it did provide us with a frame of reference for recognizing trees that were frequented by *sasabonsam*. By looking for the characteristic droppings, we were able to locate potential *sasabonsam* roosts quickly, and we identified and marked a half dozen such kapoks over the following days.

It might seem as if this breakthrough should have quickly vouchsafed us a sighting of *sasabonsam*, but unfortunately the identification of several suspected roosts, which we monitored tirelessly, did not immediately lead to visual contact with our leathery-winged quarry. This betrayed our hopes just when I had begun to think we might really find dragons, and it consequently tried our perseverance. After several days of keeping a vain vigil, Walter verbalized the irritation we were both feeling.

"Why the devil don't they show themselves?" he asked. "Don't they at least come out to eat? It's just my luck that I would find living pterosaurs, and they would all hide away like a bunch of Howard Hugheses."

We might not have seen the winged dragons, but of course they were there all along if we had only known where to look. Many wild animals can avoid being seen if they wish, and *sasabonsam* are no exception. As we ultimately learned, the winged dragons are ambush predators that wait in concealment, only revealing themselves when they strike.

There's no telling how long this discovery would have been in coming, but Walter Spink duly tempted the dragons into the open with the prospect of an easy meal. I do not by any means impugn Walter's abilities as an outdoorsman, but with all the aerial roots and hanging lianas in the way, he couldn't help getting tangled from time to time. Usually these incidents did not worry me, but finally a day came when Walter became immobilized in a knot of hanging vines while the dragons must have been watching. Sensing sudden movement in the corner of my eyes, I whirled just in time to see several gaunt, gargoyle forms peppered about the branches overhead, tensing in anticipation at the old man's distress. Their cadaverous faces leered in Walter's direction with an unwholesome fixation that could only mean one thing.

I had had my first glimpse of *sasabonsam*, and they were sizing up my associate as a potential meal.

I promptly warned Walter that he had an audience.

"Is it them?" he asked.

"Yes," I said.

"It's about damned time. Do they look friendly?"

"No. They look hungry."

Despite their obvious intention, the *sasabonsam* did not attack, if only because I noticed them before they made up their minds. I alerted our guide at the time, a positively hulking young man named Ambroise Ikolé, and we hastened to Walter's side with a *panga* to chop him loose. Though I am doubtless too scrawny to dissuade a hungry animal, Ambroise with his broad shoulders and intimidating height shifted the odds in our favor: the dragons visibly shrank from their attack poise and looked away, feigning complete disinterest in Walter now that two other full-grown men had joined him. Nevertheless, I shudder to think what would have transpired if we had not been present or had noticed them just a few moments later.

Once Ambroise and I had extricated Walter, I inquired, perhaps superfluously, after his well-being.

"Are you all right?" I asked.

"All right?" Walter squawked. "Matthew, if what you're telling me is true, I'll be just fine once I get a look at those dragons!"

With some direction where to look, Walter scrutinized the branch where the *sasabonsam* had almost blended back into the wood with their stillness. I knew that Walter had seen them, though, when his jaw involuntarily dropped, and he just gaped at the dragons in this manner, awestruck, for some moments before speaking again.

"Matthew," he said, "are you seeing what I'm seeing?"

"Yes," I said.

"Good, because I was starting to doubt my own senses. Matthew? They do look just like prehistoric reptiles, don't they?"

"Yes, they do."

"You know, I've dreamed of a moment like this since I was a small boy, longer ago than I care to admit. But enough of this…someone is going to think I'm a homosexual if I keep letting myself get so emotional."

As my alarm at the circumstances of our initial encounter subsided, I couldn't help echoing Walter's sentiments and looking at the winged dragons with more appreciative eyes. Admittedly, they followed the typical pterosaur body plan with which the reader is doubtless familiar, so they were not overly prepossessing with their wedge-shaped heads, scrawny limbs, and membranous wings. At the same time, they nearly brought me to tears despite their ugliness, for they realized a dream, one that I had thought I had put away with my childhood, of seeing in the flesh creatures that I could only have imagined before.

Finally sighting the dragons certainly fulfilled a dream that we had nursed for some time, but it also raised the question of how we would proceed now that we had found them. Among orthodox naturalists, a type specimen is usually killed and collected so that the new species can be officially described and recognized, and indeed, many commentators have questioned why Walter Spink did not simply shoot a specimen of the dragons if he found them (often with insinuating emphasis on the word "if"). As a matter of fact, I initially anticipated that Walter, aware of the convention, would similarly take a sample, but he was aghast when I suggested the possibility of shooting a *sasabonsam* to take home.

"You astound me, Matthew," he said. "I took you for an animal lover. I certainly never dreamed you were so bloodthirsty."

"It's not that," I said. "It's just that we need physical remains."

"What makes you say that?"

"The authorities back home are going to want a type specimen to prove what you've discovered."

"Oh, that. I understand what you're saying now, Matthew, but it's entirely out of the question. For all we know, there are only a handful of these animals in existence, and every individual might be needed to sustain a breeding population. The authorities will just have to accept our word."

Walter may have refused to take a specimen of *sasabonsam*, but he nevertheless conceived a course of action to follow up our new discovery.

"I'll tell you what we're going to do," he said. "We're going to stay here and observe them in the wild. I'm sure there's much more we can learn from live dragons than a dead one. Why"—the more Walter talked about his idea, the more enthusiastic he became—"we'll write up a whole scientific description. I've even thought of a formal name for them. How does *Dracopteryx cryptovenator* sound to you?"

With our luck finding *sasabonsam* and Walter's inspiration, the methodology for our study of the African dragons took form. We would live in the field and observe their behavior and physiology, much as William Douglas Burden had done for their relative the Komodo dragon. Selecting a clearing that was close enough to afford easy access to the dragons (but far enough away that they were not likely to creep up and ambush us in our very beds), we erected an ad hoc research center consisting of two fairly spacious ridge tents where we kept our supplies, took our meals, and slept. The majority of our waking time, however, was devoted to stalking and watching the winged dragons, and we soon got closer to them than any human beings have before—and occasionally closer than even we wanted.

*

Despite the novelty of their discovery, *sasabonsam* are the same as any other animal in most ways. Their lifestyle is geared toward activities that ensure their survival, and their survival depends, like other animals, on feeding. Consequently, food fathering occupies the majority of their time, and it should not surprise the reader that our earliest observations of *sasabonsam*, and indeed the majority of our observations of them, involved the dragons hunting and feeding.

It was actually the winged dragons' particular hunting and feeding behavior that enabled Walter and I to locate them again in the days following that first successful (if harrowing) glimpse of them. As we quickly discovered, *sasabonsam*, like their carnivorous counterparts from Komodo, hunt within a defined foraging area, and particularly within a smaller so-called core of that foraging area consisting of a few prime sites near their roost tree. As a consequence of maintaining such a finite hunting territory, the winged dragons were easier to find, and Walter and I could focus on documenting their feeding habits.

While the winged dragons are constantly seeking food, their manner of doing so is far from active. Being constrained by their reptilian metabolism, they cannot spend energy unnecessarily chasing prey, and they have consequently adapted an alternative hunting strategy based on ambush, much like crocodiles. In *sasabonsam,* this involves perching quietly among the branches or resting on the ground with their wings folded back behind them, as still as the gargoyles they so resemble, waiting for prey to approach them.

This seemingly lackadaisical approach to hunting was, as you can imagine, less than thrilling to watch for ten hours a day, and Walter can perhaps be forgiven for feeling somewhat let down by finding the dragons' manner so torpid.

"I'm not complaining, mind you," he said, "but somehow I expected observing carnivorous winged dragons to be a little more, well, exciting than this."

Despite Walter's complaints, what seemed like inactivity on the dragons' part was really just their hunting strategy. With their dull red, brown, or gray skin and their gaunt limbs with knobby joints, they blend surprisingly well among the lianas and branches, a camouflage that their stillness completes. When some unwary animal passes within range, however, the *sasabonsam* springs its ambush with a speed that is all the more startling because it was practically petrified the moment before. Its toothy jaws dart forward to claim its meal, which is swallowed whole if small enough or otherwise held fast until it expires, then torn apart piece by piece.

When it comes to their diet, *sasabonsam* are not particular and will eat most mammals, birds, insects, and other reptiles. As for mammals, we observed them to feed upon blue duiker (*Philantomba monticola*), bushbuck (*Tragelaphus scriptus*), western tree hyrax (*Dendrohyrax dorsalis*), and several other antelopes and rodents on the ground, as well as primates including crowned guenons among the treetops. They will eat most any of the birds I mentioned in previous chapters and also prey upon gray parrot (*Psittacus erithacus*), emerald cuckoo (*Chrysococcyx cupreus*), and paradise flycatcher (*Terpsiphone viridis*). Rounding out their diet are snakes including the poisonous Gaboon viper (*Bitis gabonica*), which they dispatch too quickly for it to strike back, several species of lizard, and larger invertebrates such as the *Amblypygi* whip scorpions that live in hollow trees and among the leaf litter. Although these dragons are able ambush predators, they are not above scavenging and will also feed on carrion when afforded the opportunity.

The foregoing insights into the feeding behavior and diet of the winged dragons owed themselves to our observation of the small group of dragons into whose foraging area we had stumbled. I use the term group loosely, for *sasabonsam* do not form cohesive social bonds such as, for example, Sasquatch. They do, however, tolerate each other enough to congregate at feeding sites, albeit with frequent squabbles over a prime ambush position or the spoils of a successful hunt. Our study group consisted of three dragons, and with continued observation we learned to distinguish the individuals by their appearance, personality, and position within the group's pecking order.

From early on, we acknowledged the dominant dragon, a male who stood taller than me when his head-crest was considered and possessed a 10-foot wingspan and dark markings almost like tiger stripes across his otherwise tawny hide. He readily took down fairly large duikers and snapped at his associates if they drew too close while he was trying to gorge himself, and between his monarchical temperament and striped skin we called him Shere Khan after the tyrant of Kipling's fictitious jungle. A second individual, who was smaller than Shere Khan (but nevertheless large compared to most *sasabonsam* we observed), kept close and consequently enjoyed first pick of Khan's leavings. We called him Tabaqui after his counterpart in *The Jungle Books.*

Just as any gathering of dragons has its dominant members, it will inevitably have weaker members who barely scrape out an existence feeding on what little does not pass to fitter animals. Our study group was no different, and one small, slate-colored individual with a small head-crest and a lean and hungry look occupied that niche. He always loitered a few steps away from the others—just out of range should they snap in his direction—and lowered his gaunt face in submission whenever they gazed his way.

In addition to being smaller and weaker than others of his kind, this runt (for lack of a better word) was also less successful as a hunter. Even when a small duiker or rodent passed his way, his strike was often just too slow, and he was constantly snapping empty jaws together just as his would-be prey darted safely away. When he could not catch livelier prey, he fed on carcasses too small to interest his comrades or rooted out insects from their hiding places, but it seemed painfully meager fare even for an animal of his fairly diminutive size.

The runt might not have been physically imposing or skilled as a hunter, but he quickly won over Walter, who developed a partiality toward him that would normally be frowned upon in a naturalist.

"Say what you will about that one," he said, "but I like him. He may not be strong or quick, but he's got the pluck to go on. He reminds me of myself, as a matter of fact."

Walter might have appreciated the runt's perseverance, but the dragon's companions gave him short shrift. If the smaller dragon ever found himself in possession of any desirable meat, one of his companions was sure to deprive him of it. Shere Khan especially, if for no other reason than to assure himself of his dominance, would strut over to the smaller dragon or alight at the kill, snap his mighty jaws a few times in his rival's direction to force him back, and appropriate the carcass.

The unfairness of the larger dragon's conduct, aimed at the favorite, positively affronted Walter.

"Who does he think he is?" he demanded. "Beastly thing. He could let the little one have something for himself once in a while."

Regardless of Walter's indignation, he was powerless to impose his morality upon the winged dragons, and this state of affairs continued. We could do little but document their eating habits and hope that the runt would make do for himself. Little did we suspect at the time that the dragon's desperation would drive him to extraordinary measures seeking sustenance, or that our place in this food chain would be tested in the process.

As our initial encounter suggested, the average *sasabonsam* will attack a human being given the opportunity, but for the most part, they do not go out of their way to actively hunt our kind. On the other hand, some dragons are too infirm or otherwise unfit to take down normal prey. Because human beings are slower, weaker, and less attuned to the forest than the wild animals they cannot catch, we present tempting targets to such individuals. While most of the *sasabonsam* ignored us so long as we kept out of striking distance, it was perhaps inevitable that their weaker and less coordinated companion—the runt I mentioned previously—would set his sights on human prey, in this case Walter Spink.

To be sure, the dragon did not immediately attack, but at the same time, he began lingering so dangerously close to us that I could not help suspecting an unwholesome interest. I would lower my eyes to make some notes, confident that the dragons were a safe distance away, only to look up and find the runt suddenly within arm's length. Walter and I would be arguing over the identity of a dragon that had just taken down a good-sized duiker when movement in the corner of my eye would betray the presence of the runt lurking nearby. Soon it seemed that the dragon was disconcertingly close whenever we turned around, often without our observing his approach, and his ruthless gaze was always fixed on Walter while his toothy jaw hung open in what could have been a smile—or a sneer.

"Well, hello there," Walter said to the dragon the first time he surprised us in this manner. "Matthew, it looks as if I have a new friend."

"I don't think he wants to be friends," I said.

"Nonsense. What else could he want?"

Call me prejudiced against cold-blooded reptiles, but I could not conceive of such a predator suddenly deciding to befriend us. At the same time, I could easily imagine him sizing one of us up for a meal. I suggested this to Walter as diplomatically as I could, but he would hear none of it and unequivocally refused to take the precaution of driving the interloper back to a more comfortable distance.

"I absolutely forbid you to chase my new friend away," he said, "and that's the end of it."

If Walter had permitted us to shout or brandish a stick, then perhaps we could have discouraged the dragon from lurking so close, and he might have abandoned his designs. Instead, our tolerance undoubtedly just emboldened him, and being admitted into our circle merely afforded him easy access to a stationary target. Soon he removed any doubt as to his intentions when he snapped at Walter's hand, which had been extended, ironically enough, in an attempt to assure the dragon that we meant no harm.

"Did you see that, Matthew?" Walter squawked (as if I had not tried to warn him). "He tried to bite me!"

After nearly losing a hand to the dragon's jaws, Walter finally acknowledged that its interest was not benign, and he made belated efforts to discourage future attempts.

"Move along!" he would say, as if to an unwanted dog, whenever the dragon ventured close. "Shoo!"

No matter how ardently Walter tried to repulse him now, the dragon had perceived that we were completely harmless, and his reptile brain had become fixated on his new prey. Strong words and sharp gestures might chase him back a few paces for a few minutes, but he would not be deterred altogether. Worse, he became bolder: where before he was merely lurking at every turn, now he actively tried to snatch Walter several times a day.

"I don't understand why he's always after me," Walter complained. "I hope you won't take this the wrong way, Matthew, but there's certainly more meat on you or Ambroise here."

With a carnivorous dragon stalking him, things might have gone badly for Walter, but fortunately the dragon was just as inept when he tried to ambush Walter as when he attacked his accustomed prey. When the runt laid an ambush behind a curtain of liana and tried to strike at Walter through the vines, he became hopelessly tangled and snapped his jaws ineffectually, just out of reach. When he tried landing on a low branch to lunge at Walter as he passed underneath, he misjudged the strength of the branch, which cracked under the added weight and threw the dragon to the ground in an ignominious heap. With these and other, similarly graceless miscarriages, the dragon resembled the cartoon coyote ineffectually trying to catch the roadrunner. His campaign might have been comical but for my fear that he would eventually succeed if he kept trying long enough.

Walter, too, realized that the dragon's bad luck and clumsiness could not guarantee indefinite safety.

"We shall have to do something," he said, "before he takes off an arm or a leg."

Though Walter agreed with me that we had to act, he and I differed when it came to our ideas for resolving the situation.

"It occurs to me," Walter said, "that the only reason any animal would want to eat an old mummy like me is if he was positively starving. It stands to reason, then, that if we start feeding him, he's bound to lose interest in my bony carcass—or at least to be too full up to think about eating me."

"Is that ethical?" I asked. "Won't it just make him dependent on us instead of hunting for himself?"

"Frankly, Matthew, that's a risk I'm willing to take under the present circumstances. And who knows? We may even make a friend of him. I have quite the rapport with animals, if I do say so myself."

Having overruled my objection in this manner, Walter divided his time in the coming weeks between documenting the living habits of the dragons and trying to tame the runt. With the aid of the people of Foulagou, we supplied ourselves daily with bushmeat and fish before venturing into the field, making sure never to be empty-handed in case we should encounter him. Whenever the runt approached, Walter stretched forth his hand, palm up and bearing a generous chunk of meat, thinking to glut the dragon's appetite and thus spare himself from further depredations.

"Here, my little friend," he would say. "I think you'll find this much more satisfying than gnawing on my old bones."

It is easy enough for a perfectly tame dog to nip at a finger while eagerly snatching a treat from its owner's hand, so you can imagine how close a wild dragon, with no particular fondness for its feeder, might come to taking fingers along with the meat. Those first few times, I was certain that Walter would lose his whole hand when the runt snapped his head toward the offering. I was gratefully wrong, but each time the reptile's jaws clacked shut, I winced.

"You needn't worry so, Matthew," Walter said after one such near miss. "I'm quite all right."

"It looked like he almost got you," I said.

"That's just because of where you were standing. If you'd been more to the side, you would have seen that it was never even close."

Regardless of his bravado, even Walter finally tired of hazarding a limb with each feeding and determined to impress better manners upon the beneficiary of his largesse. He continued offering food as before, but from this point, when the dragon poised to lunge at him, he shrieked a rebuke so loud and forceful that the whole forest seemed to hold its breath.

"No!" he squawked. "Wait! *Wait.*"

Perhaps it was the surprise of finding the old man so uncharacteristically aggressive and voluble, but in any event, the dragon was daunted by the sharp words. He recoiled as if afraid to be beaten, and when Walter withheld his bounty, the dragon went through a number of poses, trying to seize upon the posture that would induce the old man to bestow the meal. Finally he rested on his haunches with his sharp face averted submissively, just as he did when deferring to Shere Khan. Only after the dragon had relaxed in this manner did Walter toss him the chunk of meat, which the dragon caught with a great gulp.

"That's better," Walter said. "That's a good boy."

Once Walter set his mind to training the dragon in this manner, he was remarkably consistent and at least superficially successful. At every feeding, he withheld the meat until the dragon adopted a submissive posture, at which point he would toss it. (Given the runt's lack of coordination, this missile was generally fumbled and eaten off the ground rather than caught.) Before long, the dragon was so well-trained that Walter had but to make a gesture as if he was about to toss out some food, and the runt would sit on his haunches, head lowered, to earn his reward like any obedient dog.

"You see, Matthew?" Walter said when this performance had been repeated often enough to imply success. "He's perfectly tame, just as I thought. I told you that I have a rapport with animals."

There was very little I could say to this. To all appearances, Walter had an understanding with his unconventional new friend. Still, while Walter was satisfied that he was no longer in any danger, I privately nursed strong reservations about turning our backs on an animal that had demonstrated the propensity to attack one of us.

Regardless of my doubts, the dragon gave every visible indication of being quite reformed. If any of us so much as looked his way, he dipped his head obsequiously and gave the reptilian equivalent of a whimper. And no matter how many times my gaze reverted to him, thinking to catch him drawing up on Walter or poising for the attack, I only found him preening himself or fixating on some insect flitting in front of him.

Nevertheless, I was right to be concerned, as we soon learned.

Authorities differ as to whether it is actually possible to tame a reptile in the same manner as a dog or a cat. There have been instances in which reptiles have bonded with humans and coexisted without posing the least threat, as an American crocodile named Pocho did with the fisherman who nursed it back to health from a gunshot wound. On the other hand, pet reptiles have been known to attack their owners even after years of docile behavior. Regardless of whether it was possible to tame such a creature, the odds were certainly against Walter being able to accomplish the feat with a perfectly wild dragon in a matter of days.

In retrospect, it seems very likely that the dragon was biding his time all along, presenting a fawning exterior while still thinking to satisfy his meat tooth by feeding on Walter. He only awaited a suitable distraction so that he could effect his intention, and such a distraction inevitably presented itself, at which point he seized the opportunity and struck.

The source of this distraction was a new dragon that had joined the others in their feeding area, and whose lack of familiarity with the group's dynamics led him to the faux pas of repeatedly trying to feed before Shere Khan. This led to increasingly vocal clashes that promised our first glimpse of combat between two dragons. I had meant to guard Walter against treachery by the runt, but I am only human and found my attention understandably drawn by the hissing and shrieking of the displaying dragons. We were all so preoccupied with the fighting that we lost track of the runt, and my first hint that he was up to anything only came when Walter cried out.

"Matthew, help! He's got me!"

Walter Spink's subsequent publications on his work with unknown animals testify to his having survived this attack, but it was only his formal manner of dress that saved him. Sensible people might wear lightweight, short-sleeved or sleeveless shirts when trekking through an environment as sultry as a tropical rainforest, but I have already mentioned Walter's field attire, which incorporated his accustomed tweed blazer regardless of the heat. When the dragon nipped at his inattentive backside, it only got hold of the tail of his jacket. Thus, when I whirled at Walter's distress call, I found him struggling with the dragon, which clenched Walter's coattail in his greedy jaws like a dog wrestling its owner for a chew toy.

"Let me go, you brute," Walter said, "this instant!"

This tussle broke up quickly once Ambroise and I hastened to Walter's side. The runt was by no means bold enough to confront three humans, and he abruptly surrendered Walter's coattail and backed away with head lowered as if expecting to be struck. Walter came away from the encounter unharmed with the exception of his sense of having befriended the dragon, which was utterly destroyed.

"The scoundrel!" he said. "He must have been pretending all along. Well, I won't give him the chance to try that again."

Walter's resolution notwithstanding, it was impossible to guarantee that the dragon would never find another opportunity to strike, but the three of us on our guard minimized the risk. Judging from several unsuccessful attempts that the runt made against Walter after this incident, it seems clear that he would have snatched Walter given the chance, regardless of how docile he pretended to be when he knew we were watching. We called him Uriah Heep, for like the Dickens character, he always feigned humility to our faces but privately schemed against Walter.

Although no harm was ultimately done, Walter's failed attempt to befriend the winged dragon should serve as a lesson to future dracontologists against forgetting that these creatures are predators. They are conditioned by millions of years of evolution to hunt their fellow creatures rather than befriending them, and most are capable of taking down a human being. Working in proximity to these creatures without due respect for their nature—or worse yet, thinking they can be tamed—could have fatal consequences, as Walter Spink narrowly avoided learning not only in the instance I just described but many more times during our work with the dragons.

CHAPTER IV
FLIGHT AND FIGHT

Along with a taste for human flesh and fiery (or in some accounts pestilential) breath, the ability to fly on membranous, bat-like wings is a distinguishing trait of the dragons of legend. Because they possess the latter, *sasabonsam* are as close to their mythical counterparts as any creatures that have yet been discovered in the animal kingdom. They are also the only extant reptiles capable of true flight. Consequently, Walter Spink and I paid special attention to the flight mechanism and abilities of the winged dragons during our time with them.

Observing the winged dragons in flight presented no challenge thanks to our close association with the group I described in the previous chapter. As they grew more accustomed to our presence, the dragons no longer bothered to conceal themselves from us and flitted frequently between ambuscades. Thus, we quickly noted their flying style, which alternates between gliding to conserve energy and flapping, with the aid of powerful shoulder muscles, to stay aloft. We also remarked how the shape of their wings has evolved to facilitate flight in their forested habitat: *sasabonsam* have broad but short wings to afford maneuverability among trunks and branches, as opposed to the narrow and high-aspect wings that seabirds have developed for gliding long distances.

In addition to observing typical *sasabonsam* flight, we noted some variation in flying abilities between individual dragons. Most of them flew effortlessly and dodged obstacles with ease, but the same feats demanded more noticeable effort on Heep's part and were carried off much less successfully by him. Lacking the musculature of his companions, Heep often hung precariously in midair while flapping furiously to generate lift. He usually gained altitude rather than tumbling back to earth as we feared, but this required substantial perseverance to make up for the strength that he lacked.

Beyond the difficulty he had remaining aloft, Heep's maneuvering was also clumsier than that of his companions. On one memorable occasion, he outdid even himself by running headlong into a tree. Though we were not looking in his direction at the time, we heard a sickly crunch and followed the sound to the foot of a bokanga tree where Heep was collecting himself up from an undignified pile, at which point we guessed what had befallen.

"Good heavens," Walter said. "Do you suppose he's all right?"

(The dragon was thankfully unhurt, and since he had almost certainly been trying to sneak up on Walter when he had his mishap, the rest of us did not feel particularly sorry for him.)

As opposed to Heep's bumbling flight, the other dragons acquitted themselves much more gracefully in the air. If Shere Khan, Tabaqui, or any of the periodic visitors to our study area ever grazed a branch or stumbled into a landing, we did not see it. Rather, they wheeled in graceful arcs, banked adroitly around trees in their path, and swooped over and under branches, all with only the most cursory flapping. Shere Khan generally lacked traits that we might admire, but he nevertheless solicited our grudging praise by his form and grace in flight.

"He may be a brute," Walter said, "but I have to admit that he's a magnificent creature to watch when he's flying."

Nor was Walter the only one taken with the sight of the flying dragons. When I watched their boomerang shapes silhouetted against the rising or setting sun, or when I heard the *swoosh* of their muscular wings cleaving the air—up and down, up and down—I marveled at how effortlessly and, indeed, majestically they moved. It was as if I had been vouchsafed a glimpse of the living, breathing past, and it staggered me to think that I should experience it when all the vast reservoir of humanity, including people more adventurous and daring than I, had been denied. Though I was poorly equipped to express myself, I was deeply grateful to Walter Spink for sharing this hidden spectacle with me (albeit admittedly less so—and less admiring of the dragons—when I was snatching Walter away from Heep's jaws).

For all our observations of dragon flight, Walter and I found that one integral component of the process remained unknown: we could not say how they became airborne. There was much debate in those days concerning the manner by which *sasabonsam*'s pterosaur ancestors took off, and we might have put it to rest quickly but for the lack of cooperation on our winged dragons' parts. Being living animals going about their business, they neither moved in slow motion nor troubled about being in the clear when they launched. Thus, they either took wing in the blink of an eye, before we could register the means by which they did so, or they took off from the brush where leaves and branches blocked our view of their movements until they were airborne.

"Did you see how he did that?" Walter would ask me each time one of the dragons took off.

"No."

"Bother. Me, neither. How the devil are we supposed to figure out how they fly?"

Despite having access to the dragons, we could not describe an important aspect of their flight, but there was little we could do to force the revelation. We watched as vigilantly as possible for an opportunity to complete our knowledge, and we found plenty to learn about the dragons in the meantime. As a matter of fact, the exploits of one of our dragons in particular would keep us busy enough in the coming days that we soon forgot to bemoan the few things we could not yet understand about their flight.

*

Even if we could not yet fully describe the physiological mechanism by which *sasabonsam* fly, our observations afforded us plenty of information concerning their use of the adaptation. As you might expect, flight facilitates the winged dragons' hunting and feeding, but not in the way you might think. Not being active hunters, they do not fly after prey or swoop upon it as predatory birds do. Still, the ability to fly permits *sasabonsam* to feed on creatures that their terrestrial counterparts do not dare.

Even relatively powerful reptiles such as crocodiles will not attack large prey such as grown elephants or buffalo, knowing that they would provoke a fierce response with little hope of actually getting a meal for their efforts. They may seize a juvenile here or there, but in doing so they risk reprisals and may barely escape with their lives, to say nothing of losing the meal they anticipated. If confined to a two-dimensional existence on the ground, *sasabonsam* would undoubtedly be loath to assume such risks, but this is where their flight adaptation confers an advantage. They can retreat to the air when threatened on the ground, so they venture to take down juvenile members of some fairly bellicose species knowing that they can escape safely to the air with the fruits of their hunt.

Little suspecting how flight would embolden the dragons, I did not expect them to contend with the small herd of forest buffalo (*Syncerus caffer nanus*) that lived in our study area. Buffalo calves may be small enough for animals the size of *sasabonsam* to take down, but their parents average 600 to 700 pounds—heavy enough to trample even a large dragon if caught on the ground—and possess formidable temperaments. Their reputation for defending their young against animal predators and human hunters alike is legendary, and even lions and crocodiles have been given reason to regret a hasty attempt on a buffalo calf. It seemed to me that the dragons would be foolish to even try, considering the plentiful, more docile game in their hunting area.

Walter, for his part, shared my expectation when we noticed the male buffalo with his harem and several young approaching the dragons, who were as yet unnoticed in their concealment among the foliage of the shrub layer.

"They can't possibly attack," Walter said. "I'm sure our leathery-winged friends must know better than to trifle with buffalo."

Even if we did not anticipate an altercation between the buffalo and the dragons, Walter, Ambroise and I kept a safe distance away from the dragons' ambuscade out of respect for the fierce reputation of African buffalo. At that distance and with brush between us and the animals, we could not see all that happened, but a squeal heralded an unlooked-for attack and set the herd in motion. I immediately suspected what had happened, and sure enough, one of the dragons erupted into the air above the herd, clutching a squirming calf in his jaws.

"What the devil is happening?" Walter asked.

"They took one of the calves," I said.

"Good heavens! Which one did it?"

Even if I had not already recognized him, I would have guessed which dragon would have been daring enough to effect such an attack right under the noses of the calf's parents. There was, after all, one dragon who outstripped the others not only in hunting prowess but sheer brazen audacity. As it was, his tawny hide and dark stripes reassured me of my identification.

"It was Shere Khan," I said.

"I should have known it would be him," Walter said. "He's wicked enough to try almost anything."

Over the course of our observation, Shere Khan continued to prey upon fairly risky game, but soon he had a mishap that drove home the risk he took. One day he lay in ambush, as always, and seized a young buffalo as the herd passed. Immediately the dragon took to the air, but his quarry must have weighed some 200 pounds, well beyond Shere Khan's capacity to lift. For several tense moments, the dragon gripped his struggling, bleating prey and beat his wings ineffectually while its enraged parents charged. Just before the buffalo converged upon him, Shere Khan released the calf and mounted up into the canopy, leaving the angry but impotent buffalo uselessly goring the air he had just vacated.

Though Shere Khan dodged the consequences of his miscalculation this time, it occurred to us that his luck would almost certainly run out eventually if he continued taking such risks.

"As much as I hate the thought," Walter said, "he's going to get himself killed if he keeps carrying on like this."

Regardless of our growing concern, Shere Khan continued, as bold as ever, to attack whatever animal presented a target, and his hubris finally betrayed him just as Walter and I had feared. This time it was a family of gorillas against whom he trespassed when their travel-feeding brought them into the dragon's hunting ground and past his ambuscade. The brush in which the dragon hid concealed the initial scuffle from me, but I heard the by-then familiar squeal of an infant crying for its parents, followed by the sight of Shere Khan flapping his way up from the understory with a black and unmoving form clutched in his jaw.

"I can't quite see," Walter said. "What have they got now?"

"It's Shere Khan," I said, "and he's taken a baby gorilla."

"Good heavens. What a wicked creature!"

Though Shere Khan had taken the baby gorilla, he did not by any means escape with it. The silverback gorilla, reacting quickly, leapt into the air and grasped one of the dragon's legs, and then 400 pounds of ape came down, pulling Shere Khan back to earth with it. The dragon flapped his wings strenuously but could not gain enough momentum to break free of the silverback's grasp, and one mighty tug of the gorilla's arm plucked him right out of the sky.

Once Shere Khan had been grounded, a primordial combat ensued like a scene out of Edgar Rice Burroughs's land that time forgot. The silverback was immediately on top of the dragon, restraining its wings with his big black fists, but Shere Khan gave as good as he got. The dragon lunged toward the gorilla's face, snapping a mouthful of snaggled teeth inches from the pug nose so that the silverback instinctively threw his hands up to protect himself. Once free, Shere Khan surged upward in an attempt at flight, only to be drawn back into the brush and pummeled by his opponent, and only a desperate fluttering of the dragon's wings kept the gorilla from getting a strong enough grip to rend him limb from limb as it undoubtedly meant to do. With enough pecking and nipping, Shere Khan finally managed to drive the gorilla backward, at which point the dragon disengaged and became airborne. The gorilla fumbled after him and briefly clutched his left wing, but I heard a snap and the animals separated, with the ape tumbling to the ground and the dragon climbing into the treetops.

"That was a little close," Walter said, "but it looks like no harm was done. All the same, I do wish he'd be more careful."

Contrary to Walter's assessment, Shere Khan did not fly away from his altercation with the gorilla unscathed. Though he seemed well enough when he retreated, his wings must have given out at some point after his escape, for he was suffering from a broken wing—and accordingly grounded—the next time we saw him. As a result of this injury, Shere Khan would be flightless for the foreseeable future, but that would only be the beginning of our troubles with him.

⁂

Sasabonsam are generally hardy creatures, but a surprising number of injuries that do not kill them outright may still deprive them of flight. A fracture of one of the delicate wing bones, especially the radius or ulna, will make flight impossible, but other injuries such as torn ligaments or ruptured wing membranes will similarly ground a dragon. Although they affect the flight mechanism in different manners, they are all equally disabling, and one of them must have befallen Shere Khan while he was grappling with the silverback.

Though it was impossible to immediately distinguish the nature of the injury, we immediately noticed that something was wrong with Shere Khan when we made contact the morning after his skirmish with the gorilla. While Heep and Tabaqui flitted about the canopy, Shere Khan remained uncharacteristically grounded, trying not to let on that anything was amiss. Despite his pretense, however, the manner in which he moved gave away his injury unmistakably: he stalked about on his hind legs and his right arm, with his left wing dragging lifelessly at his side.

"Oh, dear," Walter said. "He's not doing well at all, is he?"

"No," I said. "I suppose not."

Initially, I thought Walter's grim pronouncement was the limit of our involvement in Shere Khan's fate, but this was only because I did not know him well enough yet. In what would become his accustomed manner of meddling in the lives of his research subjects, Walter resolved to rescue the dragon rather than leaving him to nature and hoping for the best.

"There's nothing for it," he said. "We shall simply have to take care of him."

I did a double take. "Come again?"

"We'll give him first aid, Matthew."

"I'm not sure about this. We're not veterinarians."

"Perhaps not, but I've splinted a few birds with injured wings in my time. It's basically the same principle."

"Except that this 'bird' could take off your hand while you're splinting its wing."

"Why, we'll just have to find some way around that."

Given the aggressive tendencies of *sasabonsam,* the only way we could safely offer first aid would be to sedate Shere Khan first. With some effort, we obtained a small supply of succinylcholine chloride, which is often used to tranquilize crocodiles, and injected it into a chunk of duiker meat. Shere Khan ate it greedily (if for no other reason than to keep Heep from enjoying it), and 30 minutes later, he teetered drunkenly, toppled over, and remained out even when poked with a stick. We bound his mouth shut in case he should awaken during our ministrations, and then we were free to operate on the dragon's wing.

First aid for a wing injury consists of treating for infection where necessary and immobilizing the injured wing, both of which are thankfully straightforward tasks even for dracontologists with no veterinary background. Upon triaging Shere Khan, we discovered that his wing was neither torn nor lacerated, and presuming a fracture but no risk of infection, we applied the latter treatment. Handling the broken left batwing as gingerly as if it were made of glass, we folded it against the dragon's body, and then I held it in place—anxious to be done before our patient awoke and began lashing out at us—while Walter and Ambroise wound bandages around body and wing to bind the limb in place. Amateurs though we were, we acquitted this task before the dragon could awake as I feared, and our bandages held even when the dragon awoke and resumed activity.

"That went well," Walter said, "if I do say so myself."

So long as the broken wing is treated, the loss of flight is not per se fatal to *sasabonsam.* The main concern for an injured animal is its ability to continue gathering food for itself, but as I've previously indicated, the winged dragons are equally able to hunt on the ground as they are in the trees. In the days after his injury, Shere Khan successfully fended for himself even if his hunting was circumscribed to the forest floor. As a matter of fact, the disabled dragon still mustered enough ferocity in terms of pecking and hissing to chase his companions away from their kills, as he did to both Heep and Tabaqui frequently during the first days of his convalescence.

"There's something his injury hasn't affected," Walter said. "He's still just as nasty as ever."

The dragons might not starve if temporarily grounded by an injury, but starvation is not the only threat to a grounded dragon. While it seems dubious that any of the local predators such as leopards would be specifically disposed to prey upon *sasabonsam,* they might still do so if the opportunity presented itself. Nor are predators the only concern, for there are several species of prey animals intelligent enough to bear a grudge, and being confined to the ground without their usual means of quick retreat puts the dragons at risk of reprisals from them.

Shere Khan had made many enemies in the course of his raids, but it was the silverback gorilla who found him first. Either through the operation of chance or because he had returned to avenge himself on the dragon, the gorilla stumbled upon the lurking dragons feuding over a kill and immediately recognized the villainous creature that had attacked his child. Walter and I did not see the gorilla coming until a rumbling bark announced its presence, at which point it was already barreling through the brush toward the dragons. Tabaqui and Heep retreated into the air without incident, but Shere Khan, in his flightless state, could only gallop away as fast as his three good limbs would carry him. The dragon ambled toward the post from which Walter and I had been monitoring the dragons, slowly being overtaken by the pursuing primate, and I closed my eyes in anticipation of their collision.

When the anticipated clash did not come, I opened my eyes and beheld an unexpected sight: the gorilla had stopped dead in his tracks some 40 feet away, and Shere Khan, untouched, stumbled to a stop about ten feet away from us, looking just as surprised to find himself still in one piece as I was.

Shere Khan's deliverance can be explained by the gorilla's attitude toward human beings. Far from being the ferocious monsters they are often depicted to be, gorillas are actually retiring creatures, at least when it comes to interacting with human beings. They will not by any means approach unfamiliar humans—in this case Walter and me—and thus our presence stayed the silverback from pursuing the dragon any farther.

"Why, he must be afraid to come any closer to us," Walter said.

Nor were Walter and I the only ones to perceive the situation. Shere Khan, too, must have sensed that we were the cause of the gorilla's sudden reticence, for he not only stayed within the radius of our protective presence but edged closer to Walter, eyeing the ape the whole time.

"That's it," Walter said, flourishing a gnarled hand to wave the dragon closer. "Come to me, you old scoundrel. You'll be safe here."

The dragon came to heel at Walter's side like an obedient pet, and the strategy worked: after venting his frustration with a tantrum that consisted of alternating threat barks, chest-beating, panting, and tearing vegetation, the silverback ultimately went on his way without satisfying his violent purpose. If we thought that this would be the end of the matter, however, we were wrong. Even once the gorilla had gone, Shere Khan remained leery lest it should return, and he refused to venture away from us. This might almost have been cute, but then he followed us when we finished our shift watching the dragons and began the hike back to camp.

Having realized that there was safety in loitering about the resident dracontologists, Shere Khan seemed determined to claim sanctuary, and Walter became equally determined to grant it.

"I don't suppose there's anything for it," he said. "We shall just have to let him stay with us until he can fly again."

"Walter, we can't," I said. "He's not just an injured bird. He's a dangerous carnivore."

"I daresay he won't eat us, if that's what you're worried about. At least not while he needs us to hide him, anyway. We can't just leave him to fend for himself in this condition. He may be an old villain, but he's still a prehistoric survivor. His life is precious."

Between Walter's single-mindedness and my distaste for confrontation, my objections came to nothing, and the dragon found sanctuary with us. When we did not protest his company, Shere Khan hobbled in our wake and set himself up in our camp, where we would try to nurse him back to health for release back into the wild. In retrospect, I suppose that it was the right thing to do rather than leaving Shere Khan to the tender mercies of his enemies, but that did not make the situation any easier in the coming days as we learned how difficult it is to live with an injured dragon.

*

Taking in and caring for injured wildlife presents several challenges even to experienced animal rescuers, and dracontologists trying to rescue dragons are at a greater disadvantage. The prospect of healing requires scrupulous attention to their nutritional and medical needs, which in the case of newly-discovered animals such as dragons can only be guessed through analogy to similar but better-known species. Caring for an animal through trial and error is difficult enough, but the experience is even more harrowing when the convalescent is a large carnivore who is also a fugitive from vengeful primates, as Walter, Ambroise, and I quickly learned.

Truth be told, much of our difficulty arose from Walter babying the injured dragon, for lack of a better word. He insisted that we feed Shere Khan rather than allowing him to hunt for himself, but this was easier said than done. A grown *sasabonsam* only eats about nine pounds of meat per day—more when convalescing—but keeping supplied with fresh meat in a tropical environment required daily trips into Foulagou, and Walter directed frequent small feedings rather than gorging the dragon at once. We seemed to be constantly either obtaining meat or feeding it to the dragon, and our efforts seemed somewhat superfluous given Shere Khan's facility hunting on the ground with his good legs.

"Are you sure this is necessary?" I asked Walter. "He's getting around well enough to hunt without our help."

"Nonsense," Walter said. "We need to keep him as well-fed as possible so he'll get better all the more quickly."

Aside from consuming the majority of our time, these feedings were also physically hazardous. I have already described how clumsy old Heep nearly nipped at the hand that fed him, so you can imagine how close a more dexterous dragon like Shere Khan came to taking a hand or finger at each feeding. Ambroise was a stolid helper and tried not to complain, but I had no such scruples.

"If we keep this up," I said to Walter, "someone's going to lose a hand."

"He doesn't want to eat your hand, Matthew," Walter said. "He's just spirited is all."

Spirited or not, the dragon was carnivorous and possessed strong jaws full of sharp teeth, so having him loitering around camp unnerved the more sensible members of our expedition (by which I mean Ambroise and me) even when he was not actively sniping at a limb. None of us possessed a weapon to defend ourselves except our own sharp words, and our ridge tents were hardly secure against an animal the size of the winged dragon if he invaded while we slept, as we feared he might. Walter, deeming the dragon too disabled to harm us, would not hear of us taking any precautions, but Ambroise and I felt strongly enough about the issue that we countermanded him, at least in secret.

"I do not mean any disrespect," Ambroise said, "but I do not feel safe sleeping with the dragon so close, not one bit."

"Me, neither," I said. "We could start keeping up a watch."

"Walter Spink won't like it one bit."

"Maybe you and I can keep watch without letting him know."

With this understanding, Ambroise and I made a plan and took alternating four-hour shifts at watch overnight so that the dragon never had the run of camp without at least someone keeping an eye lest he be tempted to exploit our inattention. In order to keep this arrangement from Walter, however, we both needed to be awake as usual during the day, and we had to function on just a few hours' sleep. As you may imagine, lack of sleep soon took a toll, and though he did not press me enough to discover the truth, Walter was constantly remonstrating me when I started to doze.

"Matthew, are you even listening to me? What the devil is wrong with you lately?"

As if tending to Shere Khan while simultaneously keeping him from eating us were not disruptive enough, we also suffered periodic sieges from the gorillas as a consequence of our harboring the fugitive dragon. Early in Shere Khan's convalescence, they must have tracked him to our camp, for we were awakened one day—and then on each succeeding day—by the silverback, reinforced by two blackbacks, tattooing his chest, barking threats, and tossing fruit. Though they would not venture within 20 feet of our tents and left shortly after we emerged for the morning, the noise was distracting even if we were not physically threatened.

Being awakened each morning by the sound of angry gorillas roaring for the dragon's blood was annoying enough, and Shere Khan's behavior hardly mollified them. Knowing himself safe, he made no attempt to hide, and if any animal ever teased his foes, it was Shere Khan: he flapped his wings as if to call attention to himself and honked as if daring them to come closer. This provocative behavior earned him more than one volley of fruit, but these were easy enough for him to sidestep even if he could not fly away.

"He's pretty nasty for supposedly being injured," I said to Walter, "don't you think?"

"I shall take it as a sign that he's getting better," Walter said.

Though Walter had faith in Shere Khan's recovery, the dragon did not noticeably improve in the timeframe we would have expected. A wing fracture would normally heal in about two weeks, but even once we removed his bandage, he continued to hobble about on tree legs and favor his left wing. At Walter's insistence, we continued feeding him and letting him stay in camp, hoping that we would soon see improvement.

There's no telling how much longer we would have coddled the dragon in the vain hope we would see progress, but fortunately I began to suspect Shere Khan's behavior. He seemed altogether too comfortable being fed, and with my cynical outlook, I could not help reflecting that it would be all too easy for the dragon to become accustomed to this easy lifestyle even once he had healed, and then to malinger to prolong it. As a consequence, I made a point of watching him, and my observation ultimately exposed his pretense.

Shere Khan unwittingly revealed himself when a mouse scurried across his path one day while I was monitoring him from behind the tent flap. A moment before, he had been languidly ambling about camp on three legs, but at the sight of prey, Shere Khan leapt on it with a swiftness—and the use of all four limbs—that belied all his pretense to an injury. If I had any doubt at this point that the dragon's seeming debilitation was an act meant to prolong his stay with us, I would have become certain when Walter squawked to me and Shere Khan immediately lifted his left wing to cradle it protectively at the sound of the old man's voice.

Even once I had penetrated the dragon's deception, I was hard-pressed to convince Walter.

"I really don't know about this, Matthew," he said. "He looks just the same to me, and I don't know that a dragon would be clever enough to fake this type of injury."

Ultimately, if I was going to convince Walter that Shere Khan was only playing Camille, I was going to have to devise a way for Walter to see it for himself. After some thought, I came up with just such a test of Shere Khan's physical ability, and I put it into effect at the dragon's next feeding. Making sure to summon Walter, I tossed a particularly tempting chunk of bushmeat a good 30 feet out of camp, thinking Shere Khan in his eagerness would forget to feign injury and dart toward it. Before I could congratulate myself on my cleverness, however, I found myself outsmarted: Shere Khan limped over to the meat on three legs just as if he were still crippled with a broken wing.

"I must confess to being somewhat underwhelmed by your demonstration, Matthew," Walter said.

My scheme might not have directly shown Shere Khan up for the fraud he was, but it nevertheless set him up for exposure. While the dragon was still far enough outside camp to be beyond the protection of our presence, a primordial roar rent the peace of the forest, and the silverback gorilla, who had evidently been lurking in anticipation of such an opportunity, barreled toward the dragon. The gorilla was too close for Shere Khan to reach the protection of camp before he was clobbered, but since he was only faking his disability by this point, he easily spread his wings and took off into the air, sneering wickedly at the pugnacious primate as he left it hooting impotently at his retreating tail end.

With Shere Khan flapping away before his eyes, even Walter couldn't deny either the dragon's recovery or his trickery.

"What a scoundrel!" Walter said. "I wonder just how long he's been pretending."

Regardless of how long Shere Khan had successfully deceived us, he had finally been unmasked, and he seemed to understand that his cachet with us had been used up. He resumed his habitation in the woods with his usual companions, and life in our camp became at least as normal as it had been before our adventure with the rescued dragon. Truth be told, we could not help admiring the dragon's ingenuity, even if he had used it to put one over on us, but we were nonetheless pleased to be done living with him.

Aside from exposing Shere Khan as a flying flimflam, this experience also filled one of the gaps in our understanding of the flight mechanism of *sasabonsam*. Though we had previously been denied a good look at the winged dragons taking off, Shere Khan was in the open when he flew away from the charging gorilla. For the record, the winged dragons do not take off bipedally like birds, presumably due to their great mass. Rather, they launch quadrupedally, springing forward with their hind legs and up with their forelimbs while extending their wings to generate lift.

Walter and I learned quite a bit about dragon flight during this time, but we learned even more about Shere Khan's audacious behavior. The dragon was dangerously cocky, as his injurious confrontation with the gorillas attested, and we had no reason to believe that he would be any more cautious in the future. To the contrary, he remained as bold as ever, and his continuing acts of hubris would soon cause us no end of worry and effort in attempting to safeguard the ungrateful beast from the consequences of his outrageous behavior.

CHAPTER V
LOVEMAKING, MATCHMAKING, AND OTHER FORMS OF MAGIC

Reptiles may be cold-blooded biologically speaking, but they are as hot-blooded when it comes to mating as any other creatures. Reproduction is as necessary to *sasabonsam* as any other species, and the competition for mates is no less fierce because of their reptilian nature. During our time among them, Walter Spink and I witnessed the zeal with which the winged dragons pursue mating opportunities and romance each other, and to my knowledge we were the first—and so far the only—witnesses to such behavior.

Our observation of winged dragons mating was some time in coming, and with good reason: for the longest time, we only observed male dragons. This first occurred to us when we realized that all the dragons we had seen bore some variation of the head crests I previously mentioned, which were almost certainly a secondary sexual characteristic unique to males, as such features are in many reptile species. This realization raised interesting questions about the dragons' distribution.

"There must be females somewhere," Walter said. "The species couldn't have survived this long if they were all confirmed old bachelors like me."

Sasabonsam do indeed have female counterparts, but the sexes do not mingle in day-to-day life, and only come together when actively mating. Having been the first to observe the process, we could not at the time anticipate the signs that the dragons were ready to mate, and we were mystified when the members of our study group became more aggressive toward each other, sniping at their neighbors with their toothy jaws without the least provocation.

"What the devil has gotten into them, do you suppose?" Walter asked. "They're even snippier than usual."

Increased aggression, such as that which Walter and I had already begun to notice, is the first sign that *sasabonsam* are gearing up to mate, and the second is listlessness and wandering beyond their usual hunting area. One morning the dragons were not to be found at any of their accustomed feeding sites, though the meaning of their disappearance was lost on us at the time. With some luck, we tracked Heep down, migrating like the others, and the frequent rests necessitated by his more feeble constitution allowed us to follow him, wondering the whole time where he could be going with such determination.

Even though we had no idea of his purpose, we followed Heep until he reached a rainforest clearing or *bai,* where we were arrested by the sight of more *sasabonsam* than we could have imagined. There were large dragons and small dragons, brown dragons and gray dragons, but they were all males bearing some variation of the crests we had already observed. Some stood expectantly while others paced irritably or flitted here and there about the clearing, and they produced a great cacophony with their collective squawking.

We tried counting the dragons in the clearing, but their constant shifting and jockeying for position defied our attempts.

"Bother," Walter said after being stymied for the third time. "I can't remember if I already counted that one. It's impossible to make an accurate count with them moving around like that."

Eventually we gave up trying to count the dragons, losing track at 34, but I hope that even this conservative count gives the reader an impression of the magnitude of the gathering.

As you can imagine, the sight of so many predators gathered together gave me pause, for with their numbers, they could undoubtedly have taken us down easily, and the only question would have been the division of our remains among them. For that reason, Ambroise and I (wisely in my opinion) lingered within the cover of the forest where we might go unnoticed, but Walter was too eager to observe a new behavior. When Heep stumbled into a clumsy landing and ambled toward the congregation, dipping his head obsequiously, Walter followed without regard to the proximity of a throng of carnivorous reptiles.

"What are you doing?" I asked, understandably alarmed.

"I just want to see," Walter said. "I'll only go a few more feet."

"But there are dozens of them. What if they attack?"

"I suppose I could err on the side of caution, but how the devil am I supposed to see?"

Gratefully, Walter saw reason (if only on this one occasion) and kept to the edge of the clearing with the rest of us. There, we watched the dragons from behind a natural blind of ferns and dogbane shrubs where we could study them without presenting an easy meal.

At first we could not guess why the dragons had gathered in this manner, but over the next few hours, their behavior began to suggest their purpose. They made a tremendous noise, cawing in such a conspicuous manner that they can only have meant to attract attention to themselves. Some reptilian popinjays strutted about or preened themselves fastidiously, and others fought with each other, tussling and snapping until one of the competitors backed away with head bent.

With so many male dragons posturing to appear strong or attractive in this manner, it occurred to me that this display must be meant to attract mates, but Walter second-guessed my hypothesis when I shared it.

"I don't see how they can do any mating without any females present," he said, "unless you're suggesting that they're all homosexuals, which I strongly doubt."

As if to answer Walter's skepticism, a creature appeared like none we had seen before and joined the posturing males. It happened quickly: there was the susurrus of flapping wings, and a shadow, broad and ominous as a thunderhead, scudded over the gathered throng, some members of which hopped in place or ruffled their wings eagerly at the arrival. At the heart of the host, the dragons crowded back to afford a landing site where an immense creature, roughly the same shape as the rest (sans head crest) but twice as large and as white as a Siberian winter, touched down.

"Good heavens," Walter said, anticipating my own conclusion, "it must be a female! I think you might be right after all, Matthew. How exciting to see them mating!"

As Walter and I discovered, *sasabonsam* practice lek mating, a polygynous system in which females choose from among competing males. At mating times, males congregate in some neutral location, which becomes a so-called lekking arena, where they call to attract females. Once females arrive, the males present themselves for review and make courtship displays, and the females mate with the most physically attractive specimens.

Once the great female had arrived, mating activity could begin in earnest. The magnificent creature—who was twice my height standing and possessed an exceptionally long and gracile neck, something like a giraffe's—meandered unhurriedly among the assembled bachelors, examining her potential suitors with a discerning gaze. Indeed, despite the ardor of the bachelors, she appraised them as coolly as a savvy shopper selecting ripe produce in the supermarket. If one of them interested her enough for her to linger and take a closer look, the lucky male would brandish his crest and flutter his wings flamboyantly, but even then she reserved decision pending examination of the remaining males.

Nor was this judicious individual the only one attracted by the males' display, for several more females arrived in similar fashion. They were all significantly larger than the males and pale in color, and we called them *shamantin* after *sasabonsam*'s female counterpart in legend. Whenever another *shamantin* joined the assemblage, the *sasabonsam* shuffled themselves so as to be most visible to the newcomer, skirmishing with one another for positions where they might catch her eye.

Although it was difficult to keep track of them in the multitude, the bachelors who formed our study group competed alongside the rest. Shere Khan was the easiest to recognize by his striped hide and size, the latter being greater than that of most any male dragon we saw, even in this larger crowd; by the same token, he was the most visible to females and needed no great effort to attract their attention. Tabaqui was his shadow as always, and Heep skulked near the others, recognizable by his stooping posture and bowed head. When a female passed by, Heep would straighten, as desperate to be noticed as any other member of his sex, but Shere Khan would invariably snap in his direction and drive him into the background.

"That really is uncalled-for," Walter said after one such scuffle. "Poor Heep is going to have enough trouble getting himself noticed, scrawny as he is, without that old villain chasing him out of sight."

"It's nice to see you're not holding all the times he's tried to eat you against him," I said of Walter's sympathy for the runt.

"I can't hold his nature against him, can I? And I feel as if everybody deserves to find love, even a carnivorous reptile."

Whether the system is fair or not, the males will vie with each other in this manner until the *shamantin* chooses one of them, at which point the act of mating occurs, preceded by a beautiful display. The female signals her selection of a mate by making a vocalization consisting of a series of clicks, at which point the male takes to the air, where he circles and loop de loops overhead. After anywhere from a few minutes to a half an hour, depending on her eagerness, the female joins him in the sky, more lithe and graceful than anything her size should be, and swoops about in a complementary display. The two come closer and closer in their respective flights until suddenly they are circling in unison, and then they come back to earth side by side. Once they have grounded, the *sasabonsam* mounts his *shamantin*, makes several thrusts, and then melts discreetly back into the crowd.

The first time we witnessed mating dragons, we were underwhelmed by the act itself. The copulation was so brief compared with the foreplay that it hardly seemed possible the male could have accomplished anything.

"If that's all there is to it," Walter said dryly, "then I daresay I didn't miss much being a lifelong bachelor."

Anticlimactic as they might have been, we witnessed several more, similarly fleeting copulations over the course of that first day. As is typical in lek polygyny, proportionally few of the males actually mated—from our study group, only Shere Khan was selected—and the females, once satisfied, took wing back to their own haunts without any ceremony. As the males dispersed, presumably to resume their normal desexualized lives on the morrow, I could not help reflecting that the dragons' sexual relations seemed much more straightforward than those of my own kind, but I was mistaken both in my perception that the *sasabonsam* mating ritual was simple and my belief that the current round of mating had ended.

Once the *sasabonsam* mating period begins, it continues on subsequent days with similar fervor on the part of the participants. If the season we observed is any indication, the dragon lekking period lasts for at least two weeks, during which the *sasabonsam* return to the lekking arena daily and compete for *shamantin.* Taking advantage of this unique opportunity, Walter and I hastened to the arena each morning during that time and recorded the mating practices of the dragons until early evening when they dispersed back to their roosts.

It might seem as if such a lengthy lekking period should afford mating opportunities for the less prepossessing males who had been passed over initially, but in practice this is not the case. Among typical lekking species, 99 percent of mating is accomplished by the few most attractive males, and it is no different among *sasabonsam.* Shere Khan, for example, as one of the larger and presumably more attractive males, was selected on most days, as were several other specimens who were either larger in overall size, more powerfully built, or better-endowed (meaning their head crests, of course).[8]

"I don't understand why the bigger males keep coming back," Walter said. "They've had their chance. They could at least let some of the others experience some romance."

"It's natural selection," I observed.

"I know, Matthew, but my heart still goes out to the losers. Take poor Heep, for instance. It doesn't look as if he'll ever find love."

If Walter felt indignation at Shere Khan and his kind monopolizing the mating opportunities, he experienced double the schadenfreude when the alpha males were rebuffed. One such rejection occurred at the claws of a particularly aristocratic female with an 18-foot wingspan and several brown spots on her otherwise creamy hide. When she touched down, the larger males clustered around her like metal filings drawn to a magnet, but she looked them over superciliously and declined to engage them, as if they were beneath her notice. Shere Khan put himself in her path, looking quite satisfied with himself and assured of being chosen, but the female, finding him blocking her way, shoved him aside with the most careless swipe of her right wing, leaving him gaping at her disinterested backside as she passed him over.

"Nicely done!" Walter chirped. "She certainly took the old villain down a peg!"

Not only did the spotted female pass over Shere Khan, but she was similarly aloof toward the other assembled males. She visited the lekking arena numerous times in the following days without making a selection, rejecting all the suitors that had so impressed the other females. We started calling her Elizabeth, for like the English queen,

---

[8]This conclusion is, of course, somewhat speculative on my part in the absence of a frame of reference for what a *shamantin* seeks in a mate.

she seemed determined to have but one mistress and no master.

Rejection might have been a novel experience for some of the males, but Heep, as you may imagine, was consistently passed over. Being too weak to fight his way into the front ranks and too short to be seen over the dominant males in front of him, he was rarely in a position to attract the attention of the *shamantin.* Even when the crowd around one of the females thinned for one reason or another, his scrawny figure and submissive personality failed to attract the discerning eye of the opposite sex.

Considering his unimpressive appearance and inability to compete with his rivals, all of Heep's romantic aspirations seemed vain, but to make matters worse, he also chose a paramour with whom he should have been doomed to fail. As the lekking continued, I noticed that he crowded with the other males around one particular female whenever she was present, but his fixation on her, of all the *shamantin* we had seen, was particularly self-defeating, as even Walter agreed when I shared my observation.

"I think Heep has a favorite," I told him.

"Well, don't keep me in suspense. Who's the lucky lady?"

"It's Elizabeth."

"Good heavens! She doesn't like anybody. How the devil does he think he can win her over?"

Even if his suit seemed doomed to failure, each day Heep tried to elbow his way to a position from which he could see Elizabeth and hopefully be seen by her, making up in perseverance for what he lacked in strength or physical attractiveness. No matter how many dominant males clustered between them, he dutifully basked in his would-be queen's presence, and no matter how often his competitors hissed or snapped at him, he would not be dissuaded from lingering in case an opportunity should miraculously present itself. If ever a cold-blooded reptile showed devotion without hope of reward, Heep did for his chosen *shamantin.*

Even when Heep was finally given the chance to catch Elizabeth's eye, his lack of social skills betrayed him. One day the dominant males broke into a scuffle over the choicest position from which to vie, however fruitlessly, for the female dragon's interest. In the ensuing melee, Heep jumped to the front of the ranks. Once he was there, he spread his wings, ostensibly to strike an alluring pose, but he did it with all the flourish and charm of a human flasher (and to some extent resembled one, with his wings standing in for the more traditional trench coat). Only the fact that we was too small to attract Elizabeth's eye, even when he was right in front of her, spared what little might remain of his dignity.

Between Heep's lack of desirable physical attributes and his social ineptitude, it seemed like a foregone conclusion at the time that his romantic aspirations would remain unsatisfied.

"I don't see how he can ever have a chance with her," Walter said. "The poor fool."

Although I was less vocal with my sympathy than Walter, the reader must not assume that I was not touched by Heep's situation. Indeed, having been passed over by more women than I cared to remember, I could empathize better than most. Nevertheless, I was convinced that nature follows certain immutable laws, cruel as they may sometimes seem, and that there was no way an unattractive weakling at the mercy of natural selection could find a mate. Still, the ways of love are mysterious even to savvier observers than I, and I was about to have hope for Heep finding romance, if not for myself.

The winged dragons are hardly the only living creatures with a sex drive, and at the risk of disillusioning the reader, I confess that dracontologists are not so devoted to their work that they lose all desire for physical love. While Walter, for whatever reason, asked no more of life than the opportunity to study his dragons, the same could not be said of his assistants. We did not by any means shirk our duties, whether they consisted of defending Walter against Heep's ham-handed ambushes or organizing field notes, but we remained red-blooded young men and pined for romance accordingly.

I kept my own romantic aspirations to myself as much as possible, but Ambroise confessed to his distraction when Walter confronted him over several days of sullen behavior.

"What the devil is the matter with you?" Walter asked. "You've been moping about for days."

"There's a girl I like," Ambroise said.

"What are you doing here, then? Go talk to her."

"She's doesn't like me. Not one bit."

"A strapping young man like you? What possesses her?"

Although the young lady's poor taste caused Ambroise no end of angst at first, he did not remain in that state for long. After another day or two of mooning over his unrequited love—and several discreet visits to town—Ambroise not only rallied but was positively joyful, whistling and humming to himself while he hiked with us to and from the lekking grounds. When Ambroise's spirits lifted, I suspected that it had to do with his young lady, but I could not have guessed the agent of the change.

"What are you so happy about all of a sudden?" Walter asked.

"My girl finally said yes to me," Ambroise said.

"However did you change her mind?"

"I went to the feticheur in Foulagou."

So saying, Ambroise reached into his pocket and produced a small pouch made of animal hide.

"Gracious!" Walter chirped. "Is that a love charm?"

Sasabonsam in the wild are more or less left to their natural attractiveness and the whim of fate to find a mate, but human beings have devised a variety of ways of facilitating love when it will not come naturally. Western science and culture have afforded the dubious avenues of plastic surgery, crash diets, and, for those who are as wealthy as they are homely, mail-order brides. The love charms and philters of folklore and legend, on the other hand, are significantly more romantic, and though they are by no means as common in our modern age, they are resorted to daily by the adherents of African fetish magic.

There are several varieties of love charms or *wayinoue*. These may consist of a variety of ingredients, but the cane and roots of the leopard orchid (*Ansellia africana*), the masticated juice of *molomo monate* (*Sclerochiton ilicifolius*), desiccated and ground dove heart, and (for some reason) graveyard dirt are the most common. As for the effect of these charms, they may purport to attract one specific lover, or they may be meant to make the bearer generally more attractive and desirable to the opposite sex (or the same sex, depending on one's preferences).

Some Westerners might perceive resorting to love magic as quaint superstition, but Walter found it positively charming.

"I would be the last to question the power of fetish," he said, "after my recent experiences with African magic."

Unlike Walter, I normally would have questioned the power of fetish, but Ambroise's reported success with the love charm made even me think. Perhaps my lovelorn state had made me more desperate than I had admitted even to myself, for I found myself intrigued with the notion that physical attractiveness and romantic desirability—attributes that I have never deemed myself to possess—could be manufactured, if only one knew the secret recipe. Thinking of Vanessa made this idea more and more appealing, and I justified what I did next by rationalizing that it might be interesting to test the power of fetish magic.

I decided to buy a love charm of my own.

Though I had decided to dabble in love magic, I did not by any means announce my intention; even if I was desperate enough to consult with a witchdoctor, I did not want anyone to know that I was doing so. With all the cloak and dagger of a drug addict stealing away to rendezvous with his dealer, I invented a pretext and visited the local feticheur.

Self-conscious as I already was, my meeting with the feticheur, Benjamin Talagouga, did little to reassure me. With his lazy eye, his crooked and brown teeth, and the pronounced droop on the left side of his face, the witchdoctor looked to be even more in need of a love charm than I was. Privately I wondered how such a physically unattractive man could help anyone else find a mate, and I hope I may be forgiven for not fully concealing my surprise when Talagouga mentioned a wife.

"You have a wife?" I asked.

"*Bien sûr,*" he said. "I have three, as a matter of fact."

"Your charms must be really powerful."

"What makes you think I had to use a charm? I just relied on my personal appeal."

Despite my admittedly shallow appraisal of the feticheur and my social ineptitude, I left the feticheur's shop in possession of a *wayinoue.* I had every intention of keeping the transaction to myself, the better to avoid being shown up a hypocrite, but I overestimated my stealth. Walter almost immediately knew of my visit to Talagouga, and lacking any concept of privacy, he questioned me about it.

"Matthew," he said, "I just heard that you've been to see the feticheur. Is that true?"

"Yes." (This, delivered like a criminal finally confessing.)

"Good heavens. Whatever did you do there?"

Perhaps if I had thought more quickly, I could have concocted an innocuous explanation for the visit and saved face. Since I am not a better liar, I simply confessed my errand, even though it might open me up to ridicule.

"Matthew, you astound me," Walter said. "I thought you didn't believe in things like magic."

"Well, I—"

"Now, don't think I hold this against you. To the contrary—there may be hope for you after all!"

I wish I could say that I found love as soon as the *wayinoue* came into my possession, but some claims are even more inherently incredible than encounters with prehistoric survivors. Left to my own devices, I would not even have tested it—at least not until I returned home to try it on Vanessa—but Ambroise insisted on taking me into town with him and introducing me to women. Had the charm worked as advertised, the young ladies would presumably have cooed in pleasure, if not outright swooned, at meeting me, but their reception was less than encouraging.

The following are typical of the responses when Ambroise presented me:

"I'm only looking for friends."

"No, thank you."

Mocking laughter.

Spectacular as my failure with the young ladies was, it did not ultimately evidence the failure of the *wayinoue.* On my way back to camp (with tail tucked firmly between my legs), I felt in my pocket, where I had last left the charm, only to find it empty. No amount of feeling around my person would produce it; it was as if the charm had vanished into thin air as a rebuke for my lack of faith. I could not say how or when I had lost it, so I could not in all fairness conclude that it had failed me.

Even though my test of the *wayinoue* was really just inconclusive, I nevertheless took it as a sign that I was not meant to dabble in love magic and forbore replacing it. I would have let the matter rest and not thought any more about the lost charm, but it resurfaced soon enough regardless of my disinterest. As a matter of fact, it got another test, and though I was somewhat nonplussed at the time, it comforts me now to think that someone may have gotten use of it even if I did not.

Regardless of my own romantic disappointments, our ostensible purpose remained the observation of the mating dragons. Though Walter and I had remained steadfast in our devotion to documenting the dragons even while I fruitlessly pursued the opposite sex, gradually we noticed that fewer males were assembling at the lekking grounds with each passing day. At the same time, the females appeared with decreasing frequency as well. By the day after my shaming at the hands of the young women of Foulagou, we had become convinced that the mating season was coming to an end.

Even with the end of the dragons' lekking, we should perhaps have been satisfied with the valuable data we had collected, but Walter nevertheless had one regret.

"I just wish that Heep could have found himself a mate," he said repeatedly.

While the dragons' mating fervor dwindled, Walter despaired for Heep's unrequited love, but his attitude changed unexpectedly on what would prove to be one of the last lekking days.

"Somehow I feel more optimistic about Heep's chances today," he said.

"Oh?" I asked. "Why's that?"

"Never you worry about that. Just let's see what happens."

Despite Walter's inexplicable confidence, the day's mating began like it had every other day. The males dutifully assembled, preening themselves and pecking their neighbors, and their vigil was eventually rewarded with the sight of a massive female gliding into view over the treetops. As her course became plain, the males erupted into motion like clockwork soldiers to assemble around her anticipated landing site, Heep among them. When the female turned out to be Elizabeth, who needless to say had still failed to find a male to her liking, Heep's prospects seemed just as nil as they had on every other day before this one.

Though my doubts only increased upon recognizing the *shamantin,* Walter still remained mysteriously sanguine.

"Wouldn't it be something if she wound up choosing our leathery-winged friend?" he asked.

In the absence of any explanation for Walter's optimism, I did not anticipate any deviation from the previous days' routine of Elizabeth rejecting all males, including Heep. You can therefore imagine my surprise when the *shamantin* stalked through the crowd, weaving her way among dozens of mugging *sasabonsam*, and stopped in front of the runt. There she craned her neck and cocked her head, inspecting him more closely than she ever had before, and beyond all hope, she clicked to indicate her approval. For a long moment she waited for the object of her unexpected attention, presumably as dumbfounded as I was, to realize that it was his move.

When Heep's moment came, it would undoubtedly have been romantic if he became debonair and charming, but that is not quite what happened. After an awkward pause, he finally launched, but for one suspenseful moment he hung flapping in midair and looked poised to crash. Even once he ascended, he swooped around his prospective mate in wobbly, erratic circles. Elizabeth soon joined him, and she adroitly dodged, like a graceful dancer accommodating a clumsy partner, whenever he swerved into her flight path. Each time they threatened to crash I winced, but they gratefully came back to earth without incident.

What came once the dragons touched down, the reader can imagine from my previous description of *sasabonsam-shamantin* relations, so I will not repeat it. While the dragons coupled, I marveled at Walter's seeming prescience.

"How did you know that was going to happen?" I asked.

"Yes," Walter said. "About that. There's something I meant to tell you. Do you remember that love charm you had?"

"Yes."

"Well, it must have fallen out of your pocket, because I found it. I was going to return it, really I was, but then I had a thought. You see, I just couldn't resist trying to help."

"What did you do with it?" (By now, I already suspected.)

"I gave it to our leathery-winged friend. Well, he ate it, in point of fact. But I promise I'll get you a replacement, and for what it's worth, it seems to have worked."

Of course there is no way to prove that a love charm was responsible for the consummation of Heep's romance. It is nevertheless a fact that Heep had previously had absolutely no luck with females, and the only factor that appeared to be different at this time was the gift of the *wayinoue.* As I have said before and will say again, I cannot unequivocally espouse magic as the explanation for such events, but after all I've seen, I cannot discount it, either.

However Heep's successful mating came about, it marked the climax of the lekking season. If the dwindling attendance in the lekking arena had not already convinced us of this fact, then the dragons' return to their typical behavior, no longer distracted by their mating drive, would have done so. Before we could even get back to the dragons' hunting area, Heep had taken up an ambush and lunged at Walter (only to trip on a fallen branch and face-plant without getting in a successful nip).

"I suppose there's no doubt that mating season is over," Walter said, "although it seems like he could have gone a few more days without attacking me, seeing what I did for him."

With the lekking done, we returned to our usual routine of studying the *sasabonsam* in their hunting area, leaving several questions regarding the winged dragons' reproductive biology unanswered. We do not know, for example, how frequently or regularly the dragons' lekking seasons recur, nor did we witness actual reproduction (whether by egg-laying or live birth). For my part, I was never comfortable being so close to a mob of sexually-aroused, carnivorous reptiles, and I am happy to leave lengthier observations of their mating habits to braver dracontologists in the future. Personally, I would settle for insight into the mating practices of my own species, but instead I've had to muddle through much like our friend Heep, relying on the odd love charm in a pinch.

CHAPTER VI
MEMENTO MORI DRACONIS

Despite being fierce, as I have previously described, the winged dragons of Africa remain as sadly mortal as any of the better-known or more mundane creatures of the animal kingdom. I have seen them inflict nonlethal wounds upon each other during scuffles over possession of a kill, and they are of course susceptible to both disease and the ravages of age. More to the point, although they do not appear to have any natural predators, they are, like all other living things, apt to be shot when they come into conflict with human beings.

Human-wildlife conflict may come about in several ways, the most widespread of which is undoubtedly competition between human beings and wildlife for finite resources. As human settlements expand, wild animals lose range and access to their accustomed food sources. Similarly, natural conditions such as drought and blight may drive wildlife to increasingly desperate measures to survive. In either case, herbivores such as elephants raid crops, while predators such as lions and leopards prey on livestock. Needless to say, the owners of the crops or livestock will defend their livelihoods from these depredations, at gunpoint if necessary.

When just this sort of conflict arose between *sasabonsam* and their human neighbors, Walter and I soon heard about it. Because there is no reasoning with wild animals, the naturalists studying them often become the surrogates to hear complaints about the creatures' conduct. Thus, Walter and I, as the seeming human representatives of *sasabonsam*, became the object of the villagers' grievances when the dragons interfered with their livestock, starting with a young but fierce boy who accosted us one day when we ventured into town for supplies.

"Are you the ones who watch over *sasabonsam*?" he asked.

"Why, yes," Walter said. (Mistaking the boy's interest, he straightened proudly.) "Yes, we study the dragons. I suppose you would like to hear all about them."

"No."

"Oh. Well, then what do you want?"

"I want you to do something about them. They killed three of my goats."

At this, Walter faltered.

"Why the devil are you bothering me about that?" he asked. "Even if that was so—and I'm sure it's not—it's not as if they're my pets. I'm not responsible for them."

"If you won't stop them, somebody's going to shoot them."

Walter might have objected on principle to being held accountable for the supposed crimes of the dragons, but his concern for their safety overrode his sensibilities on the subject.

"I suppose we could investigate," he said, relenting, "but shouldn't you be off doing something more age appropriate, like jumping rope or playing hide and seek?"

"No."

"All right, then. We shall look into this and see if my dragons did what you say, although I strongly doubt it."

By the time we toured the scene of the crime, the killer—whatever its nature—had long since gone, leaving only blood-dappled ground in its wake. Whatever it had been, the predator had circumvented a tall fence and left none of the pug marks that we might have expected a leopard to leave behind. Ultimately, we could not tell whether *sasabonsam* were responsible, but Walter took no pains to hide his bias.

"There's nothing here to indicate that one of my dragons took the goats," he said. "It was probably just a leopard. Now, maybe you should go play with your little friends."

"No," the boy said. "If you won't do something about the dragons, I'll find someone to shoot them."

"Very well, then. Matthew, I suppose we shall have to humor this beastly child and show him our dragons aren't responsible for killing his damned goats."

Under threat of harm to his dragons, Walter agreed to investigate the goat killings, which he proposed to do by staking out the corral overnight, when the goats were typically taken, and catching the killer red-handed (or clawed, as the case might be). Though Walter would have preferred to have been studying his dragons (and I would have preferred to have been sleeping), we kept a vigil on the corral through the night, ready with a lantern to expose the killer whenever it should appear. I might have dozed for at least part of this watch, but Walter kept me awake with a steady stream of complaints at his dragons being accused of such misconduct.

"This is completely absurd," he said more than once. "Why would our leathery-winged friends have any interest in these scrawny animals? I'm sure it's a leopard."

Even if the suspect might be a normal leopard, the prospect of meeting a large carnivore in the dead of night, outfitted only with a lantern and the scent of our fear, alarmed me enough that I convinced Walter to take protective measures. Thus, we included Ambroise among our party, bearing a shotgun against the appearance of predators. Though Walter acknowledged the wisdom of the precaution, he laid a strict injunction on Ambroise against any hasty use of the weapon.

"After all, you mustn't shoot one of my dragons," he said. "On the off chance that they're involved, that is."

Thus armed, we kept our vigil, but the blackness of night had given way to the grayscale of predawn by the time the killer finally made its appearance. In the fading gloom, we heard the thump of a heavy body landing inside the corral, but the new arrival remained concealed beyond the milling goats. My blood went cold at the thought that a large carnivore of unknown nature was but a stone's throw away from where we waited, but the predator gratefully curtailed my suspense: one of the goats let off a bleat that was strangled in its throat, and its attacker retreated with the struggling animal clutched in its jaws.

Once the intruder took off with its prey, we only saw it briefly, but this was enough for us to identify it. Flashing the lantern in its direction, I made out tawny hide cross-hatched with dark stripes. At the same time, the direction of the creature's retreat—straight up into the sky rather than over the fence—was consonant with only one animal I knew.

Though his eyesight was none the best, even Walter perceived enough of the animal's departure to know that it did not move like any cat.

"I don't suppose there's a chance that was a leopard?" he asked.

"No," I said.

"It was one of the dragons after all, wasn't it?"

"Yes. It was Shere Khan"

"Bother."

As inconvenient as it was to discover the dragons preying on our neighbors' livestock, it was perfectly natural that they should do so. When humans introduce a new resource into the ecosystem—such as by penning livestock, ripe for the taking—predators cannot help exploiting the opportunity for what appears to be an easy meal. In the process, they have precious little regard for the animosity they inspire on the part of the owners of those animals, although it may of course bring about their undoing at the hands of retaliating herders.

Now Shere Khan, with his usual indifference to the growing hostility he provoked, was embarking down the same dangerous path.

Shere Khan's depredations put Walter and me not only in an uncomfortable position, caught between the dragon and the increasingly frustrated victims of his raids, but a desperate one. Shere Khan may not have been an endearing creature, but his existence—a prehistoric creature still alive despite all belief to the contrary—was little short of a miracle, which we felt bound to protect if we could. Unfortunately, it seemed likely that that miracle would be snuffed out if we could not broker peace between the dragon and the villagers, which proved to be a difficult détente to bring about.

*

Assuaging the conflict between human beings and wildlife presents an almost insurmountable challenge for naturalists. On the one hand, they are understandably loath to have native populations forming angry mobs to hunt down and kill their research subjects. On the other hand, it is difficult to convince people of the necessity of conserving animals whose depredations threaten their own existence. Researchers must adopt a conciliatory approach that will mitigate harm to human life and livelihood while protecting rare and unique animal species at the same time, though it is rarely possible to do so without sacrifices on both sides.

One method of averting the destruction of offending wildlife is to pay compensation to farmers and herders whose crops and livestock have been raided. Once we had confirmed Shere Khan's culpability for the vanishing livestock, Walter paid the young goatherd and his family the cost of replacing the goats in lieu of them hunting down and destroying the killer, and this seemed to mollify them, at least for the time being.

"But it had better not come back," the goatherd said.

"If he does," Walter said, "for goodness sake, don't shoot him. We'll pay you for any animals you lose."

If the attacks on the goats had been an isolated incident, we might not have been quite so concerned, but it soon became apparent that Shere Khan's marauding was more widespread than we had anticipated. We had barely finished compensating the owners of the lost goats when we were again confronted over the behavior of our errant dragon, this time by a pig herder who accosted us as we headed back out of town.

"Are you the ones who live with the *sasabonsam*?" the man asked.

"Why, yes," Walter said. "Yes, we are."

"Where are they?" The man brandished a broom, and if the dragons had been with us, I think he would have struck them with it. "They've been killing my pigs."

"Good lord, Matthew," Walter said. "Here's another one."

Nor were the foregoing the only incidents of the dragon killing livestock. Over the next week, we reached the point where we could not visit town without being accosted by several herders seeking redress for Shere Khan's raids, to Walter's mounting exasperation.

"Here we've rediscovered animals that have been presumed extinct for 65 million years," he said, "and all anybody can do is complain about them. Imagine!"

As unpleasant as it was to be taken to task for Shere Khan's misdeeds, we were more troubled by the threat to the dragon's safety. Even though we compensated the villagers for any animals that he took, every exchange regarding the dragon's depredations ended with some variation of the following, usually delivered while brandishing a weapon as if in anticipation of hunting him down.

"If you don't do something about that animal, then I will."

"We'll compensate you for any animals he takes," Walter would say. "Just don't hurt our dragon, for goodness sake."

If we initially hoped that the conflict between Shere Khan and the villagers would resolve on its own once we had paid the herders for a few dead animals, we underestimated the dragon's persistence as well as his appetite. Over a period of less than two weeks, we compensated the loss of 22 chickens, 11 goats, and eight pigs. Walter couldn't quite make himself believe that one of his dragons could wreak so much carnage, but once Shere Khan was known to be behind at least some of the kills, he would have been blamed even if a leopard had actually been responsible. Consequently, Walter had little alternative but to pay all claimants if he wanted to dissuade them from turning their frustration on the dragon himself.

Compensation is one acceptable method of mollifying people whose livelihood has been threatened by wild animals, but it does not afford a long-term solution if the animals continue their raids, as Shere Khan did. Thus, it is generally used in conjunction with more proactive measures to deter the animals from further trespasses. Occasionally this is accomplished through wildlife management techniques such as culling or moving the offending animal, but Walter would have rejected any such proposition out of hand. The only remaining option was to safeguard the livestock against future depredations.

Unfortunately for us, protecting livestock from the winged dragons is easier said than done. Their flight ability makes it impossible to keep them out by way of a taller fence, and their size, ferocity, and sheer brazenness make the use of guard dogs futile (and needlessly dangerous to the dogs, who are apt to be eaten in the course of protecting their charges).

Walter summed up our dilemma nicely:

"I can't for the life of me figure out what the devil we're supposed to do to keep him away."

"Maybe you should ask Talagouga for help," Ambroise said.

"The feticheur?! Heavens, no! If he guesses what I did to his colleague, he's liable to curse me. No, we shall have to do this on our own, without magic."

In the absence of magical aid, there are several tested methods for keeping winged predators away from livestock. Night lights may deter nocturnal hunters, and the removal of roost trees, by spiking or outright felling, may also dissuade would-be predators. Other strategies include the installation of netting and bird scarers (or in our case, dragon scarers). Although these are all used to deter birds rather than dragons, the analogy between two winged predators seemed strong enough for us to adapt them for our use in dealing with Shere Khan so long as we accounted for his greater size and strength than his avian counterparts.

One by one, Walter and I tried the methods I described above, and each one failed. Shere Khan hunted regardless of night lights and regardless of the accessibility of roosting sites, nor did our dragon scarers—essentially banners with large, staring eyes painted on them—intimidate him. When we blocked his access to a corral with netting, he simply sheared through it, regardless of how strong the material. Nothing we did could secure the local farms against him, and the death toll of chickens, goats, and pigs mounted.

While Walter and I tried in vain to protect the livestock, the patience of the villagers became more and more strained. The following is typical of the threats that the herders made against the rogue dragon if he could not be deterred.

"You keep that thing away from my animals, if you know what's good for it. If it comes back, I'm going to kill it."

It seemed clear that if Walter and I could not dissuade the dragon from attacking livestock, someone was going to eventually dispatch him. We empathized with the villagers, for they were hardly in a position to sacrifice their livestock to sate the appetite of the dragon, nor could we expect them to place the life of a ruthless reptile over the well-being of their own families. But at the same time, we could not overstate the importance of conserving a species that had just been rediscovered after 65 million years' absence.

"I respect your situation, sir, really, I do," Walter said to one disgruntled herder, "but these animals are of great scientific value. They must not be hurt."

"Then keep them away from my goats."

Needless to say, our days were filled with worry, and on many nights we lost sleep wondering if we would awaken the next day to find that the dragon had been killed for his gluttony.

Our fears for the dragon's safety conferred ample motivation, and combined with a great deal of persistence, they enabled us to finally solve the problem of keeping Shere Khan away from the local livestock. Bird decoys are used successfully to keep predatory birds away from livestock by counterfeiting the presence of another predator, and we adapted this method for use on the dragon. Knowing that the only creature that might dissuade Shere Khan was a larger member of his own kind, we constructed an effigy of the mightiest pterosaur that has ever been imagined and perched it on the fence of a villager whose pigs had been attacked for several nights in a row. We retired to our camp that night, planning to visit the corral in the morning to gauge our success, but we had little hope and no idea what we would do if this attempt failed.

Our expectations notwithstanding, I am pleased to state that this strategy worked, though we had become so hopeless by this time that Walter dreaded the response when we questioned the herder about the results of our efforts.

"All right, out with it," Walter said. "How many did he kill last night?"

"None."

"Do you mean to say that the decoy worked?"

"Yes."

"Well, yes, of course it worked. I knew it would all along, seeing that I am the dragon expert."

With this success, Walter and I finally experienced some hope that we might avert Shere Khan's destruction at the hands of outraged herders. We began circulating dragon decoys to the other villagers whose livestock had been taken, and we looked forward to resuming our usual observation of the dragons instead of managing the safety of chickens and goats. If we thought our dragon was out of danger, however, we were mistaken, and our sense of relief was to be sadly short-lived.

*

It might seem that the dragons should have been safe once we devised a means to keep them away from the local livestock, and that was certainly our belief at the time. Unfortunately, disgruntled herders are not the only human beings who might wish to kill one of the dragons, and one group in particular would kill the dragons regardless of whether they actually posed a threat to person or property. In our preoccupation with mollifying the villagers, we neglected to account for the possibility that the dragons' doom might come from an unforeseen source, at least until Ambroise approached Walter looking uncharacteristically upset and reported that violence had befallen one of them despite all our efforts to safeguard them.

"There is something I have to tell you, Walter Spink," he said, "and you are not going to like it one bit."

"Can it wait?" Walter asked. "I'm in the middle of making my notes just now."

"Shere Khan is dead."

"What, now?"

"He's been shot."

"That can't be. He hasn't bothered the villagers in days, and besides, he's right over—where did he go?"

Even when the dragon did not present himself so as to refute Ambroise's news outright, Walter still tried to seem nonchalant.

"You might as well show me," he said, "but I'm sure there's been some mistake."

For minutes that seemed to stretch into hours, the three of us walked, and my mind went over the possibilities while Walter tried, each time less convincingly, to tell us it was all a mistake. I knew that Ambroise could not be mistaken, for he knew the dragons as well as Walter and I. That left only the question of who would have shot the dragon, but that was more difficult to answer; after all, half the village had threatened his life, so it could have been almost anyone. Finally, we reached the scene of Shere Khan's waterloo, and everything soon became clear.

We found the dragon where Ambroise had last seen him: sprawled at the foot of a giant kapok tree about half a mile from our camp. A shaft of sunlight lancing through a break in the canopy impaled him upon the forest floor, where he lay spread-eagled and unmoving in a bower of flattened ferns dappled with his blood, surrounded by a group of men we did not recognize.

Though we had been none too fond of Shere Khan in life, his death had a profound effect. Partly this was because he was a representative of a rare species that had not flourished since the Cretaceous, but his individual loss also struck us. Seeing his habitual sneer recast by death into a grimace drove home how much we had grudgingly admired his strength and dominance, and watching the beetles and rodents scurry past his lifeless jaws, as if flaunting his impotence to strike at them, seemed like a gross overpayment for his arrogance now that he had already paid everything for it.

While we gawked at the dragon's remains, a deep voice mumbled some instructions, and a handful of men heaved the body into an upright position and spread its wings, handling it as carelessly as if they were posing a doll. When the grandee who had been giving orders a moment before knelt on one knee next to the dragon, cradling the rifle that had killed it, while yet another man fumbled with a camera, I understood with growing revulsion what had happened to Shere Khan. After all the provocation the dragon had offered the local herders, he had ironically enough been snuffed out by a big game hunter instead.

"What the devil is going on here?" Walter, slower to perceive the situation, demanded.

"I've just shot this animal here," the grandee said.

"I see that."

"Well, isn't it a beauty?"

"He certainly was—before you murdered him!"

The practice of big game hunting has understandably met with criticism. Gone are the days when W.D.M. Bell could kill more than a thousand elephants, but modern big game hunting nevertheless contributes to the pressure upon already threatened species. The hunters argue that they benefit wildlife by paying permit fees and other taxes that may be used to fund conservation efforts, but this position is disingenuous; they could, after all, fund conservation through photographic safaris or charitable donations without any bloodshed. Often, trophy hunting merely satisfies the blood lust of the depraved or relieves the ennui of the privileged, both of which are trivial concerns when weighed against the necessity of conserving rare and endangered animals.

Given his love of animals, Walter Spink was bound to disapprove of big game hunting regardless of its object. Now that it had claimed the life of one of his treasured dragons, his usual indignation was roused to outright fury. To be quite honest, I thought he might strike the dragon's killer.

"Do you have any idea what you've done?" Walter asked, red-faced.

"Why, yes," the hunter said. "I think I do."

"Then how the devil can you look so pleased with yourself? For all you know, this creature could have been the last of his kind, and you murdered him."

Belatedly realizing that Walter did not mean to congratulate him, the hunter became defensive.

"Now, wait a minute," he said. "I killed it—what a beauty!—but it wasn't murder. I have a permit."

"I've heard enough," Walter said. "Now come along. You're going with us."

"Going where?"

"To see the authorities, of course."

At this point, I felt it incumbent upon myself to intercede.

"Are you sure we can do this?" I asked.

"Whyever not?" Walter asked. "We're performing a citizen's arrest. Now, Ambroise, tie him up. Quickly!"

Before I could protest the legality of Walter's course of action, Ambroise, who was equally affronted by the killing of the dragon, had assisted him in restraining the hunter. To his credit, our prisoner—an American cosmetic surgeon whom I shall call Mr. P.—

was hardly obligated to comply with the orders of such a questionable authority as Walter Spink and could have relied on the brute force of his entourage to overcome us. Nevertheless, he voluntarily accompanied us to the nearest gendarmerie, insisting the whole way that he was certain the authorities could clear up this misunderstanding (while frequently reverting to his permit and the beauty of his kill).

As we confirmed upon our arrival at the police station in Mamfe, the trouble with big game hunting, at least from the perspective of a dracontologist trying to protect his research subjects, is that it is perfectly legal. While all nations regulate hunting, it is usually a matter of obtaining a permit and keeping off protected areas; even traditionally protected species may be taken in certain countries. You can thus imagine the difficulty faced by researchers attempting to prevent the killing of dragons, which are not recognized as living species by the hunting regulations, much less a threatened one, any more than they are by the scientific community.

These limitations had occurred to me as we escorted the hunter to the authorities, and I waited outside the gendarmerie while Walter made his case against the hunter, anticipating that the old man would emerge in high dudgeon. After some muffled shouting, Walter appeared in the doorway, red-faced and indignant as I expected.

"Can you believe this, Matthew?" he squawked. "They won't do anything. They say that he has a permit, and the regulations don't protect 'imaginary creatures' like our dragons. Imaginary, my foot! Here we have creatures that have been presumed extinct for 65 million years, and nothing to keep every numbskull with a rifle from shooting them back to extinction. The fools!"

The shooting of Shere Khan might have been legal, but it was nonetheless catastrophic to the group of winged dragons that we had been observing. When he was alive, Shere Khan had of course dominated the other dragons, but after his death, they lost cohesion altogether. Tabaqui stopped coming around, presumably drifting toward a situation as henchman for some other winged tyrant. Heep lingered by himself, a sad scarecrow of a figure, but in the absence of trickle-down from the larger males' kills, he became scrawnier and hungrier than ever. This in turn made him so preoccupied trying to eat Walter that observing his natural behavior was impossible. In any event, there was hardly a group left for us to observe.

With the dissolution of the group, our study of the winged dragons came to an end. I suppose we might have simply located another congregation of male dragons to observe, but instead Walter proposed to move on in search of other dragons. Though I cannot vouch for the operation of Walter's mind, I suspect that he found it difficult to pursue his work with his spirits as dampened as they were by the dragon's death. Regardless of his reasons, I respected him too much to argue with his judgment, and I was secretly glad to leave behind a species that would willingly eat us if our guard lapsed, though my relief ultimately proved premature.

At the time, this lesson in the dragons' mortality—and the absence of legal protection for them—was bitter enough, but in retrospect it only foreshadowed the worries that would haunt us throughout the rest of our time among prehistoric survivors in Africa. If we had set out hoping just to find the dragons, now that we had done so, we felt a responsibility to conserve them as well. Though we hoped never to encounter the likes of Mr. P. again, we were no more successful wishing the big game hunters away from our dragons than we were convincing a certain winged dragon to stay where we left him.

CHAPTER VII
NGOUBOU AND OTHER KILLERS OF ELEPHANTS

When our observation of the winged dragons ended, Walter Spink and I turned our attention to their terrestrial counterparts, but that is not to say that we immediately found *mokele-mbembe*. Despite Walter showing his book of dinosaur illustrations to all and sundry, no one recognized the sauropods from life, and our journey across Cameroon soon took us out of tropical forest and into open grassland that was incompatible with reports of the long-necked dragon's habitat. Even if *mokele-mbembe* were not present in this part of Cameroon, however, the visit was not wasted, for we learned of the horned dragon that inhabits the savanna country and seized the opportunity to study it.

Our first intelligence of the horned dragon, which is called *ngoubou* in Cameroon, came from a young Fulani cowherd we encountered tending his family's zebu cattle in a settlement north of Ngaoundéré. The boy was ultimately certain that he had seen one of the animals illustrated in Walter's book of prehistoric life, but he initially found the volume to be quite humorous.

"What the devil are you laughing about?" Walter asked.

"Your book is funny," the boy said.

"I don't see what's so damned funny."

"It's missing animals. There aren't any cows."

"There aren't supposed to be any cows. It's a book of prehistoric reptiles. Now, have you seen any of these animals, or haven't you?"

"I've seen this one."

"Really? Which one is it?" Walter wrested the book from the cowherd. "Is it the *Brontosaurus*? Let me see."

The prehistoric beast that had been recognized was not the *Brontosaurus,* but the substitute was certainly adequate in Walter's estimation: the illustration that had finally sparked recognition was one of the horned dinosaurs.

"Why, it's the *Styracosaurus!*" he said. "Do you see this, Matthew? There are ceratopsians here, too!"

With the cowherd's identification to lead us, Walter and I investigated *ngoubou* and assembled the following profile. It is described as a quadruped the size of a hippopotamus or an elephant, with accounts varying whether it possesses a thick, heavy tail like a lizard or a thin one like an elephant or rhinoceros; Walter and I observed the former in our fieldwork. In one feature, all accounts (and our experience) agree: *ngoubou* possess a single, long horn on their faces that resembles polished ivory rather than the keratin of rhinoceros horn.[9] They also sport a bony frill at the back of their heads, which is ornamented by three to six additional horns or spikes, and a beaked snout, all of which indeed call to mind the horned dinosaurs.

Aside from the body plan described above and the single horn, *ngoubou* and other horned dragons elsewhere in Africa share at least one universal behavioral trait: they kill elephants by goring them with their nose horns. Indeed, in parts of their range, the horned dragons

---

[9]Skeptical readers might suspect from the description of the horned nose that *ngoubou* is but a misidentification of an ordinary rhinoceros. Even discounting our observation, which was certainly close enough to rule out such a mistaken identity, only one subspecies of rhinoceros, *Diceros bicornis longipes*, has ever been native to Cameroon. They are presently extinct and numbered approximately 100 at the time of our field work in Africa, so the identification of *ngoubou* as a rhinoceros is at least as problematic as its identification as a surviving ceratopsian.

are known as *emela-ntouka*—the killer of elephants—and the reptiles' presence is often known from the discovery of disemboweled elephants even if residents have not seen them in the flesh.

It was the elephanticidal tendency of *ngoubou* that suggested how we might locate them.

"If *ngoubou* kill elephants like everybody says," Walter said, "then it seems to me the easiest way to find them would be to look for the elephants they've killed."

With this inspiration, we began our study of *ngoubou* by surveying slain elephants, looking for indications that their killer might be an immense, horned reptile. We located these carcasses by a variety of methods, sometimes by touring the savanna personally looking for them but more often gleaning reports of elephant kills from the local villagers or the talking drums, then followed them up in a somewhat battered jeep we rented to get us here and there across the savanna. Dead elephants turned up with surprising (and somewhat disheartening) regularity and were easy enough to locate, but they did not immediately lead us to the horned dragons for reasons that will soon become apparent.

Despite the fierce reputation of the horned dragons among the peoples of Cameroon, they are by no means the only creatures with the audacity to kill elephants. Truth be told, the deaths of some 25 million elephants attest that there is no greater killer of elephants than humanity, and our time in Africa coincided with the height of the elephant hunting crisis that precipitated the 1990 ivory ban. Consequently, our first discoveries of slaughtered elephants were attributable to our own kind and not *ngoubou.*

Even before we realized the agent of its death, our first experience finding the remains of an elephant had a sobering effect. I cannot say why elephants are so beloved; perhaps it is their unusual combination of playful behavior with the appearance of physical age that is conveyed by their gray, wrinkly skin, or perhaps it is their perceived size and strength, an image that is shattered when they are injured or killed. Regardless of the reason, I was strongly affected by the grim reality of the work Walter and I had undertaken when faced with the reality of an elephant lying dead at my feet, and I found myself blinking back tears.

Even Walter, with all his determination to find and study *ngoubou*, found his enthusiasm clouded the first time we viewed the carcass of an elephant.

"Between you and me," he said, "I find that I don't take any joy in this, even if it leads us to *ngoubou.* If it's a sin to kill a mockingbird, then it's almost certainly a greater sin to kill an elephant. Now, you see better than I, Matthew. What do you think? Was it *ngoubou* that did this?"

"No," I said.

"Really? What the devil was it, then?"

"People did this."

"People? You mean more of those damned hunters, don't you?" (My transcription cannot capture the profound distaste with which Walter pronounced the word "hunters.") "What makes you so sure human beings did this?"

The methods by which human beings kill elephants leave distinctive wounds that are easily distinguished from those inflicted by *ngoubou.* Poor subsistence hunters use spears, which inflict multiple, smaller punctures than might be expected of *ngoubou*'s giant horn. Their more well-armed counterparts, including both ivory and big game hunters, use shotguns or semiautomatic rifles, and the corresponding bullet holes are easily recognized. Less scrupulous hunters use pitfall traps, leg snares, or pinboard traps in combination with the weapons I just described.[10] Certainly *ngoubou* cannot dig a pitfall or set a trap to catch an elephant, and these devices leave

---

[10]The pinboard is a simple but cruel device consisting of a board with spikes pushed through it. It is placed on the ground with the spikes pointing up, to be stepped on by the unwary pachyderm.

characteristic lacerations and perforations on the feet.

Aside from the type of wounds, the most certain—and also the most disturbing—indicator of big game or ivory hunters is the mutilation of the body. The killing of an elephant for its ivory is cruel enough, but it becomes even more grisly because a full third of the elephant's tusk is hidden within the tooth socket and cranial cavity. To keep their trophies intact, the hunters will hack away the animals' faces, and I have heard that some of the more depraved elephant killers will begin the operation before the poor animals have actually succumbed to their wounds.

The carcass that lay before us had been mangled in just such a manner, with tatters of gray skin and flesh where its face had once been. This, coupled with the gunshot wounds in its flank, proved that it had been the victim of ivory hunters rather than *ngoubou.*

Over the course of several weeks, Walter and I became quite adept at recognizing the victims of the ivory hunters, for at first, all the elephant carcasses we discovered were attributable to their depredations. During that time, we examined no fewer than 27 bodies, all of which were victims of human elephant killers, and our search afforded a gruesome reminder of the dark side of our own species that stays with me to this day. Though it almost goes without saying, Walter and I concluded, based upon this experience, that *ngoubou* account for an infinitesimal portion of elephant casualties compared with human beings.

"A plague on these beastly hunters," Walter said after one such discovery, "for killing all these elephants, of course, but also for making it more difficult for us to find *ngoubou.*"

After finding the hunters' handiwork so often, Walter and I became somewhat disheartened. By the time we actually found a casualty of *ngoubou*, we almost declined to investigate the carcass, thinking it would simply be more of the same.

"More hunters, I'm sure," Walter said when we spied the body from a distance. "Do you think it's even worth bothering?"

No matter how jaundiced we had become, we could not resist

the possibility that closer inspection might reveal something of interest, and it was fortunate that we heeded our instinct. As we drew closer, I noticed something unusual about the body that convinced me that human hunters were not involved in this killing, and I told Walter as much.

"Oh?" he said, brightening. "What makes you say that?"

While any number of injuries might implicate ivory hunters in an elephant's death, the practice is much easier to rule out, even from a distance. Trophy hunters and poachers do not go to the trouble of killing an elephant and then leave its valuable ivory intact, so if a dead elephant still has its tusks, it is a fair assumption that it was killed by means other than hunters. While this condition does not guarantee that the elephant was killed by *ngoubou*, it is nevertheless consonant with an attack by one of the horned dragons and warrants closer investigation.

The elephant carcass that Walter and I had discovered retained its ivory, and we approached it with growing anticipation, subject to our inspection revealing wounds that were attributable to *ngoubou.*

Wounds inflicted by the horned dragons can be recognized in several ways. Initially, the goring attack of *ngoubou* leaves puncture wounds that tend to be located in the perineal and thigh areas where the elephant lacks a bony shield that would otherwise fend off the horn, and they will be located high on the elephant's flank. They are also greater in size and depth than the injuries that the smaller savanna buffalo might inflict, tending to be at least six inches in width and corresponding to the size of the nose horn that constitutes *ngoubou*'s primary weapon. There may be substantial blood loss and signs of shock, but in some cases, death may actually come about not from the punctures themselves but infection secondary to them, as is the case with goring wounds delivered by other species.

The foregoing portrait of *ngoubou*-inflicted injuries was, of course, unavailable at the time and has been assembled somewhat post hoc from my subsequent encounters with the horned dragons and their occasional victims. Nevertheless, even without a guide, I recognized goring lacerations on the carcass in front of me, and I was at a loss to think of a horned animal other than *ngoubou* that could have delivered such sizable punctures and overcome a full-grown elephant.

While I was still considering the provenance of the elephant's wounds, Walter voiced a similar opinion.

"I think this animal might actually have been killed by *ngoubou,*" he said. "How about you?"

"I agree," I said.

"Well it's about damn time. At least we can finally be sure that there's a *ngoubou* close by."

With the discovery of an elephant bearing the seeming wounds of a *ngoubou* attack, we began to feel more optimistic about finally locating the horned dragons, but this was not the end of our search. We had turned up what at least seemed to be evidence of the dragons' presence, but this would not result in visual contact until we picked up a trail and followed it to the living animal. Nevertheless, our find offered enough encouragement to sustain us until we were actually able to find *ngoubou*, a feat that ultimately required the assistance of a skilled animal tracker.

Following the signs of large animals is practically an instinct to experienced trackers, but it is as mysterious as any juju magic to the uninitiated, of which group Walter and I were a part. Northeastern Cameroon, where we tracked *ngoubou*, consists of East Sudanian-type savanna dominated by tall elephant grass (*Pennisetum purpureum*), and when we peered around, we could see only a seemingly endless sea of rippling grass peppered with archipelagos of *Terminalia* or *Combretum* trees and shrubs. If there were signs of *ngoubou*'s passage, they were too subtle for Walter and me to perceive them.

Though Walter and I did not observe any trail that we might follow to the horned dragon, we retained the services of a tracker named Jean-Paul Kaimoi, who seemed able to divine the location of large game from the very air. Indeed, he often examined the ground, which bore no mark I could see, or cocked his ear or smelled the wind, and set off on the trail of our quarry, in much the same way a diviner might perceive the proper course of action for some desperate petitioner in the seemingly random patterns of tossed cowries or bones. After examining the *ngoubou* victim and its surroundings, he pointed east toward a track that was as invisible to us as it was plain to him, and we all piled into the jeep and began following it over the course of several days.

I will pass over the details of Jean-Paul's tracking because I do not have the knowledge to describe his process or recognize the signs that led him on; suffice it to say that he brought us to *ngoubou* just as he had promised. At the time of this discovery, we were pursuing our quarry on foot so as to avoid chasing it away by the laboring noise of the jeep's fitful engine, and we had tracked it into a veritable forest of elephant grass that was taller on all sides than any of us. I daresay that only Jean-Paul might have known even if a *Tyrannosaurus rex* had been standing ten feet away, so Walter and I were caught entirely by surprise when our tracker stopped us, seemingly apropos of nothing, and pointed northwest.

"There," he said. "*Ngoubou.*"

"How can you be so sure?" Walter asked. "I can't see a damned thing past all this grass."

Before we could question Jean-Paul at length, the presence of a large animal made itself plain even to our limited perception. There was the crack of dry brush under a heavy footfall, followed by the rustle of foliage grudgingly giving way to a large body, and we heard the snuffle of breath in and out of massive lungs. Something was screened from sight just beyond the grasses, and though we could not be as certain as Jean-Paul that it was *ngoubou*, we were compelled enough to investigate.

Whether my account is believed or not, I will remember the thrill of our first glimpse of a *ngoubou* in the wild until the day I die. The three of us crept forward, brushing through the tall spears of elephant grass with as much stealth as we could muster, until we stood upon the verge of a clearing. Walter stopped at the edge of the clearing, parting the grass like curtains to peer through, and Jean-Paul and I crowded behind to gaze over his shoulder. When we saw what was beyond, however, we felt as if we were looking through time—to a Cretaceous plain some 65 million years ago—rather than across a modern African savanna.

At first it seemed we must be facing a hill, for the sun was eclipsed, but then I realized it was the beast's massive humped back on the far side of the clearing, brushing the sky far over our heads. Gradually I perceived the movement of four muscular legs carrying the dragon through a thicket of *Stereospermum* shrubs on which it appeared to be browsing. The dragon's face was buried among the leaves, but I made out a great bony flange flaring out from the back of its head like an Elizabethan ruff, albeit one that was spiked around its circumference; nor could the brush conceal a three-foot-long sickle of horn that lanced up from the hidden face.

The appearance of the dragon was plain to me even from a distance, but Walter, between his poor eyesight and the sun being behind the dragon's back, could not quite discern it.

"I can't see, Matthew," he said. "It's not an elephant, is it?"

"Definitely not," I said.

"Oh, good. Is it a *Styracosaurus* like we thought?"

"I can't say for sure, but it definitely looks like one."

"I want to see it better."

So saying, Walter shoved aside the grass in preparation to step into the clearing, but his progress was temporarily arrested by a warning from Jean-Paul.

"You should stay in the grass," he said.

"Nonsense," Walter said. "I can't see from back here."

"If the birds see you, the dragon will be frightened away."

"What birds? I don't know what you could possibly mean."

Without regard for the tracker's advice, Walter squirmed out of the grass and into the clearing.

"I'm sure there's nothing to worry about," he said. "I'm just going to get a little closer."

Thinking himself quite subtle, Walter shuffled toward the dragon, but in our understandable awe of the dragon itself, we had initially failed to notice several gray birds with yellow bills, to which Jean-Paul had undoubtedly referred, perched on its mountainous back. We could not help remarking them, however, when they began screeching a raucous *kriss, kriss* at Walter's emergence.

"What the devil is that beastly noise?" Walter squawked.

The beastly noise was that of the yellow-billed oxpecker (*Buphagus africanus*), which has a mutualistic relationship with its hosts, which may include buffalo, antelopes, and even domesticated cattle in addition to dragons.[11] They have always been believed, up until recently, to feed on ticks living on the skin of other animals, and in exchange for their meals, they issue a warning cry to their hosts when a predator nears. Given the predatory role that human beings play in most ecosystems, it should come as no surprise that oxpeckers will often react as defensively to approaching people as they do to a lion or leopard.

In the same spirit of protectiveness, the *ngoubou*'s avian chaperones, taking no chance that our intentions were benign, raised a great hue and cry to warn the dragon of our presence.

When roused by the oxpeckers' warnings, *ngoubou* behave much like their horned mammalian counterparts. Just as a rhinoceros will charge any perceived threat, a *ngoubou*, when alarmed, will charge in whatever direction seems most expedient, either to attack or to flee, depending on the animal's caprice. At the sound of the oxpeckers' alarm, the dragon's horny face erupted straight up out of the bushes, throwing up a cloud of leaves and twigs like fireworks, and without so much as pawing the ground to give warning of its intention, the dragon galloped toward us, brandishing its mighty scythe of horn ahead of it like some knight of medieval legend galloping toward a foe with lance at the ready.

Being charged by an agitated dragon is serious business, but

[11]Elephants, on the other hand, do not tolerate oxpeckers.

Walter and I avoided disaster by luck even if we lacked the finesse to avoid provoking the dragon in the first place. Recoiling instinctively at the *ngoubou*'s sudden movement, we tumbled out of its path a moment before a gust of warm air shot past us with the dragon's immense body cleaving its way through the murmuring grass. A second later the grass stilled, and when we dared to look up, the dragon was gone.

"Good heavens!" Walter said. "It will come back, won't it?"

Contrary to Walter's hope, the *ngoubou* did not return to the site from which we had accidentally chased it, but instead of becoming discouraged, we decided to track the path of its retreat and attempt contact again. With the benefit of Jean-Paul's talent for pursuing large animals, we were thankfully able to relocate the horned dragon and achieve further visual contact the next day. This time, we found it grazing on the far shore of a stream with its beaked snout uprooting and sucking in tall stalks of grass, but though we tried to conceal ourselves in the grass across the way, the oxpeckers were again too vigilant for us.

"That's much better," Walter said. "I've given this some thought, and I think I shall call it *Dracoceros*—"

Before Walter could christen his newly-discovered dragon, a familiar screech—*kriss, kriss*—erupted like a klaxon. The dragon leapt away from us into the grass with a rustle almost like rolling surf, and it disappeared into the greenery just as completely as if the sea had swallowed it.

"Bother," Walter said. "Here we've found a living, breathing *Styracosaurus*, but it won't hold still long enough for us to get a good look. I suppose we shall have to be even more careful next time."

No matter how we tried to sneak up, we only found that the oxpeckers espied us and alerted the dragon whenever we caught up to it. Later that day, we closed in upon it shouldering smaller animals out of its way toward a watering hole, but too soon the oxpeckers called—*kriss, kriss*—and the dragon thundered away too quickly for us to keep up. The next day, we tried monitoring the *ngoubou* from behind a copse of *Lannea schimperi* when we heard the birds' warning—*kriss, kriss*—and just had time to get out of the way before the dragon crashed through our makeshift blind, knocking aside mature trees as easily as if they were bowling pins. It seems we were perpetually dodging the charge of the alarmed *ngoubou* or gazing at an empty plot of crushed grass from which it had just vanished at the oxpeckers' urging.

"Of all the tedious things to happen," Walter said after some variation of the scenes I just described had recurred a half dozen more times. "How the devil are we supposed to get close to *ngoubou* if those beastly birds are going to squawk every damned time?"

As frustrating as it was, our sightings of the *ngoubou* continued to be curtailed by its winged guardians. They detected even our stealthiest approaches and saw through any blind behind which we might hide ourselves, and we grudgingly accepted that they would continue to put the dragon to flight whenever we appeared as long as they thought we might be dangerous. The only way we would ever be able to conduct long-term observation of the horned dragon would be to avoid this avian alarm, but doing so would be easier said than done.

Even though they possess adequate senses of sight, sound, and smell, *ngoubou* rely heavily upon their oxpeckers to alert them to potential danger and will flee whenever the birds raise the alarm. Though individual birds come and go throughout the day, the dragons will have at least a few oxpeckers with them at all times, and catching them unattended is virtually impossible. There is no conceivable way to separate the dragon from its oxpeckers, so dracontologists who wish to observe *ngoubou* must habituate the birds until they will allow humans to approach without raising the alarm, although the means by which this must be done may seem ghoulish.

Unusual as the process of habituating oxpeckers may be, it

derives from traditional methods of befriending wild birds. These include speaking to the birds when approaching them and moving slowly in their presence, but the most widespread technique is to offer them food in hopes of overcoming their innate fear of humans. With most species, this means offering birdseed, but the unique diet of the oxpecker necessitates a substitution.

The nature of our offerings ultimately required some tweaking, but inspired by the thinking of the day, Walter and I initially propitiated the oxpeckers with ticks and other insects. Provisioning ourselves with these dainties presented no problem, as our blood and sweat attracted a seemingly unending supply of ticks, mosquitoes, and biting flies, but we did not immediately approach *ngoubou*. Rather, we thought it safer to test our ability to placate the oxpeckers that accompanied more docile herds of reedbuck (*Redunca redunca*) and korrigum (*Damaliscus lunatus korrigum*), which were less able to gore or trample us if alarmed. Settling within sight of the herds, we proffered open palms full of our alternative birdfeed in hopes the birds would investigate us rather than raising their accustomed commotion.

"Come along, then, my pretties," Walter would say. "I have some nice juicy ticks here for you, and there's more where they came from, if you cooperate."

Finding insects might have been easy enough, but tempting the oxpeckers with them was not as simple as we might have anticipated. Patient as we tried to be when we made our offerings, the oxpeckers refused to approach our outstretched hands, and they continued to warn the local wildlife of our intrusions.

"I don't see why they keep snubbing their noses," Walter said. "Who would have thought insectivores would be so finicky?"

Our efforts to habituate the oxpeckers would undoubtedly have continued to fail if we had been left to our own devices, but Jean-Paul's expertise again provided a solution to our quandary. You see, Jean-Paul had been not only a tracker but a poacher before a term in jail had shown him the error of his ways. Though he had sworn off killing animals upon his release, he retained knowledge of several techniques for sneaking up on wildlife and suggested the proper means to purchase the oxpeckers' silence.

"If you want the birds to come to you," he said, "you must give them what they really want."

"That's what we've been trying to do," Walter said. "If they don't want ticks, what, pray tell, do you think they want?"

"Blood."

"Are you sure? We're trying to attract oxpeckers, not vampires."

"The birds eat ticks when they find them, but what they really want is blood. That is what I hear."

"Somehow that doesn't sound right to me, but I'm willing to try just about anything at this point. I certainly won't have it said that Walter Spink was squeamish about giving a little blood in the name of science. Does anybody have a pocketknife?"

After fumbling through our collective kit, we located a small folding knife, which was promptly surrendered to Walter when both Jean-Paul and I proved reluctant when it came to bloodletting. With none of our reserve, Walter pricked his fingertip with the blade and then squeezed it until a good-sized bead of crimson welled up, at which point he sallied forth to within sight of the nearest herd, planted himself cross-legged in the grass, and wagged his wounded finger invitingly.

"If it really is blood you want," he said, "come and get it."

Although it was not so widely known at the time, the preferred food of the oxpecker is in fact blood rather than ticks, a fact that has since been scientifically confirmed. To Walter's immense surprise, several oxpeckers scrutinized him attentively from their antelope host's back rather than raising the alarm. When Walter did not make any threatening movements or gestures, one of them alit a few feet away, and when he rested his hand, it hopped forward and probed his cut with its beak.

"Well, I'll be damned," Walter said. "It worked."

Walter might have been willing to do practically anything to facilitate contact with the horned dragons, but I was considerably less sanguine—if you will forgive the pun—when the prospect of letting my own blood was proposed.

"You'd best let them feed on you, too, Matthew," Walter said.

"Do I have to?" I asked.

(Unlike Walter, I am perfectly willing to have it said that I'm squeamish about giving blood.)

"Now, don't be difficult, Matthew. It's just a little blood. Come over here. I'll make the cut for you, if you like."

Despite some nausea at the thought, I opted to cut myself rather than taking the risk of Walter, with his famously poor eyesight and shaky hand, chasing me around with a knife. I felt like I was being initiated into some sort of cult, but if I was, its bloodthirsty gods showed me their favor: the oxpeckers deigned to approach and feed on me. Truth be told, the sensation of having another living thing lapping up my blood was painless enough even if the thought was unnerving, and after a few feedings, I both overcame my initial queasiness and befriended the local oxpeckers.

Even after Walter and I had both successfully lured the oxpeckers to us, we tested our new technique over the course of several days before approaching *ngoubou* again. At least when it came to the antelope herds peppered about the plain, we found that we could divert the oxpeckers from their guard duty—and silence their alarm—with the expedient of sacrificing a few drops of blood. As our confidence developed, there was less and less reason to postpone resuming our attempts to contact the horned dragon.

"Now that we know how to make friends with the oxpeckers," Walter said (as a bird probed up his right sleeve from its perch on his palm), "we'll see if we can finally get a look at *ngoubou*."

Given our previous observations of *ngoubou*'s volatile temperament, testing the success of our efforts with the oxpeckers was a daunting prospect. When Jean-Paul reported the *ngoubou* feeding in a nearby copse of *Terminalia*, we approached with both self-inflicted nicks on our fingers and trepidation, poised to dodge a charging behemoth if need be. Once we had glimpsed the beast from a distance, attended by its ubiquitous retinue of yellow-billed birds while it stripped the leaves from the lower branches of one of the trees, we approached in stages, creeping from one shrub to another and waiting the whole time to hear the *kriss, kriss* of alarm.

Instead of warning the dragon of our approach, several of the fickle birds fluttered to our outstretched hands to partake of the fresh blood without giving their host any further thought.

"They certainly abandoned their posts easily enough," Walter said, "but under the circumstances, I'm not complaining."

Once we had bought the oxpeckers' silence, we approached to within 50 feet of the dragon without provoking a response, at which point we settled in behind a *Combretum* shrub rather than trying our luck. Even at that distance, we could hear the rumbling of the dragon's stomach, and when I peered through the foliage, I could make out the wrinkles around its wizened eye and count the parietal spikes that clawed the sky from the back of its head. Without a chorus of objections from the *ngoubou*'s entourage, we were able to take in these and other details at our leisure.

Even if the oxpeckers tolerated us, I realized after surreptitiously monitoring the *ngoubou* for some time—at a range from which I could appreciate its size and armament—that we should be cautious regardless of our success with the birds. We had been so preoccupied trying to circumvent the oxpeckers that we had hardly given a thought to the dragon's own temperament, but it was entirely possible that the dragon would detect us regardless of its chaperones' silence, at which point it might object to our encroachment and become aggressive. Consequently, my instinct was to be as quiet and unobtrusive as possible until we ascertained how friendly (or otherwise) the dragon might be.

Notwithstanding my preference to go unnoticed by the seven-ton reptile that was feeding a few dozen feet away, Walter in his excitement proved incapable of such restraint, and he tested the dragon's tolerance accordingly.

"This is much better," he said. "Did I tell you what I'm going to call it? *Dracoceros acanthocephalus.* What do you think?"

"I think we should whisper," I said, sotto voce.

"Whatever for? And why the devil do you look so pale all of a sudden?"

I did not answer Walter's question, but for the record, my pallor was attributable to the movement of the dragon, which had paused in its grazing and cocked its head attentively at the sound of voices. One sunken eye rolled languidly in its orbit until it rested on our ad hoc blind, which was too sparsely vegetated to hide us now that Walter's speech had called the dragon's attention to it, and appraised us coolly. Considering how easily we had seen the dragon bowl over full-grown trees, our position suddenly felt precarious, and I froze, as if transfixed by the baleful stare of a prehistoric gorgon, for fear of provoking it further.

"It's watching us," I hissed.

"Let it watch us," Walter said. "There's no need to give yourself a fit over it."

"Shouldn't we back away?" (Still hissing.)

"You worry too much, Matthew. Just try to act natural, as if you have all the business in the world being here."

Given my state of stupefaction, there was little I could do but follow Walter's direction, so I pried my attention from the *ngoubou* and sat studying my guidebook as nonchalantly as I could with an animal the size of a minibus casting side-eye toward us. After keeping up this pretense for several minutes without being charged by the dragon, I became brave enough to steal a peek in the corner of my eye, where I found the dragon browsing placidly again as if the sight of two dracontologists and their tracker-guide had been but a passing curiosity.

"What did I tell you, Matthew?" Walter asked upon assuring himself of the dragon's disinterest. "There's nothing to worry about. I have an instinct for animal behavior."

Years of misadventures have shown me that Walter's instinct for animal behavior is hardly infallible, but his appraisal of the *ngoubou* at least was accurate. Even once the dragon became aware of us, it made no objection to our presence so long as we did not rouse the oxpeckers or otherwise do anything provocative, and we began following the dragon each day and observing and documenting its physiology and behavior as it browsed the savanna. Over time, we even habituated the oxpeckers to the point where we could approach without having to make a blood offering, but in the meantime, a few drops of blood here and there was a small price to pay for such close access to another animal whose kind has not walked the earth openly in more than 65 million years.

CHAPTER VIII
WALTER SPINK'S NEW CERATOPSIAN DIET REVOLUTION

Once the oxpeckers' objections to the dracontologists have been overcome, it is possible to observe the non-defensive behavior of *ngoubou*. When they are not charging intruders, the horned dragons are more or less peaceable as they forage through their territories, and this makes for quite a change from observing *sasabonsam*, which demand constant vigilance lest they eat their observers. On the other hand, I do not by any means imply that the horned dragons should be approached without caution. To the contrary, Walter Spink and I quickly discovered that cohabiting with *ngoubou* required its own brand of finesse, nor did the horned dragon's disinterest in eating us guarantee our safety from other predators.

I urge caution with the benefit of hindsight, but when we first made contact with the *ngoubou*, which proved by evidence I will not elaborate to be a female, she meandered languidly about the savanna without much interest in our presence. To some extent, this blasé demeanor may have been a consequence of her size and armament: she was, after all, as large as a minivan and fairly prickled with horns and spines that should certainly dissuade most comers. At the same time, her jowly face and sunken, rheumy eyes bespoke age and world-weariness that seemed somehow appropriate in a representative of such an ancient species and may have accounted for her disinterest.

Whether it was an expression of assurance or apathy, the dragon's indifference conferred an almost supercilious air. So long as the oxpeckers did not alarm her, she was utterly indifferent to our presence, as if we were commoners and beneath her notice. Similarly, even when a herd of antelope or troop of baboons ambled into her general area, she neither avoided nor acknowledged them, but they scrambled obsequiously aside as if in deference whenever she came in their direction. Altogether, the *ngoubou* behaved and was treated like an aristocrat of the savanna, and we took to calling her the Countess.

Not only was the Countess as reserved as any human aristocrat, but she was equally intolerant of poor behavior. We learned this early in our observation when Walter was so ill-mannered as to raise his voice at my suggestion that we might need physical evidence of the *ngoubou* if our account of its existence and habits was to be believed.

"If you're suggesting that we harm my dragon just for the sake of bringing home a specimen"—Walter's voice mounted in volume with his exasperation—"it's entirely out of the question, and I think you know why."

Snuff. A loud breath erupted nearby.

"And you needn't be in a huff about it, Matthew," Walter added. "I hear you snorting over there."

"That wasn't me," I said.

"Then who the devil was it?"

As we learned on this occasion, among others, the horned dragons cannot abide loud noises. Normal conversation does not provoke them, but voices raised in argument or distress are apt to be rebuked. Initially, the dragon will snort a warning such as the one Walter and I had just heard, but if the offensive noise continues, they are apt to charge in earnest.

"I think you'd better lower your voice," I said, guessing the source of the dragon's agitation.

"Lower my voice?" Walter squawked. "Of all the—"

The dragon snorted again, this time more loudly—*SNUFF*—and followed up the warning noise by pawing the ground as if in preparation to make a run at us, at which point Walter relented before his tone provoked an all-out charge.

"Very well," he grumbled. "I shall try to be quieter, although it would help if everybody would stop upsetting me."

Despite nearly provoking the horned dragon on this occasion, Walter generally maintained his composure, and as long as he did, we were able to follow her without incident. Over the course of several weeks, we learned the extent of her foraging area and began to observe her daily routine, the majority of which consisted of finding and consuming the food necessary to maintain her seven-ton frame. As a consequence, most of our observations during this early period relate to *ngoubou*'s eating preferences.

The diet of *ngoubou* is primarily vegetable in nature, just as traditional reconstructions of their ceratopsian forebears lead one to expect. During the wet tropical summer, *ngoubou* enjoy a wide selection of lush, flowering plants and assume the roles of both grazer and browser. In addition to consuming grasses, they eat the leaves and flowers of acacia, African birch (*Anogeissus leiocarpa*), *Combretum, Terminalia, Stereospermum,* and most any leafy plants they encounter. *Ngoubou* also eat fruits such as wild melons and gourds when they are available, and they will eat bark, twigs, and roots as the deciduous trees become bare with the coming of the dry savanna winter.

While we documented the foregoing dietary preferences of *ngoubou* quietly, some of the dragon's food choices were more difficult to observe without the type of emphatic reaction that incensed her. When we witnessed the Countess routinely eating the fallen fruit of the sausage tree (*Kigelia africana*), for example, Walter barely restrained the indignant squawk that wanted to come forth at my suggestion that she might be enjoying the intoxicating quality of the fermented fruit.

"Really, Matthew," he said, "I hope you're not suggesting that our scaly friend is some kind of lush."

Walter's incredulity notwithstanding, it is by no means unprecedented for animals to develop a taste for intoxicating fruit. Tales of elephants becoming drunk on marula are almost certainly apocryphal, but deer and moose have been known to feed on fermented apples before going on impressive benders.[12] In any event, we could hardly disbelieve our eyes, and the Countess visited the *Kigelia* trees more often than we would have expected if she had eaten the fruit only casually.

"Hmmph," Walter said finally. "I'm not sure how I feel about it, but it seems you're right, Matthew. Our scaly friend is something of an inebriate."

Walter might have grudgingly accepted the idea of a dragon who enjoyed being intoxicated, but not long afterward, he was presented with a situation that could not help but elicit an outcry on his part. The horned dinosaurs have traditionally been depicted as strictly vegetarian, but the *ngoubou* defied convention—and nearly roused Walter to more shouting, the dragon's temperament be damned—when she came across a buffalo carcass in her travels across the savanna and fed upon it with as little ceremony as if she were a born carnivore.

"Bother," Walter said. "My eyesight must be even worse than I thought, because it looks like our scaly friend is eating meat."

"In this case," I said, "I don't think it's your eyesight. I see it, too."

"What the devil?!"

(The dragon snorted and tossed her head irritably.)

"Lower your voice," I said, "before she charges."

"But this can't be!" Walter squawked. "The horned dinosaurs didn't eat meat!"

Once Walter had composed himself, he interrogated Jean-Paul on the seeming carnivory of our *ngoubou* while the squelch of the

---

[12]Even among *ngoubou*'s fellow cryptids, the Himalayan *yeti* is rumored to be quite fond of alcohol.

Countess rending buffalo flesh with her beak punctuated their dialogue unpleasantly.

"Are *ngoubou* supposed to do this?" he asked.

"I have heard," Jean-Paul said, "that *ngoubou* eat flesh sometimes."

"Hmmph. You could have said something sooner instead of letting me get all worked up about it."

We watched the dragon strip the carcass to the point of gnawing on bare bone, whereupon she resumed foraging among the *Combretum* and *Stereospermum* again as if her meat-eating had been little more than a dream.

"Let's not make anything of this now," Walter said, "and hope it doesn't happen again. I don't know if the world is ready for a meat-eating *Styracosaurus*."

Despite Walter's incredulity at the prospect that his living ceratopsian might be an opportunistic carnivore, we continued documenting the horned dragon's feeding behavior to see if it would be repeated. I suppose I cannot blame Walter for being squeamish at the idea of *ngoubou* eating meat, considering how unbelievable the behavior would seem to authorities that would find a living *Styracosaurus* difficult enough to believe on its own. At the same time, the *ngoubou*'s possible scavenging did not threaten life and limb even if it challenged our preconceived assumptions regarding her behavior, and we soon found that another animal's meat-eating was far more worrisome to us than that of *ngoubou.*

It goes without saying that *ngoubou* are not the only African animals that eat meat, and far from being occasional scavengers like the horned dragons, many of these other meat-eaters are active predators. Human beings are not their usual prey, but as I have previously indicated, some carnivores will nevertheless attack us given the opportunity. Walter and I should perhaps have been on our guard against such predators, but we were so preoccupied studying the horned dragon that we ignored all other wildlife, even when reports began to suggest that an unknown predator had killed several calves at a nearby Fulani settlement.

"Do *ngoubou* ever kill cattle?" Walter asked Jean-Paul when he reported the killings.

"I have not heard that they do," Jean-Paul said.

"Then it's probably not a *ngoubou*, and we came here to study dragons, not cattle mutilations. I don't see any need for us to pursue the matter."

So long as we did not suspect a connection to *ngoubou*, we did not investigate the unusual killings. If we had, we almost certainly would have recognized the killer's spoor, and we probably would have guessed that it would eventually cross our path. You see, the predator behind the cattle killings was quite familiar to us, but our single-mindedness when it came to *ngoubou* kept us ignorant of its presence until it struck.

The attack that revealed this familiar predator came while we were returning to camp from a day's observation of the horned dragon. Walking in my accustomed place behind the others, I saw a shrub lurch into tremulous motion when Walter passed, as if it meant to uproot itself and follow him, and a set of jaws darted out of the leaves and clacked shut just shy of Walter's right arm. Before we could do more than recoil, the vibration of the bush changed, and it seemed that the animal, which had concealed itself within the branches to ambush us, had become entangled and was struggling to free itself rather than catch Walter.

If this clumsy attempt at ambushing Walter had not been enough for us to indentify the predator, he soon stumbled free of his woody cage and landed, flat on his face and spreadeagled, where we could view him in full leathery-winged glory. When his gargoyle form righted itself and his head dipped submissively upon finding us confronting him head-on, even Walter with his middling eyesight could not mistake the creature.

"Good heavens," he said, "it's Heep!"

Walter and I had seen so much of Heep during our study of the *sasabonsam* that we could not help recognizing his singular appearance and demeanor on this occasion. Indeed, I think we took his reappearance as well as any two people who have ever been attacked by a carnivorous winged reptile from their past, but Jean-Paul, who had never seen such a creature in his life, was considerably more uneasy as he appraised those toothy jaws.

"Do you know this animal?" he asked.

"Oh, yes," Walter said. "Much more than we'd like."

"Is it dangerous?"

"Not if you're careful. As you've already seen, he's really too clumsy to be much of a threat."

While the winged dragon's existence did not faze us as it did our companion, we were nevertheless puzzled at his presence so far from home.

"What I want to know," Walter said, "is what the devil he's doing here."

"He must have followed us," I said.

"Obviously, but why?"

"Can't you guess?"

"I'm too busy to guess, so why don't you just tell me?"

"You're the one he's always chased, and he attacked you again just now. I, er, think maybe he still wants to eat you."

"It's an awfully long way to travel to get a nip at a bony old relic like me, but you may be right. It's damned inconvenient, though. How the devil am I supposed to study *ngoubou* and fend off a hungry *sasabonsam* at the same time?"

Whether he was welcome or not, Heep invited himself to join our company, though I personally felt more comfortable with the vampire birds. We would have made an odd-looking menagerie, if anyone had been around to see us, with the horned dragon trudging resolutely across the savanna, followed by three humans, and the gangly scarecrow of a winged dragon hobbling along at the rear hoping one of us would be careless enough for him to catch. Aside from exacerbating the strangeness of our already-unusual situation, the *sasabonsam*'s coming would also demand changes in our day to day life observing the *ngoubou*, lest we document the feeding habits of the horned dragon at the expense of being eaten by the winged one.

*

Having a carnivorous *sasabonsam* loitering around is hardly conducive to observing its terrestrial counterparts. Try though we might to concentrate on the *ngoubou* and its behavior, Heep was never far away, watching for an opportunity to attack. Though the winged dragon lowered his head submissively and waddled away whenever we looked in his direction, he crept closer whenever our attention drifted back to the horned dragon as the ostensible focus of our work. Needless to say, a dracontologist is not much use studying the horned dragons if he is eaten by a *sasabonsam*, so it became necessary for one or another of us to be always watching so as to dissuade Heep from sneaking up and effecting the ambush he intended.

As vigilant as we were against Heep stalking us, I doubted our ability to fend him off indefinitely and would have felt more secure if we had possessed some sort of defensive weaponry. When I suggested the possibility of arming ourselves against the winged dragon's attacks, however, I was overruled by both my companions for their own respective reasons.

"I've been thinking maybe we should have some protection," I said, "in case our friend gets too close."

"Whatever do you mean, Matthew?" Walter asked. "A gun?"

"No guns for me," Jean-Paul said. "I am a gentle person."

"It doesn't matter, anyway," Walter said. "I absolutely forbid you from coming near my dragons with a firearm. We've already lost one *sasabonsam*, and I won't have anybody shooting poor Heep, even if he is a bit of a nuisance. We shall just have to be careful that he doesn't have the chance to attack anybody."

With Walter's prohibition against arming ourselves, we had no choice but to be as observant as possible and hope the winged dragon did not get the drop on us. We hired men from the village to guard our camp overnight and tried our best to monitor Heep during the day, but we had the business of studying the *ngoubou* to distract us while Heep could focus exclusively on stalking Walter. Inevitably, the *sasabonsam* sidestepped our watch and beset Walter once again.

When Heep attacked, I was alone with Walter while Jean-Paul answered nature's call, and Walter, in his zeal to follow the horned dragon, had ranged far enough ahead of me that the dragon must have felt he could strike before I would be able to intercede. Something dropped out of an acacia as Walter passed beneath, unfurling a set of telltale wings in the process, and I heard Walter's now-familiar squawk of alarm. Before I could process what was happening, much less act, Walter was backed up against the tree with the winged dragon drawing up on him, brandishing his open jaws as if inviting the old man to leap down his throat.

"Matthew, help!" Walter squawked. "He's got me trapped!"

With the *sasabonsam* just a snap of the jaws away from realizing his dream of dining on dracontologist, and me unarmed as a result of Walter's injunction, things might have gone ill for Walter. I was too far away to intervene between Walter and the dragon before the latter struck and too weak, without Jean-Paul, to intimidate or wrestle the dragon away even if I could have reached them. I fully expected the worst this time, but help came unlooked-for from an entirely unexpected quarter: the *ngoubou.*

The horned dragon barreled into the fray like a thunderstorm, resolving from a dark blur into her familiar armored dreadnought form just a few feet from the winged dragon's unguarded flank. Finding himself unexpectedly eclipsed by the Countess, Heep squawked in alarm and hopped backwards, whereupon the Countess flourished her nose horn while simultaneously advancing another step. A second later, Heep took to his heels altogether, and the *ngoubou* pursued him, leaving Walter behind at the tree, blinking in bewilderment but thankfully unharmed.

"Matthew?" Walter asked. "What the devil happened?"

"It was the *ngoubou*," I said. "She chased Heep away."

"I wonder what made her do that."

While it is impossible to vouch for a wild dragon's motivations with any certainty, I have already described how the horned dragons are agitated by loud noises within their territories. The *ngoubou* had very nearly charged more than once upon hearing Walter shouting, so it seems likely that was roused to intervene by the noise he had made when confronted with Heep. As for her decision to wreak her anger on Heep rather than Walter, who was actually making the noise, I can only imagine that she either perceived that the *sasabonsam* was the cause of the commotion or recognized a dangerous carnivore when she saw it.

Whatever the reason for his delivery, Walter had no sooner found himself safe than he worried about his erstwhile attacker's well-being.

"I'm grateful to be in one piece, really I am," he said, "but I do hope she didn't hurt him."

Walter would not be placated until he had ascertained that Heep was uninjured, so we searched until we found the winged dragon perched in a nearby *Terminalia*, presumably to be out of the *ngoubou*'s reach. A brief inspection reassured us that Heep was none the worse for wear, and knowing that no harm had come to the *sasabonsam*, Walter finally felt comfortable scolding him for attacking in the first place.

"It serves you right," he said. "Maybe next time you'll think twice before trying to eat somebody."

Despite Walter's hopes, Heep did not learn his lesson after his tussle with the *ngoubou*, but now we had a seven-ton, horned ally whenever he forgot himself. If the winged dragon came too close for comfort, Walter had but to raise his voice, whereupon the horned dragon charged and drove Heep away. The Countess's behavior became so predictable, both to Walter and Heep, that the latter would quail if the former so much as threatened to call her to his defense.

"You're a little too close for my taste. Let's not make me"—Walter projected his voice toward the *ngoubou* browsing nearby—"call on my scaly friend."

Or:

"If you get any closer"—Walter shouted the last word, eliciting an irritable snort from the Countess—"I shall call for help, and you won't like what will happen then."

Perceiving that Walter's raised voice would summon his enemy, Heep cringed back with a whimper whenever Walter spoke up, and after a few days of being blocked from stalking Walter in this manner, he appeared to acknowledge defeat. We still saw him each day, but he withdrew to a discreet distance whenever we made contact with the *ngoubou.* Since we joined the *ngoubou* shortly after dawn and lingered in her vicinity all day, the *sasabonsam* no longer had access to us to lay his accustomed ambushes.

This new freedom from attack was, as you may imagine, a matter of particular relief to Walter as the object of the *sasabonsam*'s unfriendly intentions.

"This is much better," he said one day. "Thanks to our scaly friend here, I hardly need to worry about old Heep anymore."

There is no denying that the *ngoubou*'s antipathy toward Heep was beneficial. We passed a series of calm and quiet days without interference from the winged dragon, and we might almost have forgotten the worries he had caused us up to that point. If we were tempted to relax our guard now that we seemed to be under the Countess's protection, however, we were about to learn that the horned dragon would not always be able to guard Walter against the *sasabonsam*'s designs.

*

Even when they are held at bay by the presence of a larger and tougher animal, *sasabonsam* do not give up their prey easily once they've set their minds to it. They are, as I have already said, ambush predators, and watching and waiting for an opportunity to strike is thus ingrained into their behavior. If the would-be prey is tempting enough, they will abide a chance for a successful ambush, and Heep's pursuing Walter across Cameroon testifies to how he craved a taste of the old man. Thus, he did not by any means give up his carnivorous purpose even if he stalked us in a more reserved manner.

Heep betrayed his continued interest in his elderly quarry by continuing to loiter about, regardless of whether he loitered at a greater distance than before. If I looked behind us at any given moment, I would see his gargoyle silhouette perched among the branches of a *Terminalia.* When I glanced around us thinking to enjoy the vast panorama of the savanna, I would see his hunched shoulders and wedge-shaped head interrupting the sea of grass a couple hundred feet away. Heep affected to be preoccupied stalking some small animal whenever he perceived that he was being watched, but I knew that there was no reason for him to be around unless he meant to be available should the horned dragon's watch falter.

Having guessed his intentions, I decided that Heep bore continued watching, but convincing Walter to be more cautious was an uphill battle.

"I think you worry too much, Matthew," he said when I brought my concern to his attention. "Old Heep's not going to try anything as long as our scaly friend is around."

"You can't depend on her protecting you all the time."

"Whyever not? Besides, I'm far too busy documenting the behavior of *ngoubou* to worry about our leathery-winged friend in any event."

Even if Walter felt sure of the horned dragon's unwavering protection, I was uneasy at both the prospect of blindly trusting to the behavior of the *ngoubou* and disregarding the danger presented by the *sasabonsam.* Some might say it was overly cautious of me, but I began monitoring Heep to ensure that he kept his distance and found no opportunity to ambush anyone. As it turns out, my caution proved entirely warranted, even if my vigilance was not entirely successful in precluding further attacks.

The eventual lapse in my guard arose from the difficulty of monitoring two dragons at once, at least for someone of my limited coordination. Even though Heep moved languidly when he knew I was watching, he relocated with unexpected speed if I took my eyes off him for so much as a second, in which way he could potentially get much closer before I could warn the others. He did not immediately make a run at Walter whenever I blinked, but after Heep demonstrated his ability to stalk so quickly when my attention wavered, I resigned myself to the fact that I could not participate in the *ngoubou* observation and guard against the *sasabonsam* at the same time. Given the stakes of losing track of the winged dragon, I chose to focus on him.

My surveillance of the winged dragon undoubtedly caused me to miss many interesting observations of *ngoubou,* which I only heard by way of Walter's running commentary.

"Well, there she goes eating carrion again, Matthew. So much for our hope that it was just a fluke."

"Now she's into the *Kigelia* again, Matthew. Considering how fond she is of being intoxicated, perhaps we should have called her Sue Ellen."[13]

"I really wish you were seeing this with me, Matthew, if only so you could corroborate what I'm seeing. I daresay nobody back home is going to believe me when I tell them about a meat-eating, alcoholic dragon."

Aside from depriving me of several interesting observations and Walter of a witness, my focus on the winged dragon at the expense of his horned counterpart had another frailty that proved to be of far greater concern. Though I correctly guessed that the *sasabonsam* would strike if given another chance, I overlooked the amount to

---

[13]*Dallas* was very popular back home at the time our observations of *ngoubou* took place.

which his likelihood of ambushing us depended upon the *ngoubou*'s behavior. The Countess was, after all, the reason why Heep did not come closer, and without knowing what was happening to her, I could not anticipate when Heep would actually move against his would-be prey.

Though the infirmity in my methodology seems obvious in retrospect, I did not guess it at the time, at least not until Heep finally exploited it during one of our daily interactions with the *ngoubou.* I had only Walter's reports of the horned dragon feeding and glutting herself with *Kigelia* fruit to inform me of her disposition, so I had no reason to expect that anything was unusual at the time. Still, Heep must have perceived what was going on with the *ngoubou*, for he began discreetly advancing, at which point I began to wonder if there was some reason why he might anticipate an opportunity to feed.

"Is anything going on?" I asked Walter over my shoulder.

"Going on?" Walter asked. "Whatever do you mean?"

"I think our friend"—I eyed Heep through the whole conversation, lest he sneak up on us—"is up to something."

"Really, Matthew, this isn't the time. There seems to be something wrong with our scaly friend."

Despite my resolution to keep the winged dragon under surveillance, I could not help craning my neck to learn what had so concerned Walter. For just a second I beheld the *ngoubou* tottering on legs that had suddenly turned to rubber beneath her, a state which lasted but a moment before she collapsed altogether. With all the grace of a rockslide, her seven-ton frame leaned perilously to one side and then smashed into the ground, barely missing Walter in the process.

"Good heavens," he said. "She just keeled over. I think it must have been the fermented fruit."

Observing an intoxicated dragon might normally have interested me, but in a moment of belated clarity, I realized that Heep must have anticipated the *ngoubou*'s indisposition when he began stalking closer. Half-expecting to find him on top of me, I whirled back toward the savanna where I had last seen him, only to find it empty. I had no idea where the *sasabonsam* might have gone, at least until I heard Walter cry out behind me.

"What the devil? Get away from me, I say!"

When I spun around, I beheld Walter recoiling away from Heep, who advanced, jaw snapping a brisk tempo to his sortie, while Jean-Paul, gentle person that he was, very politely asked the dragon to please go away. In the absence of a weapon to fend off his assailant, Walter took the only cover he could find, retreating behind the *ngoubou*'s frill. While Heep tried unavailingly to thrust his face between the parietal spikes that barred his pursuit, Walter cried out for his erstwhile protector.

"I could use a little help here, madam," he said. "Of all the tedious—will you please wake up?"

With all the *Kigelia* fruit that his scaly friend had ingested, this plea went unanswered. When the winged dragon kept coming, Walter had no choice but to scramble up the *ngoubou*'s mountainous flank, where he perched precariously like a sailor atop the prow of a sinking ship with the winged dragon standing in for the usual shark. Walter accomplished the climb more nimbly than I would have expected of a man of his years, and Heep was poorly equipped to follow. He tried jumping up the horned dragon's side, but after scrambling in place without gaining any purchase, he slid back to the ground and took to pacing back and forth, waiting for Walter to fall off instead.

Walter's retreat from the attacking *sasabonsam* happened much more quickly than I can describe it, too quickly for me to react, but Walter's shout finally roused me.

"I could use some help, Matthew"—the *ngoubou*'s side heaved with its breath, nearly knocking Walter off—"if you're not too terribly busy."

Responding to Walter's distress call, I enlisted Jean-Paul's assistance to drive the *sasabonsam* away.

"Please don't ask me to hurt it," he protested. "I am a gentle person."

"You won't have to," I said. "He'll retreat as soon as he finds himself outnumbered."

As I predicted, Heep withdrew when confronted by two grown men in addition to his prey, and he hobbled backward, head down like an obsequious courtier taking leave of his king, until he was safely away from us. Once the *sasabonsam* had gone, Walter slid gracelessly down the *ngoubou*'s side and joined Jean-Paul and me at the unconscious dragon's feet, fully expecting to hear that I had told him so.

"There's no need to say it, Matthew," he said. "You were right. Obviously I can't depend on our scaly friend to protect me all the time. I shall have to be more careful from now on."

Thankfully, Walter's reliance on the *ngoubou*'s protection had proved unwise but not fatal, and in the absence of injury or death, we could reflect comfortably on what we had learned. The horned dragon had certainly confirmed the proclivity of her kind to eat fermented fruit to the point of intoxication, and in the coming days, her periodic scavenging would also establish the tendency of *ngoubou* to eat carrion, our preconceptions as to the diet of a surviving *Styracosaurus* notwithstanding.[14] While we put to rest our questions concerning the *ngoubou*'s diet, however, we had by no means resolved the issue of the scrawny *sasabonsam*, who continued to stalk Walter and make our lives more interesting for some time to come.

---

[14]Although the idea may seem far-fetched based on traditional reconstructions of ceratopsians, more recent research into *ngoubou*'s fossilized forebears suggests that several dinosaurs that were once thought to be exclusively vegetarian may have eaten flesh on occasion.

CHAPTER IX
PENELOPE REDUX

The antagonism between the dragon and the elephant has been reported since ancient scribes compiled the first natural histories. Pliny the Elder wrote of the dragon and the elephant living in perpetual war with one another,[15] and the bestiaries of the Middle Ages repeatedly bore illustrations of elephants locked in combat with serpentine dragons. While the bestiaries commonly distorted the physiology and behavior of their subjects, modern accounts of the horned dragons killing elephants (and the carcasses of elephants gored by them) suggest that the belief in a rivalry between the two species has at least some basis in fact.

Even if the antipathy between the horned dragon and the pachyderm is not fanciful, the impression many locals (and even dracontologists) have of a species that kills elephants indiscriminately whenever they meet is not quite accurate. As a matter of fact, the first interaction Walter and I observed between *ngoubou* and elephants was entirely peaceful, though I did not anticipate an amicable encounter

---

[15]Pliny the Elder. *The Natural History,* translated by John Bostock, M.D., F.R.S. and H.T. Riley, Esq. London, Taylor and Francis, 1855, Book VIII, Ch. 11.

when I first spied a matriarch and her seven sisters, daughters, and nieces emerging from mixed woodland onto the same grassy plain where the Countess was foraging.

"Uh-oh," I said.

"What's the matter with you, Matthew?" Walter asked.

"There's a herd of elephants coming."

"Where? I don't see them."

After fumbling with a pair of binoculars and looking in every direction but the one in which I pointed, Walter finally spied the interlopers, at which point he echoed my assessment.

"Good heavens," he said, "there they are, and it looks like they're heading this way. This doesn't bode well at all, if half the things we've heard are true."

For several anxious minutes we divided our attention between the approaching herd and the Countess, who browsed peacefully as if unaware of them.

"They're definitely coming this way," Walter said. "Do you think we should try to chase them off?"

"If we do," I said, "we'll never know for sure what the relationship between *ngoubou* and elephants is really like."

"You're right, of course, Matthew. But what if it goes badly? Should we try to step in, do you think?"

"I think that would be a bad idea."

"Very well. I suppose we shall just have to observe from a safe distance and hope for the best."

Regardless of Walter's fretting, we were not called upon to take any action at this time. The elephants' march took them within a few yards of the Countess as we had anticipated, but they trod resolutely past her without stopping or being stopped by her. The *ngoubou* and the matriarch briefly locked eyes as the latter passed, more like two fine ladies reservedly acknowledging each other at a social event than the mortal enemies they were reputed to be, and with this minimal interaction, each animal returned to her own business.

"It seems that the enmity between elephants and *ngoubou* has been overstated," Walter said. "Not that I'm complaining, mind you. I'm certainly not eager to see bloodshed."

Despite observing this uneventful interaction between the species, we had already seen evidence in the form of a dead elephant to bear out the belief in their animosity. This seeming contradiction perplexed us for a time, but the next interaction we witnessed between the horned dragon and an elephant was more in line with our expectations.

The more stereotypically violent interaction between the horned dragon and an elephant occurred several weeks later when an elephant came upon the Countess feeding on some *Stereospermum.* Judging from its size, the shape of its head, and its solitary state, the newcomer was a male, and his course brought him toward the *ngoubou.* Though she initially paid him no more heed than she had the cows, the elephant's gender, the alacrity with which he approached the horned dragon, and the fluid dripping from his temples all suggested more than casual curiosity on the bull's part. When he approached the *ngoubou* and caressed her back with his trunk, I became fairly certain of his intentions, unusual as they were.

"What's he doing?" Walter asked. "I can't see."

"I think he's going to try to mate with her," I said.

"An elephant mate with *ngoubou*? Don't be ridiculous, Matthew. It must be something else."

Though my hypothesis might seem outlandish, it is by no means unheard-of for elephants to assault other creatures, even sexually. Elephants in South Africa, for example, have attempted to mount rhinoceros and, upon finding their sex objects unreceptive, killed them. Such antisocial and aberrant behavior usually occurs among males in musth, especially younger rogues that have grown up without more experienced, stronger bulls to teach appropriate behavior and hold aggressive tendencies in check.[16] Undoubtedly the Countess's would-be suitor was such a developmentally impaired

---

[16]This situation is generally agreed to arise from hunters killing all the older bulls in the area so as to allow these bulls to grow delinquent.

animal.

Whatever the reason for the strange bull's behavior, he soon confirmed my suspicion of his intentions by progressing from eagerly probing with his trunk to a more unmistakably sexual display. Without preamble or foreplay, the elephant placed his front feet on the Countess's broad backside and attempted to mount her.

Though the elephant undoubtedly intended to gratify himself sexually, the *ngoubou* was no passive animal that would tolerate his inappropriate behavior. Where the Countess had just shrugged off his trunk at first, she rejected him more adamantly when he tried to mount her, stumbling out from under him and whirling to brandish her sickle of horn between them as a warning against further trespass. If the bull had originally been oblivious to the horned dragon's disinterest, he readily perceived the meaning of her aggressive stance, and his lustful thoughts dissolved in favor of blind aggression as soon as battle had been offered. From that point, the interaction devolved into the sort of *ngoubou*-elephant conflict we had been led to expect.

If the skirmish we witnessed between the Countess and the rogue bull was any indication, it must have felt like Ragnarok in Mesozoic days with thousands of the *ngoubou*'s forebears working out their differences with thousands of their prehistoric enemies. Without any overtures or formalities, the elephant lunged forward with his trunk curled up under his mouth and ears flaring, and the Countess charged with head down and the point of her horn cocked forward. The parched savanna bushes seemed to shrink back from their coming as they barreled toward each other, and finally the titans collided like two freight trains, with a jolt that made the earth tremble where Walter and I watched some 200 feet away.

Once battle had been joined, the combat was both briefer and more confused than my description can convey. For a second it was impossible to distinguish the dragon from the elephant as they whirled like two great boulders trying to roll over each other, but occasionally I would perceive a flash of tusk or horn slashing through the fray. Several times they broke apart, resolving into their more recognizable individual forms, only to crash together again, in which position they lurched this way and that as if in an ungainly parody of a waltz. In the process, they flattened bushes and razed trees until they struck a 30-foot-tall acacia so hard they disturbed a beehive that hung from one of its branches.

There's no telling how long the dragon and her foe might have grappled in this manner before a victor emerged, but the bees intervened and curtailed further violence. As science has confirmed, elephants are terrified of bees and will usually avoid even feeding near a hive. When the agitated bees erupted from their beleaguered hive like a puff of angry smoke, the bull turned tail and galloped away as soon as he recognized the droning *kiai* of the affronted swarm, leaving the Countess in possession of the field of victory (albeit still too well-bred to gloat).

When the combat ended, Walter, who had wrung his hands and fretted over the safety of the *ngoubou* the whole time, scrutinized his scaly friend for injuries.

"I can't quite see, Matthew," he said. "Is she all right?"

"She looks all right," I said after giving her a once-over. "I don't think she's hurt."

"Thank heavens."

Though this first skirmish had ended without injury on either side, it nevertheless afforded valuable information regarding the relationship between *ngoubou* and elephants. Having observed that the horned dragon's attacker was a young, presumably rogue bull, we could at least speculate as to the source of *ngoubou*-elephant conflict, which seems to arise from altercations with maladjusted individuals rather than generalized antipathy between the species. The altercation also amply demonstrated that the horned dragons are perfectly capable of holding their own against an elephant, just as their reputation suggests. Considering that further conflict between the species would almost certainly mean death for either an elephant or the dragon, Walter and I had no particular desire to make further observations of this particular behavior, but dissuading further hostilities would ultimately require more active measures than simply wishing it away.

Whether we like it or not, conflict is a part of nature, and it is by no means uncommon for wild animals to fight and kill each other as elephants and *ngoubou* sometimes do. Perhaps it should comfort dracontologists to know that *ngoubou* generally conquer their opponents in these contests, as the bodies of slain elephants across the Congo basin mutely testify, but this is small consolation. Even if dracontologists need not worry that their dragons will be slain, it is hardly more desirable to see the blood of an elephant spilt. For this reason, Walter especially was ambivalent at the prospect of the dragon and the elephant resuming hostilities.

"I've been thinking," he said, "and if that rogue comes back, we should try to keep the two of them away from each other. Even though our scaly friend can take care of herself, I don't want anything to happen to the elephant. He may be something of a scoundrel, but his life is precious, too."

Walter's empathy for both the dragon and the elephant notwithstanding, accepted scientific practice emphasizes observing the natural behavior of animals without interference. This implicitly means allowing two natural foes to have at each other, even if one of them may be injured or killed in the bargain, for conflict and death are part of the natural course. Walter often straddled this line in his interactions with his research subjects, and I always felt it was my role to warn him against crossing it, though I was already learning the futility of asking Walter Spink to behave like a proper naturalist.

"I understand what you're saying, and I agree," I said, "but can we stop two animals from doing what comes naturally?"

"I'm sure we can think of something," Walter said.

"But is it ethical?"

"Why the devil wouldn't it be ethical?"

"Most scientists would urge against interfering with wild animals."

"I don't know about 'most scientists,' but it seems to me that it's more ethical to save animals' lives than to allow them to be harmed, don't you think? My mind is made up, Matthew. I'm going to save them both if I possibly can."

Walter's resolve to protect the *ngoubou* and the rogue elephant from each other was soon tested, for the bull returned the next day while we were observing the former. The Countess was minding her own business grazing the *Pennisetum* that flanked one of the Vina River's many oxbows when we heard the crackle of a branch breaking under an otherwise stealthy tread. Expecting at first to find Heep once again drawing up on Walter, we instead beheld the elephant emerging from around the riverbend. With the uncanny ability of his kind to move quietly regardless of their size, the rogue was less than 200 feet away by the time we sensed him, and the fluid dripping from his temporal glands told us that the state of arousal that had instigated his first confrontation with the horned dragon continued.

"Bother," Walter said. "There he is again. I suppose I shall have to intercede before somebody gets killed."

"Maybe we should wait a minute," I said, "and see if the oxpeckers warn her."

"That's good thinking, Matthew. They just might, at that."

Contrary to my hope, however, the oxpeckers continued to probe daintily among the dragon's pebbly scales and did not seem to notice even as the elephant halved the distance between himself and the *ngoubou*, who browsed obliviously the whole time. It's possible that the birds were simply not accustomed to treating an elephant as an enemy, but it's certain that the elephant closed to within 100 feet of their host without so much as a peep from the oxpeckers.

"A fat lot of good those lazy birds are," Walter said. "As I expected, I shall have to do something myself."

My extremities went cold with dread at the prospect of whatever reckless action Walter proposed.

"What are you going to do?" I asked.

"Nothing outrageous," he said. "You'll see soon enough."

While I steeled myself to rescue Walter from whatever foolhardy effort he made to intercede between the dragon and the elephant, the rogue closed on the unsuspecting *ngoubou*, still without evident alarm on the part of the entourage atop her hump. Just when it seemed another skirmish could not be averted, an obnoxious noise like the squealing of a tortured pig erupted so close that I almost fled before I realized it was coming from Walter at my side.

"*Kriss, kriss,* I say. Do you hear me? *Kriss, kriss! Kriss, kriss!*"

The resemblance to the original was so lacking that I didn't recognize the call at first, but as Walter fine-tuned his impression, I realized that he was at least attempting to counterfeit the warning call of the oxpeckers, evidently thinking to chase the dragon away before the elephant could catch her. Though I had my doubts as to his success even once I guessed his plan, my appraisal of the impression was thankfully academic, because the Countess ultimately could not tell the difference. Without bothering to peer around for the source of the false oxpecker's warning, she pivoted on her heels and galloped away north until she disappeared over the crest of a hill, leaving the elephant to shuffle to a baffled stop while we watched from the concealment of the shrubs.

Once the elephant lost sight of his would-be paramour, he meandered back in the direction he had come, and Walter explained himself while we tracked the *ngoubou* back down.

"In case you're wondering what you just witnessed," he said, "I'm something of a birder, or at least I was before I discovered dragons, of course. It occurred to me that I could make a passable oxpecker impression, and I don't seem to have done too badly, if I do say so myself."

Now that Walter had developed a working strategy, keeping the elephant and the *ngoubou* apart became a straightforward affair. On each of the succeeding days, the aroused male, whom we called

Antinous after the unwanted suitor who beset Odysseus's wife, appeared at the crest of a grassy hill or in the shade of a parasol-like acacia and approached the horned dragon with steam in his stride. As soon as we caught sight of him, Walter cupped his hands around his mouth like a megaphone and called *kriss, kriss* to the *ngoubou*, who reacted just as if her oxpeckers had signaled the alarm and made for the nearest stand of elephant grass or copse of trees to disappear.

"It's no use," Walter would say while the rogue stamped his feet in frustration. "You won't catch her now."

By the time he had averted several skirmishes in this manner, Walter was encouraged by his success even if I continued to nurse doubts concerning his meddling.

"You see, Matthew?" he said. "I've saved the two of them from coming to blows, and the world hasn't ended yet. There's nothing to worry about."

"I guess that's fine for now," I said, "but what happens when he comes back again?"

"Why, I shall simply have to do the same thing again, and again if necessary. He'll have to lose interest and go about his business sometime."

Despite Walter's optimism, the rogue remained in musth and lingered in the *ngoubou*'s foraging area, and only Walter's concerted effort forestalled a confrontation between them. When the elephant's visits continued over the course of another week, Walter dutifully kept him away from the Countess, and the old man was satisfied so long as neither animal was able to hurt the other. In his fixation on the well-being of the dragon and her unwanted suitor, however, Walter neglected to consider the ramifications that meddling between two beasts who wanted to fight each other might have for our own safety.

*

One unavoidable side effect of working in close proximity to a dragon who is the recipient of unwanted attention from a rogue bull elephant is the danger that the dracontologists will be attacked in the bargain. Even when we are not, strictly speaking, the object of an elephant's depredations, the rogue will still strike out at human beings if it finds them in its path. Thus, our proximity to the *ngoubou* that attracted the rogue led to a series of harrowing encounters in which Walter, Jean-Paul, and I found ourselves the focus of the rogue's aggression.

Our first personal run-in with the rogue came about when Walter stymied one of Antinous's attempts to sneak up on the Countess. As usual, Walter had chased her away with his counterfeit oxpecker call, thinking that would end the encounter, but this just left us waiting in the rogue's path without the dragon around to occupy his attention. Normally he would have gone on his way as soon as the dragon left, but this time he continued in our direction.

"Walter," I said, "he's still coming."

"I'm sure he'll stop any moment," Walter said, "now that our scaly friend is gone."

"He's not stopping."

"Oh, dear."

The prospect of running into an elephant in the wild might not seem frightening, given their traditional depiction as gentle giants, but truth be told, they are by no means as friendly as popular culture might have you believe. Even normal, well-adjusted elephants will charge humans who encroach too closely, and rogues as a rule are less tolerant and more aggressive in their conduct toward our kind. Whatever the source of their aggression, elephants are capable of inflicting deadly injury, whether by goring the intruder with their tusks, grasping and tossing him doll-like with their trunks, or simply trampling him into putty with all the force of their 13,000-pound weight. For this reason, meeting a rogue elephant in close quarters is an inherently dangerous situation.

Recognizing our precarious position, Walter, Jean-Paul, and I withdrew a split second before the elephant noticed us, and we took off running when he heard him trumpet at our heels. I dared not stop to look over my shoulder, fearing to stumble or simply slow down my escape, but the rogue's shadow on the ground, creeping forward from behind us and threatening to eclipse our own shadows, told me that he had given chase. As bookish and physically unfit academics, Walter and I were poorly equipped to outrun the rogue, but our retreat must have thankfully mollified him. After a brief chase, we scrambled out of Antinous's clutching shadow as he slackened his pace behind us, and when I dared to rest and look back, we had left him plucking languidly at the grass with his trunk several hundred feet back, evidently satisfied with our withdrawal.

"Well," Walter said once I told him he could stop running, "that wasn't so bad after all."

"How can you be so cheerful," I asked, "when we just got chased by a mad elephant?"

"There wasn't any harm done, was there? Really, Matthew, you shouldn't be so melodramatic."

Despite Walter's blasé attitude toward our situation, it quickly became clear that this first scuffle with the rogue elephant would not by any means be an isolated incident. Several more times we dodged charges from Antinous either when we chanced to meet him on our way to or from the *ngoubou*'s feeding area or when he stumbled upon us in the dragon's place after Walter had chased her away. Generally the elephant abandoned the pursuit if we promptly gave ground to him, but whenever he charged, it was entirely possible that this time he would pursue us more fervently—and with fatal results.

Being preoccupied with the possibility that we might be killed ourselves if we kept getting in the rogue's way, I tried to dissuade Walter from continuing to interfere (with predictable results).

"We've been lucky so far," I said in the wake of a thankfully half-hearted chase on the elephant's part, "but he's going to kill us if he ever catches us."

"What are you getting at, Matthew?" Walter asked.

"I think we should stay out of his way and see what happens."

"Oh, I couldn't possibly do that. I can't have him harming our scaly friend, or vice versa."

When Walter first refused to stop his meddling, I was too naturally meek and submissive to challenge him further, but my worst fears of a truly aggressive charge on the rogue's part were soon realized. This harrowing encounter began like any other, with the rogue appearing out of the bush and approaching the *ngoubou* while Walter, Jean-Paul, and I watched from a few dozen feet away, but this time Walter's usual strategy for putting the Countess out of danger before Antinous could get too close failed him. Normally Walter's false oxpecker call would set the *ngoubou* to flight, whereupon it was a simple matter for us to retreat, but this time the Countess had spent the day gorging herself on *Kigelia* fruit and ignored Walter's alarm.

"Matthew," Walter said, "she's not doing anything."

"She's passed out from the fruit," I observed.

"This is damned inconvenient timing. How the devil are we supposed to get her away from him?"

Walter kept trying to rouse the drunken dragon, but no matter how insistently he chirped, squawked, and buzzed, she remained unresponsive. While Walter unavailingly begged the Countess to move, the rogue ambled inexorably toward her. I tugged at Walter's arm thinking to lead him, still hooting, to a safe distance, but he unexpectedly reverted from oxpecker to English and shouted, this time at the elephant rather than the dragon.

"Oh, no, you don't, you scoundrel! You leave her be!"

The foregoing outburst was almost certainly involuntary on Walter's part, but it nevertheless had just the effect Walter would have intended if he had calculated it: it drew the rogue's attention from the dragon. At the noise, Antinous's pace slackened, and he cocked his head in our direction and appraised us icily. Under that malevolent gaze, I froze, thinking not to provoke the rogue into charging us, but Walter saw the very thing I feared as an opportunity and continued taunting him.

"Yes, that's right!" he called. "You heard me! If you want to fight someone, why don't you fight me?"

Walter continued shouting challenges even as Jean-Paul and I strong-armed him bodily away from the animals, and the rogue soon accepted the old man's offer of combat. He glared at us with ears flared for a moment while he made up his mind, but after the briefest consideration, he launched himself in our direction, leaving the Countess unmolested. His curled trunk and flaring ears, and the quickstep that his footsteps pounded into the earth with his hot-blooded approach, bespoke his aggressive intent if he caught us.

When faced with an elephant attacking in earnest, would-be victims have several options to improve their chances of escape besides simply running blindly and hoping for the best. Moving downwind and hiding behind a tree or bush, thus preventing the elephant from scenting them once hidden, is one such method. Other alternatives include zigzagging while retreating, as elephants have difficulty changing direction mid-charge, and running downhill, where the elephant will take greater care and slow its pursuit. These techniques may either frustrate pursuit altogether or at least slow it enough for humans to outrun the enraged beast.

Though Walter and I knew precious little about safely retreating from an angry elephant, Jean-Paul's poaching experience, which undoubtedly involved dodging more than one angry bull in his time, served us well in this regard. With no more visible fear than if he had been avoiding a yipping terrier, Jean-Paul ushered us several degrees west to a new position against the wind, where we ducked behind a cluster of bushy *Combretum.* We concealed ourselves not a moment too soon, for the rogue lumbered past seconds later, but without the ability to catch our scent, he thundered off across the savanna in the last direction he had seen us and eventually vanished with distance and intervening bush.

Once the rogue had gone on his way and the danger had passed, I mumbled several words to myself that I don't care to repeat here, and even Jean-Paul, gentle though he might be, remonstrated with

Walter on the subject of his recklessness.

"Well, I'm sorry," Walter said. "I saw him coming, and the words just came out. The important thing is that we're all fine, and once again we've kept that scoundrel and our scaly friend from killing each other."

Walter might have been willing to dismiss a near-fatal encounter with a rogue elephant so long as nobody was hurt, but now we knew that the rogue would chase to kill if we kept provoking him. Where at first the prospect of standing between a feuding dragon and elephant had been merely dubious and possibly unethical, the many charges we had suffered, some in deadly earnest, provided ample evidence that the undertaking might also prove fatal if we were not more careful. Unfortunately, Walter's refusal to acknowledge the danger simultaneously provided evidence that he would not voluntarily abandon his meddling regardless of the risk.

*

If Walter had had his way, the confrontation between the Countess and her unwanted suitor would have been postponed indefinitely, but being chased and nearly trampled by a mad elephant finally convinced me that we were apt to be killed before the rogue abandoned his wanton designs. We could hardly intercede between them at the cost of our own lives (to my thinking if not Walter's), and even if we had been willing to do so, the elephant and the dragon would ultimately have fought each other to the death anyway once we were out of the way. Though I am ordinarily diffident and avoid confrontation at all costs, I am by no means willing to give my life altogether just to avoid conflict, and I determined to put a stop to Walter's meddling before any of us made the ultimate sacrifice.

Once I had resolved myself to mutiny against Walter, a plan presented itself fairly easily. Though I had not yet been provoked to the point of physically tying or gagging Walter, no such drastic measures were necessary, for I found that Jean-Paul had a like mind and would follow my lead. Given Walter's negligible tracking ability, he could never have found the *ngoubou* on his own, so Jean-Paul and I could deprive Walter of the chance to interfere by simply refusing our assistance until the conflict between the two animals diffused itself, either by confrontation or otherwise.

Deciding on our course was one thing, but making our intentions known to Walter was considerably more daunting, so we put it off until the next day when Walter noticed that we were not preparing to accompany him for the day's observation of the *ngoubou.*

"Matthew, what are you doing lollygagging like that?" he asked. "You should be ready to leave by now."

"I'm not going with you," I said.

"Whyever not?"

"I don't think we can stop those animals from fighting each other, and I don't want to be killed trying."

"Matthew, you astound me. I would never have expected this in a million years. Well, if you mean to abandon me, then I suppose that Jean-Paul and I shall have to go by ourselves."

"I am not going, either," Jean-Paul said.

"Well, how the devil am I supposed to find the *ngoubou* all by myself?"

Even Walter knew that he didn't have the faintest hope of meeting the *ngoubou* (or surviving Heep's continued stalking, for that matter) alone, so his only choice was to remain in camp and grumble incessantly under his breath about our mutiny. Despite his irritation, however, he was even more terrified at the prospect of injury to the dragon or the elephant, and he quaked at the slightest noise as if it were the tramp of death itself coming for one of the animals he wished to protect.

"What was that?" he would ask. "Oh, I wish I knew what was happening. Are you sure we can't go and see?"

No matter how often Walter importuned, Jean-Paul and I maintained our resolve, and eventually the Countess and Antinous confronted each other in our absence. Given the size and ferocity of the two combatants, their duel must have been hellacious for its noise and destructiveness, but we were too far away to hear when it happened. We only learned of the confrontation after spending several days confined to camp, at which point we sent Jean-Paul to discreetly scout the plain, and he reported the outcome of the animals' rivalry.

"Well?" Walter asked. "Is my dragon safe?"

"She is safe," Jean-Paul said.

"And what about the elephant?"

"The dragon killed him."

Though we were relieved that the dragon had saved herself from her foe, we could hardly celebrate when her victory came at the cost of the elephant's life, and of course Walter took Antinous's death hardest of all of us. I half-expected him to burst into angry reproaches, blaming me for frustrating his efforts to save the rogue. Instead, he didn't say anything for several minutes, and I was more troubled by his silence than I would have been by his most outspoken shouting.

"Do you want to go to the dragon?" I asked.

"No," Walter said. "I want to see the elephant. Take me to him."

Knowing better than to argue with him in this strange mood, Jean-Paul and I took Walter across the savanna to the elephant's final resting place. Even if he was a dangerous rogue, I take no pleasure in Antinous's destruction, so I will not linger on the gory details of his fall other than to observe that puncture injuries the size of the Countess's horn and clear pugmarks confirmed the *ngoubou*'s role in the fatality. Though we had seen dead elephants before this, we had known this animal in life, and standing quietly at his side felt almost as if we were paying our last respects to a fallen comrade.

We stood contemplating Antinous's remains for some time, and I confess that I hesitated to address Walter for fear he would vent the resentment that I suspected he entertained. Whatever he felt while gazing at the animal that he couldn't save, he processed it privately and in silence, and he only spoke when he had mastered himself.

"I'm ready to go back to my dragon now," he said.

"Are we all right?" I asked. "I mean, are you angry with me?"

"No. I suppose not. It's not as if I didn't know that *ngoubou* have the propensity to kill elephants, and I can hardly blame you for having a care for your own safety. Let's just try to forget about this whole business."

Ultimately, the affair with the rogue elephant tested but did not destroy my friendship with Walter Spink, and we returned to our observation of the *ngoubou*, albeit with somewhat dampened spirits. As for Antinous, giving an animal of his size a Christian burial was obviously impracticable, so we left his body where he fell. At the time, leaving the elephant's carcass where it might be discovered did not strike us as particularly foreboding, but if we had guessed the trouble that would actually come from it, Walter might have thought twice, both about leaving the carcass and forgiving me so easily for allowing the elephant to be killed by the dragon.

CHAPTER X

HOW NOT TO FIND DRAGONS

The African dragons have generally been elusive, as the long history of unsuccessful attempts to locate them attests. Finding them at all requires no small amount of familiarity with their habits, tracking skill, and unadulterated luck. With all the effort that has gone into finding dragons to begin with, it might seem inconceivable that anyone would go to efforts to avoid meeting them, but there are situations in which finding dragons becomes undesirable, even to dracontologists. When we fell in with a big game hunter on the track of *ngoubou*, Walter Spink and I were called upon to develop the fine art of Not Finding Dragons.

On some level, we knew that big game hunting was afoot on the savanna from the many elephant carcasses we had observed while seeking *ngoubou*, but we were so preoccupied with the *ngoubou* once we found it that we didn't spare another thought for the hunters until the day one of them announced himself in a manner we could not mistake. We were minding our own business, which as always consisted of observing the horned dragon's behavior while fending off Heep's advances, when a distant crack both broke our concentration and chased Heep off our track and into the cover of some *Stereospermum.* Even the Countess, reserved as she was, lifted her head and gazed superciliously across the shaggy leagues of waving grass as if affronted by the uncouth noise.

"I don't suppose we're lucky enough," Walter said, "for that to be thunder or signal drums."

"No," Jean-Paul said. "It was a gunshot."

"Bother. That's all we need: another one of those beastly hunters loitering around where he might find my dragons."

After our altercation with the last hunter we encountered, I was understandably apprehensive at Walter's response to this, but he was not immediately wound up enough to make a scene. Over the course of the day, however, the hunter continued his sport, and the periodic crack of his shots made us feel somewhat besieged. The shooting simultaneously grated against Walter's temper, which festered until he could no longer restrain himself.

"I've heard just about enough of this," he said. "This beastly hunter won't be happy until he's depopulated the entire savanna! We shall have to confront him."

"What are you going to do?" I asked.

"I'm going to ask him to leave, of course."

"Is that a good idea?"

"If you have a better idea, Matthew, I'm open to suggestions, but we can't have this bloodthirsty fellow around where he might find my dragons."

With this resolution, Walter marched out across the savanna in the direction of the gunshots, where he eventually discovered the hunter among a hive of guides and bearers. As we ultimately learned through a closer acquaintance than Walter would have liked, the hunter's name was Mr. T. He was the dissolute son of a well-known and wealthy American real estate developer, and in the absence of either a discernable talent or the necessity of working for his keep, he frittered away his time on pursuits of the idle rich, including hunting large African animals for sport. Even without knowing his background at the time of their initial confrontation, however, Walter held the man in barely restrained contempt.

"I don't suppose," he said after the most perfunctory of introductions, "you'll be leaving any time soon, will you?"

"Why would I do that?" Mr. T. asked. "Goddamn, there's plenty of game right here."

"Be that as it may, I am a scientist. I'm trying to study the local wildlife, but your shooting is disturbing my dr—my animals."

"No one cares more about animals than me—"

(Walter snorted derisively.)

"—But I'm not leaving till I'm good and ready."

"Bother. That's what I thought you'd say."

Though Walter was less than satisfied with the outcome of this exchange, there was nothing he could do to remove the hunter, who lingered on the savanna shooting whatever game was so unfortunate as to cross his path. This circumstance caused us no end of worry, for the longer the hunter remained in an area frequented by the horned dragon, the more likely it became that he would detect her presence. To our great dismay, that was precisely what soon happened, and only Walter's quick thinking gave us any chance of protecting the *ngoubou* from someone who would sooner mount her head on his wall than study her behavior.

As a rule, big game hunters do not intentionally pursue unknown animals such as *ngoubou*. Like the rest of society, they have been convinced that living dinosaurs and such creatures are purely imaginary, and they have plenty of acknowledged species—elephant, antelope, rhinoceros, lion, and so forth—to occupy them without resorting to chasing legends. Even if they do not set out looking for dragons, however, they will nevertheless hunt a previously-unknown animal if they stumble upon one of them, and Mr. T. took an interest in the horned dragon when he discovered evidence of her presence on the savanna.

We received notice that Mr. T. had become aware of the *ngoubou* when he returned our visit to him, thinking to capitalize on our knowledge of the local wildlife, one evening as we returned to camp from a day observing the Countess.

"You know about the local animals, right?" he asked.

"Of course we do," Walter said. "What of it?"

"Well, I've found something strange. There's an animal here that I don't recognize."

"What type of animal?"

"Goddamn, I was hoping you could tell me. Whatever it is, it can kill an elephant."

This elephant-killing behavior immediately suggested *ngoubou* to Walter and me, but far from prematurely acknowledging the presence of the horned dragon, Walter remained admirably nonchalant pending investigation.

"An elephant, you say?" he asked. "Why don't you show us what you found?"

When the hunter began leading us to the elephant's carcass, we comforted ourselves with the belief that the animal in question had probably fallen to a scourge other than *ngoubou*. This pretense became more difficult to maintain, however, when Mr. T. brought us to the familiar scene of the horned dragon's final combat with her unwanted suitor. By the time we finally beheld Antinous's body, lying on its side with legs akimbo just as the Countess had left him, we were not surprised but dismayed to know that the elephant Mr. T. had found had indeed been killed by a *ngoubou*.

"Bother," Walter mumbled. "Even in death, that scoundrel insists on making a nuisance of himself."

As if being led to Antinous's carcass was not disheartening enough, the hunter also proved quite able to read the signs that indicated *ngoubou*'s involvement in the killing even if he could not name the species. Mr. T. pointed out the tell-tale goring of the perineal area, too high and large for the horns of any other animal.

He also noted several clean, four-toed footprints, each the size of a large frying pan, that did not match the marks of any more familiar savanna resident. If Walter and I had hoped we might still conceal *ngoubou*'s part in the elephant's death, it fizzled, and then the hunter asked the question we had been dreading.

"Now that you've seen," he said, "do you know the animal that did this?"

"Yes," Walter said after a great pause. "I know these marks."

"Goddamn! What is it?"

"It's a very rare animal called *Dracoceros.*"

"A *Dracoceros*. Goddamn!"

Despite admitting the involvement of his dragon in the elephant killing, Walter still attempted to dissuade the hunter from further investigation.

"*Dracoceros* are notoriously difficult to track down," he said. "You'll never find them on your own. You might as well just give up now."

"Maybe I should," Mr. T. said, "but if I *can* find it, well, imagine being the first person to hunt a *Dracoceros.* My guides tell me they don't know how to find them. Do you?"

"Yes."

"Will you help me?"

"You're asking me to help you?"

"Sure. Why not?"

When confronted with the hunter's awareness of *ngoubou* and the foregoing request, made with a mind to stalking and killing the animal we so desperately wanted to protect, there are any number of ways Walter could have responded. He might simply have refused his assistance, in which case Mr. T. would undoubtedly have pursued the animal on his own and possibly found it. Alternatively, Walter might have confessed the nature of the animal in question and begged Mr. T. to spare it, although the likelihood of the hunter being reasoned with in this manner seemed dubious. Instead of taking either of those courses, Walter conceived a third option, one that would never have occurred to me and took me quite by surprise.

"All right," Walter said. "I shall help you find *Dracoceros*."

"Wonderful!" Mr. T. said. "When do you want to start?"

"I daresay there's no time like the present. We shall just need a moment to pack a few things."

"Goddamn, this is even better than I hoped!"

The hunter was elated with this new partnership, but I was simply confused. Walter had hardly been shy about voicing his opinion of big game hunters, so teaming up with one of them—who was moreover on the trail of one of the dragons whose lives Walter held so dear—was decidedly out of character. Perhaps I should have suspected he had an ulterior motive, for that is exactly what I discovered when I discreetly confronted him while he gathered his dragon-hunting implements from our tent.

"Do you want to explain," I asked, "why you're so friendly with a big game hunter all of a sudden?"

"I assure you, Matthew," Walter said, "that friendship has nothing to do with it. If I refused to help him, he'd just go out looking for our scaly friend anyway, and he might accidentally find her. If I go along and help him—or at least *pretend* to help him—I can lead him away from our scaly friend."

"I understand what you're trying to do, but how long do you think you can keep him fooled?"

"Matthew, I doubt that fooling a numbskull like that will be particularly difficult, but I'm sure I won't have to keep it up very long, anyway. After a few good days of not finding anything, he'll get tired of hunting *Dracoceros* and find something else to do with himself."

Whether the hunter would be so easy to dissuade remained to be seen, but we nevertheless inaugurated an ambitious campaign of misdirection designed to keep him far from the horned dragon. Leaving Jean-Paul in our own camp to keep Heep too distracted with bushmeat to follow us, we transferred our base of operations to Mr. T.'s camp, from which we led him on many fruitless marches across the savanna. In the coming days, Walter would teach an unwitting Mr. T. everything he needed to know about Not Finding Dragons, and for a time at least the wandering hunter got no closer to finding *ngoubou* than the *Flying Dutchman* will ever get to finding its port.

*

The fine art of Not Finding Dragons requires as much attention to their habits as actually finding them, but the knowledge is turned on its ear so as to minimize the chance of an encounter. To find a dragon, the dracontologist must consider the extent of its foraging area, the times when it is active, and its biological needs. To ensure that the dragon is not found, on the other hand, demands consideration for where it does not forage and where the items that comprise its diet will not be found. This is precisely the strategy that Walter developed to ensure that Mr. T. did not meet the *ngoubou* in his stalking.

Reversing the principles that normally helped us locate the horned dragon, Walter started out by ensuring that the would-be beneficiary of his expertise sought the dragon when she was least likely to be active. We had previously observed the *ngoubou* to do the majority of her foraging during daylight hours, possibly as a consequence of her reptilian constitution. Thus, Walter absolutely forbade Mr. T. from pursuing the *ngoubou* before sunset and insisted that the only way we might meet her was by stalking her overnight.

"*Dracoceros* are entirely nocturnal," he said, "so there's no sense looking for them during the day."

The benefit of restricting our operations to nighttime was twofold: not only did night hunting decrease the likelihood that the *ngoubou* would be about when we looked for her, but it also decreased the hunter's chances of seeing her even if she was around. Between the darkness and our diminutive height in comparison with the grass that covered much of the savanna, our vision was restricted to our immediate surroundings. Even when we left the tall grass, our lanterns could only penetrate a few feet, and the odds of being lucky—or should I say unlucky—enough to espy the horned dragon with such a limited perspective were negligible.

As a consequence of stalking the horned dragon when she was least active and least visible, we were fabulously successful at Not Finding her. This failure might have led the hunter, who became increasingly frustrated, to question Walter's expertise, but Walter varied his tactics often enough to give Mr. T. hope of success and forestall him from mutinying.

"I'm starting to have my doubts about this," Mr. T. said after several fruitless evenings of nighttime stalking. "As much as I love animals, stumbling around in the dark looking for *Dracoceros* isn't getting us any closer to finding them."

"Surely you don't mean to give up?" Walter asked (and only someone who knew him as well as I would have detected the hope in his voice).

"Goddamn, no, but isn't there anything else we can try?"

"Now that you mention it, I daresay there is. We could always find a likely spot and set up a blind."

Constructing a blind and waiting near a site your quarry is likely to visit, such as a watering hole or a fruiting tree, is a perfectly acceptable hunting tactic, but of course Walter sabotaged the endeavor by setting up where the dragon was least likely to pass. After our weeks with the horned dragon, we had fairly mapped her accustomed foraging area and knew its boundaries. This enabled us to station ourselves well beyond the Countess's usual range, where we maintained a fruitless vigil for several nights before the hunter again began to complain.

"Are you sure this is going to work?" Mr. T. asked eventually. "It's been three nights, and we haven't seen anything."

"You must be patient," Walter said. "The *Dracoceros* will come in its own time."

Walter kept the hunter occupied in this manner for the better part of a week, at which point he agreed to change tactics while affecting to be as surprised as Mr. T. at our ill luck.

"I simply can't imagine why it doesn't come back," Walter said, all innocence. "We saw it here before, didn't we, Matthew?"

"Yes," I agreed.

"I suppose we shall just have to look elsewhere."

After the unqualified failure of our blind, we resumed mobile tracking, but still Walter concocted a host of passive-aggressive ways to ensure that we did not stumble across the dragon. Mainly this consisted of clomping noisily through grass and brush, but Walter also "forgot" himself and raised his voice so as to betray our coming to the local wildlife. When the hunter questioned his lack of caution, Walter crumpled into the very image of a doting old man who could not help lapsing from time to time.

"How silly of me," he would say. "I just forget sometimes."

Even if crashing around like a fairy tale giant was not enough to ensure that every animal within a mile radius fled from our path, Walter periodically emitted a jarring noise whose efficacy in keeping *ngoubou* away I have already described.

"*Kriss, kriss! Kriss, kriss!*"

"Goddamn," Mr. T. said after one such performance. "What is that awful noise?"

"You don't recognize it?" Walter asked.

"No."

"It's the call of an injured baby *Dracoceros*. The *Dracoceros* hear it and come closer to find out what's wrong with the child. I assure you, this is the best way to attract them."

"You don't say. Can you teach me how to do that?"

"Why, nothing would give me more pleasure."

Over the course of several sessions, Mr. T. practiced his imitation of Walter's oxpecker call until he could duplicate it to the old man's satisfaction. Soon the hunter was taking turns with Walter making the call, and it gave Walter no end of pleasure to have inveigled the hunter into sabotaging his own efforts.

"Can you believe it?" he whispered to me. "I've got this

numbskull doing my work for me!"

Between the oxpecker calls and the variety of tactics I just described, we succeeded gloriously in Not Finding Dragons. Perhaps the hunter should have suspected that there was more to such spectacular failure than mere bad luck, but I guess he could not conceive that a gnarled old man like Walter Spink could devise and carry out such a concerted campaign of deception. Thus, even as he became increasingly discontented, he still ascribed the dearth of dragon sightings to chance rather than design.

"I just don't understand it," he said one day. "Is it always this hard to find *Dracoceros*?"

"Sadly," Walter said, "it can be very challenging to find them. I daresay nobody would blame you if you gave up."

"Maybe not, but now that they've been so much trouble, I'm more determined than ever to find them."

The hunter persevered no matter how unproductive our search remained, and we were no closer to getting rid of him after two and a half weeks than we had been when we began our charade. Walter would have continued leading Mr. T. around his grassy purgatory indefinitely, but even Walter's burgeoning skill at Not Finding Dragons could not maintain this state of affairs forever. A variable we had not yet considered rendered Walter's ability to maintain the status quo dubious, and it was anybody's guess which would happen first: the hunter abandoning his quest, or the hunter meeting the *ngoubou,* with possibly fatal results to the dragon.

No matter how concerted their efforts and how great their skill at Not Finding Dragons, dracontologists trying to conceal dragons may nevertheless be thwarted by the dragons' own uncooperative behavior. Regardless of their accustomed habits, few animals—dragons included—are so set in their ways as to never venture out at night or never range beyond their usual territory, and the Countess began defying our efforts to avoid her by appearing at times and in places we had never seen her before. Eventually the *ngoubou* crossed paths with the hunter, no matter how much Walter tried to prevent their meeting.

Not yet suspecting that an encounter between the two was drawing near, Walter and I were surprised the first time we encountered the *ngoubou* during our night stalking. Between not expecting to encounter her so late and the tall grass that restricted our vision, we did not see her as we approached, and Walter's noisy stomping and chatter undoubtedly kept Mr. T. and his retinue from hearing her. Lagging a few feet behind, however, I caught the *chuff* of a familiar judgmental snort, at which point I paused until the crunch of grass and the quivering of the foliage to my left betrayed a large animal feeding just beyond our path. We were passing within a few yards of the Countess, and if we did not move along quickly, the hunter and his guides and bearers were bound to notice her as I had.

Having recognized disaster looming, I scurried to Walter's side and communicated this intelligence as quietly as I could.

"We have a problem," I mumbled. "She's here."

"Do you mean *the* she?" Walter asked.

"Yes."

"Bother. Which way?"

"Behind us, and to the left."

Inevitably, our mumbling caught the hunter's attention.

"What's going on back there?" he asked.

And to my consternation, Walter answered him frankly.

"My assistant, Matthew, here, has found the *Dracoceros*," he said.

At this news, Mr. T. became as eager as a shark scenting blood.

"Is that true?" he asked me.

"Umm…I think so," I said (still confused at Walter's admission).

"Where?"

Thinking the jig was up (and not being clever enough to lie on the spot), I almost answered honestly, but Walter's more nimble dissembling saved me and the *ngoubou* both.

"It's this way," he said, stabbing a finger to indicate the way.

Though Walter's words suggested that he meant to direct the hunter toward the dragon, he of course pointed in the exact opposite direction, and like an over-the-hill Holmes leading a credulous Watson on the trail of some murderer, he stalked into the tall grass and away from the dragon, drawing Mr. T. and his guides and bearers along with him. With everyone's attention focused in the direction Walter indicated, the dragon went unnoticed behind us until we had put half a kilometer between her and the hunter, and the danger of her discovery lessened with each step. After a surprisingly authentic pretense of tracking *ngoubou*, with frequent stops to scent the wind or peer at some mark on the ground, Walter finally left off the chase and counterfeited mingled surprise and disappointment.

"Why, it's not here, after all," he said.

"Why isn't it here?" Mr. T. demanded.

"I suppose it must have been a false alarm on Matthew's part, but you mustn't blame him. He means well."

With just a little grumbling on the hunter's part, we successfully kept the dragon hidden from him this time, but her recurring appearances in the coming days threatened to frustrate our continuing efforts to conceal her. Even in places where we had never seen the *ngoubou* before, we periodically came upon a trail broken through the grass or one of her familiar frying pan-sized prints so clear that it was no use denying her passage, and Walter was obliged to at least pretend to follow her sign. He always managed to lose the track before we risked catching up to the dragon in the flesh, but the whole time we stalked the savanna with Mr. T. and his entourage, we kept an anxious watch lest we meet the Countess.

Watchful as Walter and I were for the *ngoubou*, she ultimately appeared where we least expected her, and where hiding her was least practicable. After all our toil leading Mr. T. a merry chase across the savanna hoping to avoid the dragon, she surprised us by coming to him: she visited the hunter's camp, at which point a confrontation between dragon and hunter became almost unavoidable.

When the dragon came, I was the first to see, but I almost didn't notice her, partly because I did not anticipate meeting her on the hunter's proverbial front doorstep and partly because I was exhausted from stalking the dragon overnight. On my way to the tent I shared with Walter, where I meant to turn in for the day, I vaguely noticed what at first appeared to be a hill just beyond the farthest tent. Before I could quite dismiss the sight, however, the hill lurched into motion, and a horned snout lunged out from behind the tent, betraying the identity of the visitor.

At the sight of that bony scimitar, I recognized the Countess and scurried into our own tent to alert Walter.

"She's here," I said.

"Our scaly friend?" Walter asked. "It must be a mistake. She couldn't possibly be here, of all places."

"I was ten feet away from her. I don't see how I could be wrong."

"Well, you might as well show me, but I still think it must be a mistake."

If Walter had been tempted to dismiss my news at first, he was forced to acknowledge the accuracy of my senses when I showed him the Countess still browsing where I had left her.

"Bother," Walter said. "You chase her away, and I shall keep that numbskull occupied."

The flaw in Walter's plan, which the reader may already have guessed, was entrusting someone as submissive and timid as me to shepherd the *ngoubou* to safety. Unlike Walter, who did not seem to have the sense to fear a seven-ton reptile, I was by no means comfortable barking orders to the Countess. As you can imagine, my attempt to evict the dragon from camp without raising my voice enough to upset her was too feeble to do any good.

"Shoo," I said. "Go on, before somebody sees you. Go."

The Countess did not so much as raise her spiky head at my command, much less budge from her grazing, nor did my inauthentic oxpecker call rouse her. I was painfully aware that the likelihood of her being discovered increased with each moment I failed to move her, and finally an exclamation in Mr. T.'s voice told me it was too late to rectify my nonstarter.

"Goddamn! That's a goddamned dinosaur!"

When I turned at the outcry, there was the hunter, with Walter at his heels trying ineffectually to divert him. In one dreadful moment of utter dismay, I realized that we had irrevocably failed to keep the hunter away from the dragon, and then a bearer was at Mr. T.'s side, whereupon the hunter said the words that we had dreaded.

"Where's my gun?"

Once the hunter called for his gun, the confrontation escalated quickly. In a heartbeat, one of Mr. T.'s men scurried to his side bearing the hunter's rifle, which Mr. T. clutched and raised to his shoulder as deftly as if it were part of his arm. At the same time, however, Walter scrambled in between the hunter and the dragon, who continued feeding obliviously at the other end of camp.

"Oh, no, you don't," Walter said. "You're not shooting that animal."

"Get out of the way, man," Mr. T. said. "We've finally found it!"

"Yes, and that's exactly what I've been trying to prevent this whole time."

"Wait a minute…you weren't helping me?"

"Of course not, you numbskull."

The hunter tried to aim his rifle around Walter, who sidestepped dangerously into the barrel's path, where the hunter could not fire without hitting him.

"Goddamn!" Mr. T. snarled. "Get out of my way, or I'll shoot through you."

"No, you won't," Walter said dismissively.

"Walter," I tried to break in, "I *really* don't think—"

"You'll have a hell of a time shooting anything," Walter said, "without a working firearm."

Regardless of Walter's attempts to frustrate him, Mr. T. shouldered his way past the old man and leveled his rifle at the dragon. Before anything more could be said, the hunter squinted into the scope and pulled the trigger—

—And nothing happened. There was a click, but no gunfire.

"Goddamn!" Mr. T. said. "What's wrong with this thing?"

"I wasn't about to take the chance that you would find my dragon," Walter said, "so I ground down the firing pin a few days ago while you were sleeping. You can't shoot anything with it now."

There are several ways to sabotage a firearm. In war, this has frequently been accomplished by substituting exploding rounds for the enemy's ammunition, but this method can cause injury and was too sophisticated for Walter Spink to effect by himself in the bush. Instead, Walter contented himself with grinding the firing pin so as to disable Mr. T.'s rifle,[17] thereby ensuring that the hunter would not get in a shot at the Countess if our skill at Not Finding Dragons failed us. Though it was a mystery at the time where Walter could have learned such sabotage, I was equal parts flummoxed at his ability to pull off such a coup and relieved that he had done so.

While my opinion of Walter's strategy was largely favorable, the hunter, as you may imagine, was positively inflamed.

"What the hell were you thinking?" Mr. T. shouted.

"I suggest you lower your voice," Walter said. "*Dracoceros* don't react well to shouting."

"As if I'd listen to you!"

The hunter can hardly be blamed for doubting Walter's word after discovering that the old man had been deceiving him for weeks, but of course it would have been better for him if he had restrained his temper. As it was, Mr. T. continued shouting invective at Walter's betrayal, alternated with demands that his bearers produce a different weapon, with a predictable reaction on the Countess's part.

"I'll deal with you after I shoot the dinosaur. Goddamn! You're going to pay for this!"

The *ngoubou* raised her head and cocked one eye irritably in the

---

[17]This prevents the firing pin from making contact with the primer and thereby precludes the ammunition from being launched.

direction of the noise.

"Somebody get me a gun! Any gun!"

The *ngoubou* snorted and pawed the earth.

"You're going to be sorry you ever met me. Goddamn!"

The *ngoubou* lurched forward and galloped after the hunter.

Words can hardly convey the bedlam that erupted in the hunting camp when the horned dragon barreled through. The Countess crashed past Walter and me like a boulder rolling its destructive way down a mountainside and lumbered in behind the hunter when he retreated into the nearest tent. We heard thrashing and shouting punctuated by a great crack, whereupon the tent came down, draping itself over the dragon's lumpy, spiny form like a sheet concealing the disused furniture in a haunted mansion. The dragon might have calmed at this point, but by now her charge had precipitated so much shouting among the guides and bearers that the Countess tore through the first tent and galloped to and fro, chasing any man who so much as made a peep and breaking down everything in her way.

By the time the dragon had finished wrecking the hunting camp and wandered back onto the savanna in search of a more peaceful feeding area, every tent but one had been razed to the ground, and the erstwhile camp was a battlefield littered with shreds of canvas, splintered crates, and rounds of Mr. T.'s now-useless ammunition. As for casualties, the residents of the camp were unhurt with one exception: Mr. T. himself, whom the camp followers excavated bruised, broken, and incoherent from the remains of his tent.

"I'm not saying this is our fault," Walter said as he inspected the injured man, "because we did try to warn him, but I suppose we still have a duty to get him some help."

Without by any means acknowledging legal responsibility for the hunter's injury, Walter sent me back to our camp to fetch the jeep, and we drove Mr. T. to the nearby town of Makané seeking medical attention. Unfortunately, being so far away from any modern settlements, there was no Western doctor available, and the closest facsimile was the local feticheuse. The reader may remember how scrupulously Walter had avoided encountering any magic users up to this point, fearing to be cursed for his previous misconduct, but in the absence of any other source of help for our wounded acquaintance, he had no choice but to submit to whatever comeuppance the witchdoctor might deem warranted.

"I've dreaded this meeting for a long time," he said, "but I don't suppose I can leave this fellow in pain."

Walter's anxiety notwithstanding, the feticheuse, Lisette Obenga, applied herself assiduously to assessing the hunter's injuries and easing his pain without showing any interest in smiting Walter for his offense against her colleague. When she finished her ministrations and sought us out to report Mr. T.'s prognosis, her conversation with Walter not only eased his fear concerning her reception but resolved his concerns for the hunter's designs on the horned dragon.

"Your companion is all right," she said, "but with both arms broken, he will not be shooting your *ngoubou* any time soon."

"Now, wait just a minute," Walter said. "You know about our work with the *ngoubou*?"

"Of course, my friend. The spirits tell me everything."

"And you're not going to curse me or anything like that?"

"No, my friend. I am not the feticheuse you need to worry about."

"That's good enough for me."

With the foregoing reassurances as to the safety of the *ngoubou* and the goodwill of the witchdoctor, Walter felt comfortable enough at this point to resume our search for *mokele-mbembe.* We left the savanna and its horned dragons in favor of the tropical rainforest reputedly favored by their long-necked cousins, followed discreetly by Heep, as before. As the length of this memoir suggests, we found *mokele-mbembe*, but our troubles with big game hunters were far from over, nor would we find the next witchdoctor we met to be as accommodating as Madame Obenga had been.

CHAPTER XI

BANGOMBE AND THE BEAST

Notwithstanding the skepticism of the scientific community, Walter Spink and I ultimately located *mokele-mbembe* during our travels in West Africa, but for some time our only discovery was that its range has diminished considerably during the twentieth century. Where creatures matching the *mokele-mbembe* type were reported as far north as the Cameroon-Nigeria border as recently as the 1930s, they were completely unknown in that region by the time of our visit. It was only in southeastern Cameroon, Gabon, and the People's Republic of the Congo, in the vicinity of the Dja, Sangha, Bai, and Likouala-aux-Herbes Rivers, that a sauropod-like animal was familiar to the local villagers. This area marks the current northernmost extent of *mokele-mbembe*'s distribution.[18]

Even once we had entered *mokele-mbembe*'s range, finding the dragons was no easy matter. The villagers we visited could tell us

---

[18]*Mokele-mbembe*-like animals have also been reported as far south as Zambia's Lake Bangweulu, but our work with the Congolese dragon population precluded investigating further south. The full delineation of the modern range of *mokele-mbembe* thus remains for future dracontologists.

where a *mokele-mbembe* had been seen on a nearby stretch of river, but these sightings were so scattered and sporadic that Walter and I concluded that the dragons only periodically traveled by river and actually lived in the rainforest (a conclusion that was later borne out by our observations). The latter are unmapped and untraveled—at least by the Bantu tribes of the region—and consequently the villagers could offer little insight that would help us locate *mokele-mbembe* haunts so as to observe the dragons in the flesh.

Although the villagers could not direct us to *mokele-mbembe* themselves, they had a definite idea who might be able to do so.

"You should ask the Bangombe," we were told many times.

The Bangombe are one of several ethnic groups—formerly referred to as Pygmies—that have inhabited the rainforests of equatorial Africa for as long as historical records have existed, and probably long before then. Rather than cutting down the forest and raising crops in the manner of their Bantu neighbors, they hunt and gather in much the same manner as the earliest humans. They are renowned for their diminutive stature (rarely exceeding five feet in height) and their hunting prowess, and their knowledge of the plants and animals of the equatorial rainforest is unparalleled among their fellow Africans, to say nothing of Westerners. If anyone could lead us to *mokele-mbembe,* it was bound to be the Bangombe.

For some time, finding the Bangombe so as to solicit their assistance tracking *mokele-mbembe* proved to be as challenging as finding the dragons themselves. Unlike the Bantu groups, the Bangombe and their related tribes are semi-nomadic, building their camps (*apa*) of leaf-thatched huts only to abandon them and build anew in a different location when the unavailability of game or the ennui of the group necessitates a change. Although they trade with the Bantu villagers for cultivated or manufactured products, their visits are as unpredictable as the movement of their camps. Walter and I were alert for news of the Bangombe as we made the rounds of the villages, but it was only at Epena, in the Congo's Likouala Department, that our visit coincided with the arrival of three

Bangombe who had come to barter bushmeat for produce and iron.

Even once we finally encountered the Bangombe, it was by no means a foregone conclusion that they would help us find *mokele-mbembe*. The forest people generally disdain hiring themselves out as porters or guides, deeming the work undignified for hunters of their standing, nor will they undertake any task at all if it does not satisfy the caprice of the moment. This would have been so even if we made the best impression, and Walter's greeting was hardly conducive to good relations.

"It's about damned time you put in an appearance," he said (through one of the villagers acting as interpreter). "Now would you please be so good as to take us to *mokele-mbembe*?"

This form of address could easily have nettled the Bangombe, but instead they erupted into a paroxysm of hilarity, the symptoms of which consisted of laughing uproariously, slapping their sides, and holding their stomachs. They betrayed the source of their amusement by pointing in Walter's direction.

"What the devil is so funny?" Walter asked our interpreter.

"They noticed that you are the same height as they are," he said.

Walter bristled. "I don't see what that has to do with anything."

"Since you are the same height, they like you. They say they will help you find *mokele-mbembe*."

"Oh. Well, in that case, I suppose I shan't take offense."

Thus we ingratiated ourselves to the Bangombe, albeit entirely by accident. With their agreement to guide us, we made preparations in Epena that included stocking up on supplies for a long trek and hiring a young man named Henri Botalisi as porter-cum-translator, the latter being necessary until we learned the Bangombe language. Once these were complete, we followed two Bangombe volunteers, Ekianga and Mambunia, into the rainforest.

Despite being part of the great Guineo-Congolese forest that spans Africa from the Gulf of Guinea to the Ruwenzori, the Likouala wilderness comprises its own distinct ecoregion characterized by so-called swamp forest. Under a canopy dominated by *Garcinia* and

Manikara, interspersed with stands of *Raphia* palm that afford a prehistoric appearance appropriate to the presence of relicts such as *mokele-mbembe,* lurks a seasonally flooded forest floor cluttered with unusually dense undergrowth. Where the ground is not swampy, it is muddy; between the smothering vegetation, standing water, and clutching muck—to say nothing of disease-bearing insects and poisonous snakes—the going is as strenuous as it is dangerous.

The journey might have been unpleasant for Walter and me, but the Bangombe were positively joyful to be in the forest, and they sang a lively hymn of praise to it as they walked. Walter joined them once Henri explained the song's meaning, but no amount of exhortation on Walter's part could induce me to join them with my atonal voice.

"I'm not much of a singer," I said.

"You're just not 'of the forest' like the rest of us," Walter said, as if he had been traveling among the Bangombe his whole life.

Indeed I was not "of the forest," for unlike our guides, who traversed the swamp forest as easily as a hiking trail, I am by no means a woodsman. Flourishing machetes, Ekianga and Mambunia cleared a path through which they and Walter passed with relative ease, but with my greater height, I invariably ran into the cut ends of the severed branches and scraped up my face. While the Bangombe were as light and quick on their feet as forest sprites, I stumbled upon roots when my clumsy footsteps were not breaking fallen branches and twigs or miring me into the deepest mud. Compared to the Bangombe, I felt like Gulliver among the Lilliputians—an outsized lummox, out of place in a world scaled for smaller people.

Our group soldiered on regardless of the physical conditions, but finding *mokele-mbembe* was nevertheless a time-consuming and arduous endeavor. I spare the details here so that I may focus on our observations of the dragons' behavior, but I will say that we endured many frustrating, fruitless days with only our guides' vague predictions that we would find *mokele-mbembe* "soon" to sustain our spirits. Then, just when I was beginning to meditate mutiny against

Walter and the Bangombe alike, Ekianga and Mambunia brought us to a massive clearing where great stands of swamp arum (*Lasimorpha senegalensis*) and the occasional ochol (*Pseudospondias microcarpa*) shrub guarded a secluded pool, and there they indicated that we would find *mokele-mbembe.*

"Well, it's about damned time," Walter said. "Now let me see."

It seemed as if an animal the size of a sauropod should stand out even with a cursory inspection of the *bai,* but even our most hungry inspection betrayed no such animal. By this time, we had accumulated a sufficient Bangombe vocabulary to speak directly to our guides, and Walter confronted them about this state of affairs.

"There's nothing here," he said. "Where the devil is *mokele-mbembe*?"

"It comes soon," Ekianga said.

"Soon," Mambunia agreed.

We waited, and our patience—only marginal on Walter's part—was eventually rewarded with the promised observation of a live *mokele-mbembe.*

When the *mokele-mbembe* finally came, we heard it approaching long before we saw it. First the rustle of leaves, slowly swelling in volume and punctuated by the staggered thump of heavy footfalls, announced its coming from the opposite side of the clearing. We might have crept toward the noise so as to hasten our sighting, but we feared to chase the dragon away with our own movement and instead awaited its convenience in appearing. Gradually we perceived movement among the shadows beneath the canopy, as if one of the great trunks had been enchanted into motion, but as the animal neared the *bai*, light filtering from the opening betrayed a round head atop what had first appeared to be a trunk and a massive body below, treading resolutely forward on muscular legs. It was in no hurry to show itself, leisurely browsing the foliage of the trees as it passed, but finally the daylight washed upon a massive hump of flesh, red like the laterite soil that is so common in West Africa, with a serpentine head mounting skyward on a slender neck.

Such a glimpse of one *mokele-mbembe* should have satisfied the ambitions of the greediest dracontologist, but we were even more fortunate: the first dragon was accompanied by several more of its kind. The rustling continued even when the first *mokele-mbembe* had ventured into the open beyond the undergrowth, and one by one more serpentine heads periscoped into view over the foliage of the understory, moving forward in the same general direction as the first *mokele-mbembe* but at staggered intervals. When they had all revealed themselves, the herd consisted of six individuals of varying sizes with hides ranging in color from earthy reds to woody browns.

When the dragons finally appeared, they were still so far away that Walter needed binoculars to make out any detail, but for the time being, this did not diminish his satisfaction in their discovery.

"There it is," he said, "a sauropod, just like I thought. And not just one sauropod, but six of them. Imagine!"

"Are you crying?" I asked.

"Of course not. What do you take me for?"

You might think that Walter and I should not have been particularly affected at this point by the appearance of yet another living, breathing dinosaur. Perhaps our previous discoveries should have desensitized us, but I think we both inwardly prepared ourselves to come up empty-handed each time, so it was little short of a miracle when we actually found a prehistoric survivor. For my part, I hope I never become so jaded that I can gaze upon one of the dragons without feeling at least some thrill.

After indulging our wonderment for several minutes just watching the *mokele-mbembe* browse their way onto the *bai*, our thoughts turned to what to do with the dragons now that we had found them. It seemed a matter of course that we would make camp and begin long-term observation, but our guides proposed an alternative in case we had been so minded.

"You want the Bangombe to kill one for you?" Ekianga asked.

"The two of you, all by yourselves?" Walter asked. "Kill a big, huge animal like *mokele-mbembe*?"

Although the idea of a pair of diminutive Bangombe successfully engaging a gigantic dragon might understandably seem farfetched, the forest people are fiercer hunters than you might expect. The Bangombe and their kin routinely hunt animals as large as forest elephants with little more trepidation than if they were rabbits. Nor is it unprecedented for the Bangombe to contend with dragons: though we had not heard at the time, rumors spread in the late 1980s that a group of Bangombe had killed a *mokele-mbembe* at Lake Télé in the Congo, not far from our present study area. Our knowledge being what it was, our guides' offer seemed ambitious, to say the least.

"The Bangombe are great hunters," Ekianga said, Walter's incredulity notwithstanding.

"Great hunters," Mambunia echoed.

"Kill *mokele-mbembe* many times."

"Many times."

"I don't doubt that the Bangombe are brave enough to confront *mokele-mbembe*," Walter said finally, "but that won't be necessary. We only wish to see and watch them."

Once we had clarified our intentions toward *mokele-mbembe*, Walter and I settled in behind the cover of one of the ochol shrubs and watched the dragons until their travel-browsing took them back into the forest, across the *bai* from where they had begun. We were loath to allow them out of our sight, but our guides affirmed that the dragons visited the clearing, which I will call Bangándo Bai, daily, so remaining in the area would assure us of future sightings.[19] We made our camp about a mile away from the *bai* on the driest ground we could find, and each day we made contact with the dragons at the *bai* before following them during the day as they foraged their way through the forest, inaugurating the word's first detailed observation of *mokele-mbembe* in the wild.

---

[19]The foregoing is a false name designed to protect the location from discovery for reasons that will eventually become apparent.

The researcher's first consideration when beginning observation of a wild animal is how closely he or she can approach without provoking an aggressive response. Even intelligent and otherwise peaceful animals such as gorillas will attack unknown human beings who violate their space, and *mokele-mbembe* in particular have a reputation for killing human beings who venture too close for comfort when encountering them on the rivers. The wisest course of action, especially when dealing with newly-discovered animals of uncertain temperament, is to give them a wide berth.

Being well aware of the necessity of caution, Walter and I began our study of the dragons keeping a few hundred feet back and tending to conceal ourselves among the shrubs in the understory. We could see perfectly well with the help of our binoculars, and considering that the larger *mokele-mbembe* were 30 to 40 feet long and stood ten or more feet tall at the shoulder, I was content to watch from a distance. Even if the foregoing arrangement was perfectly acceptable for me, however, Walter, with his middling eyesight and thirst to know everything about the dragons, chafed at lingering so far from them.

"Do you think we can get any closer?" he asked our guides.

"No closer," Ekianga said. "Some *mokele-mbembe* attack if you come close."

"They attack," Mambunia agreed.

"Well, how the devil am I supposed to see?"

Regardless of the warnings of the Bangombe, I knew Walter well enough by this point to guess that he would press his luck if given the opportunity. Sure enough, the Bangombe periodically bored of watching the dragons graze and disappeared into the forest to hunt game, during which times Walter seized the opportunity to attempt closer observation.

"I'm sure it's perfectly safe to sneak just a little closer," he would say.

What constitutes a safe distance for observing wildlife varies from species to species, depending on the temperament of the animal in question and its speed when provoked. In the case of wild elephants, authorities urge watchers to keep at least 160 feet back, but buffalo should be watched from at least 200 feet away. There being no precedent for safely approaching *mokele-mbembe*, the only way to determine how close we could approach without offering provocation was trial and error.

Though we lacked a guide for anticipating how tolerant the *mokele-mbembe* might be of our proximity, even Walter Spink did not propose to simply saunter in their direction until one of them objected (presumably by trampling us). Instead, we approached one of the medium-sized individuals while she fed among the lower branches of an *Alstonia congensis* 20 feet above our heads, advancing in stages of a few feet at a time and using shrubs and shady trees as cover. (To be completely accurate, Walter crept ahead before I could bodily stop him without making a scene that might provoke the dragons, and I had little choice but to scurry after him in case he needed rescuing.) The whole time, I kept a close watch for any change in the dragon's demeanor that might indicate she was agitated by our presence, but she continued to browse obliviously.

"Is anything happening?" Walter asked every few steps.

"Not yet."

We approached to within 250 feet of the dragon in this manner without provoking any visible response, and I began to think that perhaps Walter and I were simply too puny for her to notice us at all, in the same way an insect might have escaped our own attention. Then I received the shock of my life when her great boom of a neck swung away from the *Alstonia* and she cocked her warty face so as to peer down at us. I froze like any thief who has ever been caught red-handed, and my hand seized Walter's arm to halt his approach.

"She's noticed us," I said.

"Gracious!" Walter said. "What's she doing?"

"So far, nothing."

"Perhaps we should try a few more steps and see how she

reacts."

I have rarely been more anxious in my life than I was taking first one tenuous step, then a second, with the dragon's eye fixed on us the whole time. I was painfully aware of the size of her mighty legs, any one of which could have stamped me or Walter into oblivion, as easily as you or I might trample a blade of grass, if our proximity riled her. Before my courage failed me, though, Walter and I safely reached a patch of swamp arum whose clusters of spade-shaped leaves stood good stead as a blind, and the dragon resumed foraging, albeit with periodic glances in our direction to reassure herself that we posed no clear and present threat.

"Well, that wasn't so bad," Walter said. "Maybe our Bangombe friends exaggerated the danger."

Over the course of several days, Walter and I tested how closely we could approach the dragons without provoking them. During that process it was not unusual for one or another of them to glance in our direction, but we could generally approach within 100 feet before they reacted, and even then it was to withdraw rather than attack. If Walter and I came to mistakenly perceive *mokele-mbembe* as docile creatures, however, we were rudely disabused of the notion the first time one of them charged us.

*

There is substantial variation in the temperaments of *mokele-mbembe*, and some of them are more apt to behave aggressively toward human beings than others. Just as certain elephants, like the infamous Torone sisters documented by Iain Douglas-Hamilton, are more intolerant of humans than others of their kind, there was one large female dragon who took exception from the very start to our loitering near the herd; we eventually named her Tiamat after a similarly fierce dragoness of legend. Even if the others would let us come fairly close without attacking, Tiamat was far less trusting of our kind, and she quickly lost patience with our growing boldness in approaching her family.

The great dragoness was probably displaying her agitation for some time before she actually attacked, but in our ignorance of *mokele-mbembe* body language, we did not recognize her straining temper until we had provoked her to outright violence. Not suspecting how closely she was monitoring us, we were less careful than perhaps we should have been interacting with the rest of the herd, which consisted of Tiamat, another adult female, and several juveniles, the smallest of which was a fairly young female (who was nevertheless the size of a rather husky horse). I can only imagine the alarm and fury Tiamat felt when the juvenile took an interest in the two dracontologists gawking at her family from among the arum and decided to investigate us.

When the young dragon first sauntered toward our blind, Walter was shortsightedly thrilled at the prospect of a closer interaction.

"Will you look at that, Matthew?" he asked. "I think the little one there likes us."

Before I could verbalize what seemed to me an obvious concern about interacting with a juvenile in the presence of its undoubtedly protective family, Walter patted his knee invitingly.

"Come on over, my little friend," he said to the young dragon. "We won't hurt you."

"I don't think that's a good idea," I said.

"Nonsense. Surely the little one is nothing to be afraid of."

"I'm more worried about the big ones mistaking our intentions toward the little one."

My concern was warranted but tardy, for I had hardly begun to glance nervously about for signs of an agitated dragon when Tiamat's attack came.

Gratefully, I did not see the charge begin, or I suspect I would have been paralyzed with the fear of it. Instead, I sensed movement, too quick for the dragons' usual browsing, and I heard galloping footfalls tattoo the ground at an increasing tempo. Without pausing to appraise our attacker, I grasped Walter by the arm with a roughness that can hopefully be forgiven under the circumstances, and I hustled him away from the juvenile in the vain hope that distance might ease the dragon's agitation. The pounding footsteps did not stop, and even though Walter and I were both running by this point, the great brown shadow at the edge of my vision still grew.

The *mokele-mbembe* would undoubtedly have overtaken us if she had followed through on her charge, for we had to negotiate a path around brush that the dragon simply burst through, but thankfully something stopped her. Though I did not immediately perceive it in my preoccupation with escape, her footfalls died away, and craning my neck, I perceived that Tiamat had aborted her pursuit about 30 feet behind us. Gradually I registered the source of her hesitation: Ekianga and Mambunia, back from rambling in the forest, stood in her path with arrows nocked to their bows while Walter and I recovered from the chase.

"Matthew?" I heard Walter call. "Are you all right?"

"I think so," I said.

"What the devil just happened?"

"The big *mokele-mbembe* charged us, but then she stopped."

"I can see that. As a matter of fact, she almost fell over herself trying to stop so quickly. But what the devil stopped her?"

"I think she's afraid of the Bangombe."

Though it might seem far-fetched, some of the fiercest animals on the planet quail before the indigenous warrior tribes of Africa. The lions of the Serengeti, for example, have learned a healthy fear of the fierce Maasai through a long history of being hunted by them, to the point where the cats will retreat, even ceding ownership of a kill, at the sight of the customary red Maasai robes. Similarly, confrontations between *mokele-mbembe* and the Bangombe such as the killing at Lake Télé have evidently recurred often enough for the dragons to afford the Bangombe similar deference, for Tiamat recoiled from the two tiny, fierce men despite being more than 100 times their size; the picture resembled the familiar but fictitious scene of the elephant quailing at the approach of a mouse.

"Why, this is extraordinary," Walter said.

"You want the Bangombe to shoot?" Ekianga asked.

"I don't think that will be necessary. Out of curiosity, is this how *mokele-mbembe* usually behave for your people?"

"Yes." Ekianga flashed a proud smile. "The Bangombe are great warriors. *Mokele-mbembe* know this."

"*Mokele-mbembe* know," Mambunia agreed.

"I daresay they do."

Were it not for this dragon-taming faculty on the part of the Bangombe, it is entirely possible that our study of the *mokele-mbembe* would not have gone forward. Regardless of whether the rest of the herd's tolerance, the presence of such a belligerent individual would have discouraged the type of close observation that Walter and I meant to conduct for fear that Tiamat might interpose a violent objection on the others' behalf. Fortunately, the dragoness's reaction to the Bangombe suggested a promising means of ensuring our safety while we interacted with the herd, which Walter promptly tested by again approaching them when we made contact the next day.

"What are you doing?" I asked. "Have you forgotten that one of them attacked us yesterday?"

"Of course not," Walter said, "but it was only that one female who objected to us, and she won't dare charge with the Bangombe here to protect us."

"What if you're wrong?"

"Well, there's only one way to find out."

Without giving me further opportunity to argue against it, Walter shuffled toward the dragons and approached a smaller female and the juvenile, who were feeding at the herd's flank. Just as she had the day before, the juvenile ambled toward Walter, and all I could do while he invited her to visit him was monitor Tiamat for signs that she was contemplating another attack.

Mokele-mbembe do not charge without warning but will instead display their growing agitation, at least to those who recognize the signs. Just as other animals attempt to appear larger to intimidate foes, the dragons turn sideways to present their full intimidating profile and raise their necks, perhaps superfluously, so as to emphasize their great height. If that does not discourage an intruder, they may uproot nearby plants and toss them away as if miming their violent intentions, or they may stamp or kick their feet, twitch the end of their tails, or even rear up briefly on their hind legs, making the earth itself quake as if with intimidation when their forefeet slam back down.

Tiamat made several of these signs while she watched the juvenile edge closer to Walter.

"I think she's getting upset," I warned him.

"What does it matter if she is?" Walter asked. "I daresay she won't attack with the Bangombe here."

Despite Walter's assurance, I continued to monitor Tiamat's reactions while the juvenile approached the old man. The juvenile took a few steps, then paused to inspect Walter with her head cocked at a quizzical angle, and Tiamat snorted. The juvenile skipped a few more steps forward before halting just a few feet from Walter, who extended his hand for her to sniff, dog-like, and Tiamat violently pawed the earth beneath her massive feet.

"It's all right, little one," Walter said, oblivious to the larger she-dragon's mounting exasperation. "I won't bite."

When the juvenile dragon finally responded to Walter's overtures, several things happened in quick succession. First, the juvenile thrust her head toward Walter's hand, at which point Tiamat had evidently seen enough. She took several steps, undoubtedly gearing up to gallop in Walter's direction, but the Bangombe sprang between Tiamat and Walter, brandishing their bows—

—And absolutely nothing happened. The dragon might easily have overtaken Walter and plucked him from the ground to dash him against a tree with one toss of her head. She might just as easily have crushed him like a discarded cigarette with one cursory stamp of her foot, too, but she did neither. Instead, she was rooted where she stood, and though she glowered malevolently at Walter's interaction with the juvenile, she would not try to pass the Bangombe and became powerless to wreak any violence.

With the Bangombe standing guard, Walter petted and cooed at the juvenile dragon until she had satisfied her curiosity and returned to the herd, whereupon he invited me to join him.

"What did I tell you, Matthew?" he asked. "I've made a new friend, and the big one didn't do anything about it. Now, come along and help me watch these dragons. Did I tell you that I've thought up a new name for them? *Mokelembembe spinki* isn't really a Linnaean name, after all. We shall call them *Dracosaurus longicollis* instead."

Having christened the dragons and satisfied himself that the Bangombe could deter any aggressive behavior from their fierce guardian, Walter settled in to study *mokele-mbembe* with the same enthusiasm that he had *sasabonsam* and *ngoubou*, and I joined him. Though we were by no means what I would call fast friends, we eventually reached a point where Tiamat accepted that we didn't mean any harm to the family she guarded so jealously and lost the will to trample us into oblivion. In the meantime, we kept our Bangombe chaperones close to ensure our safety pending our ability to establish more amicable relations with the dragons.

CHAPTER XII

THE MANY DEATHS OF WALTER SPINK

Although it almost goes without saying, considering the misadventures I have described throughout this memoir, the pursuit and study of dragons is riddled with hazards of varying degrees of severity. When the dragons themselves are not attempting to eat or trample intrusive or unwary dracontologists, researchers must still contend with inhospitable, harsh environments, politically unstable states, and uncooperative officials. Some of these difficulties present only annoyance or expense, but some threaten serious injury or illness, even to the point of death. During my time with Walter Spink studying *mokele-mbembe*, it seemed as if I was fretting for his safety every time I turned around, and the numerous times that he was declared dead did nothing to ease my nerves.

To be fair, some of my fretting carried over from our previous exploits. Even if we had not seen Heep for some time, at least while we were traveling in villages and other populous places, he followed us—or should I say Walter—as tenaciously as ever. He rejoined us, unofficially speaking of course, when we ventured into the swamp forest, where he might easily have ambushed us but for the observation of the Bangombe, whose sharp eyes detected him hidden in ambush one day.

"There is a strange animal nearby," Ekianga said.

"Strange animal," Mambunia agreed.

"I don't suppose," Walter asked, already suspecting the identity of our stalker, "it resembles a lizard, but with wings like a bat?"

"That is just what it looks like."

"Bother. It's that Heep again. We'd better be careful, or he'll get that taste of us he's been craving all along."

Knowing that the *sasabonsam* was still shadowing us put us on our guard even before we made contact with the *mokele-mbembe*, and then the bellicose temperament of Tiamat showed that we needed to be equally wary of aggression from certain members of the herd. Unfortunately, it was not always easy during those first days to tell the dragon who would charge us from the dragons who would demurely retreat, for *mokele-mbembe* tend to look alike to the untrained eye. The only way to avoid run-ins with the aggressive individual was to learn to recognize each individual dragon.

Identifying individual *mokele-mbembe* can require some skill because not all differences between them are readily apparent. They are easy to tell apart by gender due to sexual dimorphism, with males sporting a set of spines running down the back of their necks that females do not; thus we had no difficulty singling out the one male, a subadult whom we called Fafnir after the dragon in the Norse sagas.[20] Size can also help to narrow down the identity of individuals, but it is not an infallible guide. The single small juvenile, whom we called Campe (another classical dragon reference), might have been easy to recognize, but telling the two immense adult females and two subadult females apart presented more of a challenge.

When size and gender prove insufficient to identify a particular dragon, the surest method of distinguishing individuals is by

[20]Initially, we could only mark what appeared to be sexual dimorphism and guess that the spiny-necked dragon was the male, but this was subsequently confirmed by observation of other male dragons in situations where their gender could not be mistaken (to wit, mounting the females).

observing the tubercles in their skin. The dragons' scaly hide is generally pebbly in texture, but peppered here and there with larger, round growths much like the skin of many familiar reptile species such as iguanas. The pattern, size, and number of these varies between individuals, so the researcher familiar enough with *mokele-mbembe* can use them to tell individuals apart in much the same way that the unique noses of individual gorillas and unique ears of individual elephants set them apart from others of their own kind.

Having observed that the pattern of tubercles was the key to recognizing individual dragons, we were able to identify and name the remaining members of the herd. Fafnir and Campe were joined by the subadult females Echidna and Scylla, as well as a full-grown adult female we called Ceto. The latter appeared from her evident age and assurance to be the herd's matriarch, and we could distinguish her from Tiamat by a cluster of warty-looking knobs that drizzled down her cheek almost like tears.

Learning to recognize each member of the herd enabled us to guard against Tiamat, who proved to be the only one of them who was actually aggressive where we were concerned. It's impossible to vouch for the inner workings of a dragon's mind, but even with the Bangombe guarding us, she stared at us so fixedly that I for one felt as intimidated as when she openly attacked us. She also paced irritably and decimated the brush whenever we approached any of the others. The presence of the Bangombe restrained her from acting upon her aggressive impulses, but we knew just the same that she would charge us if she ever found the opportunity.

Despite Tiamat's hostility and Heep's craving for Walter's very flesh, neither of them was the cause of the near-injury that actually befell while we were observing *mokele-mbembe*. I did not witness the incident itself, for I had left Walter studying the dragons under Ekianga and Mambunia's able supervision while I was temporarily bedridden in our camp with a nasty case of giardiasis (a threat to many visitors to Africa, and not just dracontologists). If I thought I could trust Walter not to get himself into trouble in my absence, however, my naïveté was dispelled in dramatic fashion when Mambunia burst into the tent where I was resting and made the following pronouncement.

"Walter Spink is dead!"

Lest the reader misapprehend how dire the situation actually was, I must clarify that the Bangombe do not use the latter adjective the way Westerners do. In their culture, a person is "dead" when he is ill or injured, without having actually passed away; the phrase "dead forever" is used to describe the state of death as we understand it. Not being aware of the distinction at the time, my reaction must have seemed very melodramatic to the forest people: imagining every variety of morbid scenario, I quit my sickbed and followed Mambunia to the site of Walter's accident, only to hear the old man's carping from a distance and realize that he could not be too badly hurt. I found him sitting on the forest floor, covered in filth but unharmed, while he swatted away Ekianga's helping hands.

"I keep telling you that I'm perfectly fine," he was saying. "I wish you wouldn't make such a fuss."

Once Walter had laboriously regained his feet, I was able to elicit his explanation of the misadventure.

"It's really nothing, Matthew," he said, "I assure you. One of our scaly friends just stepped on me."

"Stepped on you?"

"Well, almost stepped on me. She missed, although just barely."

Even when they don't mean any harm, the dragons can nevertheless inflict accidental injury. Indeed, it is almost inevitable that such massive animals should have some mishaps when small creatures loiter about their feet. After all, humans are hard-pressed to avoid stepping on or tripping over small dogs and cats milling about their feet, so it is hardly unreasonable that we should be stepped on or tripped over by larger creatures such as *mokele-mbembe* if we do not have the good sense to get out from under foot.

"Why didn't you get out of the way?" I asked.

"Why do you think?" Walter squawked. "I wanted to see her up close."

"Are you hurt?"

"I'm perfectly fine, other than all of you fussing over me."

Walter might have hobbled away from his first close encounter with the dragons' feet unscathed, but similar incidents became a concerning fact of life. Though none of the dragons went out of their way to approach us, much less step on us, the matriarch, Ceto, occasionally meandered in our direction by mere coincidence. The first time this happened, we foolishly remained in her path, thinking she would veer way.

"Do you think we should move?" I asked Walter.

"I don't think that's necessary," he said.

"We're right in her path."

"Matthew, we're out in plain sight, and wild animals avoid human beings. You don't really think she'd intentionally approach us, do you? No, I'm sure she'll go around."

Walter's prediction notwithstanding, the dragon plodded inexorably in our direction. Though his reasoning seemed sound, some instinct made me apprehensive, and my anxiety evolved into quiet panic as she closed to within 30 feet without a hint of detouring. Finally, when she was so close I could have counted the pebbly scales tessellating her wrinkly hide, I ceded the right of way to her, tugging Walter along with me, and a foot the size of a cast iron skillet crunched down where we had been standing moments before.

"Really, madam," Walter said, "you must learn to watch where you're going!"

Though she might at first have seemed merely careless, the dragon's reaction to the sound of Walter's voice at her heels showed that she had not by any means meant to cross our path. Though we had been in plain sight the whole time, she trotted away with a honk of alarm when Walter announced our presence, and we guessed that she had somehow failed to see us.

"You know," Walter said (somewhat superfluously, by this point), "I think she may have a problem with her eyesight."

Once we realized that the dragon matriarch's middling eyesight would not serve her well enough to avoid trampling us, the occasions of her coming sparked disagreement between Walter and the rest of our group. The Bangombe and I, selfishly preoccupied with everyone's safety, would have either gotten out of Ceto's way or warned her of our presence so she could avoid us. Walter, on the other hand, thought to take advantage of the dragoness's condition to get a closer view of her, and he would neither vacate her path nor suffer anyone else to discourage her.

"I refuse to move, and I absolutely forbid any of you to chase her away," Walter would say. "Really, how the devil am I supposed to get a good look at her?"

Given Walter's intransigence, I was hard-pressed to keep him safe when the nearsighted dragon ventured in our direction. My desire to avoid conflict with Walter, even when I felt he was being reckless, warred with my feeling that I was responsible for keeping him out of danger. The latter ultimately won out each time, and I would either incidentally raise my voice or cough, chasing the dragon away, or pull Walter by the collar of his tweed jacket to safety.

"Really, you needn't worry so, Matthew," he would say. "She wasn't even close."

Whether my worrying was necessary or not, I shepherded Walter out of the path of a lumbering dragon many times during our study of *mokele-mbembe*, and we successfully avoided physical injury at the hands—or more appropriately, the feet—of our research subjects. Eventually even I became so desensitized to the process of dodging the dragons' giant feet that I thought little of it, and I certainly never held it against our scaly friends. Ultimately, any danger of accidental injury from working around *mokele-mbembe* is fairly small so long as the dracontologists exercise a little prudence, and indeed, Walter and I soon made an enemy of the human variety whose concerted attempts to disrupt our work were far more dangerous, both to our observation of the dragons and our physical well-being, than anything we experienced from the *mokele-mbembe* themselves.

*

Though their focus is on finding and interacting with the dragons themselves, would-be dracontologists must also frequently contend with opposition from human beings. Africa is fairly notorious for bureaucrats who make travel difficult, and these exist at all levels of government: even the tiniest village is apt to require a permit for research activities to be conducted on tribal lands. Even in the absence of such formalities, proper etiquette nevertheless requires that researchers present themselves to village authorities and obtain permission to pass through. While most Africans are amiable and obliging, some are inevitably hostile either to outsiders in general or dracontologists in particular, and Walter and I encountered a particularly hostile individual during our time with *mokele-mbembe* in the Likouala.

Our conflict with one of the locals came about as a result of the dragons' travel foraging, which took us near several villages, which announced themselves by the familiar muffled rumbling of signal drums carrying through the trees. Rather than risk trespassing upon tribal lands, Walter, Henri, and I visited each village, where we were conducted down tidy lanes of whitewashed brick buildings with corrugated iron roofs to be presented to each village's respective council. At each stop, the local grandees engaged us in extensive palaver that seemed to be essentially meant to gauge how much they could overcharge us for the privilege of studying *mokele-mbembe.*

These meetings left our petty cash depleted but otherwise passed without incident until we visited the village of Toukalaka. There, our ready agreement to the various fees the village proposed to assess reassured the council of our good faith, but the imposition of an additional condition almost upset our plans. In addition to charging us handsomely, the village council insisted on consulting the ancestral spirits to determine whether our errand was auspicious enough to be allowed to proceed.

To facilitate this consultation, the council summoned the village feticheuse, Lusunga Meombe, a diminutive and gnarled old woman with white hair like cotton mantling her head and a constellation of fetishes orbiting her scrawny neck on a circle of twine. Hardly needing to be told the purpose for which she had been called, the feticheuse proposed our errand to the spirits before casting a dozen cowry shells from which she might divine their judgment. Despite the cordial reception Walter and I had received from the last feticheuse we had encountered, however, Madame Meombe's judgment was by no means favorable to our errand.

"The spirits," she said, "they do not approve. The strangers should not be allowed to seek *mokele-mbembe*."

"That can't be," Walter said. "Are you sure you're reading those shells correctly?"

"I am so sorry, but the shells, they are very clear. It is nothing personal, *cher*. I only do what the spirits command, you know."

For some moments we were understandably disheartened at this pronouncement, but ultimately the consultation with the spirits proved to be a mere formality. It seems quite likely that we owed this reversal of the ancestors' judgment to our ready availability of funds to cover the permit fees, which promised to swell the community chest enough to outweigh the disapprobation of the dead. In any event, we received permission to study *mokele-mbembe* on the land of the Toukalaka villagers.

"Very good," Walter said. "Now, if you don't mind, I'll be getting back to my dragons."

Having been delivered from this brief impasse by the fruits of Mr. F.'s tax-exempt beneficence, Walter and I returned to our observation of the *mokele-mbembe* without paying the judgment of the spirits or their would-be messenger any further heed. As for Madame Meombe, she did not visibly bristle at being overruled in this manner, but Walter and I were fools if we thought the mandate of the ancestral spirits (or, if you prefer, the will of the feticheuse) could be thwarted by tempting the village council with lucrative permit fees.

Though we could not at the time fathom the source or depth of Madame's opposition, it seems clear from later events that she merely bided her time, and her continuing desire to keep us away from *mokele-mbembe* was revealed in dramatic fashion when one of the hazards of dracontology put Walter at the mercy of her unique craft.

✱

Aside from the obvious possibility of causing physical injury, the dragons may also inadvertently inflict harm by spreading disease. Reptiles, whether wild or kept as pets, are susceptible to several bacterial infections that they can in turn transmit to humans; some of the most common include salmonella, botulism, campylobacteriosis, and leptospirosis. Although they are unique in many ways, *mokele-mbembe* are not so dissimilar to the better-known members of their class that we should not expect them to be similarly susceptible—and similarly contagious. Our prolonged contact with the dragons, which sneezed, spit, and defecated indiscriminately throughout our shared environment, eventually resulted in illness, and Walter was the one who took sick.

At first, Walter's symptoms were subtle and easily dismissed. I noticed that he ate sparingly at every meal, but his appetite had never been what I would call hearty. More importantly, he gave a perfectly logical explanation for his disinterest in food when confronted.

"I simply don't have the time to eat," he said. "There's too much I still have to learn about our scaly friends."

Walter's passion for observing the dragons might have caused him to forego meals, but over the course of several days, I noticed that he made repeated detours to answer nature's call. When he allowed this situation to intrude upon his time watching the dragons, I knew that something was wrong, although he continued to deny any discomfort.

"I assure you that I am perfectly fine," he said when confronted.

Despite his protests, Walter's condition worsened over the

course of several days until his illness was undeniable. He stopped eating altogether, and he became so delirious with fever that he took to his bed. Knowing that Walter would have crawled into the field to see the dragons even if both his legs had been broken, I knew that his case was serious when even the prospect of observing dragons did not confer the strength to rouse himself.

"I'm afraid," I said to the Bangombe, "that Walter Spink is dead again."

"Dead again," Mambunia agreed.

Judging from his symptoms, I suspect that Walter had caught campylobacteriosis from his so-called scaly friends. The infection can be fatal, especially among the elderly, and what is more, any illness is cause for concern in such a rugged and remote environment as the Likouala swamp forests. As frightening as it was for me to take charge, I mustered uncharacteristic resolve and coordinated the construction of a litter and Walter's subsequent transportation to nearby Toukalaka to seek medical attention.

When we reached the village, I was dismayed to learn that it lacked a Western hospital or doctor, but I had little opportunity to fret over the situation. News of Walter's illness spread to Madame Meombe, who dispatched several assistants to spirit the invalid back to her for her own brand of treatment. At the time, I doubted her methods but not her good faith, and before I could have protested if I had wanted to, Walter had been carried into the fetish house, where I was shut outside for what seemed like several hours to await the outcome of the witchdoctor's ministrations.

Though I had been concerned for Walter, I would not have expected him to succumb immediately, regardless of his illness's severity. The reader can thus imagine my shock when Madame emerged from the fetish house, her face too bland and unimaginative to betray the gravity of the situation, and announced the following.

"I am so sorry, *cher*," she said. "Your friend, he is dead."

By this point, I had become so accustomed to the Bangombe usage of the word that I did not register the feticheuse's meaning.

"I know that," I said, "but will he recover?"

"No, *cher,*" Madame said. "He is *dead.*"

"Wait—you mean dead forever?"

"Yes. Dead forever."

Even with this grim pronouncement, I disbelieved until Madame Meombe led me into the fetish house, where I found Walter lying on the litter, completely still. Several moments of watching desperately—but unavailingly—for chest rise finally convinced me that the feticheuse had spoken true, and from that point I moved about in a fugue while others laid Walter out in a kambala-wood coffin and readied it for shipment back to the United States. Though I did not consciously make any plans, it seemed a foregone conclusion that the study of the dragons could not continue without Walter driving it.

Whatever thought I might have given to the effect of Walter's absence ultimately proved premature, for Walter Spink was not dead, all indications to the contrary notwithstanding. I would probably never have guessed the truth if I had been left to my own devices, but fortunately Henri was savvier than I when it came to the workings of African folk medicine and magic. When news of Walter's death reached him, he immediately sought me out with a sense of urgency that initially seemed superfluous.

"Where is Walter Spink?" he asked.

"The same place I left him," I said. "Why?"

"I think that he is still alive!"

Feeling very much like an accomplice grave robber, I led Henri to Walter's coffin and stood by while he pried open the lid to reveal Walter looking just as lifeless as he had in the fetish house. Regardless of appearances, Henri insisted on keeping vigil, certain that Walter would awaken. I attributed this behavior to mere denial, at least until a soft groan issued from the casket, followed shortly thereafter by Walter's tousled white head periscoping into view as he sat bolt upright.

"What the devil am I doing here?" he asked. "Is this a coffin?"

"We thought you were dead," I said.

"Nonsense. I'm just a bit under the weather is all."

The reader is doubtless familiar with the legend of the zombie, or living dead, but its basis in reality is perhaps less widely understood. To my knowledge, it is not actually possible for a witchdoctor or fetish priest to reanimate a dead body, but they can create the appearance of doing so by administering a drug that temporarily counterfeits death. Certain neurotoxins, in the correct dosage, can slow heart rate and breathing to the point where the victim appears—and may even be declared—to be dead, only to rise, Lazarus-like, when the drug wears off.[21] This is undoubtedly what happened to Walter.

Once we guessed the basis for the premature declaration of Walter's death, the three of us could think of only one person who had the knowledge of traditional medicine to pull off such a coup, though we could not yet divine her motive.

"It must have been that she-devil Meombe," Walter said. "She's had it in for me every since we met her."

Having guessed the cause of his near-death experience, Walter would not be satisfied until he had given Madame Meombe a piece of his mind, and he marched resolutely to the fetish house despite my attempts to dissuade him from making a scene. If the feticheuse was disappointed to see Walter up and walking, her face remained bland and unaffected, and to her credit, she did not resort to any coy denials when confronted.

"Yes, *cher*," she said. "It was me, but I never meant to kill you. I only wanted to keep you away from *mokele-mbembe*."

"Whatever for?" Walter asked. "If this is about that affair with the fetish, it was admittedly a lapse of judgment on my part, but I'm terribly sorry about it, and I assure you, it won't happen again."

"This is not about a stolen *mokele-mbembe* fetish."

"Then what the devil is it about?"

---

[21]The ingredients of the drug remain unknown but are suspected to include tetrodotoxin derived from certain species of puffer fish as well as alkaloids contained in *Datura stramonium.*

"When I consulted the spirits, they sent me a vision."

"Well, out with it. What the devil do you think you saw that's got you in such a tizzy?"

Fond as I am of Walter, I must acknowledge that he has a particular aptitude for giving offense, so I had imagined a number of reasons why the feticheuse might have taken a dislike to him. Whatever faux pas and misdeeds I anticipated to be the source of her enmity, however, were nothing compared with the doom that Madame claimed to have foreseen.

"I saw you, *cher,*" she said, "standing over the dead bodies of a herd of *mokele-mbembe.*"

"Preposterous," Walter said.

"You had killed them."

"As much as I respect your beliefs, madam, your vision is obviously mistaken. I would never do anything to harm my dragons."

"The spirits, they know what will happen, *cher.* I am so sorry. Will you leave, then?"

"I most certainly will not."

"Then you and I, we must be enemies."

No matter how we tried to convince her of our good intentions toward the dragons, we could not sway the feticheuse from her faith in the seeming prevision, and she continued trying to run us out of the area in the coming weeks. As to the contents of her prediction, I found them as incredible as Walter had; I certainly could not imagine Walter having the motivation to kill *mokele-mbembe*, much less the ability to carry out the intention. If the feticheuse's faith in a vision seemed misplaced to me, even I could not deny that we had made a dangerous enemy as her feud with Walter escalated in the coming weeks, nor could I ultimately dismiss her prediction as easily as I was initially tempted to do.

CHAPTER XIII
EAT AND BE EATEN

A dragon's feeding habits dictate not only its lifestyle but its relationships with other creatures, including dracontologists. Only the most foolhardy of researchers would turn their backs on a carnivore like *sasabonsam*, for example, and befriending an animal that is apt to take a bite out of you, if not to eat you outright, is out of the question. On the other hand, it is generally possible to have peaceful and even amicable interactions with herbivores that do not see humans as a potential food source. Thus, other than continued opposition from the *mokele-mbembe* herd's self-appointed sentry, Tiamat, Walter and I developed good relations with the dragons in our new study group.

Whatever our relations with the long-necked dragons would ultimately be, allowing ourselves to become complacent nevertheless seemed to be out of the question due to the presence of one particularly resolute carnivore. As I previously mentioned, Heep followed us to the Likouala, and the object of his interest was Walter, as always. Though Heep would not approach our camp, he pursued us, hidden among the *Marantochloa* and *Stipularia* that crowded the understory, whenever we ventured into the swamp forest, hopeful as always that our guard against him would falter if he followed us persistently enough.

No matter how assiduously Heep stalked us, the Bangombe kept him under surveillance and warned Walter before the *sasabonsam* could work any mischief.

"The Heep is following us again," Ekianga would say.

"Following again," Mambunia would agree.

"Yes, well," Walter would say, "he's nothing if not persistent."

"You want us to shoot him?"

"No, that won't be necessary. In spite of everything, he's really not such a bad sort."

Walter's tolerance of Heep might have made for a harrowing time in the Congo, but the *mokele-mbembe* themselves saved us from spending the next weeks constantly pulling Walter out of Heep's jaws. Just as she had when Walter and I approached the herd, Tiamat took a passionate dislike to the *sasabonsam* almost from the moment she laid eyes on him lurking behind us on Bangándo Bai, regardless of whether Heep was realistically too small and weak to pose any threat to her family. She started by warning him off in much the same manner as she had us, by pacing and stamping the arum at her feet, and her poise tensed when Heep proved oblivious to the display. We guessed that she meant to charge, and Walter could not convince the Bangombe to extend their protection to his favorite.

"Couldn't you help our leathery-winged friend," Walter asked, "the way you did us?"

"No," Ekianga said.

"Whyever not?"

"Because we do not want to help him."

"But he'll be killed!"

Walter's concern seemed wholly justified, for Tiamat launched into a brisk gallop, splintering trees in her path that looked far sturdier than the rangy *sasabonsam,* and seemed apt to pulverize Heep when she caught him. To make matters worse, Heep was painfully slow to react, so the enraged *mokele-mbembe* was nearly upon him by the time he fanned out his wings in preparation to retreat. It was only by some unaccountable luck—and after much strenuous flapping—that Heep mounted up and out of her path to disappear out of sight in the forest canopy.

Despite having escaped Tiamat's charge, Heep must have nevertheless been fairly traumatized by the experience, for he seemed to take her warning quite to heart. Though we might see him periodically on our way to or from the herd, he melted invisibly back into the brush whenever a reedy trumpeting or the crash of heavy footsteps betrayed the proximity of the *mokele-mbembe.* Nor did he appear while we shadowed the herd, despite Walter's frequent queries directed to the Bangombe, who would certainly have discerned him if he had been present.

"There is no sign of the Heep," Ekianga would say.

"No sign," Mambunia would agree.

After the Bangombe had confirmed Heep's absence in this manner for a good week, Walter allowed himself to believe that Heep had been dissuaded for good and began to see the benefit of having the dragoness chase him away.

"I almost think I owe old Tiamat a debt of gratitude," he said. "Without Heep around, we can focus on observing our scaly friends instead of worrying about being eaten."

Walter's appraisal of our changed situation proved accurate in the following days. Under the threat of reprisals from Tiamat, Heep kept away from us when we intercepted the *mokele-mbembe* herd and as we followed them in their travels throughout the day. Moreover, not having to look constantly over our shoulders, lest the *sasabonsam* sneak up on us, freed our attention so that we could focus on the long-necked dragons and make many valuable observations. On the other hand, Heep's absence alone could not confer the rapport with the *mokele-mbembe* that was necessary for us to exploit that opportunity, and that became the focus of our efforts.

✻

Even if we no longer had to contend with Heep's depredations, we still had difficulty getting close to the *mokele-mbembe* and documenting their lifestyle. Our experience with *ngoubou* notwithstanding, most wild creatures are uncomfortable with human beings getting too close, and if they do not retreat altogether, they will still be ill at ease, making it impossible to observe their natural behavior. *Mokele-mbembe* are similarly shy when it comes to humans, and they will generally stop whatever they are doing to stare warily, or even withdraw altogether, if dracontologists approach closer than 100 feet or so. Of the herd that Walter and I had located, only one of them sought out any interaction with us, and that was the juvenile whom we had named Campe.

From the very first days of our observation of the dragons, Campe proved both insatiably curious about her surroundings and fearless enough to approach us. She was always wandering away from the herd, either into the forest alone or toward Walter and me, and seemed particularly interested in shiny objects: she sauntered, fascinated, in our direction whenever sunlight glinted off my wristwatch, and she was equally captivated by our camera, which she eventually ate.[22] Unfortunately, one of the subadult females, Scylla, had adopted a protective role with respect to her younger relation, and whether Campe was tramping into the forest or toward us, Scylla stepped into her path to dissuade her from roaming any farther.

Between being blocked from interaction with the one dragon who seemed receptive and being avoided by the rest of them, Walter quickly became dissatisfied with the quality of our interactions and proposed to take action.

"If we're ever going to learn anything about our scaly friends," he said when the *mokele-mbembe* shied away for what seemed the hundredth time, "we're going to have to get them used to us so they

[22]This is the admittedly contrived-sounding explanation for why we were unable to provide photographic corroboration of our experiences with the dragons.

stop fleeing whenever we get close."

"You mean to habituate them," I guessed.

"Precisely."

The practice of habituation has been widely used by ethologists hoping to observe the natural behavior of wild animals, and indeed, it has gained notoriety in cryptozoological circles for its application with the North American Sasquatch. It is the process by which an animal becomes desensitized to an unfamiliar stimulus—such as the presence of human beings—so that it no longer responds with defensive behavior. Generally, habituation is effected by repeatedly exposing animals to the presence of human beings so as to show that we are harmless, but the same general principle underlies the concept of leaving seed for birds or salt licks for deer that make them brave enough to approach your house. It was this latter technique that Walter proposed to bring to bear on the *mokele-mbembe.*

"I daresay there's only one way to make friends with these dragons," he said, "and that's to offer them something they want enough to get over their diffidence."

"What do you think that is?" I asked.

"Why, food, of course. What else?"

Walter's guess that food would be the way to win over the dragons was undoubtedly informed by our observation that they were constantly eating. Almost all of the dragons' time, from early in the morning before we made contact with them and then throughout the day while we shadowed their slow travel-browsing through their foraging area, was spent eating. This is necessary because of not only their immense size but their generalist feeding strategy, which involves consuming essentially whatever plants they find in their path rather than seeking out higher quality and more nutritious fare. Indeed, we estimated that animals the size of full-grown *mokele-mbembe* would have to spend 16 hours a day eating to sustain themselves in this manner, and they consequently seemed to have little interest in anything else.

While it was obvious that *mokele-mbembe* were preoccupied with food, it was less clear what particular item might be tempting enough to lure them to us, for the long-necked dragons as generalist feeders eat most any plants they find with equal gusto. Though the variety of plants that Walter and I observed *mokele-mbembe* to eat is too broad to describe here,[23] they are equally content to feed upon whatever plants present themselves, whether they are palm trees and shrubs of the family *Arecaceae* or flowering *Chrysobalanaceae* or *Fabaceae*, and they consume leaves, flowers, and fruit of these plants with few exceptions. The only plant the dragons noticeably avoided was the local stinkhorn fungus, *Phallus indusiatus*, whose overpowering and unpleasant smell of rotting meat dissuades most creatures other than flies from consuming it. In any event, there was so much browse available to the dragons without the necessity of engaging with us that it was difficult to conceive of them coming to us unless we offered them something especially desirable.

The generalist feeding habits of the *mokele-mbembe* might have stymied Walter's plan to befriend them, but it soon became clear that there is a plant for which the long-necked dragons have a particular fondness. No matter how eclectic the dragons' menu might be, there was one variety of yellow fruit that we witnessed them eating consistently enough to suggest they truly enjoyed it, and perceiving a potential opportunity, Walter consulted our guides' expertise.

"That fruit they're eating," he said, "what is it?"

"It is called *malombo,*" Ekianga said.

"*Malombo*," Mambunia agreed.

The *malombo* plant is a type of liana from the *Apocynaceae* family. The name is actually used interchangeably to refer to several species, the most common of which are *Landolphia mannii* (which occurs along the Ubangi River near Impfondo) and *L. owariensis* (along the Sangha and Likouala-aux-Herbes Rivers). They have a milky sap that can be used to make rubber, bracts of white blossoms, and yellow fruit roughly the size of oranges with a diagnostic dimple on the bottom.

23A partial listing of plants eaten by *mokele-mbembe* appears in Appendix B.

It is the latter that *mokele-mbembe* chiefly prefer.[24]

"Our scaly friends seem to be very fond of this *malombo,*" Walter observed.

"Yes," Ekianga said. "*Mokele-mbembe* will do anything to get *malombo.*"

"Anything," Mambunia agreed.

"If our scaly friends crave this *malombo* fruit so much, then perhaps we can use it to overcome their reticence toward us."

Now that we knew of a plant that might adequately tempt the dragons, we enacted Walter's plan to habituate them. Though the *mokele-mbembe* browsed their trail fairly clear of the coveted fruit, we didn't have to range too far before we found more *malombo* vines snaking up the trunks of a half dozen trees with their characteristic fruit peeping at us from among the leaves like dozens of curious eyes. Once we had collected what seemed like an ample supply of these, we rejoined the herd, where Walter attempted to engage the dragons. Guessing that the younger dragons would be the easiest to win over, Walter first assayed his technique against the timid male, Fafnir, by flourishing his hands so as to call attention to the coveted *malombo* fruit while calling out to the dragon.

"Pardon me, young man," he said, "but can I interest you in some nice, juicy *malombo* fruit?"

At Walter's overture, the dragon raised his head from the red-blossomed *Stipularia* shrub that he had been browsing, probably to reassure himself that the noise did not pose a threat. He froze in place when he beheld the old man brandishing his offering of fruit, but the fact that he did not immediately retreat at the sight of a human betrayed his interest in Walter's bounty.

"That certainly got his attention!" Walter said.

"Yes," I agreed.

"Didn't I tell you this would work?"

---

[24]The research of Dr. Roy P. Mackal has revealed that *mokele-mbembe* also favor the leaves of a plant by the local name of *mabondzi*, which appears to be another species of *Landolphia.* We did not encounter such a plant in our observation of *mokele-mbembe*, but it may simply be absent from certain parts of the dragons' range.

"Yes, you told me. Now give it to him before he loses interest."

With some urging, Walter prepared to bestow his offering.

"You can have it," he said to the dragon, "if you want it. You just have to come and get it."

Despite Walter's optimism that the *mokele-mbembe* would come to him to obtain their favored fruit, the prospect of approaching a human, even for *malombo*, must have been too daunting. Fafnir refused this summons no matter how Walter cooed and flattered him, staring cautiously from where he stood.

"It's no use," I said. "I don't think he's ready to come to us."

"But this is absurd!" Walter said. "Why the devil is a big, huge dragon like him afraid of a bony old mummy like me?"

Even if his shyness seemed silly, Fafnir would not come to Walter to take the *malombo.* After trying to coax the dragon unavailingly for several more minutes, Walter finally tossed a piece of the fruit to him, and even then, Fafnir would only sample it when we withdrew several feet back. Still, he accepted our handout, albeit with a surfeit of caution lest we ambush him while he dipped his head to collect the *malombo*, and we had hope that continuing to ply the dragon with fruit might eventually facilitate closer interactions.

Having at least partly succeeded in wooing Fafnir, we adapted this same technique to win over the other dragons, but it was not always smooth going. Tiamat, for example, refused our offerings as if rejecting them was a point of honor, and Ceto simply lacked the visual acuity to find the fruit when we tossed it at her feet. Echidna, meanwhile, was so clumsy that she mashed half the *malombo* we gave her into pulp with her feet while she was looking for it, and once she even managed to blunder in the way when I launched a volley of fruit toward her. My offering bounced harmlessly off her broad chest, but there was still the concern that such accidents might cause the dragons to form a negative association with our offerings.

"You really must be more careful, Matthew," Walter said. "We're feeding dragons, not trying out for the Chicago Yankees. How are we supposed to habituate our scaly friends if you keep hitting them in the face with fruit?"

Whether it was the result of my troublesome aim or just the dragons' reticent nature, it was slow going trying to befriend the herd. After a week of our trying to habituate them with *malombo,* Campe was still the only dragon who would approach us, and Scylla's continued intervention prevented even her from mingling with us. In the absence of notable progress, Walter's frustration mounted.

"How the devil long is this supposed to take?" he asked. "I daresay we've given them enough *malombo* to fill the Great Rift Valley, and they still look at us as if we've got two heads!"

Though the process took longer than Walter would have liked, we persevered and began to see small signs of progress as the days went by. None of the dragons would eat from our hands yet, but day by day I noticed that the younger dragons browsed closer to where we crouched observing them, and they withdrew more lazily and did not retreat quite as far when they noticed us. Even so, it was some time before they accepted us so completely that they went about their usual business in the normal manner when we were around, and even when it seemed they were beginning to do so, we were reminded how delicate their burgeoning acceptance really was.

✱

Habituating dragons is not an exact science, and there is no magic number of *malombo* fruit or days spent habituating that will guarantee success. Nor are there unmistakable signs that the dragons are coming around; in our case, at least, the dragons finally took to us without apparent warning, just when we were becoming convinced that they would never accept us. And even then, it is entirely possible that some false step might derail the whole effort, as Walter and I learned even when we seemed to have succeeded.

Our breakthrough habituating the dragons came unexpectedly after several weeks of plying them with *malombo.* Walter offered *malombo* to one of his would-be friends, in this case Scylla, and tried to coax her nearer to collect them, but even when she shambled, bashfully at first, in his direction, we hardly dared hope she meant to come to him at last. We suppressed expressing our mounting excitement so as to avoid startling her, and finally Scylla ambled close and lowered her nub of head down to Walter's waiting hand, where she seized a piece of the fruit as gently as a horse taking an apple from a trainer.

"There," Walter murmured, "that wasn't so bad, now, was it? It was downright silly of you to take so long."

Even as he cooed reassurances, Walter thoroughly exploited his long-awaited close encounter with the dragon. While offering more *malombo* with one hand, he raised the other in stages, pausing at intervals to ensure that Scylla did not flinch from the movement. Thinking he was pressing his luck, I steeled myself for her to recoil and gallop away, but Walter's gnarled hand finally came to rest against the pebbly hide of her cheek, which he stroked gently without any visible objection from his new scaly friend.

"This is wonderful," he said. "Matthew, you should come try this."

"Do you think she'll tolerate me?" I asked.

"She's tolerating me, isn't she? And you're much more quiet and inoffensive than I am. What have you got to lose?"

Walter's point was well taken, and seeing that Scylla had continued feeding from the old man's palm even while he stroked her face and warbled at me, I decided to chance approaching the dragoness, bearing a handful of fruit as a token of my friendliness. When Scylla jerked her head away from Walter at my approach, I thought she might retreat, but instead she edged toward my outstretched hand and gently plucked a piece of *malombo.* The dragon's acceptance of my presence emboldened me to follow Walter's lead, and I raised my free hand to brush her lowered neck.

"What do you say, Matthew?" Walter asked. "I bet you never thought you'd be touching a live *Brontosaurus*!"

"That's certainly true," I agreed.

My words hardly captured my feelings, for I was more thrilled at being able to reach out and touch a live *mokele-mbembe* than I could ever have explained. After all, I had been a boy much more recently than Walter, and what boy hasn't dreamed of having his own *Brontosaurus*? Though I was poorly equipped to express myself, I once again found myself deeply grateful that Walter had included me in a venture that permitted me to experience such wonders.

However wonderful our first close interaction with a grown *mokele-mbembe* was, it was tantalizingly brief before the dragon's seeming acceptance of us was tested. Even as I gazed adoringly at my new acquaintance, a plaintive honk from somewhere off in the forest drew my attention and simultaneously set Scylla to nervous retreat.

"Gracious!" Walter said. "Whatever do you think is the matter?"

The source of the cry became apparent when we performed a quick inventory of the herd and discovered that one of the dragons was missing: the juvenile, Campe. We had often seen her poised to wander into the forest but for Scylla's intervention, so it seemed obvious that she had stolen away while Scylla was occupied interacting with us. The strident note to Campe's distress call suggested that she had gotten into a predicament, but the nature and severity of the danger were not immediately evident.

We did not have to wonder about the juvenile *mokele-mbembe*'s trouble for very long, for the crackle-rustle of snapping branches and disturbed foliage betrayed Campe's retreat from whatever had spooked her, at which point she promptly reappeared among her family. For some moments, the larger dragons circled protectively around her with the whirling mass of their marching legs blocking her from our view, but gradually they calmed enough to disperse and reveal the juvenile. Upon observing Campe ambling about without any obvious lacerations or bleeding, we were reassured of her safety, but at the same time, there was something off about her appearance that it took a few moments to register.

"Now wait just a damned minute," Walter said finally. "Wasn't her tail longer than that the last time we saw her?"

"I'm sure it was," I agreed.

"Then what the devil happened to it?"

"If I had to guess, I'd say that something attacked her, and she shed her tail to escape."

Just as Campe had lost most of her tail, leaving only a nub, several species of reptile, including many lizards and the tuatara (*Sphenodon punctatus*), are able to defensively shed all or part of their tails with minimal injury or blood loss. Caudal autotomy, as it is called, has also been documented among prehistoric reptiles of the genus *Captorhinus* but not, to my knowledge, among sauropods. While it is unlikely that an adult sauropod could shed its tail, it has been hypothesized that their young may have done so, and the bloodless manner in which Campe lost her tail is certainly more consonant with autotomy than having it torn away by a predator's bite.

"Maybe she did shed her tail," Walter said, "but what the devil attacked her?"

As if in answer to Walter's question, there came a *swoosh* as of flapping wings, and a grayish projectile erupted out of the understory before resolving into the form of a *sasabonsam.* From the absence of winged dragons occurring naturally in the area and the wobbly, precarious way he hung in midair before finally mounting toward the vaulting of branches overhead, we knew it was Heep. He rose slowly enough that we perceived a long, thin member—obviously Campe's tail—clutched in his jaws, and we guessed his part in the juvenile *mokele-mbembe*'s alarm. Though he would not contend with an adult *mokele-mbembe*, Campe must have wandered far enough from the herd for Heep to chance an attack.

"That rascal!" Walter said. "I should have guessed he would be lurking around thinking to cause mischief if he got the chance. I just hope our new scaly friends don't blame us for the attack."

Walter's concern was well-founded, for the unfortunate timing of Heep's attack might work against our habituation efforts even if it had not seriously injured Campe. Even if the *sasabonsam*'s stalking was entirely separate from our efforts, the skirmish between him and the juvenile *mokele-mbembe* had coincided with our interaction with Scylla, and she might fallaciously associate the negative stimulus with us. If that were the case, she might continue retreating from us, and all our efforts with her would have been in vain.

"There's nothing for it," Walter said. "We shall simply have to test her."

In order to gauge the damage Heep's attack had inflicted on our relationship with the dragoness, Walter equipped himself with a fresh handful of *malombo* before striding to within a few dozen feet of Scylla and calling to her.

"Excuse me, young lady," he said, "but what do you say we pick up where we left off before that bit of unpleasantness?"

Walter's offer hung in the air for several tense moments, but after considering the fruit thoughtfully, Scylla obligingly came to him again. While the dragon browsed from Walter's hand, we breathed a sigh of relief that our efforts had not been nullified by Heep's inopportune timing.

"Well, that's a mercy," Walter said. "I don't mind telling you, Matthew, that I would have had a few choice words for Heep if he had thrown a monkey wrench into our work."

Thankfully, no such harsh words were necessary, for Heep's attack did not retard our progress habituating the long-necked dragons. As Scylla became bolder in her interactions with us, the other members of the herd began to follow suit, and we eventually developed a rapport with the herd (with the exception of Tiamat) that greatly fostered our ability to observe their natural behavior. This improvement of our relations with the long-necked dragons happened slowly, but in the meantime, an unexpected consequence of preying on a *mokele-mbembe* would change our relationship with the *sasabonsam* and keep us occupied while we waited for his terrestrial cousins to come around.

⁕

Evolution has devised a variety of means for animals to deter predators, and *mokele-mbembe* have developed more than one such deterrent. Their size alone would make most carnivores think twice before attacking, but in the event that a predator makes such an attempt, the long-necked dragons possess an alternative defense that is guaranteed to discourage future predation. Studying the dragons when we did, Walter and I had not yet heard of *mokele-mbembe*'s secondary defense mechanism, but the Bangombe enlightened us in the wake of Heep's partially-successful attack upon Campe.

"The Heep made a big mistake," Ekianga said, "trying to eat *mokele-mbembe.*"

"Big mistake," Mambunia agreed.

"*Mokele-mbembe*'s flesh is very poisonous."

"Very poisonous."

"The Heep will die. Maybe die forever."

"Die forever."

"Whatever makes you say that?" Walter asked.

Though Walter balked at the information at first, we learned from the Bangombe what has since become cryptozoological legend with respect to *mokele-mbembe.* I have previously mentioned the killing of a *mokele-mbembe* at Lake Télé, but as our guides explained, the Bangombe not only killed that dragon but also butchered its carcass and ate the meat. According to the Bangombe, as well as other accounts of the incident that have subsequently surfaced, all who partook of the dragon meat became ill and died.[25]

"But that's horrible!" Walter said. "What's going to happen to Heep? He's a rascal, but I would hate for anything to happen to him. We have to find him and make sure he's all right."

With growing unease for the *sasabonsam*'s well-being, Walter sought Heep with the assistance of the Bangombe, and we eventually found him: a disconsolate pile of tatty wings and gaunt limbs languishing among the ferns and *Stipularia* on the forest floor. I might

[25]Given the idiomatic usage of the word for death among the Bangombe, it is possible that the diners became gravely ill rather than expiring outright.

have counseled caution before Walter approached a possibly sick animal that had already made several attempts on his life, but he shuffled urgently to Heep's side without consulting me. When the *sasabonsam* did not so much as raise his head to acknowledge our presence, Walter retrieved a stick from the muddy ground and poked the fallen dragon.

"You there—Heep"—Walter jabbed the crumpled body—"are you all right?"

If Heep had been all right, he would undoubtedly have attempted to strike out with his toothy jaws, but instead he lay still and unresponsive. We thus guessed that Heep was in genuine distress rather than feinting to put Walter off his guard, and observing the crumpled *sasabonsam* for a good few minutes convinced us. The periodic heave of the dragon's concave chest betrayed life, but he was by no means well, as indicated by his continued inactivity.

"I don't suppose there can be any doubt," Walter said. "*Mokele-mbembe* have toxic flesh, and poor Heep is ailing from it, the fool."

Having discovered Heep in distress as the Bangombe predicted, we were left with something of a conundrum: what to do with him. I anticipated Walter's likely proposal with dread, having already dealt with a convalescent *sasabonsam* once at a toll of great inconvenience and stress, and Walter did not disappoint my expectation.

"We can't just leave him here like this," he said. "It would be downright inhumane, even if he has tried to eat me a few dozen times. We shall simply have to take him back to camp with us."

"Is there anything we can do to help him?" I asked.

"Frankly, I have no idea, but he can't be any worse off than if we left him here ailing, all by himself, can he? At least we can give him food."

"I'm still worried that it's not safe to have him around camp."

"Quite the contrary, Matthew. We're safer having him tied up and knowing where he is than letting him wander around wherever he pleases. And as long as we have him restrained, we know he's not trying to harm our scaly girl. Now, are you going to argue with me or help me move this dragon?"

Given this choice (and my admitted aversion to conflict), I assisted in toting the sickly and unresisting dragon, whose jaws the Bangombe bound shut with liana rope, back to camp. Regardless of my reservations, the invalid made his journey in a manner befitting some potentate of legend, on the shoulders of four bearers consisting of me, Ekianga, Mambunia, and Henri, while Walter ushered us along with strict injunctions to avoid jostling Heep. Nor for the first or last time, we took a needy dragon into our midst, but whatever Walter's intentions in keeping him close, Heep found a way to make just as much trouble for us as our captive as he ever had stalking us.

CHAPTER XIV

I WAS A SORCERER'S APPRENTICE

When one is studying dragons in the wilderness, developing a reputation for being a little strange, if not outright crazy, is unavoidable. Many people cannot conceive of their fellow human beings choosing the company of wild animals rather than their own kind. This prejudice against those who eschew society is especially pronounced when the animals in question are cold-blooded, unsociable (to popular perception) reptiles. Fairly reputable and well-adjusted scientists have been regarded as eccentric, so you can imagine the situation in which Walter Spink—who was eccentric and unsociable to begin with—found himself.

I confess that I entertained my own doubts about Walter's sanity when he once again took in one of the winged dragons as if it were just a baby bird fallen out of its nest and in need of a little nursing back to health. I speak of his decision to care for Heep, of course, and as always, Walter did what he wanted regardless of my opinion. Even if it seemed to defy reason, Walter installed Heep in our camp with one leg tethered to a tree to keep him from working any mischief against us.

This precaution seemed superfluous for the first few days of the dragon's recovery, as Heep's illness made him quite manageable. Once we deposited him at the foot of his tree, Heep simply lay in a crumpled heap where he had been placed. He evidently moved occasionally, for periodically a glance in his direction would reveal him slightly repositioned, but his movements were too languid to merit much attention. Even when we presented him with food, he did not so much as lift his head, and needless to say, he did not do any stalking during this time.

Heep's inactive condition made it difficult at times to be certain whether he was still alive, and Walter could not resist periodically nudging the dragon's body with a foot or poking him with a stick to reassure himself on this point.

"You there—Heep," he would say. "Are you still with us?"

No matter how often Walter tried to engage the dragon, there was no response. Only the faintest chest rise—noticeable only with persistent starting—reassured us that he lived.

"I don't like this at all," Walter said after one such check. "You don't think he'll die, do you?"

"I don't know," I said.

"It seems like you could have at least tried to comfort me, Matthew."

Regardless of whether I offered any comforting words, Walter fretted about Heep's illness and moped around camp for several days. He would not let the invalid out of his sight lest the dragon take a turn for the worse in his absence, but at the same time, he bemoaned not being able to continue his observation of the *mokele-mbembe.*

"I wish he'd make up his mind to get better," he said. "All this malingering is interfering with my research."

With much fervent wishing on Walter's part, Heep did finally begin to improve, although his recovery came without warning. To all appearances, he continued languishing, and Walter continued poking or prodding him to gauge whether he still lived, until finally Walter's probing unexpectedly elicited a dramatic response: Walter jabbed Heep with his stick, and Heep's head lurched forward while his jaws snapped shut like a bear trap. He might have taken off Walter's arm if he had been more coordinated, but instead he caught the end of the stick in his mouth and chewed as if he meant to gnaw it down until he could reach Walter. (This did not work as planned, and the dragon was soon gagging on splinters while Walter safely retreated.)

"I'd say the worst is over," Walter said, "but now we need to worry about him trying to eat us again."

After his unexpected display of renewed vigor, Heep resumed eating the scraps of meat that we offered. Even with his newfound appetite, he remained fairly gaunt, but he certainly became livelier and gave us quite a run for our money when we tried feeding him; despite Heep's recent illness, it was all we could do to retain all of our limbs at feeding times. Encouraging as his recovery was, it also presented a new source of conflict between Walter and me.

"Now that he's better," I said, "don't you think maybe it's time we set him loose?"

"Oh, no," Walter said. "We couldn't possibly."

"Why not? I think he's ready to survive on his own."

"Maybe so, but it's safer for everyone—us and the other dragons—if he's tied up someplace. Think of him as a sort of pet."

By the time of Walter's internment of the winged dragon, I had become fairly desensitized to his eccentricities, so it did little but confirm my existing view of him. It did not occur to me how unheard-of it really was for someone to take in such a creature, or that it might inspire gossip among people who did not know Walter as well as I. When Henri visited town on his days off, however, he related our misadventures with the dragons, and as word of this new exploit inevitably made the rounds of the local villages, Walter's reputation would take a turn that I could never have foreseen.

*

For some time, we had no idea of the rumors that were circulating about Walter among the villagers. Nevertheless, word of Walter's exploits as a would-be dragon whisperer spread, and the people developed unusual ideas about him, not least of all because he kept a live *sasabonsam* the way a witch keeps a black cat. Finally our ignorance was rectified during one of our weekly supply runs to Toukalaka, where Walter noticed that the village children watched him furtively, glancing away if his gaze swept in their direction.

"Am I losing my mind," he said, "or is every child in this village watching me?"

Now that Walter mentioned it, I noticed their scrutiny, too.

"And if I look at them," Walter said, "they run away as if they're afraid of me."

"I see it, too," I said.

"Not that I want to be friends with a bunch of children, mind you, but it's still damned strange."

At first we could not guess the reasons for this odd reception, but eventually a particularly fearless young girl sauntered up to Walter, cocked her head inquisitively, and asked the following.

"Are you a sorcerer?"

"A sorcerer?" Walter squawked. "Why the devil would you say that?"

"Everybody says that you are a sorcerer. Is it true?"

For a moment, I was not sure how Walter would react. Some people would have been deeply offended, considering the possible negative connotation of being associated with the magical arts. Had he known what was to come, Walter might have been one of them, but instead he was positively delighted.

"Actually, you're quite right," he said. "I am a sorcerer, and you can tell all your little friends I said so."

Having confirmed the villagers' growing speculation, Walter continued in the following days to enjoy his new cachet as a local wizard. Even in our camp, he would periodically shake his head and chuckle or murmur to himself.

"Me, a sorcerer. Imagine! Just like Merlin the enchanter!"

Other than stroking Walter's sense of self-importance, this newfound notoriety did not initially change our daily lives, but being perceived as a sorcerer promised to be more useful when Walter became convinced that he was under magical attack himself. You see, once the Toukalaka feticheuse, Madame Meombe, announced her intention of running Walter out of town, the old man took to blaming his every misfortune on her magical machinations. If he so much as tripped on a root, Madame must have put it in his path, and if he suffered a paper cut, Madame must have sharpened the paper so as to inflict it (or so he maintained). Similarly, if any of his personal effects—which are reputed among magic users to give power over their owners—came up missing, that, too, was attributed to the scheming sorceress.

"Matthew," he said one day, "have you seen my hairbrush?"

"I don't think so," I said.

Walter clucked his tongue. "I don't like this one bit."

"What's the problem? You can borrow mine."

"That's not the point. I think that she-devil Meombe took it."

"Why would she do that?"

"Why do you think? To get some of my hair so that she can curse me."

My response, as you can imagine, was polite but skeptical.

"Just you wait," Walter said. "Something terrible is going to happen. I know it."

While I cannot wholeheartedly endorse the idea that magic works on a physical level, I have no qualms about acknowledging that it works on a psychological one. Purported victims of black magic have been known to worry themselves to death when threatened by a witchdoctor, regardless of whether magic could have effected the deed. Similarly, when one believes oneself to have been cursed, psychosomatic processes may explain the symptoms that the victim, under the influence of his belief system, credits to magic.

Whether psychosomatic or magically-induced, Walter began to

experience symptoms. These consisted of sharp, sudden pains in various parts of his body, and at first they concerned me greatly due to their similarity to the signs of certain life-threatening (but purely physical) ailments. The first of these pains struck while we were watching the dragons; I heard a yelp and whirled to find Walter clutching his left arm.

"Matthew," he said, "there's a sharp pain in my arm and chest."

"Did you hurt yourself?" I asked.

"No, it just came on all of a sudden."

"Oh, God." I envisioned Walter keeling over then and there, miles from any hope of medical aid. "Do you think it's a heart attack?"

"What? No, of course not. I'm being cursed. That she-devil Meombe is probably poking nails into a doll."

Whatever its source, the phantom pain eventually receded (to my great relief), but it recurred in the coming days. Strangely, it was not connected with any injury, nor were there any objective signs of illness such as redness, swelling, or fever; the pain itself was the only symptom. Moreover, the pain did not stay in one part of Walter's body as I would have expected of a medical condition: one day his chest pained him, and the next he might complain about leg pain. After several days of Walter complaining without a visible injury or illness, I hope I can be forgiven if I privately thought he imagined the pain, having convinced himself that he was cursed.

Even if I doubted their source, Walter's complaints began shortly after his confrontation with the feticheuse and continued even after we learned of his newfound reputation as a magic user, at which point Walter's attitude toward the would-be attacks changed. Where before he had felt powerless to dissuade the feticheuse from her designs, now that Walter was considered a sorcerer himself, he was emboldened to confront her.

"You know, Matthew," he said, "it occurs to me that my reputation as an enchanter might also solve our problems with that beastly feticheuse."

"What are you going to do?"

"Why, I'm going to make her think twice about cursing me."

Knowing I could never dissuade the old man (but feeling distinctly foolish the whole time), I accompanied Walter and Henri into Toukalaka to confront a sorceress whose powers I doubted about pain that was quite possibly a figment of Walter's imagination. Upon our arrival at the fetish house, Walter delivered the following ultimatum, undoubtedly having conceived the idea that Madame Meombe might hesitate to tangle with a fellow sorcerer.

"You may have heard that I am something of a sorcerer myself," he said. "Now, up to this point, I've restrained myself out of professional courtesy. But if you don't leave me in peace, then I shall become angry and use my magic on you."

With this seemingly preposterous bluff, Walter returned to his beloved dragons and left Madame to contemplate his warning. Though I could not at the time have explained my unease, I questioned the wisdom of this particular strategy when Walter and I were alone.

"Are you sure that was a good idea?" I asked.

"She's already cursed me," Walter said. "What else can she do?"

"That's not it. I just have a bad feeling about capitalizing on your, er, reputation."

"Well, now who's being superstitious? Really, Matthew, everything will be fine. You worry too much."

There's no telling whether Madame actually believed that Walter had the power to retaliate against her, although I suspect she was too clever to fall for his threat without some demonstration that he could actually follow through. In any event, Walter did not suffer from the phantom pains in the coming days, and he believed that he had daunted the feticheuse into abandoning her designs. If Walter was tempted to exult in having leveraged his reputation so successfully, however, he was about to learn that being perceived as a sorcerer is perhaps more dangerous than being targeted by one.

*

Magic users—and suspected magic users—tread a dangerous path in Africa, just as they have in most parts of the world at one time or another. Would-be sorcerers earn praise and accolades when they seemingly cure the sick or end a drought, but gratitude for the benefits mingles with mistrust of the supernatural powers. When ill fortune befalls, even perfectly normal illness or injury, witchcraft is apt to be suspected, in which case reputed magicians will be among the first to be accused. Needless to say, the suspicion of witchcraft is especially strong when the would-be sorcerer has previously threatened the selfsame ill fortune that has occurred, and by threatening to use his perceived sorcery against Madame Meombe, Walter placed himself in just such a position.

Little suspecting that Walter's threat might come back to haunt us, Walter, Henri, and I made our usual visit to Toukalaka the week after our most recent confrontation with the feticheuse. This time, however, I immediately felt a change in our reception: even the adults looked at us askance now, and I had the distinct impression we had done something gravely wrong, though I could not have said what. My impression of having transgressed was heightened when the village council summoned us immediately upon learning of our arrival, but Walter was oblivious to the change of atmosphere.

"I assume they've thought up another fee for us to pay," he said.

Walter's misapprehension was promptly corrected, however, when we arrived at the village meeting house and the council's speaker addressed him gravely.

"You have been accused of witchcraft," he said.

"What?" Walter squawked. "Who the devil would accuse me of witchcraft?"

With this request, Walter's accuser was promptly brought forth, at which point the situation became clear. The mantle of white hair and necklace of fetishes gave away her identity as Madame Meombe, but otherwise I would hardly have recognized her when she staggered forth, bent as if walking into a strong wind. When she raised her head to face Walter, I could see that her eyes were sunken in dark circles and her cheekbones stood out as if with long illness.

"As you can see, *cher*," Madame said, "I have been unwell. The spirits, they tell me that a witch has made me ill."

"What the devil has that got to do with me?" Walter asked.

"The spirits, they tell me that you are the witch."

When Meombe delivered this pronouncement, I immediately guessed that she had contrived her seeming illness and the accusation of witchcraft to twist Walter's own threat against him. Judging from his reaction, Walter realized this, too, albeit too late to recall his hasty words.

"Bother," he said.

Regardless of Walter's tardy regrets, the council's questioning proceeded.

"Did you threaten to use your magic against her?"

"Well, yes," Walter said. "But I was only bluffing. I don't actually have any magical powers."

Even if I knew it was the truth, the village council was understandably reluctant to accept Walter's claim of powerlessness when he had expressly fostered his reputation as a sorcerer just days before. It was quickly agreed that a trial would be necessary to determine Walter's guilt or innocence of the crime of witchcraft.

There are any number of ways to try accused witches, with trial by ordeal being by far the most common, and two particular types of ordeal appear to predominate in Africa. The first involves heating a *panga* or similar blade over a fire and then touching it against the leg of the accused, who is adjudged a witch if the blade burns him or her. The second ordeal consists of orally administering a poisonous concoction called *mwavi* or *kikovero* (depending on which part of Africa) to a chicken and waiting to see if the chicken dies, in which case the accused is convicted. As you can doubtless imagine, both varieties of ordeal are biased in favor of finding the accused guilty, and refusal to submit to ordeal is deemed an admission of guilt.

There being no possibility of avoiding the ordeal, Walter was bound for immediate trial, where his guilt would be determined by *mwavi.* We gathered that Madame Meombe was to administer the ordeal in her capacity as feticheuse regardless of what some might consider an interest in the outcome, and she vanished for some minutes. Before we could hope for a reprieve, the feticheuse hobbled back into the meeting house, grasping a gourd in one hand while a struggling chicken, clutched by the legs in the other hand, beat its wings ineffectually against her hip.

"Really, madam," Walter said. "Trying me for witchcraft is one thing, but if you're going to hurt that chicken, I shall have to take exception."

"The bird only dies if you are guilty," Madame said.

"Oh, good. It should be fine, then."

Once it had begun, the *mwavi* ritual itself was surprisingly brief. As dispassionately as a veterinarian dosing a sick pet, Madame held the chicken fast against her breast with one hand and poured the gourd's contents into its mouth, splattering droplets of a noisome liquid all over herself and the bird in the process. Then she released the bird to circle jerkily around her feet, oblivious to the intense concentration that the crowd—Walter and myself included—now fixed upon it.

"If he is a witch," Madame commanded the bird, "die."

While the whole village watched the bird for signs of distress, I felt as if someone were sticking pins through the heart of my own poppet. This was not for fear that Walter actually was a witch, mind you, but due to the inherent bias in the test. The method of trying witchcraft was so apt to find Walter guilty—if you poison a chicken, then it is pretty likely to die—that only blind luck (which we hardly possessed in spades) could provide for an acquittal.

My concern with Madame's witch hunting methods proved justified when the chicken abruptly tottered and toppled over, where it lay unmoving with its petrified feet jutting at uncomfortable angles.

"There must be some mistake," Walter said. "I'm no witch."

"I am so sorry, *cher*," Madame said. "You must understand that I am not the one condemning you. It is the spirits."

Convicted witches may be punished in a variety of ways. The practice of burning witches alive is known in Africa and Europe alike, but the African practice of burying the convicted witch up to the neck in the path of voracious driver ants—rarely in use nowadays—appears to be unique. Other methods include drowning, lynching, or poisoning. Regardless of the method, the penalty for witchcraft has historically been death.

Knowing the capital nature of the offense in many cultures, I dreaded to hear the sentence, but Walter did not allow himself to be daunted.

"Fine," he said. "Now that you've convicted me, what do you mean to do? Kill me?"

Walter's defiance notwithstanding, a death sentence seemed like a concrete possibility for several excruciating minutes while the councilors mumbled their deliberations over Walter's punishment. Nor did the grave voice of the speaker, whom they deputized to deliver the sentence, offer any reassurance.

"You have been found guilty of witchcraft," he said, "and you must pay the price for what you have done."

This time, Walter visibly swallowed and refrained from commenting.

"The fine is 200,000 francs."[26]

Walter blinked. "You're not going to execute me?"

"No. We do not do that."

Thinking himself lucky to have gotten off so easily, Walter paid his fine and hastened away before the council could reconsider its judgment and impose a stiffer penalty.[27] To his credit, Walter learned his lesson at this point and stopped holding himself out as a sorcerer, no matter how much the pretension might have flattered his ego, and

---

[26]This amounts to approximately 350 U.S. dollars in today's currency.

[27]To be fair, the killing of witches is not sanctioned by the legal system of any African country, although vigilante killings of suspected witches occasionally take place.

determined to call less attention to his work with the dragons in the future. Unfortunately, his newfound humility could not recall the unwanted attention he had already attracted to himself and the dragons, about which we would shortly learn.

✱

If it seems like being accused and tried for witchcraft is the worst that could have come from Walter's infamy as a sorcerer-cum-dracontologist, then the reader has failed to anticipate the most damaging consequence of Walter's exploits becoming widely known, just as Walter and I did at the time. Far worse than risking his own hide, as far as Walter was concerned, would be to attract harm to the *mokele-mbembe* themselves, and that is just what Walter inadvertently did by failing to keep a lower profile. Traveling by means of the signal drums from village to village up and down the Likouala-aux-Herbes, news of an eccentric American's discovery of dragons reached a man whose interest in them was far from benevolent, and he accosted us in Toukalaka in the wake of Walter's trial.

"Excuse me," a man's voice called as we hastened out of town, "but are you Walter Spink?"

Upon investigation, the speaker proved to be a middle-aged but hale white man with graying hair and a week's worth of matching stubble stippling his jaw and cheeks, accompanied by a retinue of village men bearing packs and crates.

"I am Walter Spink," Walter said, squinting as if it would help him recognize the stranger. "Do I know you?"

"No," the man said.

"Then how the devil do you know about me?"

"I've heard the most interesting stories from the villagers—"

"I can only imagine."

"—And I was wondering if they're true."

"Who the devil are you?"

Although the stranger was not literally the devil, he might as well have been, at least as far as Walter was concerned. His name was James Phillip Hartley, and as we ultimately confirmed by asking around the villages, he was one of the big game hunters whose kind had already taken the life of one of the *sasabonsam* and made an attempt on the *ngoubou.* We only learned details of Hartley's background later, but he had already made himself the bane of African wildlife through six countries, having reportedly shot more than 110 elephants, 23 rhinoceros, 89 lions, 42 leopards, and sundry buffalo, all for the cheap thrill of saying he had done so.

Even without knowing Hartley's history at the time of their meeting, Walter sensed that he should not be forthcoming about our work.

"Out of curiosity," he asked, "what have you heard about me?"

"I've heard a hell of a lot of things," Hartley said, "but the most interesting thing I've heard is that you've discovered a living dinosaur."

"A living dinosaur? How preposterous. There's no such thing."

"All the villagers think you found one."

"Yes, well, they just convicted me of witchcraft, too, so you shouldn't believe everything you hear about me. Now, if you don't mind, we shall be on our way."

With this curt dismissal, Walter undoubtedly hoped to convince Hartley that the supposed dragons of the Likouala were not worthy of further investigation, but of course we were not fortunate enough for the hunter to be dissuaded so easily. As later events showed, Hartley's interest remained piqued by the prospect of prehistoric survivors, and he lingered in the area, seeking *mokele-mbembe* independently regardless of whether Walter denied its existence. When he finally caught up to the dragons, there would be more at stake than just Walter's reputation.

CHAPTER XV

A BESTIARY OF CONGOLESE BEHEMOTHS

Unbeknownst even to many people who are otherwise fairly well-versed in cryptozoology, there are several distinct but obscure species of dragon in the Likouala in addition to the better-known *mokele-mbembe.* Other dracontologists, before and after Walter Spink, have collected accounts of animals that resemble prehistoric beasts—but not of the sauropod type—and bear names such as *emela-ntouka* and *nguma-monene.* During our time in the region, Walter and I were so hard-pressed to fully document the behavior of *mokele-mbembe* that we hardly had time to study the Likouala's lesser-known dragons, but we did periodically come across signs of them and even achieved several visual sightings.

We owed our first encounter with one of *mokele-mbembe*'s dragon cousins to the inquisitiveness of the *mokele-mbembe* herd's youngest member. I have already described Campe's tendency to roam away from the herd, usually in pursuit of food but sometimes merely to investigate some interesting new animal. Normally she did not venture very far and was quickly reunited with the other dragons, but finally she went too far and became separated from them altogether.

Campe's disappearance came to our attention some time after it actually happened, when we made contact with the herd one morning and found it one member short.

"I could be wrong, Matthew," Walter said, "but it looks to me as if there are only five dragons when there are supposed to be six."

"I think you're right," I said, and added after taking inventory of the dragons who were present, "Campe is missing."

"Heavens! You don't think Heep got her, do you?"

While Walter had every reason to believe that Heep was the only predator in the area large enough to seize Campe, his concern on this score proved unwarranted. At Walter's request, Mambunia sprinted to camp and confirmed upon his return that the *sasabonsam* was still tethered just where we had left him.

"If she hasn't been eaten," Walter asked, "then where the devil is she?"

Even if Campe did not seem to have been taken by a predator, the herd was nevertheless skittish without her. One or another of them was constantly glancing over a shoulder as if fearing to disappear next, and even while they browsed, they shifted anxiously from foot to foot. Occasionally one of the adult females lowed mournfully to the indifferent trees as if pleading with them for Campe's return, but this technique neither produced the errant juvenile nor eased the dragons' distress.

With his beloved dragons in such a disconsolate state, it was not long before Walter decided to take action.

"You know, Matthew," he said, "it occurs to me that we could find our scaly girl. You'll say it's unethical or hopeless, but I just can't bear to think of her lost and alone in the forest."

Though I have typically advocated against human interference in the lives of dragons and other unknown animals, even to save them, I have occasionally found that my conscience would disturb me even more at the thought of doing nothing. The possibility of leaving a child of whatever species to the mercies of the forest and its many hazards presented just such a troubling situation, and high-minded scientific principles seemed less important when weighed against Campe's safety. Under those circumstances, I agreed with Walter's proposal, and I think he derived as much pleasure from my agreement as he ultimately did from finding the lost dragon.

"Matthew, I'm impressed," he said. "Maybe I'm finally rubbing off on you, after all."

Having mutually decided to intercede on behalf of the lost dragon, Walter and I temporarily left the *mokele-mbembe* herd. With the assistance of the Bangombe, we meant to backtrack the herd's course so as to determine where Campe parted ways with the other dragons, from which point we would pursue the juvenile dragon's trail until we intercepted Campe herself. We would have been perfectly satisfied to just find Campe, but over the course of our search, we also discovered that the long-necked dragons are by no means the only dinosaur-like creatures that persist in the swamp forests of the Congo.

*

Many animals are rarely seen in the wild and are far more likely to be detected through traces they leave behind. Despite being fairly recognizable, the North American mountain lion is better-known from scratches, scat, and pugmarks than personal observation, and the North American Sasquatch is notorious for leaving only footprints without putting in any in-person appearance. Similarly, Walter and I only guessed that dragons other than *mokele-mbembe* were nearby when we discovered footprints that clearly did not belong to the more familiar long-necked variety.

Mokele-mbembe footprints can be distinguished from those of other dragons by several key features. Size alone will identify the prints of a fully-grown *mokele-mbembe*, for they are the size of a large frying pan and dwarf those of most other creatures, but this is less helpful in the case of juveniles whose feet are more commensurate in size to those of other species. On the other hand, *mokele-mbembe* of any age have the same three clawed digits at the front of their prints, and this feature is fairly diagnostic. As you can imagine, Walter and I became quite familiar with the shapes of *mokele-mbembe* prints as we retraced the herd's course to the site of Campe's departure and then followed the juvenile's trail.

As a result of our growing knowledge of *mokele-mbembe* footprints, Walter and I were quick to notice when we came across the print of a strange animal mixed among Campe's. Whatever the species of the print's owner, it was larger by far than the young *mokele-mbembe*'s and scalloped along the front with the impressions of four splayed but rounded toes. Try as we might, Walter and I could neither reconcile it with our experience of the long-necked dragons' prints nor identify it with any other animal we knew, and we were obligated to consult our guides' expertise.

"What the devil kind of animal made this print?" Walter asked.

"It is an animal," Ekianga said, "called *emela-ntouka*."

"*Emela-ntouka*," Mambunia agreed.

Our Bangombe informants confirmed that horned dragons very much like *ngoubou* exist in the Likouala region under the name *emela-ntouka*, which translates quite literally as "the killer of elephants." As the name implies, the horned dragons of the Likouala periodically kill elephants just as their cousins of the Cameroon savanna do, and they use the same weapon: one great horn on their snouts. Despite these similarities, *emela-ntouka* appear to be a distinct species, for they are never, to my knowledge, reported with parietal spikes like *ngoubou*.

The discovery of a possible new species of horned dragon in the Congo was of course quite compelling, but under the circumstances, our errand precluded us from doing much more than observing the print in passing.

"As much as it breaks my heart to forego the opportunity to study another new dragon," Walter said, "we really must find our scaly girl before something happens to her."

Even if Walter could not indulge his interest in *emela-ntouka* at the time, our pursuit of Campe soon disclosed the track of yet another variety of dragon, this time under circumstances more conducive to investigating its maker. We followed the juvenile *mokele-mbembe*'s track until it met that of another animal, this one with prints that were wider than those of the sauropod dinosaurs but bore five toes—too many for any species of dragon we had yet seen. Walter and I did not recognize them, but the Bangombe identified them as belonging to yet another dragon.

"Good lord!" Walter said. "It's like we've stumbled into Conan Doyle's *Lost World* or Burroughs's *Land That Time Forgot.* What's this one called?"

"*Mbielu-mbielu-mbielu.*"

Unlike *mokele-mbembe*, which are recognized by their long necks, and *ngoubou* or *emela-ntouka*, which are known for their horned faces, *mbielu-mbielu-mbielu* are distinguished by a row of plates running down their backs. The feature is so diagnostic as to have inspired their name—"the animal with planks growing out of its back"—and is about all that is commonly known about the creatures among the peoples of the Likouala, although these dragons are believed to be strictly herbivorous in behavior. Even this minimal description of a dragon with a line of plates standing in a row down its back, however, raised an interesting possibility as to the creature's identity, which Walter was eager to test.

"I don't know about you, Matthew," he said, "but I only know of one creature in all of history that had anything like planks growing out of its backside."

Walter could not test his identification of *mbielu-mbielu-mbielu* in the usual manner because he had left his book of prehistoric animals in our camp, but unlike *emela-ntouka*, it seemed that we might have the opportunity to see the plated dragon in the flesh. Whereas the horned dragon had merely crossed Campe's track, the juvenile *mokele-mbembe*'s track intersected that of the *mbielu-mbielu-mbielu* and then proceeded alongside it, as if the two creatures had met and then traveled together. Assuming the dragons had continued their seeming association, we could fulfill our errand to reunite the long-necked dragon with her family and satisfy our curiosity as to the plated dragon at the same time.

"I'm most concerned about out scaly girl, of course," Walter said, "but I certainly wouldn't mind if we caught a glimpse of *mbielu-mbielu-mbielu*, too."

With his usual enthusiasm, Walter drove us on in pursuit of the *mbielu-mbielu-mbielu* and the young *mokele-mbembe*, who continued to travel together. While the dragons undoubtedly meandered and loitered here and there in their foraging, we pursued them directly and began to overtake them, as evidenced by fresher signs along the track. Soon we would catch up, at which point we would find that interacting with a live *mbielu-mbielu-mbielu* can be much more difficult than tracking it down.

The most delicate stage of tracking any animal is approaching it once you've finally found it. Many animals will not tolerate human beings approaching too closely, and most animals react poorly when surprised by our kind. This is true not only of dangerous carnivores but seemingly unassuming vegetarians: hippos, for example, react as violently as any predator when surprised by humans at a riverbend. Where the behavior of an animal is completely unknown, as in the case of the African dragons, even more caution is necessary to avoid agitating it when coming up from behind.

The possibility that we might not want to approach the *mbielu-mbielu-mbielu* too closely once we caught up to it only occurred to me when the Bangombe reported that the dragons had passed through just a few minutes ahead of us, whereupon I realized that I had never considered how the plated dragon would behave when confronted by two nosy dracontologists and their guides.

"Do you think *mbielu-mbielu-mbielu* is dangerous?" I asked Walter.

"You know," Walter said. "I never really thought about it.

Perhaps we should ask the Bangombe."

We settled the question by consultation with our guides, who averred that *mbielu-mbielu-mbielu* were not reputed to be particularly pugnacious.

"*Mbielu-mbielu-mbielu* do not attack people," Ekianga said.

"They do not attack," Mambunia agreed.

With this reassurance, I was more at ease as we neared the end of our pursuit, and suddenly the Bangombe announced that we had come upon the *mbielu-mbielu-mbielu* whether I was ready or not.

"*Mbielu-mbielu-mbielu* is right ahead," Ekianga said, pointing.

"Right ahead," Mambunia agreed.

Despite our guides' assurance of the dragon's presence, neither Walter nor I could make out an animal in the direction they had indicated. If it was there, the dragon must have circled behind the shrubs and stunted trees at our approach, for looking ahead we only saw some ten-foot-tall ochol trees poking up over the heads of the shrubs, with here and there a massive spatulate leaf of a type I didn't recognize fanning out behind the ochol.

"Where is it?" Walter asked. "I don't see anything."

Even as he spoke, Walter took a step forward, at which point the foliage came to life as if enchanted. The unfamiliar leaves lurched into motion behind the ochol, and I perceived that they were plates attached to a tall hump of back, all of them furred with a verdigris of algae so that they blended among the plants. Having perceived the body, I was able to trace its front end dwindling to a reptilian head, and at the same time, a long, thick member bristling with thorny spikes swung out from the opposite end of the body and arced toward us, passing so close to the top of Walter's head that his hair stood on end with the wind of its passage even as Walter himself simply gawked.

"Just as I thought, Matthew," Walter said, seemingly oblivious to his close call, "it's a *Stegosaurus*."

More than one dracontologist has speculated that *mbielu-mbielu-mbielu* might be a surviving *Stegosaurus* or *Kentrosaurus*, based largely upon the diagnostic plates that serrate its backside. While I cannot vouch that *mbielu-mbielu-mbielu* are bona fide stegosaurs or descendents thereof, the resemblance is certainly suggestive: when the plated back is rounded off with the small head and spiked tail, the animal we encountered could have detached itself from the appropriate page of Walter's book of dinosaur illustrations. Given the physical resemblance and Walter's enthusiasm at finding a putative *Stegosaurus*, quibbling over phylogeny seems petty.

Even as Walter remarked upon the likeness of the dragon to the stegosaurs, the *mbielu-mbielu-mbielu* thrashed the thorny tail that contributed to the resemblance. With a jerk of its hindquarters, the plated dragon swung its spiky bludgeon in an arc like a mace, and it would have gone badly for us if we had been in its path. Though we had fortunately withdrawn far enough at the first swing that the second one found only air, the leafy shrapnel that exploded from the injured brush could have been our flesh and blood if we had not moved back as quickly as we did.

The way the dragon kept lashing its tail at us suggested agitation even though we lacked a frame of reference, and this reception was especially puzzling in light of our guides' representations that this was not a dangerous animal.

"Why the devil is it so touchy?" Walter asked. "I thought these plated dragons were supposed to be friendly."

"*Mbielu-mbielu-mbielu* are usually peaceful," Ekianga said.

"Peaceful," Mambunia agreed.

"Something unusual must have happened," Ekianga added.

"Something unusual," Mambunia agreed.

Before we could wonder for too long at the *mbielu-mbielu-mbielu*'s uncharacteristically aggressive behavior, its likely source revealed itself. There was a familiar honk, and Campe emerged from the brush behind the plated dragon and trotted in our direction, paying the angry *mbielu-mbielu-mbielu* no more heed than if it really were one of the shrubs.

"There you are, you naughty girl," Walter said. "You have no idea how much worry you've caused everybody, but I suppose I shall have to forgive you."

Even with Walter remonstrating her, Campe would have come to his outstretched hand and investigated his person for concealed treats, but the plated dragon forestalled their reunion. With an irritable *chuff*, the *mbielu-mbielu-mbielu* darted in front of the juvenile *mokele-mbembe* to stand between her and Walter, flourishing its mace of a tail threateningly in case physically blocking us had not already communicated its intention to keep us away from the smaller dragon.

"This is extraordinary," Walter said. "It's as if it's protecting our scaly girl. Do you suppose this is why it's being so aggressive?"

It is common knowledge that wild animals are particularly touchy when humans approach young of their own kind, but it is not unheard-of for animals to adopt and protect representatives of another species. While this is commonly seen among animals in captivity, such as when an ape in a zoo bonds with a kitten, it occasionally occurs in the wild as well; one particularly striking example is that of a wild lioness on Kenya's Samburu Reserve, named Kamunyak by ecologists, who adopted a series of baby oryx antelopes and even went so far as to defend them from predators and other lions. Given the *mbielu-mbielu-mbielu*'s aggressive reaction to the prospect of our interacting with Campe, it seemed that a similar relationship had developed between them, and we guessed that the plated dragon was a female and called her Raksha after Mowgli's adoptive animal mother from *The Jungle Books.*

Regardless of the reason for *mbielu-mbielu-mbielu*'s protectiveness for a member of another species, it was most certainly inconvenient for our plans. All things being equal, we would have taken custody of Campe and ushered her back to her family, but the plated dragon would not have it. Any time the juvenile *mokele-mbembe* made as if to approach us, or we attempted to approach her, Raksha threw herself in between and nudged Campe sternly back with her snout while shaking her spiky tail at us like an angry fist.

"As grateful as I am to you for helping our scaly girl, madam,"

Walter said, "I think you're taking it too far. After all, you're no more a mother to her than I am."

Walter's attempts to reason with the plated dragon were as effective as you probably expect, and she continued to isolate Campe from us until even Walter acknowledged the futility of trying to come between them.

"It's no use, Matthew," he said after many frustrated attempts to coax Campe to himself. "There's no getting around her."

"What do you want to do?" I asked.

"There's nothing we can do but stay close. She'll have to eventually realize we don't mean any harm, and then maybe she'll let us take our scaly girl home."

Despite Walter's hope that the *mbielu-mbielu-mbielu* would get used enough to our presence to relax her guard, she showed no signs of relaxing her vigilance in the coming days. When Raksha continued to guard Campe against our attentions, we took to following the two dragons at a discreet distance, spending our nights in the wilderness sleeping in leaf-thatched huts à la the Bangombe, so as to keep them under surveillance pending an opportunity to deprive the *mbielu-mbielu-mbielu* of her ward. There is no telling how long we might have waited for the plated dragon to become habituated enough to relax her jealous watch, but it became unnecessary to win her over when the presence of a seemingly greater threat to her fosterling drew her attention away from us.

*

Though human beings may be unwelcome, they are not the dragons' natural predators, and it stands to reason that dragons will quickly forget about us if one of their natural enemies appears. The problem with relying on such a distraction is waiting for an animal to come along that is fearsome enough to worry a grown dragon, for typical predators such as leopards and crocodiles would be too small to overcome all but the smallest juvenile dragons. Even after all that

Walter and I saw during our time in Africa, I hesitate to say for certain whether a flesh and blood predator stalks the likes of *mokele-mbembe* and *mbielu-mbielu-mbielu*, but the *mbielu-mbielu-mbielu* that had adopted Campe nevertheless saw something that was so terrifying to her that it occupied her full attention to the exclusion of all else.

When Raksha first perceived this new threat and responded with her accustomed tail-lashing display, Walter and I were so used to the dragon's defensive behavior being directed toward us that we mistook its object.

"I don't understand why she's in a huff this time," Walter said. "We haven't gone near either of them all day."

While Walter was speaking, however, I noticed that Raksha's attention was not directed toward us but over our heads and into the forest. It goes without saying that anything that could give a dragon of her size and armament pause would positively scare the hell out of a puny human like me, and with growing dread, I tracked the focus of the dragon's gaze and beheld the cause of her unease.

"I don't think her display is meant for us," I said.

"What the devil do you mean?" Walter squawked. "And why the devil are you so pale all of a sudden? You look as if you'd seen a ghost."

I don't know whether it was actually a ghost, but at the same time, I can vouch that the *mbielu-mbielu-mbielu* was not jumping at shadows because I saw something, too. I would frankly have slept much more comfortably if I could have convinced myself the thing was a ghost or apparition and not a flesh and blood creature, but even now, having had 30 years to reflect on the experience, I cannot be certain. All I can do here is describe what I perceived and let the reader speculate as to its nature.

Between the gloom of the forest and the distance between us, I could not discern the fine details of the thing's appearance. Even so, I made out a bipedal, almost bird-like silhouette, albeit a bird that was two stories high and dangled short, clawed forelimbs from its chest in lieu of wings. The shape of its immense head, too, was more reminiscent of a crocodile than a bird, right down to the crooked jaw that hung open and was serrated with the silhouettes of a phalanx of teeth like knives. Like any boy who has ever been fascinated by prehistoric life, I recognized the silhouette; it resembled one of the carnivorous theropods that stalked *mbielu-mbielu-mbielu* and *mokele-mbembe*'s prehistoric ancestors, but the reasoning part of my brain knew it could not be what it seemed because popular prejudice and the fossil record gratefully show that such terrors are long since extinct.

Even if I was loath to name the form that had appeared to me, Walter had no such reservation when he saw it.

"Gracious, Matthew!" he said. "That looks just like a *Tyranno*—"

"It's not," I said.

"But you didn't even let me say!"

While Walter and I tried to process this phantasm, for want of a better word, its behavior did little to help us resolve its reality. Other than staring down the affronted *mbielu-mbielu-mbielu*, it made no move to approach, and there was no confrontation between the animals that might have conferred objective reality upon the thing. Instead, the *mbielu-mbielu-mbielu* stood her ground, thrashing her spiky tail the whole time, and seemed determined not to take her eyes off the apparition for fear any inattention might provoke it to an attack that was all too carnal. This standoff had the effect of leaving Campe effectively unattended, as I gradually realized while the initial shock of my sighting wore off.

"Whatever it is," I said, "it's got all of Raksha's attention."

"And with good reason, too," Walter said. "I'm fairly fascinated by it myself."

"My point is that she's not watching Campe. If we move quickly, we can get her away from here."

"Oh, of course. How silly of me."

Having been recalled to his original purpose, Walter resumed trying to coax Campe toward him while her adoptive mother kept the would-be predator at bay.

"Come here, you naughty girl," he said. "I just may have a treat for you."

While Walter beckoned to the young *mokele-mbembe*, I monitored the *mbielu-mbielu-mbielu* lest she perceive what Walter was about and decide to interpose an objection. Fortunately, whether she noticed or not, Raksha was no more willing to turn her back on the seeming theropod than I would have been, and Campe sauntered to Walter's outstretched hand and sniffed up his sleeve for food, at which point the Bangombe supplied a liana rope that Walter passed around the juvenile dragon's neck and used to lead her away. Not only did the plated dragon permit this, but her fierce display covered our subsequent retreat (on the chance that the thing in the forest was a flesh and blood creature that might otherwise have pursued us).

Even though we were poised to make a clean escape, Walter could not help hesitating, and he cast a longing look back over his shoulder at the fearful apparition.

"I would love to stay and get a closer look," he said finally, "but then again, if that's what I think it is, we'd better get our scaly girl away from here."

We ushered Campe back into the forest and ultimately to the protection of her own kind while the *mbielu-mbielu-mbielu* was still bristling and thrashing her tail at the would-be intruder, and we did so with an alacrity suitable to the thing's theropod appearance even if I doubted it could be what it seemed. When we last sighted them, Raksha was still lashing her spiny tail and glowering at the thing in the forest, which still had neither advanced nor withdrawn. We did not witness the resolution of the standoff, and I cannot guess its outcome, but we successfully returned Campe to the herd while Raksha was distracted, regardless of the nature of the distraction.[28]

Once Campe had been reunited with her family, we could comfortably speculate regarding the seeming theropod without the

---

[28]Walter convinced himself that Tiamat became more tolerant of us from this point, presumably in gratitude for the service we had rendered, but it is equally possible that she just finally got desensitized to our company.

immediate threat that it would eat us if it proved to be real. The nature of the thing's appearance prevented us from saying whether it was a flesh and blood animal or some strange folie à trios shared by ourselves and the plated dragon, and the Bangombe afforded no assistance in sorting out the truth, denying that they had seen anything. Ultimately, it was anybody's guess what we had really seen, but Walter favored the least likely but most thrilling (to him at least) explanation.

"I don't care what you say, Matthew," Walter said. "It was clearly a *Tyrannosaurus*."

"How could a *Tyrannosaurus*"—I stumbled over the name in my hesitation to even consider the possibility—"be here?"

"How the devil should I know? But it certainly looked like one."

"I just can't believe it, whatever it looked like."

My skepticism at this point might seem strange, considering that I had already had encounters with dragons resembling pterosaurs, ceratopsians, sauropods, and stegosaurs, only to draw a seemingly arbitrary line at the putative carnosaur. I could reason that it is more credible for relatively peaceful vegetarians to survive unnoticed for so long than a massive carnivore, and that would be true, but it would not be the full extent of my opposition to the idea. I do not mind confessing that I was terrified at the possibility that such a creature might be stalking the very same swamp forest as we were, and doubting its existence became a defense mechanism. I slept better by explaining the seeming *Tyrannosaurus* away as a ghost or hallucination and would have been perfectly content to end our research with the many Congolese dragons we had already discovered.

CHAPTER XVI

BATTLE (AND OTHER INTERACTIONS) OF THE SEXES

Ordinarily, male and female *mokele-mbembe* do not mingle in the wild, as I have previously said. Juvenile males live and forage with their herds, at least until they reach maturity, and adult males may be periodically—and briefly—encountered at feeding or watering sites. Otherwise, males live either alone or in small bachelor herds and do not seek out females any more than the females seek them out. The obvious exception is the one activity for which the presence of both sexes is something of a sine qua non, by which I of course mean mating. This is yet another activity that Walter Spink and I were the first Westerners to observe.

It was some time into our association with the herd when we observed mating, and for the first months of our study of the forest dragons, we had not seen a male other than young Fafnir. For that reason, we had no idea how the herd would react if one appeared, and Walter misapprehended the situation when Tiamat made her customary threat display by way of greeting a male dragon.

"Good heavens," he said. "Is it the *Tyrannosaurus*?"

Although something large was moving through the forest,

snapping branches from the hoary trees with the massive hump of its shoulders as it passed, its profile was immediately distinguishable from the bipedal theropod Walter (oddly) hoped to see. I recognized the familiar quadrupedal body plan with the long neck and tail, held parallel to the ground, of another *mokele-mbembe.* The sawtooth profile created by a row of spines along its neck told me that it was a male.

With this recognition came a promising opportunity to observe new behavior in the dragons.

"It should be very interesting to see how the herd reacts to him," Walter said once I had identified the newcomer.

Evidently the other dragons were less intrigued with the newcomer than Walter and I were. I have already indicated that Tiamat greeted the male defensively; even after she had assured herself of the stranger's nature, she kept herself between the herd and the interloper and eyed him warily at all times. As for the rest of the herd, Ceto remained oblivious as we would have expected, but the juveniles, too, went about their browsing without paying him any heed. The male, for his part, was content to prowl far enough back to avoid provoking Tiamat to outright attack, and after loitering about for a good hour or so, shadowing the herd's slow progress through the forest, he went on his way.

"I must say," Walter said, "that was rather anticlimactic."

We might have ascribed this first encounter to chance, but we reconsidered its significance when male dragons suddenly seemed to be coming out of the woodwork. On the second day after this meeting, and again on the third day, a male *mokele-mbembe* approached the herd while it was browsing. Moreover, the varying patterns of the neck spines showed that a different individual visited the herd each time. To see multiple males in close succession when we had seen none for many weeks seemed to be the product of more than mere happenstance.

If the males were intentionally seeking out the herd, there was one likely reason, which Walter and I quickly guessed.

"I don't know about you, Matthew," Walter said, "but I can only think of one reason for all these males to be loitering around all of a sudden. They must be looking to mate."

Like many species, *mokele-mbembe* have periodic mating cycles. Females experience cyclical estrus periods during which they become sexually receptive and fertile, alternating with long stretches of unwillingness to mate. These are staggered, so that only one of the females in a given herd will become estrous at a given time. Males similarly go through intermittent states of heightened sexual activity similar to the rutting of some mammalian species. Rutting males are attracted, and indeed males' rutting state may be activated, by the pheromones of an estrous female.

Although we guessed fairly easily that one of the females in the herd must be in estrus to be attracting the males, identifying which of them it was took somewhat more effort. *Mokele-mbembe* females do not exhibit visible symptoms of estrus such as enlarged genitalia (that we could perceive) or lordosis.[29] The only objective signs of estrus are the presence of aroused males and the act of actually mating with one of them, and the females in our herd all appeared to be equally indifferent to the prospect.

In the absence of outward signs of estrus, Walter and I had to make an informed guess, but we reasoned that Echidna and Scylla were probably the only females of breeding age in the herd other than Tiamat, who was too hostile toward the males to be a likely candidate. Our initial thought as to which of these two was actually ready to mate, on the other hand, was mere speculation.

"It must be Scylla," Walter said.

"What makes you so sure?" I asked.

"You see how she mothers the little one, as if she's practicing to be a mother herself. It's almost certainly a sign of sexual maturity."

This hypothesis was not entirely unreasonable, but it was not borne out when further observation finally showed us which female was actually in estrus. Though we could not for the life of us discern

---

[29]Lordosis refers to the posture involving downward arching of the back that is assumed by females of some species, usually mammals, during mating.

any outward sign that either Scylla or Echidna was ready to mate, our observation of the males' behavior soon gave us the missing piece of the puzzle. Although they would not attempt to physically approach in the face of Tiamat's obvious objection, the males gazed wistfully and trumpeted repeatedly as if to call the receptive female to them. When our two putative bachelorettes were close together, it was impossible to discern which was the object of the longing glances and calls, but when they separated, it became plain from the focus of the males' attention which female they pursued.

Echidna was the object of the males' entreaties.

Even though Walter and I realized that Echidna was attracting the males, the dragoness herself remained disinterested. No matter how perseveringly the males called to her, she was far more interested in the pressing business of feeding her face, which burrowed greedily among the foliage without so much as a spare glance for her admirers. (Nor did she seem particularly alluring with her cheeks and throat puffing out, bullfrog-like, as she stuffed herself with browse, but this did not dissuade the males any more than her inattention did.)

The males might have persisted regardless of their success (as males of our own species are wont to do), but Tiamat left them little choice in the matter. After affording them a certain amount of time to press their suits, her patience would inevitably be exhausted. At that point, she pawed the earth and bellowed her own display, occasionally punctuated by a mock charge, and the males would finally leave.

"I never thought I would hear myself saying this," Walter said, "but old Tiamat and I finally agree on something. Those interlopers need to move along and leave our scaly girls alone. Now, why the devil are you looking at me that way?"

"I'm just surprised," I said. "I would have thought you'd welcome the opportunity to witness mating behavior."

"Normally, I would, but this is different."

"How so?"

"I just feel responsible for the young ones. Their biological father is not in the picture, and I feel as if I'm standing *in loco pater*. And no father wants to think of his girls growing up and doing…that."

Regardless of Walter's desire to keep her innocent, Echidna was nevertheless physically mature, judging from the persistence with which she continued to attract the males. Whether now or in some future estrus cycle, it seemed inevitable that she would eventually overcome her oral fixation and heed the call of her other instinct. Aside from the desirability of propagating an obviously rare species, another concern would soon urge that she do so as soon as possible: the hazard of having several sexually charged—and frustrated—male dragons loitering in the vicinity of the herd while we studied it.

*

In most rutting species, males experience several behavioral changes while rutting in addition to the obvious one of pursuing females. During their sexually active period, they may wallow in mud, mark their presence with urine, or make unusual calls. More importantly, they may also become more aggressive as a consequence of their increased testosterone levels. This last trait is almost universal among rutting animals, so it should come as no surprise, given the other similarities of their mating style, that *mokele-mbembe* males also become more temperamental at mating times.

The males had not demonstrated any overt aggression at their first few appearances, but as Echidna remained in estrus—and her suitors remained unsatisfied—we began to perceive that the males were irritable, to say the least. Occasionally one or the other of them would knock over a tree or uproot a bush and toss it aside with abrupt, jerky gestures that bespoke frustration. When one of them was in our path before we could make our morning contact with the herd, we (wisely, to my thinking) avoided provoking them, knowing that they were already on edge.

"I think maybe we should take the long way around and give him plenty of room," I said the first time we found one of the agitated dragons in our way.

"Is that really necessary?" Walter asked. "It will take a long time."

"Maybe, but they're bound to be temperamental. Under the circumstances, I think we should keep our distance."

"I suppose you're right, but it's terribly frustrating. It's bad enough having hundreds of males mooning over my scaly girl without them delaying me in getting to my work."

By exercising a little caution, Walter and I managed to avoid being the direct recipients of the males' aggression, but lest we decide we had misjudged their dispositions, they amply demonstrated their short tempers in their interactions with each other. Over the course of Echidna's estrus, it was common for two or more of the males to intercept the herd at the same time, and it was only natural that several males vying for the affection of one female should be unfriendly toward each other. Consequently, there were frequent squabbles and skirmishes between the males seeking Echidna's favor.

There were two major contenders in these various clashes, and seeing them close together in combat enabled us to distinguish them by physical features and temperament. The largest, whom we called Typhon, was missing several spines along his neck, and numerous scars cross-hatched his pebbly hide. His appearance vouched for his weathering many skirmishes, and his slow but steady and deliberate way of moving and engaging the other dragons bespoke his age and experience. His chief competitor was Nidhogg, a robust younger male with few scars and a precipitate manner that made him appear cocky; he frequently instigated a confrontation when Typhon, more confident in his prowess, would have coexisted peacefully. A third male who regularly appeared, Smok, was gaunt for a *mokele-mbembe*, with a shorter neck and blunter spines, but he was too unassuming to confront the others: he gave them a wide berth, and he retreated submissively, lowering his head as if in deference, if any of his competitors so much as grunted at him.

Just as male deer lock antlers, male *mokele-mbembe* competing for mates have their own signature combat style. The ritual begins with the combatants exchanging bellows so vehement they seem like they should flatten the trees in their path. This is often enough to dissuade the competitor from pressing his suit—it certainly discouraged Smok, who withdrew even when he was not its target—but when it is not, a physical confrontation ensues. This may consist of the dragons locking their necks together and wrestling, or rearing in tripodal fashion on their hind legs and tails while shoving each other with their forelegs. The first to give way is the loser, and he will cede the field of combat, at least until the mating dance resumes the next day.

No matter how many times we watched Typhon and Nidhogg come together in the manner I just described, I could never help wincing, anticipating a clap like thunder. Though there was no such explosion, I would open my eyes to find them straining against each other, muscles moving like great boulders under their skin. They stumbled back and forth, still locked together, and moved forward or backward depending on whose strength favored him at a given moment. Finally the weaker male would collapse backward, often toppling over on his side like a landslide of flesh, and leave the winner in possession of the position closest to the herd while the loser ignominiously righted himself and retreated.

Nidhogg eagerly initiated these skirmishes, spoiling to confront his rival, but he almost invariably exhausted his strength so early that Typhon successfully repelled him merely by conserving his full strength until his competitor ran out of steam. Perhaps Nidhogg should have been discouraged after a few such losses, but hope sprung eternal in the brash bachelor's breast; he continued to assay his strength against the older male, and the forest fairly trembled with their combat for several weeks.

With two dragons repeatedly coming to blows so close by, trying to observe the herd was not only difficult but potentially dangerous, an opinion that I shared with Walter to little avail.

"I think you're overreacting, Matthew," he said. "They're too busy fighting each other—and mooning over my scaly girl—to take any interest in us."

While it was true that the dragons' aggression was not directed toward us during these squabbles, this did not by any means rule out our danger. Just as a pair of brawling humans might take out furniture or mistakenly land a blow upon an innocent bystander, the feuding dragons were apt to knock over a tree on top of us or simply trample us under foot without ever even noticing. We scrambled out of the way whenever we sensed hostilities rising, but the speed with which a confrontation might erupt between the dragons made it impossible to guarantee that we would have enough notice to escape.

After successfully retreating out of the way often enough, Walter and I were finally caught between the two twitterpated dragons without warning, and we were nearly trampled during their combat. We had been following the herd as usual, and we had become so desensitized to the males that we took no alarm when Typhon joined us to moon over the estrous female. Unfortunately, I was so distracted by Walter's complaints about hundreds of unworthies pursuing his scaly girl that I did not hear Nidhogg approach until his challenge rung over our heads.

"There they go again," Walter said. "Bothering my poor, scaly girl with their unwanted affections. Matthew, what the devil is wrong with you?"

Though Walter had not yet noticed anything wrong, I had perceived that the younger dragon was approaching from our left while the older dragon bellowed his response to the challenge from our right. By a trick of our ill luck, we were within their most direct path by which the dragons might confront each other. Despite my realization, I hesitated to move or shout a warning to Walter for fear of provoking the very charge I meant to escape, and my paralysis lasted just long enough for the dragons to finish trading threats and initiate combat in earnest.

Nidhogg and Typhon lurched into motion and came at each

other like medieval knights tilting, with their long, spiny necks jutting straight ahead of them like lances. The earth quaked as if it meant to give way under our feet, and I don't think we could have run even if we had had the presence of mind. I had just enough time to throw myself protectively over Walter, but then there was nothing left to do but listen to the swelling thunder of the footfalls advancing toward us from both sides.

When the footfalls stopped and I remained intact, I dared to open my eyes and found myself in shadow where one of the mountainous bodies eclipsed the sun. Slowly I glanced up to behold the dragons' mighty necks locked together like mating snakes two stories over our heads. As they strained against each other, the dragons shifted their feet alternately to press their advantage or hold their ground, and in this manner they slowly revolved around Walter and me. This made escape to either side problematic: every time I thought the dragons had left a gap through which we might retreat, a giant sidestepping foot came down where we would have been if we had bolted. Finally there was nothing to do but to make a break for it as soon as an opening appeared and hope for the best, in which way we successfully fled the field of combat, leaving the dragons to settle their differences (in Typhon's favor, as always).

Though we escaped unharmed, this incident drove home to me how dangerous it really was to have the males loitering around picking fights with each other. If Echidna did not select a mate soon, we were apt to be crushed under foot during one of her suitors' incessant skirmishes.

Out of mounting concern for being trampled, I watched Echidna closely in the following days in hopes of seeing her take an interest in the males, and initially I was encouraged. Though she had always ignored her petitioners before, now she paused in her browsing to crane her sinuous neck and inspect them when they beseeched. I was leery of misleading myself through wishful thinking, but still it seemed as if instinct was beginning to overwhelm her disinterest, and I felt cautiously encouraged that she would finally venture beyond the protection of the herd and that nature would take its course from there.

I should have known it wouldn't be that easy.

Regardless of dawning instinct, just when Echidna took a step toward one of the mooning bachelors as if in preparation to explore some newfound attraction, her attention was called elsewhere. Abruptly she ambled in the opposite direction, and she did so eagerly, with none of the vacillation that characterized her contemplation of her would-be mates. For a moment her massive body and pumping legs blocked the object of her interest from my view, but soon I beheld Walter coaxing her toward himself with a handful of *malombo.*

"That's a good girl," he said. "Come on over here."

The dragoness obligingly approached the old man, who stroked her face lovingly with his left hand while she plucked the fruit from his right.

"There, girl," he said, "isn't that better than mingling with those nasty men?"

"Walter, what are you doing?" I asked. "I think she was about to pick a mate."

"I daresay she was, Matthew. I'm trying to stop her."

"Whatever you might feel, I don't think it's ethical for us to interfere if she's ready to mate. And more importantly, we're going to be killed by the males if they don't mate soon."

"I'm sure you're exaggerating, Matthew, but I'll take it under advisement."

When we ended the conversation, I thought I had made my position clear, but I should have realized that "taking it under advisement" meant that Walter planned on ignoring me (as he usually did when my advice conflicted with his immediate desires). Sure enough, Walter tried to collect *malombo* on our way to contact the herd the next day, but fortunately his previous day's efforts had exhausted the fruit within his reach.

"Will you help me here, Matthew?" he asked. "I can't quite reach this *malombo.*"

"Are you planning on using it to distract Echidna?"

"Of course. Why do you ask?"

While I normally went along with Walter's various schemes under protest, I was nevertheless convinced that his meddling was once again putting us in imminent physical danger. Under those circumstances, and having already successfully challenged Walter during our observation of the *ngoubou*, I was braver than usual when it came to confronting him about micromanaging the mating dragons. More importantly, Walter was in no position to execute his scheme without someone of my height, so putting an end to his meddling was simply a matter of restating my position and refusing my aid.

"You astound me, Matthew," Walter said. "I had no idea you felt so strongly. I can't very well do this without you, so I suppose I shall have to reconcile myself to letting my scaly girl grow up."

"I think that's the right thing to do," I said.

"Yes, well, between you and me, I do hope you won't make a habit of opposing me on every little thing."

Having come to an understanding, Walter and I resumed our daily observation of the herd, and Walter proved true to his word; though he undoubtedly willed Echidna to choose chastity with all his might, he did not coax, cajole, or otherwise try to influence her. For my part, I privately wished for her to choose her mate. I am sure that the dragoness acted without regard for any of our wishes, but she still did as I had hoped: after some importuning from her suitors, she left off feeding and mingled with them, albeit in her accustomed indecorous manner, stumbling several times on the way to them.

"I suppose that settles it, then," Walter said. "She's going to mate with one of them."

Despite Walter's opposition and her own initial reluctance, Echidna finally came around to the prospect of mating. She might have been taken somewhat by surprise by her first estrus, but it seems clear that nature in its wisdom has conferred instincts to help newly fertile *mokele-mbembe* females navigate their maturity. Without necessarily grasping what was happening, Echidna was still drawn to the loitering males, and the only thing left standing between the she-dragon and the consummation of that instinct was the act of choosing her mate, which would happen in due course now that the other obstacles had been overcome.

Nature has devised a variety of criteria by which females might select their mates. The size and physical endowment of the males may be the basis of her selection, as in the case of *sasabonsam.* Depending on the species, mate selection may instead be based upon which male gives the most impressive call, or males may battle, with the winner acquiring the right to mate with his chosen female. Given the many skirmishes we had already observed, Walter and I suspected that the latter would play a part in the selection of mates among *mokele-mbembe*, although this did not prove to be true.

Regardless of whether our hypotheses concerning *mokele-mbembe* mating practices was accurate, Walter and I settled in to observe the anticipated climax of the dragons' mating ritual with enthusiasm. In this regard, I will say one thing for Walter: though he was not particularly gracious in defeat, he recovered from his disappointment quickly. When he could not dissuade Echidna from mating, he took an equally passionate interest in her choosing a quality mate from among her beaux.

"Now that she's about to choose one of them," he asked, "which one of them do you think it should be?"

"I hadn't really given it any thought," I said.

"I for one hope she picks Typhon. That Nidhogg is too vain and preening for my taste."

"One of the younger dragons might have a better chance of getting her pregnant."

"Nonsense, Matthew. You'd be surprised how virile an older male—whether human or dragon—can actually be. Besides, Typhon's won against Nidhogg every time. She's bound to mate with him."

(I would secretly have preferred for Echidna to favor my fellow omega male, Smok, but I kept my preference to myself.)

While her observers anticipated her choice in great suspense, the dragoness ambled past each male in turn, appraising them coolly. Though it was highly unlikely either of us could influence her choice, Walter volubly urged his favorite, crying out encouragement like a spectator at a horse race, when she inspected Typhon.

"That's it!" he said. "That's a good girl. Go to that one."

Regardless of Walter's exhortations, Echidna was no more minded to heed his wishes than if she had been a human adolescent and he her father. After considering Typhon (and without looking too closely at Smok), she indicated her choice by meandering toward Nidhogg and stopping just a few feet away from him, where she nickered almost like a horse. Nidhogg, for his part, accepted her interest with ennui, as if her affection were simply his due and the ritual of obtaining it a bore.

"I thought she would have shown better judgment," Walter said, shaking his head, "but I suppose there's no accounting for taste."

Once the female *mokele-mbembe* chooses a partner, the act of mating is relatively straightforward and does not involve further courtship. Without regard for anything approaching privacy, the coupling dragons step aside from the herd merely to afford ample space for their movements. The male then mounts the female from behind, bracing his front feet against her shoulders and straddling her tail with his pelvis while his external penis snakes into the female's cloaca. A few minutes later, the male climaxes, and the dragons part.

Echidna acquitted herself during this coupling with the awkwardness we would have expected, given her inexperience in the act and her accustomed clumsiness. When Nidhogg approached from behind and tried to climb her back, she honked in confusion and fled as if thinking the collision had been accidental. Even once she understood what the male meant to do, the mechanics of getting into position presented consternation; several times, for example, Echidna thrashed her tail just as Nidhogg tried to straddle her, and only his upper legs poised against her shoulder prevented him from toppling over. Nevertheless, they copulated with presumed success, for Nidhogg finally managed to assume the position against her backside, thrusting with youthful urgency, before eventually retiring away in apparent satisfaction. Once the male had left, Echidna remained where she was, not so much basking in the afterglow as processing a ritual she still did not quite understand.

While the dragoness reflected on her new experience, Walter continued to bemoan her choice.

"I still wish she'd chosen Typhon," he said.

(Privately, I wished that she had chosen Smok.)

Walter and I might both have saved ourselves some disappointment if we had not made an unwarranted assumption about mating among *mokele-mbembe.* Though we expected a dragoness to mate only once and with only one male, we ultimately learned that the estrus period of a female *mokele-mbembe* may linger for at least another week even after she has copulated. During that time, her suitors will continue to pursue her, and she will mate again, often with different partners.

Not suspecting that Echidna might couple again, we were surprised the next day when a sprightly trumpeting announced Typhon's return, followed shortly thereafter by Nidhogg and then Smok, albeit the last without fanfare. We were even more surprised when Echidna again engaged with her suitors, stepping with what appeared to be more assurance this time. To Walter's mingled amazement and satisfaction, after contemplating her choices, the dragoness accompanied Typhon on a brief courtship walk before mating with him.

"I'm not quite sure how I feel about this," Walter said. "It seems a little loose, but at least she chose the right one this time."

Regardless of Walter's mixed feelings, the dragons continued their courtship. Each day the three males returned, and Echidna took one of them for her lover in the manner I described previously; even

Smok had his chance. Gradually, however, Echidna's ardor for lovemaking dwindled, and feeding soon preoccupied her to the exclusion of troubling over the male dragons. For another two days, the males returned, still plighting their troth, but eventually their visits shortened and then ceased altogether.

Once Echidna's suitors had finally gone on their way, we had more leisure to consider the evolutionary significance of the mating practices we had observed, and the potential of the dragons' mating scheme was not lost on Walter.

"You know, Matthew," he said, "I just realized something: with all this mating, she's almost certain to get pregnant! I could be a grandfather, in a manner of speaking."

Ultimately, Echidna's courtships afforded us valuable opportunities to learn about mating among the long-necked dragons, although many of our tentative conclusions will only be verified by further studies among other groups of *mokele-mbembe*. One thing that was confirmed beyond doubt during our study of the mating dragons, however, was Walter Spink's penchant for interfering in the lives of his research subjects. In retrospect, Walter's meddling on this and other occasions foreshadowed the lengths to which he would ultimately go when he believed his dragons were in danger, but I remained blissfully ignorant of its significance until our coming trials roused Walter to action of which I would not have thought him capable.

CHAPTER XVII
ODYSSEY OF A COWARDLY DRAGON

Coming of age for a male *mokele-mbembe* involves not only reaching a certain level of physical development but leaving his maternal herd and learning to fend for himself. This was evident early on from the absence of mature males within our study group, which called to mind the structure of elephant herds, where adult bulls are similarly excluded. The timing of this rite of passage remains mysterious, but Walter Spink and I were afforded a glimpse of the manner in which the transition occurs when Fafnir, having attained the dragon equivalent of majority, was exiled from the herd.

The coming of this event was difficult to foresee as a consequence of Fafnir's already marginalized position within the herd. From the very beginning of our observation, he had fed at the edge of the group and followed last behind the others when they travel-browsed. Initially we had attributed this to Fafnir's reticent personality, but in retrospect the dragonesses may have been pushing him to the edge of the herd for some time in anticipation of driving him away.

When the time finally came for Fafnir to leave, we began seeing more unmistakable signs from the other dragons. Apropos of nothing, Tiamat randomly charged one day, loosing a fearful bellow in the process.

"Good heavens!" Walter said. "Do you think she senses a predator?"

"No," I said upon appraising the situation.

"Then what the devil is she hollering at?"

"It's Fafnir."

Even as Walter and I watched, the great dragoness galloped in the male's direction as if she meant to trample him. There is no telling whether she would actually have harmed him, but fortunately Fafnir quailed so easily that he immediately yielded. With a faint trumpet of protest, he retreated a good 100 feet or so and cowered submissively, at which point Tiamat aborted her attack as capriciously as she had begun it and browsed the fruit of a nearby *Coelocaryon botryoides* as if nothing had happened.

The altercation had diffused so quickly that we might initially have chocked it up to an intra-family spat over possession of prime browse, but it became obvious that something more was at play when the same occurred on succeeding days. Tiamat repeatedly chased Fafnir away from the herd, sometimes more than once in a day, and sometimes even Scylla or Ceto echoed the dragoness when she bellowed for the male to keep his distance.

"Something is definitely going on," Walter said. "It's like they're trying to banish him from the herd."

"I think that's just what they are doing," I said.

True to my expectation, the females forcibly evicted Fafnir from the herd when he neglected to leave on his own despite their not-so-subtle hints. After several days of communicating to Fafnir that he was unwelcome as I described above, the dragonesses finally chased him out for good. Always the physical aggressor in these skirmishes, Tiamat urged Fafnir away from the herd in her accustomed manner, but this time was different from their previous spats. Now Ceto trudged on into the forest, pulling the rest of the females along in her wake, but Tiamat stood guard behind them to dissuade Fafnir from following. Once the herd had traveled a suitable distance, Tiamat ponderously came about and followed them, leaving Fafnir alone.

If it seemed plain to Walter and I that Fafnir was not meant to accompany the rest of the herd, it was less clear to the dragon himself. When Tiamat took to her heels, Fafnir evidently felt that the usual performance was over, as it had been each time before, and he could now rejoin his family. As soon as the dragoness heard the rustle of the male's approach through the brush behind her, however, she stopped, turned sideways, and roared an unmistakable injunction over her shoulder against him following. These steps were repeated several times, with Tiamat resuming her slow but steady walk and pausing to hurl imprecations back at Fafnir if he pursued. Finally, Fafnir understood the prohibition and stayed in place, but he bleated at the females' backsides as if begging them not to leave him alone.

"How can they do that to him?" Walter asked. "Just look at him. He's terrified!"

"I think maybe it's just their nature," I said.

"Even so, I don't see why they need to be so cruel about it."

Regardless of Walter's opinion of their methods, the dragonesses plodded inexorably away without another look back at the male they left behind. Fafnir's pleas were so piteous that they should have moved the very trees to weeping, but the herd ignored them and was eventually screened from his sight by intervening forest.

Once he was alone, Fafnir seemed to be at a loss what to do with himself. He finally stopped crying out once he registered that his aunt, mother, and sisters were beyond hearing, but he did not immediately move on in search of a bachelor herd as we might have expected. Instead, he ambled listlessly back and forth around the immediate area, occasionally plucking at a leaf or flower without gusto. There was no telling how long he might mope at the site of his banishment in this manner, for the coming of night necessitated that we return to camp and leave him to his fate.

"I suppose by morning he'll have gotten over it and moved on,"

Walter said. "I wonder if we'll ever see him again."

Though we wondered over Fafnir's fate at the time, we found the disconsolate dragon the next day just where the herd had left him, haunting the trees like a disquiet spirit rambling about a decaying mansion. We would hardly have been human if we had not been moved to compassion by his lingering distress, but Walter was inspired to not only empathy but action.

"We should follow him," he said, "at least until he gets used to the bachelor life. We'll learn about the lifestyle of a solitary male *mokele-mbembe*, and we can keep an eye on him until I feel sure he can fend for himself."

At Walter's urging, we inaugurated our study of a male dragon adjusting to the more solitary lifestyle of his maturity. Temporarily eschewing the herd, we focused our attention on the newly-liberated Fafnir, thinking to assure ourselves that he would ultimately learn to fend for himself. Unfortunately, Fafnir was slower to take to his solitude than we anticipated, and though we could never have foreseen it, our presence inadvertently provided him with a new crutch to lean upon rather than weaning himself of his dependence upon his former family.

*

By the time he is cast out from his herd, the subadult male *mokele-mbembe* has already learned most life skills. He can identify which plants are edible and which plants should be avoided for toxicity, so he can feed himself. He is large enough by this time that most other animals will give way rather than confront him, and even if they do not, he is powerful enough to defend himself. The only real adjustment is doing all these things by himself rather than with the herd.

Being deprived of their female relatives may be more traumatic for some young bulls than for others, but it was certainly devastating for Fafnir. Though we had prepared ourselves to follow him through the forest, he lingered in the area where he had been abandoned, periodically calling out in the vain hope of convincing his long-gone family to return for him. Still, we visited him daily, thinking that he would inevitably accept his new position and begin his solitary peregrination through the forest so that we could study it.

Fafnir might eventually have set forth on this own, but Heep's intervention sent him on a course nobody could have predicted. As I previously mentioned, Heep had not only become healthier but livelier under Walter's care, to the point where he nearly took off a hand or foot if anyone turned their back on him. Finally he managed to chew through his tether and mount an ambush outside our tent flap that was nearly successful in catching Walter for good and all, at which point we had chased him out of camp and not seen him since. We had kept our eyes open, suspecting that he would not be far, but we did not expect him to venture near Fafnir after his previous altercations with long-necked dragons.

Even if we had not been looking for him, we belatedly realized that Heep was nearby when Fafnir thrust his neck out to browse a *Honckenya ficifolia* shrub, at which point a pair of leathery wings erupted into flapping life where the winged dragon had been hidden, accompanied by a ferocious hissing.

"What the devil is Heep doing here?" Walter asked.

Despite the *sasabonsam* surprising the *mokele-mbembe*, it might seem that there should have been no contest between the two dragons. After all, Heep was of roughly human size and gaunt to boot, whereas Fafnir was 25 feet long, stood double Heep's height, and could have sent him flying with a fairly cursory kick. It has long since been established in the world of beasts, however, that it is not physical size or strength that determines such skirmishes but self-confidence and ferocity. Fafnir lacked both, and he recoiled step by step as Heep, tiny though he was by comparison with his foe, advanced, hissing and snapping his jaws all the more boldly to make up what he lacked in size and strength.

"Why doesn't our scaly friend fight back?" Walter asked. "One good bellow, and I daresay Heep would turn tail and run."

"You know Fafnir," I said. "He's scared of his own shadow."

"Well, we'll just see about this."

When Fafnir refused to stand up for himself, Walter marched toward the dragons with no more trepidation than if he had been a schoolteacher rolling up his sleeves to wade between two brawling schoolboys. Careless for his own safety, he thrust himself between the dragons and stabbed an accusatory finger toward Heep, little guessing that the action he was about to take would change not only Fafnir's future but our own.

"Now, that's enough," he said. "What possesses you, frightening poor Fafnir like this? If you want to attack someone, then you can attack me. Otherwise, you'd better move along."

When confronted in this manner, Heep effected his accustomed groveling manner with head bowed and eyes averted (though we knew full well that he was entirely unrepentant) and backed away. Once he had put some distance between himself and Walter's chastising words, he took to his heels and launched himself into clumsy flight off into the forest.

"That's the end of that," Walter said, marching back toward me, "and good riddance, for now at least."

Contrary to Walter's expectation, however, our relationship with the newly-liberated dragon did not revert to normal upon Heep's retreat. Walter might have meant to quit the scene of the confrontation alone, but Fafnir followed him and only stopped, like a comically oversized shadow, when Walter himself realized that he was being accompanied and paused to glance over his shoulder.

"What do you suppose this is about?" Walter asked.

"I'm not sure," I said.

"Go on." Walter waved a dismissive hand toward the dragon. "You're safe now. There's no reason to cower behind me."

Despite Walter's attempts to shoo him away, Fafnir remained rooted where he stood and locked his gaze upon Walter as attentively as a pet doting upon its master. Further attempts on Walter's part to encourage the dragon to go about his own business rather than attending our every move were similarly unavailing, and for some time Fafnir simply watched Walter from a few feet away. As you can imagine, observing a dragon whose behavior consisted only of waiting for us to do something was less than thrilling.

"How the devil can I study his behavior if he won't do anything but stare at me?" Walter asked. "What do you suppose is the matter with him?"

"I think I have a guess," I said.

"Well, out with it. There's no use fumfering."

"Now that you've rescued him, I think he's formed an attachment."

"I hardly think that conclusion is warranted."

Walter's doubt notwithstanding, it is not unheard-of for even a wild animal to become attached to its human rescuer. We have all heard of the baby elephant, separated from its mother, bonding with the first human it meets, but the phenomenon goes farther than that. I previously mentioned Pocho the crocodile, who chose to live with the fisherman who nursed him back to health; similarly, a Magellanic penguin began devotedly spending most of his year with the Brazilian bricklayer who rescued him, resisting all attempts at being ushered back into the wild. In these rare cases, the rescued creature associates as eagerly with a human as its own kind, and even Walter could not dispute that his relationship with Fafnir had changed the moment he delivered the dragon from Heep's harassment.

"I still don't see how this can be," Walter said, "but just to humor you, we'll test it."

When we investigated the extent of Fafnir's interest in Walter, it became apparent that the dragon had developed some kind of fixation with his perceived rescuer. When Walter lumbered away from me, the dragon followed on his heels like a baby duckling queuing behind its mother (albeit a baby ten times its adopted mother's size). If Walter darted behind a tree, the dragon bleated plaintively until Walter reappeared, at which point he became quiet and content again. In warding off Fafnir's foe, however superfluous the service seemed to Walter and me, Walter had inadvertently made the stray dragon fairly dependent upon him.

"I think you might be right, Matthew," Walter said. "I seem to have made myself a new friend, after all."

"What are you going to do about it?"

"For the time being, I don't see much need to do anything. But if he's just going to follow me around anyway, we might as well go back to camp where I can get some of my writing done."

As Walter anticipated, his newfound devotee shadowed us when we hiked back to our camp, and at this point I had my first misgivings. Walter might have been tickled at the idea of having a dragon all his own, but I was uncomfortable at the prospect of treating a wild animal like an admittedly oversized pet. Aside from the ethical questions this raised, I suspected—quite rightly, I might add—that the presence of a live dragon in our midst would disrupt our work far more than it could possibly facilitate it.

Living with a subadult male *mokele-mbembe* can be difficult, as I suspect most readers will have imagined on their own without the need to learn from our experience. Like Gulliver to our Lilliputians, they can knock down whatever feeble shelters we might erect as easily as grass, even if they do not intend it. When in such close quarters, there is also the constant prospect of being underfoot regardless of how friendly the dragon's temperament might be. Unfortunately, Walter would not hear of the downside to incorporating Fafnir into our living arrangements until he saw for himself how ill-suited the match was.

I second-guessed Walter's decision to bring Fafnir into camp as soon as he joined us, at which point it became apparent that our setup was not scaled to accommodate the dragon. Walter, the Bangombe, and I sauntered easily enough through the gap between the leaf-thatched huts where Ekianga and Mambunia slept in the style of their people, but the opening was too narrow for Fafnir. This might not have been a concern but for the fact that the dragon did not allow the structures to stop him; instead, he stomped on through and flattened both huts in the process. Even once we had rebuilt camp around him, he was so easily startled that he was constantly whirling this way or that at some sound or movement and thrashing his tail in the process, in which manner he knocked over our tent twice in the first day alone.

When the dragon was not knocking over our modest homes, he was quite literally eating us out of them. He would not budge more than a few feet from Walter, and this made for conflict when he tried to make up the half-ton of browse he ate daily from whatever plants were at hand. Being understandably unable to distinguish the *mongongo* leaves thatching Ekianga and Mambunia's huts from those that were fair game for eating, Fafnir was constantly getting caught snatching a mouthful of roof or wall for a snack, to the mounting frustration of the huts' owners.

Aside from his seemingly insatiable appetite and physical destructiveness, Fafnir also disrupted the peace of our living arrangements by crying ceaselessly—and volubly—whenever he was separated from Walter. This might not have been so trying if it had been restricted to a few moments here and there when Walter sought some privacy to relieve himself, but it was excruciating when we tried to sleep. Though Walter might calm him long enough for us to retire into our tent, Fafnir was sure to call for him several times a night like a fussing baby—a fussing baby with the volume of a speeding freight train, I might add. Despite my hope that the dragon would become accustomed to sleeping without Walter nearby, the event seemed unlikely to come about any time soon.

Fafnir continued being difficult in the following days, and his behavior chafed the residents of our camp. My own inconvenience only amounted to a little lost sleep, which I took stoically and kept to myself, but the others were more strongly irritated by Fafnir's transgressions. It seemed that someone was speaking out against some new misdeed every moment, and since the dragon was insensible to English, French, and Bangombe, it was Walter who fielded these complaints.

No matter how strongly his companions condemned the dragon, Walter was quick to defend his new pet. Unfortunately, this amounted to little more than making excuses for his ward's conduct, which did little to assuage anybody's frustration.

When the dragon browsed a hole in Ekianga's roof:

"He's just hungry, that's all," Walter said. "How is he supposed to know that those leaves aren't for eating?"

Or when the dragon's nightly caterwauling drew complaints:

"He's can't help it," Walter said. "He's frightened to be alone in the dark."

With Walter defending him in this manner, Fafnir soon learned to scurry fearfully to the old man's side whenever he heard a raised voice, much like a pet retreating to its master's protection, and Walter invariably obliged by reproaching the complainant.

"You mustn't raise your voice around him," he would say. "Look how you've scared him."

Walter continued coddling the dragon's misbehavior, and Fafnir continued making himself a nuisance about our camp, for about a week. The rest of our group became increasingly irritable, and though I feared that Henri and the Bangombe would finally throw up their hands and leave us, Walter refused to acknowledge their concerns.

Even if it took him longer than the rest of us, Walter finally realized that Fafnir could not continue living with us, albeit only when the dragon's mischief affected him directly. It had been all well and good when Fafnir grazed upon the roof or walls of the Bangombe huts, but he went too far for Walter's taste when he intruded upon our tent. One morning Walter and I awakened almost simultaneously to the rasp of tearing paper, only to glimpse Fafnir, just his head and neck poking through the tent flap, seizing a sheaf of papers from Walter's notebook with his mouth before swallowing them with a toss of his head.

When the dragon disturbed the sanctity of Walter's priceless notes, Walter finally refused to brook his trespass.

"What the devil are you doing?" he squawked, chasing the dragon out of the tent without so much as pausing to dress. "Do you know how long it's taken me to compile the information in those pages? And now it's lost! Oh, this is simply dreadful!"

After blustering in this manner for a few minutes, Walter calmed and beckoned the dragon back to him.

"There, there," he said. "We're still friends. I know you didn't mean it."

Though Walter forgave his Gulliverian friend, this incident removed the blinders that affection had imposed on his perception, and he ultimately came to the same conclusion that the rest of us had long since reached.

"You know, Matthew," he said, "I'm beginning to think that it's a bad idea to let our scaly friend here live with us. We should probably return him to the wild."

However belated it seemed to the rest of us, Walter had finally realized the inherent incompatibility of human beings and dragons. He had learned the lesson at the cost of a few pages' worth of research notes, but realizing that we could not cohabit with the dragon was only the beginning of a longer struggle. Now that Fafnir had become used to following Walter around, persuading the dragon to go off on his own would be a more involved process than just withdrawing his welcome.

*

Convincing an immature but nevertheless massive dragon to resume its normal existence in the wild, once it has become attached to a human being, is easier said than done. Obviously you cannot simply explain politely that it belongs among its own kind, nor is it apt to conveniently decide to leave all on its own. You must find some way to wean it off its dependence on human beings, which requires either making the wild seem more attractive or human company less appealing, all the while taking care to avoid inflicting additional trauma in an already less than optimal situation.

Walter might not initially have realized how sensitive our situation with the dragon was, but he had these concerns in mind when I asked him how he meant to return Fafnir to the wild.

"Well, I can't just shoo him away," he said. "It would be cruel, and I don't think it would work, anyway. No, we need to find him someone—or something—else to attach to, someone—or something—that can teach him how to function as an adult dragon."

"Another male *mokele-mbembe*?" I suggested.

"My thoughts exactly."

Our strategy for reuniting Fafnir with his own kind derives from our knowledge of elephants, among which newly-liberated males seek out other, more experienced males and may even form small bachelor herds with them. Given the many other behavioral similarities between the two species, Walter and I suspected that the same might be true of the dragons, but the only way to test our hypothesis would be to introduce Fafnir to another male dragon, which of course meant tracking one down.

Finding an adult male *mokele-mbembe*, in the absence of an estrous female to attract them, would have presented an insurmountable obstacle if Walter and I had been alone. Fortunately, the Bangombe were still with us, their disgruntlement with the destructive dragon notwithstanding, and they were eager to track another *mokele-mbembe* down if it would rid them of the nuisance.

With the help of the Bangombe, Walter would willingly part with his dragon, but he was nevertheless exacting when it came to choosing Fafnir's prospective associate.

"Now, you must be very careful about finding an adult dragon for my scaly friend," he said. "I don't want one of those brash, young ones. They're apt to scare him away altogether, timid as he is. No, you must find him an older male with the experience and patience to teach him. Do you understand?"

With these instructions, the Bangombe left us for several days, during which Fafnir repeatedly dismantled and we repeatedly rebuilt our camp, before returning to announce that they had found a male *mokele-mbembe.*

"Did you find a nice older one like I told you?" Walter asked.

"Yes, yes," Ekianga said. "Good *mokele-mbembe.*"

"Good *mokele-mbembe,*" Mambunia agreed.

"I certainly hope so."

With sundry assurances from the Bangombe that their proposed mentor for Fafnir was the most suitable dragon available, Walter and I accompanied them to his foraging area. Still unwilling to be parted from his guardian, Fafnir toddled happily behind us, oblivious to our plans for him. Then the crackle of branches yielding to the passage of a huge body signaled the proximity of the other dragon, and suddenly Fafnir quailed and needed coaxing to follow us any farther.

"Come along, now," Walter said. "You needn't be frightened. We've just found a new friend for you. Come along."

Stopping every few steps to urge Fafnir along in this manner, we were by no means stealthy, but fortunately our noisy coming did not disturb the other dragon. Soon we beheld the auburn mountain of his back breaching in the midst of the understory, and when he finally withdrew his head from the canopy and arced his serpentine neck our way to inspect us, we recognized Typhon by the unique pattern of missing spines.

"This is wonderful!" Walter said. "I couldn't have chosen better myself. He's sure to set a good example for our scaly friend."

Even if the older male satisfied Walter's criteria, introducing two bachelor dragons does not guarantee that they will form a bond, any more than introducing a random male and female of any given species will automatically induce mating. Individuals of the same species may have wildly varying temperaments, and any number of instincts, ranging from territoriality to plain dislike, may frustrate the match. For that reason, there was no telling how Fafnir and Typhon would react to each other.

Despite our inability to guarantee the outcome, the meeting between Fafnir and the older dragon seemed promising at first. A less circumspect male might have chased the newcomer away, but Typhon seemed to guess Fafnir's situation and even rumbled gently, as if to invite him closer. Unfortunately, we had failed to reckon with how cowardly Fafnir really was: hardly even curious about another of his own kind, he cowered behind Walter. The situation might almost have been comical—like an elephant hiding behind a mouse—but for the urgency of reuniting Fafnir with other dragons.

"Go play with your new friend," Walter said. "Go on, I say."

No matter how Walter exhorted him, Fafnir would not take so much as a step closer to his would-be companion. At one point, Walter even thought to give the dragon a push, but he might as well have been pushing a mountain for all that Fafnir budged. Finally Walter threw his hands up in frustration.

"Of all the pestiferous dragons!" he said. "He won't budge, Matthew!"

When Fafnir refused to engage with him, Typhon must have sensed the futility of waiting any longer. After lingering for a good half hour, he finally heaved into motion and plodded off into the forest, feeding as he went, without making any further effort to coax Fafnir along.

With Typhon departing—and Fafnir no closer to leaving our side—even Walter had to concede our failure.

"I just don't know what to do," he said.

"You might need to use some stronger language," I said.

"Matthew, I can't be cruel to him."

"It might be kinder in the long run if you do."

Walter's reluctance notwithstanding, several more unsuccessful attempts to broker a friendship between Fafnir and the older dragon must have made him truly desperate, for he finally followed my advice (which was always a last resort). Fafnir continued to devotedly trail along behind us wherever we went, but now Walter periodically stopped and tried to discourage him from accompanying us.

"You're a pestiferous dragon," he would say, "and I've just about had enough of you. I think it's time for you to stop following me around. Shoo!"

Even when Walter shooed his pet dragon away, he was less than emphatic at first, and this undoubtedly contributed to Fafnir not taking his commands seriously. After a few more attempts, however, Walter's failures hardened both his will and his words, until finally he effected such genuine displeasure that no one could mistake it, regardless of their species.

"Now, that does it!" he squawked, rounding upon the dragon.

Fafnir flinched and recoiled at his tone.

"I've tried to let you down easy—goodness knows I have—but enough is enough. I don't want you following me anymore. Shoo, I say! Shoo!"

Walter punctuated this exchange by lunging at the dragon as if he meant to strike him, and Fafnir retreated several steps.

"That's better," Walter said. "Now stay there, and don't let me catch you following me."

If Walter thought he could shrug off the dragon's devotion with the expedient of a few harsh words, he failed to reckon with the strength of Fafnir's devotion. The dragon might cower at Walter's strong words while they were being delivered, but as soon as Walter turned his back, Fafnir was trotting happily behind him again as if nothing had happened. After more attempts than I care to count, Walter was no closer to chasing off the dragon than when he began.

"I don't know if this will ever work, Matthew," he said finally. "You see how I try to drive him off, but it's no use. I'm just not capable of being mean enough, I suppose."

Walter's efforts to chase the dragon away might have continued to fail indefinitely, but Fafnir was eventually dispatched back to the wild by an agency beyond our control or expectation. This happened during one of the now-routine spats between the old man and his dragon, which continued no matter how demoralized Walter became.

This time as always, Walter recriminated Fafnir for his recalcitrance and all but begged him to leave, little suspecting that the outcome would be any different than his dozens of previous attempts.

"How many times do I have to tell you you're not wanted?" Walter asked. "It's time you went on your way. Now!"

To this point, the exchange had been typical, but this time a clap like thunder unexpectedly punctuated Walter's admonition.

"What the devil?" he squawked.

While Walter blinked and blustered in confusion, Fafnir bleated and galloped away from the old man as if stung, smashing recklessly through any bush or tree that was unlucky enough to block his path. After some confusion on my own part, I recognized the thunderclap as a gunshot, and I feared from the dragon's reaction that he had been hit. I had little time for speculation, however, because presently a horde of village men passed nearby in pursuit of the dragon, led by a familiar, bearded white man bearing the rifle whose fateful shot had sent Fafnir running.

James Phillip Hartley had caught up to the dragons, but Walter wasted no time before thrusting himself in the hunter's way.

"Who the devil do you think you are," he demanded, "shooting at my dragon?"

"Get the hell out of the way, man," Hartley said, sidestepping even as Walter barred his path. "Don't you see that it's getting away?"

"That is precisely what I want to happen."

Hartley would undoubtedly have taken a second shot at the retreating dragon rather than engaging with us, but when he raised his rifle, Walter stepped in its path, heedless of the danger. This type of ferocity from someone of Walter's advanced years doubtless flummoxed the hunter, for he lowered his weapon and gaped while Walter stormed toward him, red-faced, until they were chest to chest.

"If you think I'm going to just stand by and let you shoot my dragon"—Walter seized the rifle while the hunter remained dumbstruck—"you've got another think coming."

So saying, Walter stalked back my way, clutching the rifle, before

I could even think to intercede, much less act.

"What the hell are you doing with my gun?" Hartley demanded.

"I'm confiscating it before you murder any more innocent creatures," Walter said. "If you want to summon the police, be my guest, but I daresay you'll have a time of it finding a constable way out here."

Walter's indifference notwithstanding, Hartley and his bearers could easily have swarmed Walter and retrieved the firearm, but most people are averse to forcibly overcoming an elderly person (a fact that Walter relied upon more than once in our time together). Thus, Walter stormed away unmolested and in high dudgeon to dispose the rifle in the nearest stream while the alternating thrash and crackle of Fafnir passing through the ferns and breaking through the shrubs dwindled with the dragon's successful escape. Without the means to dispatch the dragon, the hunter had no motivation to follow regardless of how plain a trail it had left, and Fafnir was saved.

Once the hunter had departed and Walter had calmed down, we tried tracking Fafnir to assess his condition, but the coming of night stymied our efforts. Our attempts to locate him in the coming days were similarly unsuccessful. Walter repeatedly insisted that the dragon was fine, but his certainty seemed put on.

"You know Fafnir," he said. "He's probably just hiding because he's frightened, don't you think?"

Whether he was frightened or wounded, Fafnir wound up in the wild where he belonged, and when he did not reappear, we resumed our observation of the herd while Walter continued to tell himself his erstwhile pet was somewhere safe. Though I would not for all the world have crushed Walter's brittle hope, it seemed probable to me that Fafnir had been hit, and there was no telling what sort of injury the shot had inflicted or whether it might become infected. It occurred to me that Walter might not have done the dragon any favor by preventing a clean kill, but I kept such grim thoughts to myself, at least until Fafnir's odyssey reunited him with us under grimmer circumstances than even I had feared.

CHAPTER XVIII

THE HUNTING BEHAVIOR OF THE LIKOUALA REX

Though dracontologists are generally loath to acknowledge it, there has been at least one report of a bipedal, carnivorous reptile bearing a strong resemblance to the *Tyrannosaurus* type existing in a remote area of modern Africa.[30] I speak of the almost notorious Kasai Rex, which is known from the 1932 account of a Swedish plantation owner named Johanson (or Johnson, depending on which version you read). Johanson reportedly witnessed a 40-plus-foot reptile, which he likened in so many words to a *Tyrannosaurus*, attacking and killing a rhinoceros while he was travelling in the Kasai Valley in what is presently the Democratic Republic of the Congo. The absence of subsequent sightings or even a native tradition of such a creature—and the plainly falsified photograph that accompanied the original report—have led even the most optimistic of cryptozoologists to reject the Kasai Rex as a fabrication.

Because of the absence of reliable evidence for such a creature, I

[30]There are also reports of such a creature in Australia, where an animal known as the *burrunjor* is said to raid livestock and leave behind tantalizing theropod-like tracks.

hope I can be forgiven for doubting the existence of a *Tyrannosaurus* in the Congo even after the sighting I previously described, Walter's conviction on the subject notwithstanding. As if the testimony of the fossil record, which is completely devoid of post-Cretaceous theropod remains, was not enough, common sense suggests that a 40-foot carnivorous reptile could not have lived such a quiet lifestyle as to go unnoticed up to the present date. Whatever resemblance the lurking thing in the forest, which we had seen so briefly, bore to such a creature was therefore obviously a result of poor lighting conditions and imagination, or so I had told myself when I initially dismissed it.

Considering my misgivings about acknowledging the presence of a carnivorous dinosaur in the Likouala, you can imagine my consternation when our previous vision repeated itself.

When the thing that resembled a *Tyrannosaurus* reappeared, Walter and I were observing the *mokele-mbembe* herd as always. I don't know what made me glance in the right direction at the right moment, but I peered over the brown hills of the dragons' backs, past sinuous necks that wound up into the treetops, and beheld an irregular shape breaking the monotony of straight trunks marching off into the distance. To my growing dismay, I recognized the large head with triangular snout preceding a heavy body poised, birdlike, on two muscular legs. I kept looking, undoubtedly hoping on some subconscious level that persistent squinting might resolve the unwanted intruder into a misshapen tree, but Walter called out to me and broke the spell; I blinked, and the thing was gone.

"What the devil are you looking at, Matthew?" Walter asked.

"You didn't see anything?"

"No."

"Oh. It was nothing."

Thinking it best not to arouse Walter's interest when I could not, due to the brevity of my sighting, be sure what I had seen, I kept the matter to myself. Truth be told, I was probably rationalizing, for my worldview was immeasurably more comfortable without having to accommodate a living *Tyrannosaurus*. In any event, I convinced myself that I had temporarily been deceived by a trick of the light and kept mum on the subject of the thing that looked like a theropod, although I tread cautiously from that point in case there was more to it than I had been willing to admit.

My position that I had misinterpreted a more innocuous object became considerably more difficult to maintain in the following days when the same phantasm insisted on reappearing. On the third day after the sighting I just described, I again witnessed the thing lurking while the herd browsed. This time Walter and I were between the herd and the seeming *Tyrannosaurus*, so I had a clearer view of gnarled arms ending in claws like sickles and a jaw that curled in a perpetual sneer, as if the thing were delighted at the distress that its appearance caused me. The jaw dropped open to brandish an armory of teeth like ivory daggers. Using the nearby trees for scale, it seemed to me that it was 40 feet long if it was an inch.

This sight alone was so fearful that my stomach clenched, but the thing did not venture closer; nor did the dragons react to it as I would have expected if there had been a threat. Between the predator's distance and the proximity of the herd, whose numbers seemed to keep it at bay, I managed to control my alarm. This did not, however, stop me from leading Walter into the midst of the herd where we might be most secure if the thing risked an attack.

"What the devil are you doing, Matthew?" he asked.

"I was, er, having trouble seeing," I said.

Walter did not question my excuse, and when I looked again, the thing was gone, though it might have merely concealed itself rather than leaving altogether. This thought naturally did little to comfort me, and I kept up a watch as if our lives depended on my vigilance (which they might, assuming for argument's sake only that this thing was not a figment of my imagination).

Now that I was alert for the thing, it seemed to reappear even more frequently, sneering at me the next day from behind the fan of fronds atop a mid-sized *Elaeis guineensis*. Despite my doubts that it could be a flesh and blood creature, it was physical enough that a party of turacos erupted into agitated flight when its toothy face brushed the branches adjoining their perch. It was also physical enough to feed upon flesh and blood animals: when a bongo wandered close, the seeming theropod's mouth lashed downward with the ruthless precision of a steel-jaw trap and seized the antelope whole, swallowing it with one toss of the angular head.

The seeming theropod gave many such small hints of its reality, and the more I considered the situation, the more difficult it was for me to dismiss what I had seen as a figment of my imagination. I am not an expert on hallucinations or other altered mental states, but even I know that they do not arise in a vacuum, and I could not conceive an objective reason why I would experience them. Lacking any history, I had no reason to believe I was medically predisposed to delusions, nor had I taken any drug with hallucinogenic potential. Similarly, though I might doubt my faculties on occasion, even I could not have consistently mistaken some inanimate object or common animal for a giant carnivorous reptile. Loath as I was to admit it, the circumstances raised the distinct possibility that I was seeing a flesh and blood animal that bore a striking resemblance to a *Tyrannosaurus rex.*

Reluctant as I was to embrace the idea of a flesh and blood theropod wandering around the Congo, I nevertheless tried to view the possibility scientifically. To the extent there was any chance I was not imagining it altogether, I made observations of its habits, and more and more I could not help thinking of it as a flesh and blood animal. For want of a better name than *that thing*, I mentally referred to it as the Likouala Rex.

Now that I was looking for the Rex, I saw it constantly, more than half the days that we spent among the herd. While Walter was distributing treats of *malombo*, I would glance around us until I found its hulking shadow lurking among the trees. As the herd continued its slow march through the forest, I would look over my shoulder and perceive a flash of that craggy death's-head of a face leering at me when the Rex's slow but steady pursuit brought it through a shaft of light, only to lose it when the shadows coalesced again. Assuming that it was a real animal, it was probably nearby even when I did not see it, though I avoided indulging that thought for reasons relating to my peace of mind.

Whenever the Rex was visible, I attempted to observe its behavior, the majority of which consisted of hunting and feeding. Judging from what I witnessed, I quickly concluded that it was not by any means a pursuit predator that actively runs down fleeing prey in the manner of a lion or wolf. Rather, such animals as it took under my observation—usually antelopes on the forest floor, but occasionally a monkey leaping between branches within reach of its jaws—were stalked and then ambushed.

The Likouala Rex's ambush predation may disappoint readers who, like me, were raised on a steady diet of art and film depicting theropods and sauropods locked in mortal combat, but nevertheless, the two species of dragon do not ordinarily confront each other. While I previously described how the *mbielu-mbielu-mbielu* displayed fiercely when she sensed the Rex, the *mokele-mbembe* did not so much as acknowledge it, or at least the Rex prowled far enough away from the herd that it did not demand Tiamat's warnings. It was as if the *mokele-mbembe* and the Rex had an understanding: they were evenly matched in size and ferocity, so neither engaged the other.

Although the Likouala Rex did not openly engage the herd, I nevertheless suspected that it would prey upon a *mokele-mbembe* if the opportunity presented itself. There was certainly no reason for its interest in the herd other than as a meal, and even when the Rex pretended to go about its business, it was still conspicuously available to exploit any weakness on the other dragons' parts. It might not actively chase and kill an adult *mokele-mbembe*, especially not with the herd protecting it, but a dragon killed or disabled by other natural causes, or separated from the herd, would undoubtedly be fair game.

The dragons in our herd were in too good health and physical condition to afford the Rex a meal any time soon, but I was less assured that none of them would stray from the herd so as to become its prey. The smallest and hence most vulnerable of the juvenile dragons, Campe, was both inquisitive of her surroundings and fearless in the manner of the very young. She was constantly investigating a new smell or sound that drew her away from her guardians, and once the Rex entered the equation, I found myself fretting that she would unwittingly ramble too close to those merciless jaws.

For some time my worry proved needless, for Campe was not permitted to indulge the curiosity that might otherwise have lured her into danger. As I have already described, Scylla took it upon herself to look after her younger sister, undoubtedly practicing out of instinct to be a mother herself. Whenever Campe looked apt to leave the herd, Scylla stepped into her path and gently prodded her back into line. This was the case most of the time, but just as Scylla's faltering watch allowed Heep to attack the juvenile once before, there finally came a day when the subadult dragoness was too preoccupied in her own browsing to fulfill her function as guardian, and Campe ventured away from the herd.

When Campe tramped toward the forest where the Rex lurked, lured along by a pair of bush pigs and their young that had been flushed out by the herd's passage, I was already watching the Rex and could not help noticing. For a moment, I dared hope she would not pass close enough to trigger the predator's ambush, but to my dismay, the Rex marked Campe's approach and crept stealthily to intercept her. The leering jaw dropped open, and its tongue lolled out hungrily among its teeth while its fingers twitched eagerly. If Campe ventured a few paces further, it would have her and be off before her family was any the wiser.

Regardless of what might have happened naturally, I have already mentioned my difficulty leaving a young and fairly helpless animal to be injured or killed, even if proper scientific procedure urges noninterference. Certainly my conscience disturbed me more at the thought of letting a child, however big and scaly, blunder into the clutches of what is, by all appearances, a bloodthirsty predator. Under those circumstances, I decided to save Campe from the Rex.

Dissuading Campe from approaching the Rex might have presented a challenge, given that she was several times my size, but past experience had taught me that there was one lure that Campe could not resist: my wristwatch. She had always been fascinated by it when I didn't want her to have it, and hopefully the fascination would remain even if I willingly offered it. Flourishing the watch so that it would catch the light, I called to her.

"Hey, girl. Do you want this?"

Between my voice and the glint of metal in the corner of Campe's eye, the juvenile dragon abandoned her pursuit of the bush pigs as eagerly as she had started it, giving chase after this other coveted bauble instead. Just to assure myself of her safety, I backed into the midst of the herd, drawing her along by keeping the watch just out of her reach.

"Anything wrong, Matthew?" Walter asked, noticing my interaction with the young dragon.

"No," I said. "Everything is fine."

Once I had shepherded Campe back to safety, I glanced back at the Rex in the forest, although I almost wished I hadn't. The steely gaze with which it fixed me, as if aware that I had deprived it of its anticipated meal, practically withered the foliage between us.

Though it seemed to displease the would-be predator, none of the dragons strayed enough during this time to place themselves on the Likouala Rex's menu. Given the persistence with which the Rex shadowed them, however, I had a sinking feeling that it would be there to profit by their misfortune if any of them ever faltered. I hoped I would not be present to witness when it happened, but as usual, events transpired without regard for my preferences.

*

You may be wondering what Walter Spink was doing while I investigated the Likouala Rex. Certainly he would have been thrilled at the prospect of a living theropod and applied himself to its study with his accustomed fervor. On the other hand, his enthusiasm would undoubtedly have been reckless: he was apt to test the Rex's reality by sauntering within range of its jaws and trying to stroke its scaly hide. Between my fear of what Walter might do and my ambivalence whether the Rex was just a figment of my imagination, I reasoned that it was best to keep the whole affair to myself until I could be sure.[31]

Initially it was not particularly difficult to keep Walter oblivious to the Rex's appearances. Between his poor eyesight, the distance of the Rex from the herd, and the gloom under the forest canopy, Walter was unlikely to perceive the Rex without intentionally looking for it. If the other dragons had reacted to its presence, he might have spied the Rex out when his attention had been called to it, but it continued to lurk far enough away for the herd to disregard it. Occasionally, Walter noticed that I was preoccupied watching something, but it was easy enough to distract him.

"What are you looking at, Matthew?" he would ask.

"Nothing," I would say. "I was just daydreaming."

"Well, snap out of it. I need your mind on our work."

Feigning mere distraction kept Walter from realizing that I was scrutinizing the Rex, and even when it seemed that Walter was about to look right at it, in which case there was a distant chance he might make it out among the trees, I could usually redirect him before he could do so.

"We should find some more *malombo*," I would say when Walter's attention drifted toward the Rex's ambuscade, "just in case Echidna is eating for two."

"Oh, of course," he would say. "That's good thinking,

---

[31]Nor did I risk alerting Walter to the Rex by attempting to enlist the Bangombe in my efforts.

Matthew."

Or:

"That bird over there," I would say. "Is it an emerald cuckoo?" (*Chrysococcyx cupreus;* this being a bird that Walter had been trying to spot since we had settled in the Likouala.)

"Oh," Walter would say, forgetting all else. "Let me see!"

Though I was able to keep Walter preoccupied with such tricks, I knew that I would only be able to monopolize his attention for so long before he finally sensed the Rex's presence. Eventually some lapse in vigilance would prevent me from diverting Walter in time, and there would be nothing left to do but follow him in his quest to document the behavior of a supposed living *Tyrannosaurus.* Fortunately, I was not the only source of distraction that kept Walter from noticing the Rex, as I discovered one day when Walter abruptly cried out while we were with the herd.

"Good heavens!"

Walter pointed excitedly with a quivering finger, and thinking the jig was up with respect to the Rex, I guiltily tracked the object of his attention. Imagine my confusion in the absence of a hulking bipedal reptile, or any other living thing that could possibly have caused Walter such alarm, for that matter.

"Do you see it?" he asked.

"See what?" I asked.

"It looked like that beastly hunter, but he's gone now. Isn't that strange?"

Though I had not shared Walter's vision, I did not think much of it at the time other than being relieved that he had not discovered the Rex. Even when a variation of this scene repeated itself in the coming days—Walter repeatedly insisted, to his horror, that he had seen the hunter, or "that Heartless fellow" as he occasionally called him, but they were always gone before I could react to his alarum—I was merely grateful that he was so preoccupied. To the extent that I gave the source of Walter's sightings any thought, I suspected that his lingering distress at the altercation between Fafnir and the hunter, mingled with fear lest the rest of the herd should suffer a similar fate, had strained him to the point where he jumped at every shadow, but Walter himself suspected a different agency.

"I think we both know what's happening here, Matthew," he said. "It's that she-devil Meombe. She's sending me these visions to try and frighten me away. Well, if she thinks she can run me off, she's got another think coming."

Regardless of whether Walter's distraction was supernatural or merely psychosomatic, it continued to divert his attention, and I was thankfully left to puzzle out the mystery of the Likouala Rex on my own. Perhaps I could have resolved my dilemma more quickly if I had shared by observations with Walter, for the possibility that I had hallucinated the whole thing would have been eliminated if Walter had seen the Rex, too. Things being as they were, however, the Rex remained illusory to me, even when I had an encounter that would normally have confirmed its terrifying reality.

It is not possible, based upon my limited observations, to describe the diet of the Likouala Rex with certainty. I witnessed it catching and consuming a bongo, so it is likely that it preys upon other forest antelopes such as yellow-backed duiker (*Cephalophus silvicultor*), bushbuck (*Tragelaphus scriptus*), and sitatunga (*Tragelaphus spekii*). The blue duiker (*Philantomba monticola*) may be too small, at 12 pounds, to attract its attention. It opportunistically preys on primates such as De Brazza's monkey (*Cercopithecus neglectus*) and the crowned guenon (*Cercopithecus pogonias*) as well, but these, too, are too small to be any more than a minor component of its diet. Given the size of its accustomed prey, it goes without saying that a Rex would also prey upon a human if given the opportunity, and moreover, I confirmed its interest in human prey firsthand.

The Rex did not have the chance to sample dracontologist for some time, but it was nevertheless apparent that it was aware of

Walter and me. Unobtrusive and insignificant as we might be compared with the giant *mokele-mbembe*, the Rex must have made out our scent, for I frequently caught it leering directly at us with a fixation that I can only describe as unwholesome. A chill scurried, rat-like, down my spine whenever it locked its gaze upon me in this manner, and its sneer seemed to say, *I know you're there, and I am patient.*

Being scrutinized by a 40-foot predator with only Bangombe arrows and profanity to ward it off in the event of an attack is disconcerting, to say the least. Granted, I had only seen the Rex in the vicinity of the herd, where we benefitted from Tiamat's jealous guard against its encroachment. Nevertheless, it stood to reason, if it were a flesh and blood predator as I was coming to believe, that the Rex had a substantial hunting range and might be met anywhere. Thus, I lived in constant fear of meeting the Rex unprotected in the forest, and over time I began to quake at every movement in the corner of my eye and recoil from every shadow.

When my edginess continued long enough, even Walter overcame his own preoccupation with the *mokele-mbembe* and the phantom hunter long enough to notice.

"Matthew," he asked, "why the devil are you so jumpy all of a sudden?"

"What makes you think I'm jumpy? I'm fine."

My awkward protest might have been fairly transparent to a more astute observer of human behavior, but Walter did not see through it; or at least he was unwilling to detract from his dragonwatching to investigate further. In any event, he did not pursue the subject, and I tried to conceal my anxiety so that he would not divine its source.

No matter how anxious I was, it is impossible for any human being, however motivated, to be vigilant every moment of the day. Even if it were possible, human perception has its limits: we cannot see every direction at once. Whether it was the frailty of my human faculties, plain bad luck, or something more sinister, I eventually encountered the Likouala Rex without any of the *mokele-mbembe* nearby to make it think twice about attacking me.

When I met the Rex, I was thankfully alone, for rescuing Walter while effecting my own escape was certainly more than I could have managed. Ekianga and Mambunia had gone hunting, and Walter took Henri into Toukalaka to confront Madame Meombe over the visions of the big game hunter with which he continued to be oppressed. Taking uncharacteristic pity on my frazzled condition, Walter had excused me from participating.

"I have an idea that will put a stop to that she-devil Meombe's schemes for the foreseeable future," he had said, "but you might as well stay here. You've been so jumpy this past week, I daresay you could use some rest."

Though Walter's observation was accurate, I ultimately found it impossible to relax at camp, having become so used to being always on the move with the herd. When rest would not come, I decided to take a walk to the *bai* to watch whatever animals might come to drink, and just when I had become relaxed enough to drift into a pleasant daydream of Vanessa, the Rex surprised me.

Even when the Rex sprang its ambush, I did not immediately recognize it. Given its height and how close I was—perhaps 50 feet—its legs were the first thing I saw, and they might have been tree trunks. It was only when one of the seeming trees lifted off the ground and lurched toward me that I realized this was a living thing, and with mounting dread, I craned my neck to behold the familiar and much-feared death's-head glowering down at me. The Rex advanced nearly six feet with one step while I was still gawking, and now its sneer seemed to say something different: *I have you now!*

There is a lamentable dearth of precedent or advice to guide the dracontologist confronted with a hunting theropod. When accosted by most animals, experts suggest standing your ground while making noise and waving your arms to appear larger, but the benefit of this strategy against a carnivorous dragon two stories high seems patently dubious. Thus, when I finally registered what was happening, I simply ran, and I stand by my choice.

Running from the Likouala Rex might serve its ordinary prey well enough, as I have previously observed that it is not a pursuit predator, but overtaking a fleeing human is by no means as challenging as running down antelope; nor is the Rex averse to following through with an ambush if it has to run a few paces. The Rex tracked my retreat without even seeming to exert itself, stepping adroitly over the clutter of plants in the understory, while it was everything I could do to hurdle fallen logs and dodge the branches and fronds that seemed to grasp toward me as I passed. I did not dare look back for fear of slowing myself, but each crash of a foot down through the understory sounded louder and closer.

With the Rex closing and my retreat frustrated by the thick brush, I would undoubtedly have discovered the hard way whether the Rex was a flesh and blood carnivore, but my clumsiness offered deliverance where my fear-addled brain had not. While running with no more plan than to hope the Rex would lose interest—and painfully aware that it not only retained interest but was overtaking me—I vaguely registered the foul carrion smell of the ubiquitous stinkhorn fungi. Far from actually conceiving the idea that the rotting meat scent in the air might overwhelm my own scent, however, I simply tripped on a root and tumbled face-first to the ground in the midst of the noisome fungi. As I recovered my senses, I perceived in the corner of my eye that my resting place was screened from sight by a natural bower of leaves and fronds, and it belatedly occurred to me that I might elude the Rex by remaining where the foliage hid me while the stinkhorns simultaneously masked my scent.

Despite being hidden to both sight and smell, the minutes I spent on the ground felt like hours, and they were some of the most excruciating minutes (or hours) of my life. I would not have moved at that point in any event for fear of exposing myself, but even if I had wanted to, the thump of footsteps approaching from somewhere over my shoulder would have dissuaded me. The footsteps stopped, and in my mind's eye I could almost see the cruel death's-head of a face with its dagger teeth stooping toward my hiding place and trying to nose me out among the brush. Now and then I heard the snuffle of breath, sometimes just over my head and sometimes farther away, and fought to suppress both my trembling at the Rex's proximity and my gagging at the stench of the stinkhorns, certain all the while that the Rex would discover me in the next moment.

The Rex did not find me, but I do not for the life of me remember hearing the thud of footsteps to suggest its retreat. Nor do I know how long I lay among the stench and dirt holding my breath, but eventually I noticed that I had not heard my pursuer for some time. Finally I summoned the courage to raise my head, and my secular leanings notwithstanding, I was tempted to sing a hymn of joy when I confirmed that the Rex was nowhere to be seen.

After having such a close shave with the Likouala Rex, I perhaps should have accepted once and for all that it was a flesh and blood animal, but the postscript to this encounter shattered what little certainty I might have developed. Interestingly, it was the denouement of Walter's feud with the feticheuse Meombe that suggested, more tantalizingly than I would have liked, an alternative explanation for my sightings of the Rex. Walter delivered news of his confrontation with the feticheuse a few hours after my close call, when he returned from Toukalaka in such high spirits that I knew he must have scored some victory over his nemesis.

"I finally got the best of that she-devil Meombe," he said. "I accused her of witchcraft for sending me visions of those beastly hunters, and she was tried and convicted."

"I suppose that's good," I said, "but wouldn't they just sentence her to a fine like you?"

"That's precisely what they did."

"Then why are you so happy?"

"Don't you see? Meombe can't pay a fine—most of her clients pay for her services in live chickens or fresh produce, mind you—so they put her in jail until someone pays for her! I daresay she can't do anything to me from there!"

Aside from outwitting the feticheuse, Walter and Henri made a discovery in the fetish house during the course of the witchcraft investigation that threw my perception of the Rex into question. While raiding Meombe's sanctum, they had confiscated several items that Walter adjudged to have magical significance. These included Walter's own hairbrush, which had presumably been taken in order to hex him (just as he had been saying for some time), and two crude stuffed dolls that seemed to glance back at us askance from the uneven positioning of their button eyes.

"What are these?" I asked, though I anticipated Walter's guess.

"Why, poppets, of course," he said. "What a lay person might refer to as 'voodoo dolls.' She was undoubtedly using them to send me all those waking nightmares of that beastly hunter."

Among those who believe in fetish, it has long been accepted that practitioners can send visions and nightmares to their enemies. One example is the so-called dog magic, still practiced in West Africa, by which the witchdoctor purportedly sends a debtor nightmares of being chased by dogs until he pays his creditor. Of course, announcing to a suggestible person that you have sent him nightmares will more often than not induce those nightmares regardless of magic, but the question of cause is fairly academic to the interested parties if the result is obtained.

The possibility of the feticheuse using magic to conjure fearful visions had obvious implications for Walter's sightings, but it occurred to Walter that I, too, might have been targeted.

"You'll notice that there are two poppets, Matthew," he said, "so it behooves me to ask: have you seen anything strange lately?"

When Walter confronted me with his discovery, it occurred to me regardless of my skepticism toward fetish that Walter's explanation for his own hallucinations might apply with equal force to my sightings of the Rex. On the other hand, I am not suggestible enough to psychosomatically experience such a phantasm, and I was no more eager to espouse the idea of literal magic than I had been to conjecture a living *Tyrannosaurus*. Indeed, had my sighting been of anything but a Rex, I would not even have been tempted to entertain the possibility of black magic. In any event, there was only one thing I could say if I did not want to hear Walter carping about the matter ad nauseam.

"No," I said. "Not that I remember."

If the discovery of the poppets alone did not cast doubt on my experiences with the Rex, then you can imagine my disquiet at the fact that the Rex stopped appearing at this point—coincidentally just when Walter had relieved Meombe of the dolls. To my skeptical mind, choosing between a living *Tyrannosaurus* and an African curse was like choosing between Scylla and Charybdis, but at least the absence of the Rex in the coming days gratefully allowed me to postpone making a decision on its reality. Truth be told, even if I wasn't sure what to believe, I would have been happy to live in doubt if it meant that I never saw that leering death's-head again.

CHAPTER XIX

THE ROGUE DRAGON OF BENE

Any species may produce a rogue animal, but the definition of the term is somewhat nebulous. Some animals are called rogues after they raid crops or interfere with vehicular traffic, but others are rogues because they attack or even harm people. In any event, an unusual relationship with humans beings and their works—confronting us rather than avoiding us like the rest of their kind—defines the rogue. When it comes down to it, the word refers to any animal that does not behave in a manner that is convenient to human beings.

There was no reason to believe that a *mokele-mbembe* could not go rogue under the right circumstances, but it seemed to Walter and me that such incidents should be rare because the dragons do not live in close proximity to the local villages. On the other hand, we were so notorious for our connection with the dragons that the villagers brought us any information concerning *mokele-mbembe* activity, and so we were apprised quickly when a seeming rogue dragon appeared in the Likouala.

The news of a marauding *mokele-mbembe* reached us through a deputy from the village of Bene who had been dispatched to seek our counsel as dragon experts (or at least the closest facsimile thereof). A *mokele-mbembe* had reportedly visited the village's weekly market, where it had both chased away the paying customers and purchased all the fruit at the discount sellers grudgingly afford a behemoth that can literally trample their objections (viz: free). Those few souls brave enough to try shooing the trespasser away were discouraged by a threatening lunge or a mighty bellow, and the animal went about its business in the market until it had satisfied its craving for produce, at which point it had lumbered back into the forest and vanished.

In his somewhat rosy view of the dragons he studied, Walter was skeptical of this account.

"This doesn't sound like any dragon I've ever seen," he said. "It must be some mistake."

Walter may have doubted that the dragons would have raided a human settlement, but even he recognized the importance of easing relations between the *mokele-mbembe* and their human neighbors as a conservation measure. If a rogue dragon bothered the villagers without being discouraged, it was all too likely that the villagers would turn against the dragons in general, even individuals who had nothing to do with the rogue. With the foregoing in mind, we journeyed to Bene to examine the scene of the alleged attack and verify whether a dragon was in fact involved.

When we arrived in town, we confronted a scene that resembled the aftermath of a hurricane more than that of an animal attack. Where a tidy row of sago palms had once chaperoned humble but neatly-kept houses, most had been stripped bare and their fronds scattered across the street, and at least one wooden shed had been razed to the ground. In the marketplace, the ground was cobbled with pieces of splintered wood, shreds of basket, more palm fronds, and the smashed remains of what little fruit the dragon had not seized in tribute.

The destruction alone could have been accomplished by any number of animals, but fortunately the invader was considerate enough to leave tracks scattered about the village it had sacked. These were roughly circular in shape but for the outline of three distinct clawed toes, and they were about 24 inches in diameter. We quickly recognized them, from our many observations of live dragons leaving such prints, as the marks of a *mokele-mbembe*'s passage.

"I suppose there's no getting around it," Walter said. "This is undoubtedly the work of a *mokele-mbembe.* I still think it's nothing to worry about, though. We've studied dragons for months, and this is the first we've heard of overtly aggressive behavior like this. It will probably never happen again."

So saying, Walter returned to his observation of the herd and did not expect to hear any more of the putative rogue.

If Walter was initially inclined to dismiss this rampage as an isolated incident of aberrant behavior, the idea of a bona fide rogue dragon became more plausible when similar attacks recurred. A small cocoa plantation was raided and most of the trees either knocked over or browsed clean, and a pirogue full of fisherman was chased downriver by a long-necked beast that it surprised around a bend in the Likouala-aux-Herbes River. Aside from the descriptions of the creature, which clearly indicated a dragon, prints found in the wake of several altercations were the same shape and size as those we had previously found, suggesting that the same individual had been involved each time.

"Go ahead and say it," Walter said to me after we had found the same tracks several times. "I was wrong. We seem to have a dragon exhibiting so-called 'rogue' behavior after all."

"What do you mean to do about it?" I asked.

"We shall simply have to find this dragon and study it so we can figure out why it's behaving this way. I hate to leave the herd, especially if there's a chance one of our scaly girls is pregnant, but I suppose there's nothing for it."

At the time, the appearance of the rogue dragon was little more than a behavioral curiosity to investigate, and Walter applied himself to its study with his accustomed diligence. We temporarily transferred our operations to Bene, the site of the first attack, and we solicited and investigated news of additional incidents with the rogue, eager to observe it in the flesh. In retrospect, however, I wonder if either of us would have been so keen to pursue the rogue if we had guessed what we would ultimately discover.

*

Tracking down a rogue dragon is extremely difficult as a consequence of its unpredictable behavior. It may strike at a location once, never to return, with nary a clue as to where it will go next. Even if it makes multiple visits to any one site, it may still vanish just when the dracontologists arrive thinking to meet it. Nor does a familiarity with the habits of dragons in general help in forecasting the rogue's movements, for the rogue by definition does not conform to the behavior typical of its kind.

For some time, it seemed as if Walter and I were doomed to just miss the rogue wherever we sought him. With the help of the signal drums and our usual informants, we learned quickly when the dragon was loitering about a manioc field or wandering the streets of a village, and we hastened to the site seeking a glimpse. No matter how speedy we thought we were, however, the dragon had always moved on by the time we arrived, leaving only footprints, debris, and the mystery of its unaccountable behavior in its wake.

"How the devil are we supposed to study it," Walter asked, "if it won't stay still?"

Regardless of Walter's frustration, the rogue led us a merry chase for the next week. We pursued it up and down a 10-mile stretch of the Likouala-aux-Herbes and up several tributaries so poorly known that they do not appear in maps to this day. There was little we could do but follow every lead and hope our luck would change, but the suspense of trying to intercept a roving dragon was excruciating.

These repeated disappointments made Walter so cross that I thought he would abandon the pursuit and return to the more tractable herd, but we managed to be in the right place at the right time before that happened. We had stopped in a small village overnight on our way to the remote site of a recent river encounter with the rogue, and luck was with us: the rogue struck in that very village, saving us the trip upriver to meet it.

When the rogue appeared, it took us completely by surprise. As we were going about our morning ablutions, we heard a tremendous row of people shouting, punctuated by a long, loud roar. We immediately recognized the familiar tenor of an agitated dragon, and scrambling into our clothes as quickly as we could, we staggered in the direction of the noise, which came from somewhere beyond the whitewashed houses. By the time we rounded the last corner, the dragon must have accomplished its purpose, for we beheld its broad red backside being pursued back into the forest by the curses of a devastated manioc field's owner.

"Don't go yet!" Walter cried. "Let me get a look at you first!"

Strangely, Walter's call was heeded, and judging from what we soon discovered, the dragon may actually have recognized Walter's voice. When Walter shouted, the dragon paused in its retreat and turned just enough that it could bring its eyes to bear upon us by craning its neck. As soon as I saw its face, I was dumbstruck with recognition, and Walter with me, for this was no strange dragon suddenly come into our study area but our erstwhile companion.

"Gracious!" Walter said. "Do you see that, Matthew? It's Fafnir!"

Having recognized the rogue, Walter and I could only speculate later as to how Fafnir assumed the role. Adolescent males without the mentoring of older, experienced males to model proper behavior are particularly susceptible to going rogue. This phenomenon has been observed, for example, among young bull elephants where all of the larger bulls who might otherwise keep them in line have been extirpated by hunters. Though it had not occurred to us sooner, Fafnir, who had similarly been cast into the wild without the benefit of a proper role model, would also have been prone to falling into roguish habits without anyone to correct him.

Whatever the cause of Fafnir's behavior, Walter's entire attitude changed once he recognized the dragon.

"Come over here this instant," he said to Fafnir, kindlier now, "and let me take a good look at you. Why, I think you've grown since I last saw you."

Even if Walter was overjoyed to be reunited with his dragon, Fafnir himself was more ambivalent. After inspecting us coolly for several moments, he resumed his trek into the forest without sparing us another glance, and all of Walter's pleading was inadequate to induce him to linger.

"Wait," Walter cried, "don't' go! Come back! Come back!"

Our first glimpse of Fafnir since our unexpected parting was brief, but it invigorated our determination to pursue the rogue. Aside from our obvious purpose of dissuading him from raiding villages and making a nuisance of himself, we also meant to reassure ourselves that he was healthy and well in the wake of his altercation with the hunter. Perhaps we should have realized from the circumstances of our reunion that he was not entirely the same dragon he had been when we had known him, but instead we reckoned on our familiarity enabling us to overcome his bad behavior and put him on the right path.

Because they do not fear us like the rest of their kind, rogue animals tend to be dangerous to human beings. Where most animals will flee when confronted by humans, the rogue is apt to charge anyone who interferes with his depredations. Indeed, some rogues, for reasons that can only occasionally be divined, intentionally attack and chase humans on sight. The threat of injury depends upon the size of the animal, but it goes almost without saying that a rogue *mokele-mbembe*, if it was so inclined, could smash bone to dust, rend flesh, and kill without even exerting itself.

Even if he had the capacity to inflict serious injury, Fafnir's raids on the villages were fairly bloodless for the first weeks of his spree. Usually a bellow was enough to scatter everyone out of his path, and even when the dragon gave chase to one of the villagers, he left off after a few galloping steps and let them flee while he resumed whatever business—usually feeding—had brought him into town. Destructive as he was to property, he seemed harmless to person, and this would of course have been consonant with our knowledge of his personality.

"I don't know why everybody is so damned worried," Walter said. "Now that we know it's Fafnir, I think it's safe to say he doesn't have the heart to actually hurt anybody."

Walter's perception of Fafnir's gentleness was threatened, however, when one of the dragon's raids resulted in a casualty. An octogenarian from Maloka, Paul G., fled too slowly when the dragon visited his village, and the dragon trampled him in mid-stride. By the time Fafnir had passed far enough away for the broken body to be safely retrieved, the old man was unrecognizable—and beyond help.

The death of a villager at Fafnir's hands cast his behavior in a new light that did not appear so innocent. It occurred to me then that Fafnir's experience with the hunter might have changed his temperament, but Walter would hear none of it.

"I'm sure it's only an accident," he said. "It's hard for an animal of that size to avoid stepping on every little thing. They've almost stepped on you or me more than once, and there was nothing malevolent about that, was there?"

"I guess not," I said, "but this seems much more aggressive."

"Nonsense. Our scaly friend is alone and frightened, so he's acting out a little. Everything will be fine once I find him."

Walter clung to his certainty that all would be well once we intercepted Fafnir as we continued our pursuit, and the only way to test his belief would be to confront the dragon. Nevertheless, Fafnir eluded us as before, and in the meantime, another villager was killed, this time in a more unmistakably aggressive manner: the dragon snatched up a woman in his mouth even as she fled, shook her like a dog worrying a rat, and dashed her against the side of a building, where she broke her neck.

"I know what you're thinking, Matthew," Walter said in the wake of this news, "and you're wrong. He's frightened and disoriented, that's all. I'm sure he didn't know what he was doing."

"He couldn't have accidentally done this," I said.

"Well, even if he meant to do it, so what? He might have killed a few strangers, but he knows me. I'm sure he wouldn't hurt a hair on my head. We just need to find him so that I can lure him away from the villagers, for their good and his as well."

Walter's assurances notwithstanding, I became more and more certain that Fafnir's misfortunes had worked a change for the worse, and even Walter's tenderness might not be enough to recall the dragon's loyalty. At the same time, however, I shared Walter's sense of responsibility for our former dragon's actions, nor could I think of a better plan to dissuade him from further raids. We therefore continued chasing a rogue dragon in the hope of befriending it, uncertain whether we would be rewarded for our troubles with the same fate as his previous victims.

While naturalists such as Walter Spink seek to peaceably dissuade rogue animals from further acts of destruction and violence, there are others who would simply destroy them. Beleaguered villagers desperate to end the rogue's spree by the most expeditious means urge the latter course, and they can only afford to be so patient with their lives and livelihoods at stake. And if the naturalists cannot avert the raids quickly enough, a third group is willing to heed the residents' cries for blood: the big game hunters, who are eager for any excuse to shoot an animal and pat themselves on the back as heroes.

With the possibility that one of the big game hunters might be called upon to dispatch the rogue, we might have anticipated that James Phillip Hartley would take his own brand of untoward interest in Fafnir. Sure enough, we encountered him again in Epena while we were on Fafnir's trail in the wake of his most recent sortie against a cocoa plantation. Walter noticed him first and recognized him with all the relish one might reserve for the recurrence of a chronic illness.

"That looks like that Heartless fellow who shot our poor Fafnir," he said, "although I wouldn't mind being wrong."

"I think you're right," I said.

"Bother."

Despite his obvious distaste for the man, Walter guessed the purpose of Hartley's visit, coinciding as it did with the dragon's raids, and confronted him.

"You there!" he squawked. "I know just what you're planning, and I won't have it. You leave my dragon alone!"

"Your dragon has been causing a hell of a lot of trouble," Hartley said.

"It's no reason for you to shoot him."

"Your dragon is the most dangerous animal around. It has to be stopped before it hurts anyone else."

"You're wrong. Once I find him, I shall calm him down and lead him someplace he won't bother anybody."

Walter's opposition notwithstanding, Hartley was not dissuaded, and now we repeatedly encountered the hunter while we pursued Fafnir's trail. When we came into a village to assess the aftermath of Fafnir's raid, we would hear the deep hum of his familiar voice from beyond the houses, or we might simply round a corner and find him crouched over a line of footprints in a flattened field. Though we abhorred his attitude toward his fellow creatures, we were forced to concede that he was resourceful and enjoyed connections that made it entirely possible he would intercept the dragon ahead of us.

"We need to hurry up and find our scaly friend," Walter said, "or that Heartless fellow will shoot him before we have the chance to do anything about him."

Finding the hunter always ahead of us added urgency to our quest to find the rogue dragon. We woke earlier, journeyed farther, and tried the patience of more than a few guides in our hurry. While Walter single-mindedly pursued his reunion with Fafnir, however, my feelings continued to be more mixed; I could not shake a sense of foreboding despite Walter's confidence that the dragon would receive us as old friends. As much as I wanted to success in our search, I dreaded the dragon's uncertain temperament, and I was ultimately right to do so.

✷

Once an animal has been branded as a rogue, there are only a few possible outcomes. Occasionally, with enough resources, the rogue can be relocated far enough away from human beings that it can no longer trouble anyone. More often, however, the rogue is put down, usually because it requires less effort and delivers quicker results than more peaceful methods. Knowing this possibility, Walter was so desperate to locate Fafnir that he pursued the dragon without any consideration for his own safety, even when we finally engaged the rogue *mokele-mbembe* again, this time in a small village called Tushunguti.

I will never forget the sight of Fafnir galumphing toward us down the main street of Tushunguti if I live to be a hundred years old; it would certainly have dissuaded me from approaching him if I had been minded to do so in the first place. Though I knew he was large, he seemed positively humongous against the backdrop of one-story houses, which his immense body seemed apt to shoulder out of his way. Nor was he our good old Fafnir who quailed and ran for cover in the face of creatures a fraction his size: now he lumbered inexorably forward, and his neck lashed snake-like after the people who fled his coming. Even as we watched, he chased a man so eagerly toward one of the houses that he crashed into it, knocking it over upon himself in the process, only to break forth from the pile of rubble and resume his rampage none the worse for wear.

When the dragon continued to advance, Walter met him like a figure out of legend. The lore of *mokele-mbembe*'s distant cousin, the Loch Ness Monster, says that Saint Columba confronted the monster when it threatened a swimmer in the River Ness in 565 CE; with no more trepidation than if he had been scolding a naughty child, Columba commanded the monster to "go no further, nor touch the man," whereupon the monster spared its victim and fled. With all the assurance of Columba but none of the spiritual authority, Walter Spink sauntered forward into the dragon's path, leaving me gaping from behind the corner of one of the houses during their confrontation.

"You there! Fafnir!" he cried. "You leave those people alone!"

At the sound of Walter's voice, the dragon aborted his pursuit of a fleeing woman and fixed his gaze upon the old man who stood goading him from down the street.

"Stop this at once," Walter said. "Look at all the trouble you've caused, and all the people you've frightened. Now, come here and we'll take you somewhere safe where you won't bother anybody. Come on."

While Walter spoke, Fafnir listened with head cocked attentively, and when the old man finished the dragon lumbered toward him. Though he seemed to respond to Walter's command, his bearing remained tense, and he advanced with the same aggressive, lurching movements with which he had pursued the villagers rather than the leisurely or playful canter of a submissive dragon returning to his old friend's side.

Even as Fafnir closed upon Walter, it occurred to me that his behavior might be caused not by the absence of a loving role model but the madness of a painful injury. Now that I saw him more closely, I perceived the round, scarlet pit of a bullet hole against the cinnamon hide of his chest, the handiwork of Hartley's inexperience finding a dragon's vital spot. The wound radiated a starburst of wavy black lines and wept a milky green pus, and it must have been excruciating. This observation suddenly suggested a different explanation for the dragon's recent actions.

Rogue behavior can come about in several ways. Some rogues are behaviorally maladjusted as I previously described, but other animals go rogue due to a painful injury, often inflicted by ham-fisted hunters. The rogue elephant of Aberdare Forest, for example, behaved aggressively as a result of a musket bullet lodged in the nerve center at the base of its right tusk. More importantly, Iain Douglas-Hamilton documented several of the Manyara elephants becoming violent for similar reasons, during which times they were just as apt to attack habituated humans as they were strangers.

Like the rogue elephants, it was entirely possible that Fafnir was maddened by pain to have become so uncharacteristically aggressive. If that was so, he would doubtless be as merciless to Walter as he had been to the villagers, and I tried to warn Walter even as the dragon barreled toward him.

"Walter," I said, "something's wrong. You need to get out of his way."

"Nonsense, Matthew," he said.

"I don't think he's going to stop."

"I tell you, I can get through to him, and I'm not budging."

Before Walter could argue any further, Fafnir was upon him with no indication of yielding and loosed a mighty bellow that was anything but friendly. Walter would almost certainly have stood his ground, convinced that his influence could stay the dragon's violence even as he was trampled to death under its angry feet, but for Hartley's unlooked-for appearance. In the blink of an eye, he was in the street training his rifle at the looming dragon, and before I fully comprehended what I was seeing, he fired.

The hunter's aim was truer this time than it had been in his previous engagement with the dragon. Almost simultaneously with the blast, Fafnir's head snapped backward with the force of the bullet to his head, and suddenly his humongous body went limp as a rag doll and collapsed into a 12-foot-tall heap in the middle of the street.

Mercifully, he did not suffer but expired almost instantly, the life fleeing his body with one impotent twitch of his tail followed by stillness.

While the dragon came to rest, Walter just blinked his black bean eyes at the spectacle, hardly able to process this turn of events.

"What the devil happened?" he asked. "Who did this?"

Having approached the dragon to nudge its head with his boot and reassure himself of its mortality, Hartley answered before I had a chance to explain.

"If you're talking about that fantastic shot," he said, "it was me."

"You! I should have known it would be you who'd shoot a poor dragon, but I still can't see how you're so damned proud of it."

"Well, it was a hell of a shot, and it saved your life."

"It was entirely unnecessary. I would have gotten through to him if you'd only given me a few more moments. I know I would have gotten through."

Despite his words, I suspect that Walter knew, deep down, that his effort would have been futile and Fafnir's death inevitable regardless of how much time the hunter afforded, but he would never have given me, Hartley, or anyone else the satisfaction of acknowledging it. Instead, he hurled imprecations at the hunter, finding it easier to show anger than to experience the loss, at least in the short term. For as long as he lived, Walter would never speak of his feelings at Fafnir's death, but long hours that he spent alone in his tent with the rest of us shut out of his presence testified to his grief.

As if we were not already grieving Fafnir's loss, we also had to witness the celebrations with which his death met. The villagers emerged from their houses to cheer their deliverance while Hartley stood cradling his rifle with one boot planted on the dragon's lifeless neck, and the hunter undoubtedly felt himself very heroic posing in this manner. I could not completely begrudge the villagers their relief, knowing the terror the dragon had brought into their lives, but the feeling that we alone mourned Fafnir sharpened the loss to a point beyond Walter's tolerance.

"Let's go back to camp, Matthew," he said at last. "I can't bear to see any more."

With accordingly heavy hearts, Walter and I left the village and resumed our work with the surviving members of the herd, and we could only reflect upon the senselessness of the entire affair. Fafnir's fate is sadly the same as that of most animals once they have made themselves a nuisance to humans, even when a human being's conduct turned them rogue, as in our dragon's case. Even as we grieved Fafnir, we tried to take some consolation in hoping that the hunter's appetite for dragon blood had been slaked and that the rest of the herd at least was safe from his attentions. Unfortunately, the average big game hunter is just as implacable as any rogue dragon, and even this minimal solace was denied us.

CHAPTER XX

DESTROY THE THINGS THAT YOU LOVE

Dragons in the wild face a multitude of threats to their well-being. The jury may still be deliberating the existence of a living *Tyrannosaurus*, but illness, injury, and the butchery of the big game hunters are very real dangers; poor Fafnir's fate clearly demonstrates the latter. Preoccupied as he was with protecting his beloved dragons from such obvious hazards, Walter Spink overlooked the possibility that our presence in the dragons' lives might play a role in their undoing, at least until his own conduct finally endangered them.

After Fafnir's death, it was only natural for Walter to fixate on the threat posed by the big game hunter. Though I will undoubtedly be criticized for the analogy, the big game hunters of the world are much like its addicts of controlled substances; their fix may involve spilling blood rather than consuming drugs or alcohol, but they are similarly insatiable, no matter how many animals they kill, and continually seeking the thrill of another, more impressive kill the way a junkie pursues a greater high. Their kind depleted the great herds of Africa in the late 19th and early 20th centuries and would no doubt hunt the dragons back to extinction without regard to the miracle of their surviving this long. Knowing the mentality of the big game hunter, Walter and I hardly dared believe that Hartley would be satisfied shooting just one *mokele-mbembe*, regardless of how fervently we hoped it would be so.

Our hopes were dashed when we learned, just days after Fafnir's death, that Hartley still sought *mokele-mbembe* regardless of his success. Henri had gathered the news on his weekly supply run to Toukalaka and reported it immediately upon his return, knowing how it would concern Walter.

"Hell and damnation!" Walter said. "A thousand deaths aren't enough for that Heartless fellow. I daresay he won't be satisfied until he's cleaned out the whole damned forest."

Now that he knew with certainty that the hunter sought to track down and destroy more dragons, Walter became positively paranoid for the herd's safety. Constantly afraid that the hunter would come upon the dragons, Walter was watchful to an extreme that shamed anything I have seen before or since. Like those of a tiny, hunted animal, his eyes darted here and there across the *bai* or through the forest, and he repeatedly glanced over his shoulder as he followed the dragons while convincing himself that every smell, sound, and movement betrayed the lurking hunter.[32]

"What's that noise? Has he found us?"

"I thought I saw something moving over there in the trees. What is it? Is it him?"

"Why is everything so quiet all of a sudden? Good lord, it's not him, is it?"

These were all, gratefully, false alarms, but even once the source of a noise or movement had been identified, Walter would not be assuaged unless the herd left the area. Indeed, at times he simply decided, without any reason that was apparent to me, that the dragons had lingered for too long and were unduly pressing their

---

[32]Needless to say, Walter's unparalleled alertness worked against our old friend Heep, who try as he might could not sneak up on the old man.

luck. In either situation, his solution was the same: to move the dragons away from the imagined danger.

"We should get our scaly friends away from here," he would say, "just to be safe."

The first time Walter proposed to move the dragons, I thought he was overestimating our talent for managing them, but he was either daring enough or foolish enough (depending upon your point of view) to actually pull it off. His method involved sauntering casually up to Ceto, who was too nearsighted to mark his coming as long as he didn't speak—and who was easily startled at hearing an unexpected noise within her space. Coming close enough to touch, Walter smacked her leg (her flank being out of his reach overhead) and squawked in a shrill voice that panicked me, to say nothing of the dragoness.

"All right, then," he said. "Move along, old girl!"

When Walter shouted at her heels, the matriarch could have reflexively kicked the noisy pest rather than moving as he wanted, but Walter's estimation of her personality proved accurate. Whenever he unexpectedly assailed her in this manner, Ceto invariably lurched into retreat. More importantly, where she led, the rest of the herd followed, and in this manner Walter was able to move the dragons whenever he became paranoid for their safety.

Whether Walter's management had its desired effect or the hunter simply missed them, the dragons were safely out of Hartley's crosshairs during this time. After a week of being on alert in this manner without encountering Hartley, we were encouraged, but we entertained no illusions that he would be dissuaded by a mere week's bad luck. Sure enough, the hunter devoted the same ingenuity to his bloodthirsty goal that Walter did to protecting the dragons, and he conceived an alternative means of finding them—one that, to our great distress, involved us.

*

Even for an experienced hunter, *mokele-mbembe* are difficult to track in their natural habitat. They tend to retrace their own routes or to follow elephant trails and to travel in single file, thus minimizing the signs of their passage. At the same time, the undergrowth of the Congolian swamp forest in which they live is unusually dense, so a tracker could be just a few feet away from a *mokele-mbembe* trail without noticing. Unless the hunter is fortunate enough to befriend the Bangombe as we did—a rare circumstance—he might wander the forest for a lifetime without finding the dragons.

It was undoubtedly the difficulty of tracking in this environment that initially spared the herd from Hartley's designs. Unfortunately, this failure only inspired him to rethink his technique, as we learned on our way to rendezvous with the herd one morning. One moment, we were traipsing through the forest with no particular care to the noise of our chatter or the path of broken foliage we left behind, and the next Ekianga called a stop and listened like an animal that has scented a predator upwind.

"What the devil is wrong now?" Walter demanded.

"Someone is following," Ekianga said.

"Following," Mambunia agreed.

"Gracious! Where?"

By dispatching Ekianga to circle back, silent as a leopard, while we trudged noisily on our way, we induced our pursuer to follow so that the Bangombe could get a look at him. Minutes later, Ekianga returned to us and reported what he had seen: a white man with gray hair and beard, carrying a rifle.

"It's that damned Heartless fellow," Walter said. "He must be following us hoping we'll lead him to our scaly friends."

"What are you going to do?" I asked.

"Well, I'll be damned if I lead him to my dragons."

Though he hated to lose a day with the dragons, Walter was more unwilling to risk Hartley finding them, so we backtracked to camp and stayed there. In the coming days, knowing the hunter was lurking about did not dissuade us from our observation of the dragons, but it did make us more careful. Having successfully averted danger to the herd, at least for the time being, we took pains not to make ourselves conspicuous or leave a visible trail that might lead the hunter to us—and thence to the dragons.

"I know a few ways to avoid being followed," Walter said, "although it's been a while since I've had to use them."

There are a variety of ways for human beings to avoid being tracked in the wilderness. Aside from holding one's tongue, it is also necessary to step carefully so as not to crash through branches, break twigs, or splash through water, any of which noises might call attention to an otherwise stealthy march. Similarly, walking through streams or standing water where possible precludes leaving footprints that may be found even after one has passed through. Careful attention to not disturbing the environment, such as using a stick to part foliage rather than breaking through, also minimizes the possibility of pursuit. It is entirely possible, with enough care, for a human being to move about without leaving any visible traces, as many indigenous peoples do even today.

We enlisted these and other methods to hide the routes we took to the dragons, but some members of our group were more skillful in this regard than others. The Bangombe had no problem whatsoever moving silently without so much as breaking a twig, being one of the indigenous peoples that have so successfully avoided detection. Though I would not learn the reason for many years, Walter, too, had learned to move stealthily through the forest when he was so minded. No, the member of our group who had the most trouble rising to this challenge was yours truly.

Not being much of an outdoorsman, I rarely knew I had done wrong until Walter called my attention to my various errors. I would be minding my own business (and laboring under the impression that I was being suitably quiet and stealthy) when a squawk from Walter would disabuse me of my complacency.

"No, no, no, Matthew!" he would say. "Don't you see that you just left a print, right there plain as day for anyone to find?"

Or:

"What are you doing, Matthew? You're leaving a trail—just look at all those bent branches!"

In addition to earning me increasingly strong rebukes from Walter, my missteps necessitated much circling back and meandering to restart our journey to the dragons afresh so that my carelessness could not betray the herd. Sometimes Walter aborted our journey to meet the dragons altogether rather than risk their lives to my incompetence, but more often he dispatched Mambunia to esquire me back to camp where I wouldn't be any trouble while Walter and Ekianga sought the herd alone. Some days Walter abandoned me in camp from the very beginning rather than wrangle me through the forest.

"I'm sorry, Matthew," he would say, "but you're something of a lummox, at least when it comes to trying to move quietly in the forest, and I simply can't afford to take the chance on you alerting that beastly hunter to our scaly friends' whereabouts."

Even when I did not run afoul of Walter, and no matter how careful we were, there were days when we detected Hartley on our trail when we set forth to contact the dragons. Occasionally Walter or I heard the rustle of leaves at his passage or the plash of his footstep in the standing water of the swamp forest, but usually the Bangombe sensed him following and alerted us. However the hunter came to our attention, Walter immediately called a halt and confronted him.

"We know you're out there," he would say, "so there's no use hiding. By now you must realize I'm not going to lead you to my dragons. It's time you gave up and left them alone."

Walter's delivered his speech in whatever direction he thought the hunter was hidden, but Hartley generally stayed quiet even when confronted in this manner. Perhaps he thought to make us second-guess our perception that he was near, but if so, he underestimated Walter's caution. Even if he had not been certain of being followed, he would have aborted his visit to the dragons until such time as he could do so relatively certain that he was not pursued. Once we had reason to believe the hunter was following, we turned back and spent the day in camp, where Walter tried to reassure himself that Hartley could only pursue the dragons unsuccessfully for so long before becoming discouraged.

"He'll have to give up eventually," he would say.

Regardless of Walter's hope, the hunter did not give up in the coming weeks, nor did he seem apt to do so any time soon. There were stretches of four or five days at a time when he caught up to us and we were forced to abandon our plans to see the dragons, and this went on for several weeks. That alone should have convinced Walter that the hunter would not be put off, but if it didn't, Hartley's response one day when Walter confronted him in the forest made it clear that he intended to follow us as long as it took to find the dragons.

"You're going to a hell of a lot of effort," Hartley said, stepping out from behind an arum, "but it's not going to do any good. I won't give up."

"Why must you chase my dragons so?" Walter asked. "You've already killed one. Shouldn't that be enough?"

"I want more."

"These animals are a miracle. They've survived 65 million years longer than all the rest of their kind, and we have no idea how many there are."

"What the hell does that matter to me?"

"What's that to you? Of all the—their lives are precious. Why must you kill them?"

"Because I can."

"Not if I can help it, you can't."

"You might try. You might even keep me off their track for a while, but sooner or later, I'll still get them."

The hunter was true to his word, and he continued tracking us in the coming days until we felt hunted ourselves. Under these circumstances, I confess that I couldn't see any end to our situation other than the hunter eventually finding his quarry, and all of us found our faculties and tempers strained. Walter especially, who already suffered grief and guilt at his inability to save Fafnir, seemed poised to fracture under the pressure. I surreptitiously monitored his behavior for the signs of some sort of breakdown, but for the longest time, he remained in good spirits no matter how persistently we were pursued. It was only later that he became convinced that there was no saving his dragons, at which point his behavior began to suggest he was contemplating something desperate and dangerous.

Human beings have the strange ability to resist believing something regardless of all evidence, only accepting it when they choose to do so. No matter how many times we caught the hunter on our trail, and no matter that Hartley had declared his intention to pursue us as long as it took to reach the dragons, Walter Spink still believed he could save them. On the other hand, Walter had an unusual faith in the power of African fetish magic, and remembering a witchdoctor's vision of doom convinced him he could not protect his dragons where the hunter's persistence had not.

I saw you, cher, *standing over the dead bodies of a herd of* mokele-mbembe, Madame Meombe had said. *You had killed them.* At the time, Walter had ridiculed the prediction, for the idea of him intentionally harming his beloved dragons was too preposterous to entertain. Now that it seemed Walter might inadvertently bring about the dragons' destruction by leading a big game hunter to them, however, he recalled the feticheuse's warning, and it seemed not only more plausible to him but inevitable that he should bring the dragons' doom to them.

I learned that Walter had reconsidered the significance of the feticheuse's vision after he spent several days acting more sullen than I had seen him since after Fafnir's death. Having already been concerned with his mental state, I probed until he confided the reason for his sudden low spirits.

"It's occurred to me that that Heartless fellow is going to get my dragons, after all," he said, "no matter how I try to protect them."

"What makes you so sure?" I asked (pretending I had not come to the same conclusion some time before).

"Because the feticheuse foresaw it."

"I don't understand."

"She had a vision of me standing over a group of dead *mokele-mbembe.* At first, I thought she believed I was going to kill them with my own hands, which was preposterous, but what if the vision means that I am going to lead that beastly hunter to them so that he can kill them?"

"I thought you didn't believe her."

"I didn't, but I'm starting to think I was wrong."

Normally I would have discounted the feticheuse's prediction, but it was not the time to debate the paranormal with Walter, and moreover I agreed with the assessment, if not the manner in which he reached it. For some time, I had conceived a chance to avert the dragons' fate but had kept it to myself, knowing Walter would receive it poorly. Now that he saw we could not dodge the hunter indefinitely, I chanced making the suggestion.

"Maybe we can stop it from happening," I said, "if we stop visiting the dragons."

"Believe it or not," Walter said, "I've thought the same thing, but I fear he would just find another way to track them down. No, the only way to save them would be to stop him from looking for them, and I haven't the faintest idea how to do that. I'll tell you one thing, though: I really will kill the dragons myself before I let that murderer mount their heads on his wall."

Once he convinced himself of the futility of resisting the hunter's designs on his dragons, Walter only sank further into despair. When we were in camp, he barely ate, and he neglected to keep up his notes. Even on the days when we visited the dragons without incident and were able to conduct our observations, Walter took no particular relish in his interactions with them. Rather, he viewed their destruction as a fait accompli, and he mourned them as if they had already been slaughtered and were mere ghosts haunting the forest. For example, when Campe probed Walter's pockets in search of food (which he had stopped bringing in his despondency), he did not move, and only his words to me evidenced that he even knew she was there.

"She would have gotten so big in a few more years."

And when I remarked that Echidna was eating enough for two dragons, hoping to rouse Walter's interest in the prospect of studying dragon birth, he hardly acknowledged me.

"Her babies would have been so beautiful."

After despairing in this manner for some time, Walter began withdrawing even from my company. He stopped taking me with him to view the dragons altogether, and if I inquired after his day's observations upon his return to camp, he would only say that the dragons were all right, "at least for now." He was obviously quite depressed, but even so, I did not anticipate him doing anything truly rash until I received an ominous response to one of my inquiries after his well-being.

"I'd be lying if I said I was doing particularly well under these circumstances, Matthew," he said, "but it doesn't matter. It will all be over soon. I know what I have to do."

Whatever Walter thought he had to do, he would not explain himself no matter how persistently I questioned him, but his wording made me anxious. It seemed clear that he was meditating some action, and in the absence of more information, I could only speculate as to what it might be. By the time I learned Walter's plan, I had envisioned a half dozen scenarios, none of which actually matched the outrageousness of what he ultimately did, and became positively frazzled with the waiting.

After a few suspenseful days, Walter made his move, though I did not know what he meant to do until after he had acted. One morning he visited the dragons, leaving me in camp as always, only to return early and in unusually good spirits. Nevertheless, I guessed that something was amiss from the way Ekianga, who had accompanied Walter, avoided my gaze. I suspected coming misfortune even more when Walter proposed to return to the herd and offered to bring me along, abandoning his usual caution.

"Aren't you worried I'll call attention to us?" I asked.

"It doesn't matter very much if you do," Walter said.

As if his words were not ominous enough, I noticed that Walter had also abandoned all care for the amount of noise he made traipsing through the forest. Not only did he step recklessly wherever he pleased and leave disturbed plants in his wake, but he spoke noisily and made so much rustling as he moved that it almost seemed intentional.

"He's going to find us," I said, referring to the hunter, "if you keep making so much noise."

"I daresay it doesn't matter if he does."

With Walter bush-whacking in this manner, the hunter found us just as I feared. Ekianga announced that we were being followed, and if I hadn't already suspected that something was terribly wrong, Walter's reception of Hartley would have removed all doubt.

"It's about time you caught up," he said in the hunter's direction. "I've been waiting for you. Come on out, and I'll take you to the dragons like you wanted."

At this, Hartley emerged from the brush and advanced cautiously, cradling his rifle protectively as if he were unsure of the old man's intentions.

"There you are," Walter said. "Come on, now."

Walter resumed trudging through the muck, but Hartley hesitated, scratching his gray beard in puzzlement.

"What the hell is this?" he asked. "Some kind of trick?"

"You want to see my dragons, don't you?"

"Yes. I just don't understand why you're being so accommodating all of a sudden. You know what I mean to do to them."

"Oh, there's nothing you can do to them now. Come along."

With this cryptic statement, Walter led the way to his beloved dragons with inexplicably good humor at the prospect of presenting them to an armed hunter, and I followed with mounting certainty—and corresponding dread—that something was terribly wrong. I could not think of a reason why Walter should suddenly change his course in this manner unless he had had a break with reality and meant to actually sacrifice the herd to the hunter, or…

Human beings are all too willing to destroy the things that they love best, especially if they are convinced that it is the only way to avert a worse fate. Perhaps the most dramatic example is that of Margaret Garner, a fugitive slave in pre-Civil War America who killed her own daughter to spare her the misery of being returned to the slave-owning southern states. Under the right circumstances or under enough strain, an otherwise unconscionable act can seem like the only alternative.

I saw you, cher, *standing over the dead bodies of a herd of* mokele-mbembe. *You had killed them.*

In a moment of dreadful clarity, it seemed as if the feticheuse's vision might be literally true; then we emerged onto Bangándo Bai, where we had first seen the dragons, and I knew what Madame had seen, for it was before my eyes. There was Walter Spink, meandering triumphantly among five hills the color of African earth that proved to be the lifeless bodies of five *mokele-mbembe.*

Lest the reader toss aside this memoir in premature frustration, I will reassure you that the dragons were not dead, even though they seemed to be from all external appearances. Not a chest heaved with continued breath, nor did a neck or limb stir when the hunter nudged it with his boot. Tiamat, who disliked human beings with a passion, did not so much as tremble at the sound of voices, and Campe, who was unabashedly curious of all newcomers, did not crane her neck inquisitively to see what we were.

The dragons remained in this state long enough to convey the impression of death, and while I was still reeling at this vision, the hunter blustered at Walter in his frustration (even though he meant to do the exact same thing to the dragons).

"What in the hell did you do?" Hartley asked.

"What does it look like?" Walter asked. "I spared them from serving as target practice for the likes of you. How do you like them now? It's not such great fun if you can't be the one to slaughter them, is it?"

Walter continued to gloat until the hunter left in disgust, and meanwhile I labored for several agonizing minutes under the same misapprehension of the dragons' condition as the hunter. This continued until Walter was certain that Hartley was out of earshot, at which point the old man disabused me of my needless grief.

"That Heartless fellow is gone now, Matthew," he said.

"I noticed."

"Well, if you know, then why the devil are you still sniveling? It's not as if they're really dead."

"Aren't they?"

"No, of course not! How could you think I'd do such a thing?"

When he finally realized my misunderstanding of the dragons' condition, Walter not only affirmed that they were perfectly healthy but explained the reason for their deathly appearance. For some time, he had been despondent with the grim realization that Hartley would not give up hunting the dragons while he knew they were alive, but just when it seemed there was no hope, he conceived a solution.

"I realized that I had to convince that beastly hunter that the dragons were dead, and then he would have no reason to look for them anymore. The trouble was how to make them look dead without actually killing them, but then I thought of that she-devil Meombe and what she did to me."

The reader will doubtless recall how the feticheuse caused Walter to appear to be dead by administering toxins that slow the heart rate and reduce breathing to counterfeit its appearance. In a moment of inspiration, it had occurred to Walter that he might use the so-called zombie medicine to trick the hunter into believing that Walter, in a moment of desperation, had killed the dragons himself. Meombe, who was still jailed pending her ability to pay her fine for purportedly bewitching Walter, cooperated in exchange for Walter paying her fine and arranging her release.

"As for my dragons," Walter said, "they'll all wake up in a little while none the worse for wear, and you and I will have our own herd of zombie dragons. Imagine!"

Walter Spink might not have murdered the dragons outright, but as I have said, he did endanger them, as we were about to learn. You see, by incapacitating the dragons, he delivered them from the hunter, but he simultaneously left them exposed to any other predator that might come along. With the amazing timing that only unfortunate events seem to possess, a different but familiar foe came upon us while we were still waiting for the dragons to revive, and there was no hope of Walter and me protecting them from this one.

We did not notice the newcomer immediately, but we heard a growling whose origin Walter initially mistook.

"For heaven's sake, Matthew," he said. "Eat something already."

"That wasn't my stomach," I said.

"Then what the devil was it?"

Though Walter could not conceive the source of the noise at first, I had a sinking feeling just what type of predator would be lurking about hoping to avail itself of the herd's incapacity, and I was sadly correct. Movement in the corner of my eye betrayed the position of something red and towering emerging on the far side of the *bai,* and when I looked head-on, I found the anticipated muscular legs and dangling forearms, and above them the huge, leering death's-head face brandishing dagger teeth. It was the Likouala Rex, and its patience had finally been rewarded with a crack at the dragons while they were unable to defend themselves.

While I considered the implications of the Rex's inopportune appearance, Walter finally perceived the intruder.

"Didn't I tell you it was a *Tyrannosaurus*?" he asked. "There can't be any doubt now."

"Whatever it is," I said, already backing away, "I'm more worried what it will do if the others don't wake up."

My concern being quite valid, Walter and I tried unsuccessfully to shake the *mokele-mbembe* awake while the Rex goose-stepped daintily toward us, sneering wickedly as if in assurance that our efforts would be in vain. Try as we might, we were unable to stir the sleeping dragons, and as the Rex came inexorably closer, we did the only thing left to us: we yelled at the top of our lungs. To be candid, my shout was one of terror (and a few octaves higher than what is popularly considered masculine), but Walter's was one of defiance.

"You stay away from my dragons," he shouted. "Shoo! I just saved them, and I'm certainly not about to deliver them over to your tender mercies!"

As you may expect, our show of noise did nothing to intimidate a predator of the Rex's standing, but it had an effect on another animal that we had not expected to be lurking nearby. In response to our shouting, the forest behind us erupted in a roar that sounded part lion and part elephant, following by the mounting thrash and crackle of a large creature forcing its way toward us through the understory; seconds later, a quadrupedal dragon with one long horn stabbing skyward from its snout burst forth into the clearing. It was much like *ngoubou,* albeit without the spikes fringing its frill, but we knew this creature because we had encountered its sign before: *emela-ntouka.*

Though the species are not identical, *ngoubou* and *emela-ntouka* almost certainly share a common ancestor, and it is not surprising that they share certain behavioral traits. I have already mentioned that both animals are known for killing elephants, but the similarities go further. As Walter and I learned, both *ngoubou* and *emela-ntouka* become agitated upon hearing loud noises and charge the source of any such racket, just as the Countess had done many times and the strange *emela-ntouka* did on this occasion.

The *emela-ntouka* might initially have been provoked by our noise, but several hundred million years' worth of instinct took over when it registered the presence of the Rex on the *bai.* The horned dragon bellowed a challenge, which the Rex, too tempted by a five-course *mokele-mbembe* feast to retreat, answered with a sibilant noise from its leering mouth. Without further formality, the horned dragon charged across the clearing toward its foe, spraying shreds of leaf and clods of dirt to either side as it passed, and the Rex loped forward to meet it. On its way to the Rex, the *emela-ntouka* lowered its head so that its horn lanced straight out in front like that of a tilting knight, and with a clap that rent heaven and earth, the combatants came together in the middle of the clearing like two reptilian locomotives.

While the dragons confronted each other, I worried over the safety of my own kind. With the help of the Bangombe, who had no more power to dissuade the Rex with their poison-tipped arrows than Walter and I with our voices, I tried to tug Walter into cover in the forest, but he resisted.

"I just don't think that's necessary, Matthew," Walter said. "Our horned friend there looks fit to chase that monster away."

If Walter thought the battle would resolve itself so easily, he was wrong. Initially the horned dragon knocked the Rex off its feet and trampled it while down, but after a few moments of frantic scrambling during which we could not make out where one dragon ended and the other began, the Rex was on its feet again. It leapt toward the *emela-ntouka*'s backside, aiming for its vulnerable neck, and though the horned dragon tossed its head in time to put its frill in the way of the Rex's jaws, the Rex clung fast to its back for several perilous moments before the *emela-ntouka* bucked forward and spilled the unwanted rider.

Two dragons trying to destroy each other in this manner are unlikely to eat or gore any nearby dracontologists, but there is still the danger of being trampled under foot as their brawl takes them to and fro. It occurred to me that we should stand clear of the tussling dragons, but Walter would have none of it.

"If we leave," he said, "what's to stop them from trampling our scaly friends?"

In his concern for the unconscious dragons, Walter would not be moved, and the grappling dragons inevitably gyrated in our direction. I felt certain Walter would be crushed when he stood between them and the sleeping herd, but Walter remained defiant and oblivious to his danger.

"Oh, no, you don't," he said. "Keep away. Shoo! Shoo!"

Walter's cries notwithstanding, the dragons whirled closer in their combat, but before they could overwhelm him, another combatant threw herself into the melee: Tiamat, who had finally awakened without our noticing. She lumbered in from the side, and the force of her 20-ton impact knocked the other dragons onto a new course that took them away from Walter and the remaining members of the herd.

With three dragons now involved, the brawl was over quickly. For a few moments the *bai* was a tangle of legs, tails, horns, and teeth like some half-formed chimera out of ancient myth, and we lost track of which dragon was which. Suddenly there came a shrill yelp like that of an injured dog—albeit a thousand times louder—and a sharp crack, and the huddle of dragons spit out a ball of red that unfurled into a heap some 50 feet away. The Rex lay on its back kicking impotently at the air while the other dragons watched, but finally it managed to hoist itself painfully to its feet, yelping once again when it put weight on its left leg. The Rex's leg was almost certainly broken, and rather than contending any further with its foes, it limped off into the forest.

"It's never going to be able to hunt in that condition," Walter said. "If the wound doesn't kill it outright, then it will still starve to death."

"I think you're right."

"Should we go after it? Its body would be priceless to science."

"There's no way in hell I am going after that thing."

While Walter and I debated further follow-up, the Rex wandered off into the forest, presumably to find some place quiet to dic, and the other dragons returned to their respective business. Having forgotten the nuisance that drew it onto the *bai* in the first place, the *emela-ntouka* trudged resolutely back into the understory without awaiting any thanks from the *mokele-mbembe.* Tiamat, for her part, hastened back to inspect her family, whose tails and legs were twitching with the first signs that they were reawakening.

Even when the dragons began to stir, Walter and I were too cautious to count them safe until they were all up and on their feet. Knowing better than to linger too close with Tiamat nearby and already somewhat agitated, we kept the dragons under surveillance from a distance until all five had gotten over their initial disorientation and resumed feeding as if nothing had happened, at which point we returned to our own camp for a much-needed break. Though nobody had been hurt as we feared, we nevertheless learned a sobering lesson of the danger our discovery posed to the dragons, and that we might best protect them by leaving them alone.

CHAPTER XXI
ODDS AND ENDS

History teaches us that wild animals almost invariably suffer from the presence of human beings in their lives. We either find some reason to start killing them—usually food or sport—or commandeer their habitat to accommodate our own bloated population. Even though Walter Spink and I had nothing but the best intentions where the dragons were concerned, we had still nearly destroyed them by attracting the hunter's attention. Despite our success rescuing the dragons, I became reluctantly convinced that we might endanger them again if we did not leave them.

Having come to this realization, I suggested to Walter (with great trepidation) that we should conclude our study before any other mishaps befell, and to my immense surprise (and relief), he agreed.

"Believe it or not," he said, "I've come to the same conclusion myself. There's just one thing I need to do before we even think of leaving our scaly friends unattended: make sure that Heartless fellow has finally gone on his way."

We began asking after James Phillip Hartley in the nearby villages, and initial reports were encouraging. The Toukalaka villagers reported that the hunter had left for Epena, where we hoped he meant to catch a flight to Impfondo and thence travel out of the Likouala. When we followed this lead up in Epena, however, we learned that Hartley had ventured into the rainforest several days earlier and had not yet returned.

"What the devil is he doing?" Walter asked.

Though we waited in Epena several days, Hartley seemed to have disappeared, and he was not the only member of our circle of acquaintanceship who vanished during this time. After passing a few peaceful days in the wake of our confrontation with the hunter, we noticed that it had been some time since Heep had made any attempt on Walter's life, and he was more than due for one. This started us looking for Heep in earnest, but even then, the winged dragon was still nowhere to be found.

"I suppose I shouldn't complain," Walter said, "but I felt safer knowing where he was. Now he could come at me at any time."

Contrary to his concern, Walter was ultimately safe from being eaten by Heep, and the dragons were safe from being shot by Hartley. In retrospect, they had both disappeared at about the same time, and this was no coincidence, although the newspaper articles regarding the hunter's disappearance told only half the story.

BIG GAME HUNTER MISSING IN CONGO[33]

> BRAZZAVILLE, PEOPLE'S REPUBLIC OF THE CONGO. An American big game hunter has gone missing near Epena, Congo and is presumed dead.
>
> The hunter, James Phillip Hartley, 54, from Dallas, Texas had hunted big game on six continents. He went into the rainforest of the Congo's Likouala Department hunting antelopes and elephants but never came out.
>
> Hartley's disappearance was discovered when his

[33]Barnes, S. *The Times.* October 22, 1984: B1. Print.

> guides and bearers returned to Epena and reported him missing. Despite a search, Hartley's body has not been found.
>
> As of this time, authorities believe that Hartley fell victim to one of the predators of the Likouala, which is home to leopards and several species of crocodile, at least one of which is known to attack human beings.

The truth about Hartley's fate must have been deemed too incredible to print, for his guides and bearers told us a much more detailed story upon their return to Epena. I can vouch that Walter interviewed them personally and in my presence, and they reported, without prompting, that Hartley had been attacked and dragged away by an animal of a type they had never seen before. Walter and I immediately suspected the killer's identity, which Walter tested with the help of his trusty book of prehistoric creatures.

"I don't suppose that the animal"—he speared one of the pictures with a bony finger—"looked like this?"

"As a matter of fact, *tata,*" one of the guides said, "it looked just like that."

The animal that the guides identified as Hartley's attacker was, of course, a pterosaur, which meant only one creature.

"You know what I think, Matthew?" Walter asked. "Old Heep got a look at that Heartless fellow—a handsome white man with a beard, like me—and decided to eat him, thinking he was me. But unlike me, that Heartless fellow wasn't on his guard for a carnivorous dragon, and Heep got him. It's ironic, don't you think? The hunter becoming the hunted."

"You don't seem too broken-hearted," I said.

"Why the devil should I be broken-hearted? I said it was ironic, not tragic. Serves him right for all the animals he's killed."

Whether there was poetic justice in the hunter's fate is a matter of opinion, but the facts nevertheless supported Walter's hypothesis that Heep mistook one older white man for another and satisfied his craving for Walter by dispatching Hartley. We never saw the winged dragon again during the rest of our time in Africa, and this was such a departure from his dogged persistence pursuing Walter that it certainly seemed he must have gratified his hunger somehow. Regardless of what the dragon or the hunter might have been thinking in those last moments, the effect upon our lives was the same: we could concentrate once again on the *mokele-mbembe* for however long we remained in the Likouala.

*

The lives of dragons have their ups and downs much like those of the dracontologists who study them. They are born dewy-eyed and hopeful, only to go through alternating periods of hardship and ease on the winding path to their lonely graves. Recently the affairs of the herd had taken a turn for the worse with Fafnir's loss and the hunter's pursuit, but Echidna's pregnancy promised a period of peace and renewal. Though we agreed that our leaving the dragons was for the best, we wanted to see the baby born first, thinking to reassure ourselves that the dragons' period of hardship was truly over.

Despite the promise of new life, so little was known about *mokele-mbembe* reproduction at the time that we could only speculate how Echidna's pregnancy might proceed. One question in particular preoccupied us.

"Do you think she'll lay eggs or give birth to live young?" Walter asked.

"I guess she'll lay eggs," I said, "like most reptiles."

"There's no way to be sure. No other reptile on earth is quite like our scaly friends."

This question could not be resolved by precedent from *mokele-mbembe*'s sauropod ancestors or the lore of *mokele-mbembe* witnesses, neither of which offered much information concerning the dragons' reproductive methods. In the case of the former, competing theories in favor of their laying eggs or bearing live young have yet to be resolved into any consensus. With respect to living *mokele-mbembe*, on the other hand, the Bangombe and related tribes maintain that baby *mokele-mbembe* are born live much like baby elephants, but this belief is based upon second-hand tales rather than direct observation. Thus, Walter and I could do little but watch Echidna and see what form the birth actually took.

Watching to see if Echidna laid eggs involved constant attention whenever she appeared to be squatting, and this conferred unparalleled and often uncomfortable familiarity with her bodily functions. Though our interest in her activities was scientific, I felt little better than a peeping Tom, and for once I was the one who anthropomorphized one of our research subjects instead of Walter.

"I feel like we're invading her privacy," I said.

"Don't be ridiculous, Matthew," Walter said. "I don't think our scaly friends even have a concept of privacy."

Whether the dragon minded or not, Walter and I scrutinized her carefully for many weeks without seeing her lay eggs or dig out a scrape in preparation to make a nest.

Echidna's failure to lay eggs during this time period did not by itself predict that she would birth a live baby, for the time period between mating and egg laying varies between different reptile species. The crocodile, presumably *mokele-mbembe*'s closest relative, lays eggs four to six weeks after mating. Another large reptile, the Komodo dragon, may lay its eggs as soon as one month after mating. While it was entirely possible that *mokele-mbembe* would take longer to lay eggs, it nevertheless seemed that the longer Echidna went without laying eggs, the more likely it became that she would bear her child live.

"If she doesn't lay any eggs in the next month or so," Walter said after two months of our monitoring her, "I daresay it's safe to conclude she's going to birth her baby live."

When the prescribed timeframe passed without any nesting, Walter and I tentatively hypothesized that the Bangombe tradition about *mokele-mbembe* reproduction was correct, and this was borne out when the baby was actually born.

Regardless of our uncertainty as to how it would come into the world, the prospect of a baby dragon would normally have filled us with joy, but in this case our joy was somewhat clouded. Though Echidna was physically healthy, she had never been a mother before, and this concerned us greatly. New mothers of any species may inadvertently neglect or injure delicate newborns, and with her accustomed clumsiness, coupled with inexperience, we could not quite assure ourselves that Echidna would take to her new role with finesse.

"If she doesn't get over her awkwardness by the time the baby comes," Walter said, "I'm afraid she's apt to accidentally step on it."

While Walter fretted over Echidna's aptitude as a mother, the weeks rolled on, and finally her labor came a few short weeks after Hartley's disappearance. *Mokele-mbembe* do not evidence external signs of pregnancy coming to term, so there was little forewarning of this event. A morning simply came when Echidna was unusually restive, alternating between lying down and standing up but obviously having difficulty getting comfortable either way. This began to suggest that her time had come, but before we even had a chance to work ourselves up into excitement, the baby abruptly slid out of the dragon's cloaca and onto the ground with an unpleasant sucking sound.

"Is that it?" Walter asked. "Somehow I thought there'd be more to it."

As Walter observed, the birth of a baby *mokele-mbembe* is not particularly ceremonial, nor is it particularly beautiful. Far from the idealized image of the newborn uncurling, neat and clean, to look at the world with alluring and overlarge baby eyes, the baby dragon is expelled, still in the fetal sac, with a squirt of blood and amniotic fluid. For some moments, the baby lies on its side wriggling under the clinging sac like a ghost wrapped in a sheet until one of the adults pulls the sac away.

While the newborn stirred in its sac, Echidna gaped without understanding what was expected of her, and she stood watching while Tiamat and Scylla dealt with the task of releasing the baby from its wrapping. Tiamat swung her neck low, and with a gentleness surprising in an animal of her size, she clutched a loose flap of the clinging film in her teeth and tugged it away to reveal a dragon, perfectly formed and about the size of a Great Dane. Once exposed in this manner, the newborn more properly presented the heartwarming image that is depicted in fiction, right down to the alluring and overlarge baby eyes.

The presentation of a seemingly healthy baby did not hearten us as much as we might have hoped, for it was at this point that Echidna sustained our fears for her mothering ability. Upon seeing the newborn revealed, she lost interest and meandered over to a nearby *Alstonia* to browse without paying her baby any further heed.

"It looks like it's as we feared," Walter said. "She just doesn't seem to have the mothering instinct. I wonder what will happen to the baby?"

"I'm sure the others will help," I said.

True to my prediction, Tiamat and Scylla came forth to intervene with the baby where its mother failed, but the baby seemed determined to pine if it could not have its biological mother's care. Standing up being the first order of business, Tiamat used her head to lift the newborn to its feet, from which point it was meant to stand and perhaps even venture a few shaky steps, but it flopped back on its side as if its legs were made of rubber as soon as the old dragoness withdrew her supporting head. The baby was similarly uncooperative when Scylla made the same attempt, and it lay on its side crying while its aunt and great aunt could only pace fretfully.

"So much for that hope," Walter said. "Maybe we should step in and try to help."

"I don't think that's a good idea," I said. "Even if they know us, they're bound to be unusually protective with a newborn present."

"I suppose you're right, but what's going to happen to the

baby?"

Walter's concern for the newborn might well have proved warranted, what with a disinterested mother and a newborn too stubborn to be succored by a surrogate, but nature safely guided the course of events despite our misgivings. Perhaps hearing her own child bleating for help stirred instincts in Echidna that ran deeper than her disinterest at the sight of it, or perhaps she just became idly curious at the distress call. In any event, Echidna advanced toward the source of the noise, shuffling with exaggeratedly short steps as if fearfully approaching some beast of uncertain temperament, and then she lowered her great spar of a neck and thrust her questioning eyes into the face of the wailing newborn, at which point it quieted.

"Well, I'll be damned," Walter said.

Now that Echidna had taken an interest, the baby's prospects brightened considerably. In just minutes, it was on its feet and stalking tentatively among the sedge and ferns, already probing everything leafy with its mouth. It was not altogether out of the woods, though, because there was still the very real possibility that its own mother would clumsily step on it, as Walter and I feared when she began walking with the newborn perilously close to her big feet.

"Oh, I just know she's going to step on it," Walter said when a foot came down inches from the milling baby. "I can't bear to watch!"

Regardless of Walter's anxiety at several near-misses, the newborn cantered safely about its mother's feet without incident. Echidna may have been famously clumsy, but the baby was nimble and quick and easily dodged her footfalls. Indeed, it almost seemed to make a game of it, skipping about under and behind her and circling her feet. After a good few hours of Echidna tending solicitously to her new baby without trampling it, our fears for the situation finally began to ease.

"I don't know about you, Matthew," Walter said, "but I have a feeling things will turn out all right, after all."

With this encouraging turn of events, mother and child thrived in the following days, and the herd acclimated to the presence of the new arrival. Walter and I visited them daily, and though we knew better than to approach the newborn for fear of provoking the other dragons, we got a close enough look to observe a line of blunt little knobs running down the back of its neck where spines would eventually develop: it was a male. Now that the baby's survival seemed assured, Walter felt secure enough to name it Orthrus after the first offspring of its parents' mythological namesakes. The herd seemed to have come through its hard times and into a period of peace, but for us there was a down side to this change: we were running out of reasons to rationalize continuing our surveillance and postpone leaving them.

It seemed like the birth of a new dragon and Echidna's promising change of heart toward her responsibilities should have overjoyed Walter, but his happiness at the herd's improved fortunes nevertheless wrestled with some sadness. I frequently caught him staring wistfully at the dragons or sighing softly, and I imagined it was the prospect of leaving his dragons that gnawed at him. For some time, he stubbornly insisted that nothing was wrong, but an exchange with Madame Meombe on a visit to Toukalaka both reminded Walter what he had to do and explained his melancholy.

"You haven't forgotten your promise, I hope?" Madame asked.

"Of course I haven't," Walter said. "Just a few more days, and I shall be leaving just like you wanted."

"It's not me, you know. It's what the spirits wanted."

If we had not already concluded in our hearts that the dragons were better off without our presence, the feticheuse (or the spirits), having the same inspiration, had wrested Walter's promise to leave the Likouala as part of the price for assisting him to outwit the hunter. Walter had negotiated to be allowed to linger until he could see the baby dragon born, but now his performance of the agreement had come due. Reluctant as he was to leave his beloved dragons, however, Walter would not dream of going back on his word.

"After all, who knows what she'd do to me if I reneged?"

Despite his intention to honor his accord with the feticheuse, Walter lingered a few more days, during which time we split our efforts between packing up our camp and visiting the dragons until finally we were ready to leave. Before starting the trek to the nearest village, thence to bid the Likouala farewell, Walter insisted on seeing the herd one last time, and the Bangombe led us to Bangándo Bai, where the dragons obligingly made their morning appearance. There, Walter watched Campe and Orthrus scamper back and forth around the legs of their older counterparts, whose necks probed into the treetops, preoccupied with food. To the dragons, nothing of particular moment was happening, but Walter paused on the threshold of leaving them.

"Once we leave," he said, "I don't suppose we'll ever see them again."

Suspecting the permanence of this farewell, Walter dallied watching the dragons for some time. There's no telling how long he might have vacillated before finally moving on, but Tiamat gave him a suitable push out the proverbial door: she bellowed and galloped toward him, stopping short only when Ekianga and Mambunia slid to Walter's side and trained their bows on her. Though there was no harm, Walter was drawn irritably from his reverie.

"All right," he said, "the point is taken. I suppose we should get going now, Matthew."

With Tiamat's not-so-gentle urging, we left, and thus ended our study of the African dragons. We certainly wished we could have stayed longer, but we could not dispute that the dragons were better off without us. Nor could we justifiably feel shortchanged: how many people can claim to have had even a fleeting glimpse of living pterosaurs, sauropods, and (maybe) a *Tyrannosaurus,* much less the lengthy and close interaction that had been vouchsafed to us? By the time we made our plane home, we had reconciled ourselves to our departure and even begun to look forward to announcing our discovery upon our return to Fairview, little suspecting the indifferent response our tales of living dinosaurs would receive.

*

Accounts of prehistoric survivors in West Africa might have been fairly popular in the 1890s and early 1900s when the continent was popularly perceived as savage and primeval, but Walter Spink and I found the 1980s public much less receptive. Walter's account of repeated encounters with *sasabonsam, ngoubou*, and *mokele-mbembe* met with polite condescension at best and ridicule at worst, and my own inaction at the time, which I am ashamed now to confess, did nothing to improve the situation.

The rejection of Walter's discovery began almost as soon as we arrived back in the States, where Walter began spreading news of his dragons, thinking to convince the world that they were real and needed protecting. When he reported to our patron, Mr. F. was delighted (even if he credited Jesus for the discovery more than Walter felt was strictly fair), but the same could not be said of the various newspapers and wildlife advocacy groups that Walter contacted. The polite ones took down Walter's name and number and simply omitted to ever call him back, but most simply accused him of hoaxing and refused to hear him out altogether. Physical remains of a dragon might have gone a long way to convincing them, and we had encountered such remains more than once, but Walter's refusal to exploit them left us with nothing but seemingly far-fetched tales.

When the media would not take Walter's word for the discovery of living dragons, he naturally turned to me, thinking that my speaking up regarding our mutual experiences would bolster his credibility.

"If you come forward with me," he said, "I'm sure we can convince them I'm not just a crazy old man who's been out in the sun too long."

The possibility that I might be called to witness Walter's discovery had occurred to me, and I viewed it with mixed feelings. I wanted to speak up on his behalf, knowing that everything he said was true, but when the time actually came, I faltered.

"Walter, I'm sorry," I said. "I can't."

"Wonderful! Now we shall—wait a damned minute. What do you mean, you can't?"

Though Walter was taken aback by my response to his request, you must understand my position at the time. Walter as a retired person had no need to nurture a professional reputation, but I was just starting my own career. I had already been dismissed from the museum for espousing Walter's heretical position on living dinosaurs, and I had only just gotten a teaching job at a local community college and feared to strain my new employer's goodwill. Thus, I was not brave enough to come forward with what I'd seen, being in the ironic position where telling the truth might actually discredit me. Indeed, I wonder how often the unpopularity of a perfectly true account has caused it to be withheld in this manner?

When I refused to corroborate his account, Walter convinced himself that my silence condemned his discovery. Regardless of whether that was so, Walter's attempt to announce the existence of several dinosaurs in modern Africa fell flat. Aside from his own, unpublished memoir of the experience, few reports of the amateur dracontologist who claimed to have discovered living dinosaurs reached the public, and their almost satirical tone guaranteed that no one would take them seriously enough to inquire further.

Between unavailingly trying to convince the media of his discovery and undoubtedly nursing a grudge against me for my cowardice, Walter did not contact me for some time. Just when I had reconciled myself to the idea that my monster hunting days were over, however, Walter relented and called me.

"Does this mean you forgive me?" I asked.

"Believe it or not," he said, "I don't have a large circle of friends, so I can't afford to hold a grudge. Besides, I can tell you feel guilty enough as it is, and I have every intention of availing myself of your guilt to get my way from now on."

With this reconciliation, Walter and I maintained a friendship in the coming years, and we did more monster hunting together, albeit during the summers when my teaching schedule permitted. Other projects kept us from resuming our studies of the African dragons, and the dragons themselves—*mokele-mbembe, sasabonsam, ngoubou*, and *emela-ntouka* alike—lived their lives in the comparative safety of not being known to exist. It was probably for the best that the dragons remained unknown to exploitative Westerners during the poaching crisis of the 1980s, when they would undoubtedly have been hunted near to extinction as a novelty for the European and American bourgeoisie. Now that wildlife in general, and that of the Likouala region in particular, is being increasingly protected, and Walter Spink's success documenting the behavior of the North American Sasquatch has attracted interest to his other work with unknown animals, we can only hope that the time has come when humanity will both acknowledge the African dragons and guard them against being relegated back to the state of extinction from which Walter Spink's efforts retrieved them.

THE ACCIDENTAL CATCH OF THE DAY

A SHORT STORY OF WALTER SPINK'S EXPLOITS IN AFRICA

The following incident took place while Walter Spink and I were first seeking dragons in Africa, shortly after our arrival in Cameroon. While it does not strictly relate to our study of mokele-mbembe *and its cousins, it nevertheless represents an encounter with a previously unknown species, which may be of interest to some readers.*

M.P.

Africa's surviving dinosaurs are so well-known (in legend, if not scientifically) as to have inspired books all their own, this memoir included, but Africa's traditions of aquatic but nevertheless dragon-like beasts have received less attention. Such creatures have been reported from South Africa up the Atlantic coast past the Gulf of Guinea, including one unidentified but prehistoric-looking animal with a long tail, short neck, and flippers that was found on Bungalow Beach in Gambia in 1983. Though such creatures were not our object during our time in Africa, Walter Spink and I did have the opportunity to examine one of them quite closely.

Our close encounter with the African sea dragon owes itself to the practice of blast fishing among some African fishermen. This technique involves the use of explosives rather than nets or hooks; the fishermen toss small, homemade bombs containing dynamite, kerosene, or fertilizer into the sea, where they explode. The blast can kill every fish within 30 to 100 feet, causing a harvest of dead fish to float to the surface to be scooped up more quickly and cheaply than they can be obtained by traditional artisanal fishing. Despite being quicker than traditional fishing, blast fishing is significantly more dangerous—as our informant's appearance would testify—and, more to the point here, likely to injure animals that are not commercially fished.[34]

While dragon-like animals are obviously not the target of blast fishing, the beast we found must have been one of its collateral victims. Probably it blundered into the midst of the fishing operations just as one of the explosions went off, for it surfaced, lifeless, among a flotilla of dead fish in the wake of a blast, then it drifted until it beached. The fishermen who discovered the body had heard about two visiting dracontologists on the talking drums and sought us out so that we might see the creature if we wished.

When the fishermen's one-armed deputy sought us out, Walter was initially loath to abandon our search for terrestrial dragons.

"I've never heard of a *mokele-mbembe* being found so close to the open sea," he said. "What does this thing you found look like?"

"It definitely looks like a crocodile—"

"There you go. I daresay we're not interested in crocodiles."

"—But twice as long as our canoe, with flippers instead of legs."

"Are you sure?"

"Oh, definitely."

"Now, that might almost be a dragon. I suppose we should have a look, after all."

Now that Walter had taken an interest, the fisherman conducted us back to his boat and thence to the location where the seeming sea dragon had beached. This last stage of our journey was accomplished by dugout canoe traveling down one of the many narrow, mangrove-hedged canals that wind their way into the Bight of Biafra via the Rio del Rey. Our approach coincided with low tide, during which the brackish water withdraws to reveal the trees' stilted, downcurved roots marshaled like an army of knobby-legged spiders and here and there an open mudbank, and it was on one of the latter that we found the washed-up sea dragon.

Even glimpsing it from a distance as our canoe approached the

---

[34]The practice of blast fishing has been condemned for the danger it poses to sensitive marine ecosystems, and it has been banned in many countries.

bank, we could tell that the animal was unusual.

"I may not always see so well, Matthew," Walter said, "but even from here I can tell that this beast is like nothing anybody has seen in 65 million or so years."

Walter's appraisal was well-taken, and in fact the lore of sea monsters is replete with the discoveries of carcasses that resemble prehistoric creatures. These may be found stranded on beaches as our monster had been, or they may be hauled from the depths accidentally by fishermen. The Japanese fishing trawler *Zuiyo Maru*, for example, encountered a decaying beast whose apparently long, thin neck and prominent flippers at least superficially resembled those of a plesiosaur. These discoveries can usually be explained as the decomposing remains of basking sharks, which lose their lower heads and dorsal fins during decomposition so as to be easily mistaken for a prehistoric creature.

While many would-be plesiosaurs are rotten sharks, the animal Walter and I found was as preserved as if it had just fallen asleep but looked just as prehistoric as anything previously reported. Its limp body with flippers splayed out at odd angles resembled a bear-skin rug, albeit one composed of scaly black hide and 25 feet long from the tip of its snout to that of its tail. Aside from its great size, its most arresting feature was a mouth, large enough to snatch an average-sized man, which brandished a palisade of crooked teeth like ivory daggers. Its long, flat head resembled the nightmare offspring of a giant crocodile and a killer shark, but it lolled impotently in the position in which the unsympathetic tide had left it.

"I'm not completely blind, Matthew," Walter said, "and I know you've had your reservations about declaring the existence of any prehistoric survivors. But even you have to believe the evidence of your senses."

"I do," I said. "And for what it's worth, it looks like a prehistoric animal to me, too."

"What do you think it is?"

"It looks a lot like a pliosaur."

"My thoughts exactly."

This identification, however ambitious it might sound, was entirely warranted by the appearance of the stranded dragon. The pliosaurs were a type of short-necked plesiosaur that very much resembled a crocodile with flippers rather than legs, and their group included monsters such as the 21-foot-long *Liopleurodon* and the 30-foot-long *Kronosaurus.* Up till now they have been largely believed to have died out by the end of the Cretaceous along with the dinosaurs themselves, but several sightings of superficially similar creatures, including a 60-foot-long aquatic animal "like a crocodile" with "four limbs with powerful webbed feet" that was seen by the crew of a German submarine in 1915,[35] support our observations of the beached pliosaur.

Whatever the thing actually was, Walter did not afford me much time for musing before he put me to work.

"Matthew," he called, "what are you doing lollygagging over there? I need your help here."

At first I could not conceive what we might do besides lollygagging at the body, but A.C. Oudemans, in a seminal 19th century work entitled *The Great Sea Serpent*, provided instructions for future discoverers of dead monsters such as the one we confronted in the mangrove swamp. In addition to preserving the body for examination by the proper zoological authorities, Oudemans recommends measuring and sketching the remains. Neither of us being a particularly gifted artist, Walter and I set about the former task with Walter's trusty tape measure.[36]

Without questioning Oudemans's advice, measuring the thing proved difficult for several reasons, not the least among them being my reluctance to lay a hand upon its scaly hide. Though I had seen no

[35]Heuvelmans, Bernard. *In the Wake of the Sea-Serpents.* New York: Hill and Wang, 1969, 396. Print.

[36]Oudemans also suggests, in the event it is not possible to preserve the entire skeleton, to keep at minimum the skull, the bones of a fore and hind flipper, several vertebrae, and a length of skin. For reasons that will become clear, even this minimal preservation proved impracticable.

indication of life, those teeth as long as my hand seemed to be always in the corner of my eye, and I knew they could in life have amputated a careless arm or leg with a lazy flick of the huge jaws. When I finally screwed up the courage to touch the thing while placing the tape measure, we still struggled with the size of the creature, which necessitated our climbing over and around it like mountaineers scaling a fleshy Everest. In the end, we made do as circumstances permitted, and such measurements as we were able to take appear in Appendix C of this work.

In addition to taking measurements, we also examined the community of ectoparasites living on the creature's hide. These ranged in size from minuscule copepods no more than a few millimeters long to larger isopods up to five centimeters, all of which looked like ticks, some of them disturbingly large. Grotesque as it may sound, we took samples of these, and in fact our foresight in this regard paid some dividends, even if they did not quite offset our overall disappointment.

Though we took measurements and samples in the short-term, our ultimate goal was to preserve the remains of this creature as a type specimen, which is of course the bare minimum requirement for a new species to be scientifically recognized. Had we succeeded, I suspect that Walter would have been so eager to publicize the find (and earn, to his mind, much overdue accolades) that he would have postponed our search for *mokele-mbembe.* Ultimately, this experience was little more than a footnote in our larger study of the dragons, for our plans for preserving the sea dragon's body as a specimen did not come to fruition.

Our inability to preserve the sea dragon was disappointing, but considering the manner in which we lost it, I consider us lucky to have escaped without losing an arm. While Walter was probing among the thing's dagger teeth as if for a lever that would ratchet the huge jaws open, I felt a recurrent whisper of warm air against my arm from the direction of the toothy mouth and recognized it as gusts of hot breath. Without consciously formulating any plan, I seized the hand with which Walter was probing for a means of ingress into the mouth—how close he came to seeing more of its gullet than even he would have wanted!—and yanked him away just a second before the massive head heaved itself from the ground and snapped its jaws ineffectually where the old man had just been standing.

The sea dragon's resurgence took us completely by surprise, but we should perhaps have been more prepared for the possibility that the animal was not dead. It was all well and good for us to accept that small-scale, homemade explosives would do for the fish littering the mudbank, but this was a mighty predator of several tons' mass. It is not uncommon for larger animals such as whales and sharks, often the collateral victims of blast fishing, to merely be stunned by the blast fishermen's hand-crafted depth charges, and that was obviously the case with our creature as well.

Whatever the cause of its former torpor, the sea dragon was now quite alive and snapping as best it could in our direction, and we were fortunate that it was so large. Being pinned down by its own weight, the would-be pliosaur could not pursue us along the mudbank, and we were safe as long as we stood clear of its head. Even then, I was taking no chance of becoming a live sea monster's next meal, and I dragged Walter down the mudbank to where the fisherman was already launching the dugout.

"What are you doing?" Walter demanded. "We can't abandon a discovery of this magnitude!"

"If it eats you," I said, "you'll never have your chance to announce the discovery."

"I suppose you have a point, but still…"

Walter wisely cooperated in getting well out of biting range in the dugout, from which we observed the creature, thrashing and snapping, from a safe distance. I can only imagine what Walter, whose enthusiasm often overwhelmed good sense, might have proposed to do with the live creature, but the incoming tide decided its fate for him. More quickly than we would have thought, the mudbank disappeared under the lapping water, and the pool around the creature deepened until, with a tremendous splash, the thrashing monster dislodged itself and slid into the main channel and out of sight.

Once it had submerged in the brackish water, we did not see the creature again, and under the circumstances—where we would only have been separated from this monster by a flimsy dugout—I was less than heartbroken. Walter, for his part, was much more disappointed to lose sight of the thing, but he, too, was soon preoccupied enough with *sasabonsam* and *ngoubou* to ease his mind at the loss of the putative pliosaur.

Though our sighting of the sea dragon proved brief, we did salvage a more permanent discovery from the encounter, as we learned when we returned to the States and took account of the parasites we had sampled. Many species of parasite are endemic to only one host species, as in the case of the copepod *Dinemoleus indeprensus*, which is known only in the megamouth shark. One of the isopods we pried from the mystery beast's leathery hide also proved to be a new species not known in any other animal, so it provided at least circumstantial evidence of an unknown species. The isopod is known as *Anilocra spinki* for its discoverer, but of course it goes without saying that Walter was hardly flattered at having a marine parasite named for him. Fortunately, the new species he would discover when our research some years later turned to sea serpents and other unknown marine animals would be larger and much more impressive.

APPENDIX A
A BRIEF GUIDE TO AFRICAN DRAGONS

Detailed descriptions of the behavior and habits of the assorted African dragons appear throughout this volume. For ease of reference, I have also chosen to include a brief summary of the appearance, range, and behavior of each species studied by Walter Spink and me during our time in Africa.

Long-Necked Dragon
(*Dracosaurus longicollis*)

Local Name:	*Mokele-mbembe.*
Description:	Quadrupedal reptile with long tail and long, snake-like neck with small head, generally resembling a sauropod dinosaur; color ranges from rust-colored red to brown; length (adult) up to 40 ft. (12 m.); males have spines running down back of neck.

Similar Species: Unknown; similar animals referred to as *nsanga, jago-nini,* and *n'yamala* may be same or related species.

Diet: Greenery, flowers, and fruits, especially *malombo* (*Landolphia mannii* or *L. owariensis*).

Habitat: Rainforest and swamp forest; use rivers and pools for travel between feeding sites.

Range: Southern Cameroon; Gabon; People's Republic of the Congo; Democratic Republic of the Congo.

Behavior: Sociable with others of their own kind; females and immature males live in matriarchal herds consisting of adult females and their collective offspring, while mature males live alone or in small bachelor herds; herbivorous and generally peaceful, but some individuals will attack human beings who approach too closely.

Horned Dragon

(*Dracoceros acanthocephalus*)

Local Name: *Ngoubou.*

Description: Quadrupedal reptile with long tail; has one 3 ft. (1 m.) long horn on snout and frill at back of head containing three to six parietal spikes; generally resembles a ceratopsian dinosaur (*Styracosaurus*).

Similar Species: *Emela-ntouka* (*Dracoceros smilopsis*), which lives in swamp forest and lacks parietal horns or spikes of the other horned dragon.

Diet: Grasses and most other plants; occasionally scavenges carcasses.

Habitat: Savanna.

Range: Northern and eastern Cameroon.

Behavior: Solitary; not hostile toward humans but easily provoked to flight and intolerant of loud noise; occasionally kills elephants by goring with nose-horn.

Winged Dragon
(*Dracopteryx cryptovenator*)

Local Name: *Sasabonsam, olitiau.*

Description: Reptile with lizard-like body and head and membranous wings, generally resembling a pterosaur; males have up to 10 ft. (3 m.) wingspan and are dull red, brown, or gray in color with a crest on top of their heads; females have up to 20 ft. (6 m.) wingspan and are lighter in color, often white or cream, with no head crest.

Similar Species:	Unknown; similar animals referred to as *kongamato* (modern Zambia) and *batamzinga* (Kenya) may be same species.
Diet:	Carnivorous, including insects and small- to medium-sized mammals and reptiles; also eat carrion.
Habitat:	Rainforest containing mature kapok (*Ceiba pentandra*) trees in which winged dragons roost.
Range:	Northern Cameroon.
Behavior:	Males congregate in small groups but are not social, and females only associate with males during mating periods; ambush predators that blend in with forest to stalk and surprise prey; will prey upon human beings given the opportunity and should be observed and approached with extreme caution.

Plated Dragon
(*Dracothyreophorus panoplonotus*)

Local Name:	*Mbielu-mbielu-mbielu.*
Description:	Quadrupedal reptile with parallel rows of spade-shaped plates down back and a long

	tail ending with four spikes, generally resembling a stegosaur; up to 30 ft. (9 m.) in length; gray skin with green algae covering dorsal plates and top of back.
Similar Species:	None known.
Diet:	Reputed to be herbivorous; specific dietary preferences not yet known.
Habitat:	Rainforest and swamp forest.
Range:	People's Republic of the Congo.
Behavior:	Mostly solitary; generally not hostile toward humans but may react defensively to humans in the presence of young.

APPENDIX B
LIST OF PLANTS CONSUMED BY *MOKELE-MBEMBE*

Mokele-mbembe are fairly notorious for their consumption of *malombo*, the yellow, orange-sized fruit of a type of liana. *Malombo* refers to two different species: *Landolphia mannii* and *L. owariensis*, which occur along the Ubangi River and the Sangha and Likouala-aux-Herbes Rivers, respectively. Although *malombo* is the preferred food of the long-necked dragons, they are generalists and will eat almost any plant material. The following list is not intended to be exhaustive but contains those species that Walter Spink and I observed *mokele-mbembe* to eat and were able to identify.

Albizia laurentii
A. zygia
Alstonia congensis
Anopyxis klaineana
Anthocleista liebrechtsiana
Anthonotha pynaertii
Anubias heterophylla
Baikiaea insignis
Elaeis guineensis
Entandrophragma palustre
Ficus mucoso
Garcinia smeathmannii
Gilbertiodendron dewevrei
Honckenya ficifolia
Irvingia smithii
Leptonychia batangensis

Berlinia grandiflora
B. sapinii
Bridelia ripicola
Chrysobalanus atocorensis
Coelocaryon botryoides
Coffea congensis
Crotonogyne giorgii
C. poggei
Cyrtosperma senegalense
Dacryodes edulis (fruit only)
Dialium pachyphyllum
Dichaetanthera africana
D. strigosa
Dichostemma glaucescens
Malotus oppositifolius
Marantochloa congensis
Mimusops andongensis
Paramacrolobium coeruleum
Pseudospondias microcarpa
Raphia hookeri (leaves only)
Sarcophrynium schweinfurthianum
Stipularia africana
Symphonia globulifera
Syzygium gilletii
S. guineense
Uapaca heudelotii
Voacanga thouarsii
Xylopia aethiopica

APPENDIX C

BODY MEASUREMENTS OF THE BIAFRAN SEA DRAGON

(Specimen examined near Bamusso, Cameroon)

Item measured	*Length*
Length of head from nose-tip to occiput	4.3 ft. (1.31 m.)
Length of neck from occiput to shoulders	6.18 ft. (1.88 m.)
Length of trunk from shoulders to tail-root	7.4 ft. (2.26 m.)
Length of tail from tail-root to tail-end	8.42 ft. (2.57 m.)
Distance from shoulders to thickest part of body	3.11 ft. (0.95 m.)
Length of fore-flapper	4.5 feet (1.37 m.)
Length of hind-flapper	4.17 ft. (1.44 m.)
Circumference of head (at occiput)	4.71 ft. (1.24 m.)
Circumference of neck	4.08 ft. (1.24 m.)
Circumference of thickest part of body	18.84 ft. (5.74 m.)
Circumference of tail-root	2.83 ft. (0.86 m.)

ABOUT THE AUTHOR

Ryan J. Lyons is the author of *Sojourn with the Sasquatch*, which made the 2018 Long List in the paranormal category of the Chanticleer International Book Awards. His novels combine his interest in cryptozoology and the occult with his belief that animals, like humans, can be characters with personalities and stories worthy of telling. Ryan lives in Central New York with his husband, and they run an unofficial group home for pets with special needs. *Drums and Dragons* is his second published novel.

www.ingramcontent.com/pod-product-compliance
Lightning Source LLC
LaVergne TN
LVHW050928080826
845145LV00001B/245

* 9 7 8 0 5 7 8 5 1 5 9 6 0 *